Losing You

Susan Lewis

Losing You

CENTURY · LONDON

Published by Century 2012

2 4 6 8 10 9 7 5 3 1

First published in Great Britain in 2012 by
Century
Random House, 20 Vauxhall Bridge Road,
London SW1V 2SA

www.randomhouse.co.uk

Addresses for companies within The Random House Group Limited can be
found at: www.randomhouse.co.uk/offices.htm

The Random House Group Limited Reg. No. 954009

ISBN 9781846059506

A CIP catalogue record for this book is available from the British Library

The Random House Group Limited supports The Forest Stewardship
Council (FSC®), the leading international forest certification organisation.
Our books carrying the FSC label are printed on FSC® certified paper. FSC is
the only forest certification scheme endorsed by the leading environmental
organisations, including Greenpeace. Our paper procurement policy can be
found at www.randomhouse.co.uk/environment

To my wonderful partner, James, with all my love.
And to my two endless sources of inspiration,
Michael and Luke.

Losing You

Chapter One

'Guess what? I have had *the* most brilliant idea!'

Lauren Scott's exquisite amber eyes were sparkling with mischief as she breezed into the kitchen, where her mother was engrossed on the computer.

'Really?' Emma Scott responded, quickly closing down the email she was reading to reveal a job-search website beneath.

'Yeah, really.' Unwinding a soft brown scarf as she slumped down at the table, all long, booted legs and clouds of icy air brought in from outside, Lauren said, 'So don't you want to know what it is?'

'Mm?' Emma clicked to open another page of the website.

Lauren ogled her patiently, her irrepressible good nature lighting her from inside, as it always did, and lending her fresh young complexion a deliciously warm glow in spite of her wind-rouged cheeks. As she removed her woollen hat the sumptuous waves of her honey-blonde hair tumbled randomly around her shoulders and halfway down her back, and caught the light overhead in a way that made it glint like gold. Her enthusiasm for life was as infectious to others as it was a surprise to her mother, who couldn't claim to have passed on any such sunny gene herself. However, Emma was willing to accept that she'd played a part in the arresting shades of Lauren's eyes, plus the high cheekbones and pixyish chin – and very probably Lauren's inherent compassion for others, since Emma had always considered it important to be as supportive to friends and family as she would wish them to be to her. (Although Emma's considera-tion hadn't always been returned, particularly where her mother and ex-husband were concerned, she simply breezed on past the defaulters and felt thankful for those who did show up in her times of need.)

In most other ways such as height, hair colour and the dazzling smile that lit up Emma's world, Lauren was just like her father, while Emma's resemblance to her own father was equally striking, if photos were to be believed, and she saw no reason why they shouldn't be. This meant that she was five foot six – a good two inches shorter than Lauren – with an olive complexion, lustrous raven-coloured hair, and could easily be passed by in the street, her attractiveness unnoticed. She had no problem with that, since, unlike her long-dead father who'd been a successful musician in his time, she'd never harboured any desire to stand out in a crowd. However, she couldn't deny loving the little frissons of pleasure she experienced whenever a man she felt drawn to seemed to sense the connection.

She'd definitely chosen the wrong man for that lately, so the least said about him the better, and she certainly wasn't going to answer his email.

'Mu-um! You're not listening to me.'

'I am. I am,' Emma insisted, finally tearing her eyes from the screen. 'Oh God, Lauren, look at you, your lips are blue you're so cold. Where have you been?'

'Only over to Melissa's and I helped some kids build a snowman on the way back. Anyhow, I've got to tell you about my idea because it's totally sick and you are so going to love it.'

Understanding that sick was enjoying a temporary redefinition in teenage-speak as fantastic, or amazing, or totally brilliant, Emma sat back in her chair and folded her arms. 'OK, you have my full attention,' she declared, while reflecting (with fingers tightly crossed) how blessed she was to be able to call this golden child her own. So many of her friends back in London had been driven half out of their minds by the stress of teenage hormones, addictions and even, in two unlucky cases, hush-hush abortions. In fact, before moving away, Emma had reached a point where she'd started to feel almost embarrassed by Lauren's comparatively problem-free journey through what were supposed to be the most turbulent adolescent years. 'Still time for it all to kick in,' she'd often heard herself saying to one mother or another, as if Lauren developing issues would somehow make them feel less singled out as the victims of the dreaded teenage revenge.

'I have decided,' Lauren pronounced, fixing her mother with the kind of look that told her there was to be no argument, 'that *you* should come to India with me in September.'

Emma blinked, blinked again, and stumbled into an incredulous laugh.

'You've always wanted to go,' Lauren reminded her, 'and ever since Donna and I started making our plans I've felt terrible about not including you . . .'

'Lauren, I'm your *mother*! You're not supposed to include me, especially not on your gap year.'

'It'll just be for the first couple of weeks, till Donna comes to join me. All right, I could easily delay my flight and go at the same time as her now she's having to be bridesmaid for her sister, but then I thought, why don't *we* – you and me – have a holiday together doing some of the things *you* want to do in India before I take off with Donna?'

Emma was shaking her head in amazement. 'You and your crazy ideas,' she chided, knowing Lauren meant it and wondering how many other girls her age would seriously want their mothers travelling India with them.

'Isn't it brill? I knew you'd love it. So shall we check to see if we can get you on the same flight as me, and then we can work out what we'll do and where we'll stay when we get there. I mean, I know you won't want to do all the backpacking stuff, but I'm cool with five-star . . .'

With a splutter of laughter, Emma said, 'I'm sure you are, but I'm afraid the closest we'll ever get to that is dreaming.'

'That's OK, we can find less expensive places to stay like ashrams or hostels. And we can get trains and rickshaws and go in search of ourselves, or enlightenment, or *love* . . .' Electrified by the theme, she went on, 'Imagine if you found someone like what's-his-name, you know the mega-zillionaire who that actress was married to?'

With dancing eyes, Emma said, 'I suspect you mean Liz Hurley and Arun . . . I'm blanking on his surname . . .'

'It doesn't matter, he might still be free, and if he is, once he knows about you . . . Actually, I'm starting to think the sooner we get out there the better, because we don't want him being snapped up . . .'

'Stop it,' Emma protested, getting up and squeezing past Lauren to go and put on the kettle.

'No, come on, Mum, you've got to think out of the box here, not that this house is a box, exactly, well it is, but a lovely box and I'm totally happy in it if you are, but I definitely think we need a holiday and you need a man . . .'

'Lauren . . .'

'OK, Arun what's-his-name might be a bit radical, but you have to admit that us going to India together is seriously cool.'

Emma couldn't deny that if she allowed herself to she might easily become every bit as excited by the idea as Lauren seemed to be, since spending a fortnight living a lifelong dream, especially with her daughter whose company she adored, had even more appeal – in fact way, way more appeal – than becoming the future Mrs Nayar – that was his name – as if there was even a remote chance of that! She was getting as bad as Lauren with her flights of fancy.

'You've got some money now you've sold the business,' Lauren was running on. 'OK, I know you're going to say it isn't much . . .'

'Because it isn't. In fact, I was lucky to come out with anything at all, as you well know, and I need every penny now while I look for a job.'

'Which you'll find no problem, because who wouldn't want you? You're brilliant at everything and everyone likes you and . . . oh Mum, please don't tell me you're going to say no. You can't. It's what you want, I know it is, and think about it this way, if you come with me you won't have to worry about me being in a foreign country all on my own till Donna turns up.'

A very good point – a very good point indeed. Even so . . . 'I'm going to need some time to think about it.'

'What's to think about? Why don't we just go ahead and book?'

'Because we've hardly been in this house a month, we overspent at Christmas and if I do manage to find a job I don't know if I'll be able to get the time off.'

'But it's only January, September's ages away yet, so if you tell them you've already booked something they're sure to be all right about it.'

Dropping a kiss on Lauren's head as she reached over her to take two mugs from a cupboard, Emma said, 'I promise I'll think about it, and if I find a job by, let's say, the end of February and they're willing to let me go, then we'll get straight online to reserve the flight.'

'Yay! I knew you'd go for it,' Lauren cheered, grabbing her mother round the waist. 'I reckon it'll be brilliant for you after all the stress of packing up the business and selling the house . . .'

'Both houses,' Emma reminded her, and immediately wished she hadn't, since it was Lauren's precious father and his crooked – yes, *crooked* – accounting and dubious investments and demanding new wife who'd virtually turned them out on the streets.

Looking dismal, Lauren said, 'It's a real pity Dad couldn't let you hang on to the cottage. He really wanted to, well you know that, but with all the debts that had mounted up . . .'

'We don't need to go over it all again,' Emma interrupted, trying not to sound clipped or bitter and failing on both counts. Her feelings towards Will and Jemima Scott-Robbins (yes, he really had gone double-barrelled since marrying the wretched woman, pretentious, ludicrous, sad bastard that he was) were for her to deal with and not to be laid on Lauren. Not that Emma wasted any time harbouring the bitterness that most said she was totally entitled to after her ex had virtually destroyed the small, and until he got his hands on it, successful catering business she had started *alone* some fifteen years before. She'd never felt right about his insistence that he should resign from his job as an insurance assessor to help expand her company, and she could only wish now that she'd cleaved to her instincts.

5

The debts they'd managed to accrue until he'd abandoned ship – and marriage – to take up with Jemmy, as he called his mistress-now-wife, had turned out to be so staggering that, with a recession upon her and banks fleeing from the rescue, there had been nothing Emma could do to save her dear little empire from crashing. Nor had she been able to hold on to their smart house in Chiswick, unless she'd wanted to declare bankruptcy and turn her back on the debts she owed people she'd known, and who'd trusted her, for years. And the tiny, two-bed cottage his father had left to *both of them* just after they were married, had also been liquidised in order for them to reach a settlement that would help Will to provide a decent home for his new, young family. (The fact that *Jemmy* was absolutely rolling in it hadn't seem to count for anything at all.)

In the end Emma had come out of the ordeal with the grand sum of two hundred and twenty-five thousand pounds, which might sound massive, but almost all of it had gone towards the small, three-bed estate house she and Lauren had recently moved into; the rest – around fifteen thousand – she was counting on to get her through until she was earning again.

The really good part of it all was that she was mortgage-free – at least for now, and if she found a job soon there would be no reason for that to change.

The worst part was that she'd worked so hard to build her business, only to end up back where she'd started.

Nevertheless, she wasn't going to age and enrage herself by focusing on the injustices she had suffered at Will Scott's grabbing little hands; indeed, she did her level best never to think about the TBs (Thieving Bastards as her brother Harry liked to call them) at all. What was the point when they were no longer a part of her life? Nor, mercifully, were they enjoying their marital bliss in either of the homes Emma had created and loved with a passion. Instead, they were luxuriously shacked up in Jemmy-baby's towering town house in Islington along with Ms Scott-Robbins's twelve-year-old twins from a previous marriage and two- and three-year-old Chloe and Dirk (*Dirk!*) the adorable (according to Lauren) fruits of Jemima's union with Will.

So with the TBs fully ensconced in London where Jemima practised her sharkery – another of Harry's little witticisms, Jemima being founder and head of some whizzo IT firm – and Emma now settled in only just affordable North Somerset, there was next to no chance of running into them.

Thank God.

In fact, the only contact Emma ever had with Will these days was the occasional text concerning Lauren, usually to ask what she might want for her birthday or Christmas, when he always went preposterously over the top with his gifts. He didn't have to buy his daughter's love, or try to absolve his guilt with five-hundred-pound cheques, or a brand-new car as he had for her eighteenth, because Lauren adored him anyway. Nor did he have to keep making pathetic excuses (another source of his irritating texts) about why it wouldn't be convenient for him and Jemima to have Lauren living with them in London during the week while she finished her last year of school. Lauren was more than happy to stay with Donna and her family, who'd readily thrown open the double front doors of their massive house in Hammersmith, or with Emma's mother, Phyllis, with whom Lauren had a far closer relationship than Emma had managed in her entire life. There was also Emma's wonderfully eccentric and still outrageously flirtatious Granny Berry – her father's mother – who lived some of the time in an airy riverside apartment in Chelsea, and the rest with Alfonso, a dashingly romantic Italian poet, in his rambling Tuscan retreat just outside Siena.

'It's a pity you didn't know your mother before your darling father was so tragically taken from us,' Berry often sighed tipsily to Emma. 'She was a real beauty in her day, you know, and actually not a bad singer in spite of what the critics used to say. They were really quite cruel about her at times, claiming that it was only because of your daddy that she was in the band. That was probably true, I suppose, but none of the other members had a problem with it, and it was always Daddy who did the real vocals, she was only ever part of the backup.' At this point Berry would usually smile mistily and take another sip of Chianti, before going on to say, 'Everyone loved him. I don't mean just his fans, I mean his friends and the people he met on tour, or in the recording studios. You should have seen the turnout for his funeral. Well, you and Harry were there of course, but you don't remember it, do you?'

Emma always felt terrible that she didn't, but since she'd only been three at the time it was hardly surprising. In fact, she had very few memories of her father, and since her mother would never talk about him, she had to rely on Harry's hazy recollections, and the wonderful stories Berry often told about him. And of course there were the two Top Ten hits he'd had with his band, back in the sixties, the royalties from which still provided her mother with a modest income today.

'Your daddy absolutely adored Phyllis,' Berry would insist. 'It was after he died that she changed. Such a terrible tragedy. It broke all our hearts, and I don't think she's ever got over it. It's hard to know though, isn't it, when she won't ever discuss it.'

A part of Emma actually detested her mother for the way she'd so stubbornly and selfishly refused to talk about her father; it made the dozens of silver-framed photographs around her mother's house of a man clearly besotted with his children seem more of a punishment than a kind and loving way of remembering him. She wouldn't even allow Emma to play his records, which was unbelievably mean, Emma always thought, when she never used to tell Harry off if he put them on. Since Harry had been almost eight when the terrible accident had occurred, he had his own memories of their father, which he readily shared with Emma when she was small, though never when their mother was around. What he didn't remember very clearly, however, was their father going out into the garden after an almighty storm to start tidying up, according to Berry. He hadn't realised until it was too late that the broken cables he'd grabbed hold of were live power lines brought down by the wind. Apparently her mother had seen it happen, the frenzied jolting of his body as thousands of volts pumped their lethal energy through him, burning him to death from the inside out.

It was when she considered how horrendous that day

must have been for her mother, aged only twenty-eight at the time, that Emma found herself able to feel some sympathy and even tenderness towards her. Not that she ever showed it, she'd learned long ago that her mother wouldn't welcome it if she did – in fact there had even been occasions when her mother had managed to make her feel as though she was in some way to blame for what had happened.

'Ah no,' Berry had assured her, 'it's not just you. In her way she blames everyone, especially God, which makes you wonder, doesn't it, what's going on in her prayers when she rocks up to His place on a Sunday.'

Emma was sure she'd never made Harry feel to blame, in fact she knew that her mother loved Harry much more than she'd ever loved her, mainly because she'd never tried to hide it. Emma would go as far as to say that her mother seemed to like everyone much more than she liked her own daughter, including Will when he'd come into the family. She'd even stayed in touch with Will during and after the divorce, and had gone with Lauren several times to visit the new family in Islington.

How disloyal could a mother get? She'd even seemed to take some pleasure in remarking to Emma, after one of her visits, how well Will seemed to be doing for himself now, as if up to then she, Emma, had been responsible for holding the lying, swindling, double-crossing swine back. Life was looking blindingly rosy for Will since he'd made a meteoric rise through the ranks of Jemima's company to the position of vice president, whatever that overblown catch-all of a title was supposed to mean. What it meant to Emma was a) he could afford to provide very generously for Lauren, which indeed he did; and b) the sly-witted, money-grubbing Jemima was stupid enough to be setting herself up for the exact same fall that had left her, Emma, face down in the muck after she'd promoted her husband beyond his capabilities.

What a fool she had been! And what a salutary, and expensive, lesson in love and how never to trust yourself when in it!

'So what are you doing on the computer?' Lauren wanted

to know, turning the laptop round so she could see the screen. She read aloud, '"The Rainbow Centre for Children affected by cancer, life-threatening illness and bereavement."' Her eyes were both questioning and knowing as she turned them to her mother.

'It's a local charity,' Emma explained as she set two mugs of coffee on the table and squeezed back into her chair. She was actually becoming quite fond of this new build they'd recently moved into, with its mock Georgian windows and shiny front door, but she had to admit that its bijou interior, after the space they'd had in Chiswick, was taking some getting used to. The kitchen table, not much bigger than a dartboard, was set up against the wall beneath a row of fake-ash cupboards, and had just about enough space in front and to one side of it to accommodate two chairs. The back door, which was at the end of a small hall outside the kitchen, opened out on to a brave little patio (brave for claiming such a lofty status when it consisted of no more than a three-by-three layout of paving stones) and a boxed-in cabinet for the bins was around the corner, next to the side gate. Beyond the patio was a largish dirt patch that constituted the back garden, which Emma intended to turn into a lawn and vegetable patch when the weather improved. At the front of the house were two gravelled areas, four-by-six, fenced in by some fancy black wrought-iron work, and home to a pair of ornate stone pots (currently empty). A jaunty crazy-paved path connected the pavement outside to the front door – no gate yet, but it was due to be fitted by the end of the week.

From the kitchen window, which was above the gleaming new stainless steel sink with single drainer, they could, if so inclined, chart the progress of cars coming and going from their loosely laid-out cul de sac that looped around a central green with Victorian-style lamp posts and a couple of carved wooden benches; or wave hello to a friendly neighbour who might be ambling past with a pushchair, or a dog, or an ageing relative with a Zimmer. (Not much activity going on out there today given the weather, but Emma imagined that would change come spring.)

Since the cottage Will's father had left them was less than a mile away this was an area Emma and Lauren already knew quite well, having spent most summers and school holidays over the past eighteen years enjoying their picture-book country abode and the village nearby. This shining new estate had only been completed in the last year, making many of their neighbours either first-time buyers, or older couples downsizing because their children had left home – or because the recession had done for their larger incomes or businesses. Already Emma had found herself commiserating with a hairdresser who'd been forced to close down the salon he'd opened with a five-hundred-pound loan from his dad almost twenty years ago; a PR executive who'd lost so many clients he'd had to wind up the company that he too had built from scratch; and even a lawyer whose firm had laid off more than half its staff. (She wasn't sure why, but she'd never imagined lawyers being subjected to the devastatingly brutal blow of redundancy.) Finding new positions wasn't proving anywhere near as easy for any of them as this new coalition government had promised when it had started making all the cuts, and as the unemployment lines lengthened it was becoming clear that hope was turning into as rare a commodity as cash.

'So do they have any jobs going at this charity?' Lauren wondered as she sipped her coffee.

'None that pay,' Emma replied, turning the computer back to carry on reading the website, 'but once I've found a job I think I'd like to be involved in some capacity anyway.'

Taking out her mobile as it bleeped with a text, Lauren appeared faintly flustered as she checked to see who it was from.

Amused, Emma said nothing, while guessing it was a new boyfriend, or at least someone she had her eye on.

Seeming to sink with disappointment, Lauren gave a groan of frustration. 'It's Parker Jenkins again. Mum, what am I going to do? How do I get him to accept that it's over between us? It's been nearly three months now and he's still asking if we can get together to talk things through, but there's nothing to talk about. I just don't want to go out with him any more.'

Remembering a time, barely eight months ago, when all Lauren had been able to think about was how to get Parker Jenkins to notice her, Emma said, 'Why don't you tell him you've met someone else? That should get the message across.'

Two vivid spots of colour flew to Lauren's cheeks. 'Because I haven't,' she protested. 'What makes you say that?'

Emma shrugged. 'Just a hunch.' Yes, she definitely had someone in her sights. 'Why not just ask him to stop texting because you've moved on and it's time he did too?'

Lauren looked amazed. 'That sounds a bit mean.'

'Lauren, that halo of yours can be a real pain at times. Tell him to get over it and start looking for somebody else, because that's what you're doing.'

'I so am not. And I'm starting to feel really sorry for the poor blokes you're lining up on that dating website. I bet you haven't said in your profile that you've got a sadistic streak with a penchant for shrivelling egos.'

With a choke of laughter, Emma said, 'I don't even belong to one of those websites . . .'

'Oh come on, don't think I didn't see the way you shut something down when I walked in, because I did.'

With a sigh to try and cover the fluttering of her nerves, Emma said, 'You have a very fanciful imagination, young lady.'

'I don't think so. Anyway, it would be great if you met someone. I wouldn't have to worry about leaving you here on your own all week . . .'

'I'm a grown-up, I can take care of myself and if you're going to worry about me while you're in London, then I'll have to worry about you and frankly I think I'm going to be too busy for that.'

Getting to her feet, Lauren said, 'Just my luck to have a mother who doesn't worry about me.'

'I know, life is so hard for you.'

'You're right, it is. I'm going upstairs to write in my journal.'

Emma's eyes came up. 'Secrets?' she teased.

'Wouldn't you like to know?' Lauren teased back.

'I'm glad you're keeping it up.' She'd given Lauren the journal on her eighteenth in the hope of encouraging her to record some of her memories in her own hand, or, like so much that was done digitally, they would almost certainly end up being lost.

'Actually, I quite love it,' Lauren told her, taking a yoghurt from the fridge. 'Are we still going to the cinema tonight?'

'Is that what we'd planned? Aren't you going clubbing with Melissa and her friends? You usually do on Saturdays.'

Lauren shrugged. 'I don't really feel like it tonight. I know, why don't we get a DVD and curl up with a takeaway in front of the fire?'

Thinking longingly of the log fire they used to build at the cottage, Emma said, 'Sounds good to me, but if we're going out we'll have to take your car because mine is short on petrol and my credit card is currently maxed out.'

'No problem, but remember mine keeps cutting out. Did you book it into the garage, by the way?'

'Yes, it's in for Tuesday, so it should be sorted by next weekend. What time train are you getting tomorrow?'

'Um, I'll probably go about four, I think.'

Emma was about to say she might join Lauren in London for a few days and stay at Berry's when she remembered the cost of the rail fare and quickly reined herself in. There was the expense of getting around to consider too, plus the price of the lunch she'd be sure to have with whichever friends might be free, and the shopping she probably wouldn't be able to resist, plus little extras for Lauren that always seemed to pop up. There was no way she could allow herself to stretch to all that when she hadn't even managed to get an interview yet, never mind a job.

Determined not to feel depressed about her current state of unemployment, or lonely without her friends around her, she returned to her computer, tensing as a plane thundered overhead on its way into Bristol airport. This was a jarring fact of her new life that was taking a while to get used to, the roar of jet engines that seemed to shake the house to its foundations. By way of trying to deal with it she and Lauren had taken to deciding that it must be the ten thirty easyJet from Malaga, or the twelve o'clock KLM from Amsterdam. Occasionally, as a further distraction, Emma would go on to create little stories in her head about the passengers and crew and why they were on board that particular flight.

As the noise of what might have started out as the eleven fifteen from Cyprus faded into the distance it was replaced by the haunting melody of Lauren practising her flute upstairs – a single, hypnotic thread of beauty emerging from the heart of a hellish din. She was preparing for a performance she was giving as part of her A-level course at the end of the month, and though Emma knew she was biased she simply couldn't imagine how Lauren was going to end up with anything less than an A star. She was on target to do just as well in English and humanities so there was every chance she'd find herself reading music at the university of her choice, London's Guildhall School of Music and Drama.

This coming week was going to be the first since moving here that Emma would be in the house alone, as Lauren had already broken up for the Christmas holidays by the time they'd rented a van to transport their belongings from London. Prior to the move they'd been staying at Berry's Chelsea apartment which was a bit of a squash when Berry was there, but fun all the same, simply because Berry usually managed to make everything fun. In fact, Emma had only moved into this house now, months before Lauren was due to sit her A2s, because it simply hadn't been fair to carry on putting upon her grandmother the way she had since the house in Chiswick had been sold. Generous and welcoming as Berry always was, having her open-plan kitchen-cum-sitting room turned into a bedroom for Lauren every night must have been a royal pain in the proverbial.

It was lucky, Emma was musing to herself, as she resisted clicking back through to her email, that she wasn't a complete stranger to these parts, or she and Lauren would have to be putting themselves out there to try and make new friends as well as a new life. At least she would, because Lauren's world wasn't going to change all that much, with her being in London each week, and still at the same school. In fact, it probably wouldn't be long before she started wanting to stay on for weekends, so she, Emma, had better start bracing herself for that.

Just in case any important emails had turned up in the last ten minutes inviting her for a job interview, or requesting more information than she'd provided with her CV, Emma decided she really ought to check her inbox. There was a new message waiting, though not from a potential employer, or from Philip Leesom whose name alone was causing her some disarray – it was from Polly Hunter who lived at the far end of the local village. She'd known Polly for over seventeen years now and was, in a way, possibly even closer to her than she had been to many of her friends in London. Maybe it was not living in each other's pockets that had allowed their friendship to grow the way it had, or perhaps it was simply the natural affinity that had drawn them to each other in the first place. That had happened during a quiz night at the local pub when she and Will had found themselves teamed up with Polly and her adorable, unbelievably handsome husband Jack. Whatever the reasons, it was mainly because of Polly – and her daughter Melissa who Lauren had, in a long-distance fashion, more or less grown up with – that Emma had chosen to move to this part of the world when it had become clear that she could no longer afford to stay in London.

Disaster! Despair! Polly had written. *At father-in-law's in Devon right now. Back Tuesday. Please say we can get together. Does 6 work for you?*

Not sure whether she should be concerned or amused, given Polly's penchant for drama, Emma sent a message back assuring her she'd have a bottle ready and waiting. She and Polly had been through a lot together over the years, traumas and crises that had seen one or other of them dashing up or down the motorway desperate to be there for whichever one was in need. Fortunately there hadn't been anything too disastrous since Emma's divorce, and she could only hope that there would never again be anything like the horrific shock of Jack's sudden death. The illness and suicide that had taken him was a few years behind them now, but nothing could ever be as bad as that, Emma was thinking, simply nothing, unless of course anything happened to one of the girls, but that went without saying and wasn't something any sane parent would ever allow themselves to dwell on.

Since there was still not a single response to her numerous job applications, she decided that perhaps she could allow herself to read Philip's email again, if only to lift her spirits, and then she really must delete it.

Just want to wish you good luck in the new house and if you're ever in London, please be in touch.

That was all, quite simple and straightforward, nothing to get excited about, a polite, brief message that could have been sent by anyone, because he hadn't even signed off. It was only his name in the address box that told her it was from him. What it also told her, if she allowed it to, and she probably ought not, was that he was thinking of her and would like to see her again.

Actually, it probably didn't mean that at all. Why would it, when they didn't even know each other that well, and had certainly never been out on a date, or anything even remotely like it. (Unless the Saturday afternoon just before the end of last term counted, when they'd run into each other at the library, got chatting and ended up going for a coffee.) Other than that they'd only ever met at the school where Lauren was in Philip's English class and most of the girls, including Lauren, had a mega crush on him. It was hardly surprising when he was a Tom Ford/David Beckham lookalike, and so charming in an intense and interested way that it was impossible not to be drawn to him.

He was also single, which was probably what made him so irresistible as far as the girls were concerned, and Emma had to admit it worked for her too, even though he was a good ten years younger than her. Nevertheless, she wasn't going to allow herself to respond to his email. OK, it might appear rude and unfriendly, but hopefully he'd put it down to how snowed under she was by the move and starting a new life.

16

Almost laughing to herself as she realised she was behaving more like a teenager than Lauren, she simply hit the delete key and was about to abandon the computer to go and finish off at least some of the unpacking when another message came through from Polly.

Make that two bottles with vodka chasers!

Chapter Two

'I love you,' Polly sighed wearily as Emma passed her a
brimming glass of Sauvignon Blanc on Tuesday evening at
six. She was a petite, attractive woman with wispy blonde
hair and large brown eyes, and had always managed to
look much younger than her age (today, like Emma, she
was fast approaching forty-two), until the loss of her
husband had etched the sadness of its story into her creamy
complexion. 'You don't know how much I need this. Honest
to God, I swear I could be losing my mind along with
everything else. Anyway, cheers,' and after clinking Emma's
glass with her own she took an enormous, gratifying sip
of the deliciously chilled wine before letting her head tip
back against the sofa. This was a characterful item of furniture that Emma had brought from the cottage, and though
unabashedly shabby, it still managed to exude a dignified
sort of elegance with its fading claret stripes and hand-
carved bowed legs.

'Well come on, out with it,' Emma prompted, sinking
into her only armchair which, Polly had remarked when
they were moving it in, looked as worn as an old tart, or
as grand as a pissed-up duchess, she wasn't sure which
and anyway who cared? 'What's going on?'

Groaning loudly, Polly kept her eyes closed as she spoke.
'Just give me a minute. I need to try and get my head
round it all so I can work out where to begin. Actually, it's
more what's *not* going on,' she decided in the end, sounding
unusually downbeat for her. 'Oh God, listen to that phone.
Is it yours or mine? If it's mine it can go through to
messages.'

'One of us needs to change our ringtone,' Emma told

18

her, heading off to the hall to check their coat pockets. 'It's yours,' she called out. 'Are you sure you don't want it?'

'Absolutely positive,' Polly called back, and downing another generous mouthful of wine she helped herself to a handful of cheese and onion crisps from the bowl Emma had set on the table. 'I don't know how the heck I'm managing to eat when I feel so awful,' she grumbled. 'Maybe all this stress will help me to put on some weight.'

'Will you please stop hedging, and tell me what on earth's going on,' Emma demanded, going to sit down again.

Polly's eyes closed as she swallowed hard. 'I have to shut down the nursery,' she blurted, and then winced as though the words themselves were as painful as the reality.

Emma gaped in disbelief. 'You're kidding me,' she cried. Polly had run the local nursery for as long as Emma could remember, and had turned it into as integral a part of the community as the village hall and the pub – the post office, too, before it had been forced to close down. What a royal pain it was trying to get by without that – however, one way or another, they were all managing, but it was hardly likely they would without Polly's Playtime. In fact with no nursery hereabouts the world would very probably go straight to hell in a handcart. Everyone, but everyone, with small children depended on it; they couldn't work if they weren't able to leave their precious cargo at one of the best-run nurseries in Bristol (this was official, according to a survey carried out for a local magazine a couple of years ago). And what about Polly's impressively capable staff? This was going to leave them without jobs. No, it simply couldn't be happening. Then, suddenly suspecting the worst, Emma's heart slowed horribly as she said, 'Oh my God, please don't tell me someone's been caught doing things to one of the . . .'

'Oh Christ no!' Polly jumped in quickly. 'No, no, no. It's nothing like that.' She looked quite faint. 'Just imagine . . . No, we can't even go there. In fact, I'm starting to feel a bit better now because no way is what's happening as bad as that.'

Feeling awful for even suggesting it, Emma said, 'That's probably your phone again.'

Polly pulled a face. 'I should go and turn it off, because they're all calling to find out if the rumours are true. God knows how it's got out there already, but obviously it has.'

'But you surely can't be serious about closing.'

'I don't have a choice. I'm broke – or apparently I will be if I carry on running at a loss the way I have been this past year.'

Stunned, Emma said, 'But you're always full and you've got a waiting list as long as the M4.'

'Not any more. It started falling off months ago, and now, thanks to this bloody recession, I'm almost never at full capacity and at least half of those who've stayed are struggling to pay me – if they pay at all, and unfortunately a lot don't. Or can't, is what I should probably say.'

'How come you've never mentioned any of this before?' Emma protested.

'Because you had enough going on with all your own stuff, you didn't need me loading all my crap on you as well. Anyway, I kept telling myself it would get better, things would turn around, a miracle would happen. How delusional was that, because it turns out I can't even meet this month's wages now, and nor can I avoid the eviction notice I had served on me last Friday.'

Emma's jaw literally dropped. 'But you use the church hall,' she protested. 'How can they evict you?'

'Really Christian, isn't it, chucking me out like a dirty old sinner just because I'm a few weeks behind with the rent. OK, it might be months, but most of us live in this parish, for heaven's sake. You'd think they'd try to help us through our rough patch, but no, apparently it can't be done. The vicar assures me he feels really terrible about it, but it's no longer in his hands, he's simply carrying out orders from on high. I asked if he meant God and if he did then what had happened to suffering the little children to come unto me.'

Emma choked on a laugh. 'I bet that went down well.'

Polly's smile was weak. 'He gave me one of his withery, vicarish, looks that I think was supposed to tell me that

I'm not nearly as funny as I think I am, and maybe I'd like to mend my ways by coming to church on Sunday. Instead, I took myself off to see my father-in-law, who as you know does my yearly accounts, and so he delivers the crushing no-brainer – if my clients don't pay their bills, I can't pay mine.'

'So why aren't they paying?'

'Why do you think? This bloody recession, and they've got to know, all these parents who keep ringing me up, that I can't go on running my business as if it's a flaming charity for ever. I mean, I feel sorry for them, obviously, it's terrible to lose your job, or to have your hours and pay cut, and if you don't give your kids to a minder how are you going to find more work, or hang on to the bit you still have? I swear I understand their problems, but they have to try and see it from my point of view too. The last thing I want is to find myself refusing to take little Cathy or Brett until the bill is settled, but that's what's been happening. I've even had to physically push some mothers out of the door, or run after them down the street with their baby bawling in my arms saying I can't take him until she pays. Honest to God, I'm turning into the person everyone loves most to hate, and when those that do pay find out I no longer have any premises they'll probably whisk their little darlings out of my grasp faster than you can say *what's the name of that other nursery, the one that won this year?* Give me some more wine, please, or just hand me the bottle.'

Dutifully refilling both their glasses, Emma picked up the newspaper she'd knocked to the floor, as she said, 'I wish I could offer to help, and honestly I would, if I weren't . . .'

'Don't even think it. I know you're as strapped as I am, and anyway it's not your responsibility. It's mine. And if I had any sense in my head I'd have made it clear as soon as the first bill wasn't paid that I don't do credit, but hey, what do I do instead? I say, oh never mind Mrs Must-have-a-career or Mr Single-parent, or Sir Benevolent of Brokesville, I'm sure it'll all work out, just you leave little Christie or Fabio with me and pick them up at your usual time. Well,

I'm afraid that can't happen any more. From the end of this week Polly's Playtime will have gone the same way as Polly's bloody business sense, straight down the pan and all the way out to drown in the sea.'

Having been in virtually the same position when the businesses she'd catered for around Brentford and Isleworth had started going under, Emma couldn't have felt more empathetic. 'Pol, we have to do something,' she decided. 'Maybe if I lend you a few hundred . . .'

'Please, don't even think it. Banks are for lending money, not friends.'

'And if you can get a loan out of any one of them right now you'll make headlines.'

'True, but we have to face it, they need every penny they charge us for our accounts and everything else to pay out all those multimillion-pound bonuses and inflated salaries. So, come on, it's wrong of us to expect them to put us, the customer, the taxpayer, the people who bailed them out of their shit, first. Whatever will we think of next? No, I just have to accept that the only way out of this mess for me is to remortgage the house, if I can, but even if it does turn out to be possible how can I be sure of making the repayments when they kick in, when I can't be sure my clients themselves are going to stay in work? No, the fact is I'm stuffed, and the sooner I face it the sooner I can move on.'

'But what about the clients who *are* still paying? At least it'll be some sort of income.'

Polly didn't deny it. 'Actually, I'm planning to keep those kids on for the time being, provided the parents are happy about me running things from home, but it'll still mean having to lay off the staff which I'm really dreading, because I love them all so much and now they're going to be out of work too. Where's it all going to end, Emma? What the hell is happening to this country? More wine, please, before I top myself. Or no, I probably ought to check my calls first, because that wretched phone's obviously not going to stop and I suppose it could be Melissa trying to get hold of me.'

As she disappeared into the hall, Emma picked up her glass and stared pensively down at the faux coal fire that she'd finally learned how to light without blowing herself up. This sitting-cum-dining room was by far the largest space in the house, with windows either end looking out front and back, and a pale-coloured carpet throughout that she might have chosen herself if it hadn't come with the house. Though the furniture had mostly come from the cottage it didn't really suit this modern interior, but she didn't particularly mind, and at least it was something to be going on with until her fortunes changed.

Probably best not to hold her breath for that.

Hearing Polly's muted voice as she rang someone back, Emma felt quietly stunned all over again, not only by the crisis in her friend's business, but by the way she had asked for, 'More wine, before I top myself.'

After what Polly had been through with Jack it was hard to believe she could trot out such a flip remark as though its only reality was an attempt at dramatic effect. In fact, Emma knew, it was yet another indication of Polly's incredible inner strength and refusal to make her future all about her past. Jack would have wanted it that way, there was no doubt about that, which was perhaps what made it easier for Polly to go on the way she had.

It hadn't been depression that had driven Polly's beloved husband to take his own life, or the loss of his job, or the breakdown of his marriage, it was the shocking, and then terrifying, diagnosis of motor neurone disease. It had taken them months to come to terms with the truth of it, going through second and even third opinions, spending hours on the Internet finding out all they could about it, and finally, as the symptoms became more and more pronounced, the acceptance that it really was a part of their lives now, and always would be, because there was no cure. In the end, unable to face what it was going to mean for Polly – and Melissa – when he was no longer able to do anything for himself, Jack had taken it upon himself to spare them the agony of watching his disintegration and go while they could still remember him as a strong, capable and loving husband and father.

'I wouldn't have minded looking after him,' Polly would cry, usually when she'd had one too many, or the loss crept out of the shadows to smother her. 'It would have been better than not having him at all.'

The point was, as Polly knew very well, that he'd have minded, very much, which was, perhaps, what made the act selfish, but however it was labelled Emma knew that in her heart Polly could never, and would never, believe that he'd done it with anything but love for her and Melissa in his heart.

How tragic their story was, Emma was thinking, as Polly, still on the phone, came back into the room to sit down, and how meagre it made a divorce seem. Not that it was a contest – no one in their right minds would ever want to be top of the league when it came to suffering – but the way Polly had coped during these past four years had shown Emma what true strength and courage was all about.

And now this damned recession had come knocking at Polly's door, which just went to prove that there was no justice in the world, because if one person should be exempt from this ghastly downturn after everything she'd been through, it absolutely ought to be Polly.

'OK, sweetie, I'm sorry,' Polly was saying, as she reached for her wine. 'It's true I ran away after nursery today, and I know I shouldn't have . . . I swear it never occurred to me that they'd start ringing you, but don't worry . . . No, I promise, I'll get back to them as soon as I finish speaking to you . . . Melissa, I'm doing my best here, OK? We all are . . . All right, it's not your problem, I get that, but . . . Yes, I am at Emma's.' She glanced at Emma and rolled her eyes. 'No, Lauren's in London, I thought you knew . . . OK, don't bite my head off, I was just saying . . . Melissa, Melissa, I'm forty-one years old, which makes me perfectly capable of deciding how much I have to drink . . . All right, I'll stay here tonight if it makes you happy. I take it you're at Lucy's and her mother's dropping you at school . . . Right, her father . . . And I'll be there to pick you up . . . OK, darling, love you too, no, of course I'm not mad with you, as long as you're not mad with me.' She gave a laugh. 'Call before you go to sleep,' she said, and as she rang off her eyes returned to Emma. 'Is this the point,' she queried, 'at which the parent–child role reversal starts to take place?'

24

Chuckling, Emma said, 'If it is, why don't we send them out to battle the world on our behalf while we go back to school?'

Polly seemed to light up. 'What a damned good idea. I mean they're already there, aren't they, because when you know everything, the way they do, you can't get anything wrong, can you? So it's absolutely right for them to be in charge. According to my father-in-law they're already running the country anyway – and I guess from his perspective the current Cabinet does look like a scene from *The Simpsons*. Or maybe he's thinking of the way we've all gone soft on our kids in comparison to the discipline of his day. Who knows? Who cares? Let's just drink to us and pretend that when we wake up tomorrow everything's going to be fab and gorgeous and the way we really want it to be.'

Upending the bottle again, Emma said, 'Question is, how *do* we really want it to be?'

Polly groaned. 'Don't get me started. Just tell me how your job search is going. Any interviews lined up yet?'

Deflating horribly, Emma replied, 'With agencies, yes, but none of the jobs I've applied for through websites have yielded a single positive response. Of course, they never say why I'm not invited in, just that they're sorry but on this occasion my application hasn't been successful.'

'So what sort of thing are you applying for?'

'Just about anything, from assistant restaurant manager, to lettings negotiator, to call-centre operator. The trouble is, I don't have any prior experience at any of them, or IT skills, or a degree that seems to mean anything at all these days, or I presume it doesn't, because so far no one actually wants to meet me. How can they not want to meet *me*?'

Polly looked suitably baffled. 'There are clearly greater things waiting for you out there,' she decided. 'Remind me, what's your degree in?'

'English, much good it's ever done me. But what did it matter when my little sandwich round got going, my stop-gap, as it were, between uni and some greater glory. The trouble was it took off and off and off, until I had a dozen people working for me including two events organisers and a full-time clown, and by that I don't mean my ex-husband. Or maybe I do. Yes, I definitely do. Anyway, it's all in the past now, and unfortunately a failed business doesn't make me the most desirable new employee on the block.'

'But you don't put all the collapse stuff on your CV, right?'

'I'm learning not to. Anyway,' Emma went on, reaching for the paper, 'I was going through the *Evening Post* just before you got here and here's what I've circled so far: a store manager for Dixons (must be passionate about their products).' She glanced up. 'I can be passionate about plugs for thirty-five grand a year. Next: an assistant cook at a care home, must have natural rapport with the elderly and own transport; a customer service administrator for a bakery – just over seven quid an hour for that, which I know isn't a lot of bread – sorry, terrible pun, but I couldn't resist. Anyway, there seem to be vacancies, but there are so many of us going for them that either because of my age, my gender, my background – who the hell knows what the problem is – I'm apparently not even worth interviewing.'

Sighing, Polly said, 'It's so depressing, isn't it? How did we get to be this age and find ourselves in such a mess?' Leaning forward to pick up another section of the paper, she said, 'Oh dear, look at this and we think we've got problems.'

'What is it?'

'An appeal from the parents of that poor girl, Mandie Morgan, who was murdered over Thornbury way about six months ago. Twenty-two, she was. So young. Can you imagine how you'd feel if it happened to one of ours?'

Turning cold at the mere thought, Emma said, 'I take it they don't know who did it.'

Polly shook her head. 'If they do they can't have enough evidence to arrest him or they'd have done it by now. God, it really wrenches at your heart to think of what that poor couple must be going through.' Sighing sadly, she turned another couple of pages and started to smile. 'Now, here's a job I'd *love*,' she declared, turning the paper round so Emma could see the headline. *Golden Angels Make Pensioner*

Fred's Day. 'Exactly who *are* these golden angels, as they're calling themselves, is what I want to know? Everyone's asking the same thing. They keep cropping up and no one seems to have any idea where they're coming from.'

'I've never heard of them,' Emma confessed. 'What do they do?'

'Well, as far as I can make out they drop into Asda, Lidl, Morrisons, you name it, completely out of the blue, and pay people's grocery bills.'

Astonished, Emma reached for the paper.

'They've been trying to work out if it's because you've bought a certain product, but it doesn't seem to be, and anyway, if someone like Heinz or Kelloggs or one of the big companies was behind it they'd surely be making a big deal of it.'

Emma nodded agreement. 'So how many of these angels are there?' she asked, scanning the article.

'No one seems to know. The press have only managed to get hold of one of them and she wouldn't fess up to who she was working for. What she did say was that the golden angels were only about putting a smile on people's faces during these difficult times.'

Emma's eyebrows rose. 'Well, they're definitely doing that,' she remarked, looking at what surely must have been the happiest face in the paper. 'A ninety-three-quid bill just taken out of this old chap's hands and settled by a stranger. Amazing. Who on earth would do something like that?'

'As I said, it's what everyone's asking. They reckon it's someone local, because it only seems to be happening around the Bristol area. I wish they'd drop in on me, I know that. Anyway, fascinating, isn't it? I think they've been turning up at garages too, since the price of petrol went through the roof. You know, if I could afford to work for nothing, which I presume they do, I'd go and buy myself a pair of wings tomorrow.'

Emma looked startled. 'You mean they actually dress up as angels?'

'Well, no, I don't think so, or not that anyone's ever said, but you get my drift. The trouble is, I wouldn't even know where to apply, because the whole thing's so shrouded in secrecy that not even the supermarket managers seem to know who's behind it.'

Looking at the paper again, Emma remarked, 'Well, all I can say is he or she must be pretty well off to be doing something like this.'

'And the owner of a pretty big heart too, so, let's drink to them, whoever they are. Long may their angels fly and even longer may their loot last.'

Chapter Three

'Is that all you can say to me?' Sylvie Lomax cried furiously, her French accent slurring awkwardly around the words that were already being formed with difficulty. She'd been beautiful once, and vestiges of it remained, but right now temper and excess were torturing the loosening flesh of her pale cheeks, and turning her bloodshot blue eyes to watery pools of confusion and anger. 'You're sorry, but you're not changing your mind?'

'OK, how about this?' Russell Lomax shot back angrily. 'I'm not prepared to waste any more time going over this again and again . . .'

'I'm not yesterday's paper that you can just throw out . . .'

'Try some new lines, I'm getting pretty sick of that one.'

Looking as though she'd been struck, she said, 'You are turning into a monster. You are not the man I married . . .'

'I've heard those too. Now, I'm leaving and if you ever pull a stunt like last night's again I swear to God I'll call the police.'

Anguish was rushing through her so fast that she stumbled against the table as she tried to grab him. 'Russ, stop,' she cried wretchedly. 'Please. I know I shouldn't have . . . Russ, please don't go. We need to talk . . .'

With his back still turned he closed his eyes in furious frustration. 'There's nothing left to say,' he growled. 'You have to get a grip, Sylvie . . .'

'I'm trying, you know that, but I love you, Russ. I can't go on without you.'

He didn't turn round, but for the moment he couldn't quite make himself walk away.

Sylvie's face was starting to tremble with all the terrible emotions crushing her heart: fear, desperation, jealousy, hate, love at its very worst and most painfully intense.

When he finally turned round her husband's handsome face was still taut with anger, and there was no light of forgiveness or even affection in his harsh brown eyes. 'You know I want a divorce . . .'

More panic surged through her. 'No! I am not giving you a divorce. You are my husband . . .'

'You are the one who walked out on me,' he reminded her cuttingly. 'This is *your* flat, the one that *you* bought so you could live your own life, away from me.'

'Not away from you, only independently now and again. It is for when I want to see my friends and do some shopping.'

Though Russ knew very well that its purpose was to provide her with somewhere she could down as much wine or vodka as she pleased without anyone trying to stop her, he didn't bother to point it out. She knew he knew and he really didn't want to get into yet another row about that right now.

'It isn't where I want to be all of the time,' she went on plaintively. 'I need to come home, Russ . . .'

'No. What you need is to find yourself a lawyer so that we can both get on with our lives.'

'No! No, no, no. I am not giving you a divorce just so you can marry the little tart you 'ave been screwing in *my* bed, in the house that *I* bought . . .'

'*We* bought,' he corrected, 'and I've told you a hundred times, if you want me to sell it . . .'

'Of course I don't want you to sell it. It's our home, it is where our children . . .'

'I can't have this conversation again,' he cut in savagely. 'You know very well that our marriage isn't working and hasn't been for years . . .'

'That isn't true. It has been for me . . . Russ, please. My whole life is with you, and our sons. They need us to be together, you must understand that. You cannot deprive them of their mother.'

Despairing of the repetition, he said, 'The boys are

twenty-one and twenty-three years old. Neither of them is even living at home any more.'

'Oliver is.'

'Temporarily, while he looks for a job.'

'So you are allowing him to be under the same roof as you and that bitch. This is not a good situation for him. I will not allow my son to be exposed to your debauchery.'

Knowing from bitter experience that it was a waste of breath trying to tell her he wasn't having an affair when she'd already managed to convince herself he was, he said, 'This has nothing to do with Angie.'

'How can you say that when she is in my home, stealing my husband, making up to my sons, using my things . . .'

'OK, I'm out of here.'

'Noooo! You can't just leave! Please, Russell, *please* let me come with you. I swear it'll be different this time. I'll do whatever you want . . .'

'All I want is for you to let me go.'

'But I cannot do that. I love you . . .'

'Sylvie, your drinking, your jealousy . . . they're out of control . . .'

'I will get help.'

'That's what you always say, but you never do and I've had enough. I want to live in a world where I can breathe and not have to keep watching what I say in case you take it the wrong way, or feel afraid of even looking at another woman, never mind speaking to her . . .'

'I swear I will change. Please give me another chance. I know you still love me, really. I can see it in your eyes. We've been through so much together . . . Twenty-five years, two children, my cancer . . . Remember how afraid you were that I would die?'

His eyes closed again. Though he'd known it was coming, at least this time the cancer card had taken longer to play – usually it was one of the first out of the deck.

'Don't look like that, please,' she implored. 'I know you care, because it's not in you to stop just like that. OK, I have not always been easy, but after Papa died . . . Grief does things to people, Russ, you said that yourself. Remember how you felt when your own father passed?

For a long time you didn't know who you were or where to turn. I was there for you then, the way I've always been, so please don't just throw me out now when I need you the most.'

Feeling the knife of guilt twisting deeper and deeper, he came to put his hands on her shoulders and waited for her anxious, teary eyes to come to his. 'This isn't about your father, or your cancer, or grief. It's about the fact that I don't love you any more – or not in the way I used to . . .'

'Don't say that!' she yelled. 'Don't, *don't*. She's put you up to this. You're besotted, delusional . . .'

'Sylvie . . .'

'Don't you realise that all men your age go through a mid-life crisis? No, don't look like that. I know this is not what you want to hear, but it is what's happening to you. We married young; you didn't get to play the field, so you're doing it now. I understand that, and I'm trying to deal with it . . . Moving here, to this flat, was me trying to give you some space to be you, but we can't go on living apart. It's not right, Russ. It's not who we are. We belong together.'

Letting his hands drop to his sides as she distorted the truth to suit herself yet again, he said, 'I have to go. Please don't vandalise Angie's car again . . . No, don't deny it, I know it was you and honest to God, if you carry on the way you are . . .' He didn't even want to think about what might happen. 'She was extremely upset . . .'

'*She* was upset . . .'

'And scared . . .'

'She's sleeping with my husband and *she's* the one who's upset?'

Knowing he'd be insane to go any further with that, he simply said, 'Charlie's coming to see you sometime in the next couple of days.' Charlie was their elder son, now living in London. 'He's worried about you and frankly, Sylvie, he could do without the distraction when his bar exams are coming up in less than a month.'

Her eyes filled with disbelief. 'You told him what I did?'

Though he knew he shouldn't have been surprised by the question, he found that he was. '*You* told him, Sylvie.

You rang him at three o'clock this morning . . .' Suddenly he almost felt sorry for her, as shame and bewilderment seemed to crush her. A drunk's amnesia could be a blessing until someone came up with a reminder.

'Why is he coming?' she whispered. 'He doesn't have to.'

'You're his mother. He loves you and he needs to know you're all right. Please tell him that you are, Sylvie. His future is at stake and he's worked so hard . . .'

'Why are you telling me something I already know? He's my son. Nothing matters more to me than him – and Oliver. They know I love them equally, which is more than I can say for you.'

'For God's sake, don't start that again . . .'

'Oh, I'm sorry, I forgot. You've never had a favourite between them, have you? Charlie was never the . . .'

'Sylvie! If Oliver feels that I love him less than Charlie then the blame lies squarely with you, because neither one of those boys means more to me than the other.'

'Try telling Oliver that . . .'

'No! *You* try telling Oliver that, because you're the one who's fed him all the crap about him being the spare after the heir. For Christ's sake, we're not royalty . . .'

'But Charlie *is* your favourite.'

'*Charlie is not my favourite.* I love both my sons more than my own life and if I hear those words coming out of your mouth again, so help me God, I'll push them back in a way we'll both end up regretting.'

Stepping away from him, she said, 'You never used to be like that. There was never any violence in you before.'

Throwing up his hands, he sighed. 'I don't know why I came here. Talking to you is like wading in quicksand and I'm in over my head. I'm drowning, Sylvie, in who you are, what you're trying to do to us all, what's made you like this . . .'

'*You* made me like this. If we were still together . . .'

'Sort yourself out, Sylvie, because I'm done with trying. I have a business to run, two boys to care about and . . .'

'. . . a whore to satisfy! Does she know you take Viagra?'

He blinked.

'Does she?'

'If I were you,' he said quietly, 'I wouldn't go any further with that, because I swear you won't want to hear . . .'

'Oh,' she spat, 'so it's my fault, is it, that you are impotent? Is that what you're telling yourself?'

'OK, this really is over now. Please be sober when Charlie gets here, and if Oliver comes round try to remember that he's way more sensitive than you give him credit for and . . .'

'Don't lecture me about my own son. I know Oliver a thousand times better than you ever will.'

Since this was an utterly futile argument, he turned, walked to the door and tugged it open.

'Doesn't it bother you,' she shouted, 'that I will have to go on the game to support my children?'

Stunned, he turned back again.

'I don't have any money,' she cried, 'and I'm not qualified for any other kind of work, because all I've done for years is give you the sex you want and bring up your children.'

'For Christ's sake,' he shouted, coming back to her. 'Will you look at where you are? This is one of the best addresses in Bristol, and your net worth is about three times more than mine since your father died. Actually, why the hell am I getting into this? I don't know what makes you say the things you do, Viagra, prostitution . . .'

'They are true . . .'

'. . . but you're making me think you're losing your mind.'

'If I am, it is your fault for making me stay here. I am like a prisoner, unable to go to my home . . .'

Turning away, he went back to the door and would have left had she not charged after him and blocked his way. Her eyes were glittering with desperation and fear, her chest was heaving as she tried to catch her breath. 'If you go now I will tell everyone what I know about you,' she hissed.

He frowned in confusion.

'You know what I'm talking about.'

'I really don't.'

'Oh yes you do. You are lying to everyone, pretending you don't know things when you do.'

A small glint of suspicion, and unease, sparked in his eyes.

'If you do not want me to go public with the truth you will change your mind and let me come home.'

Standing her aside, he grabbed the handle and tugged open the door. 'You need to sober up,' he told her savagely.

'What's the matter with you?' she yelled, pulling on the door as he tried to close it behind him. 'Why have you changed so much?'

'Go back inside.'

'No, because this is not where I belong. You can't leave me here. I have no one without you. My father is dead and my sister is in Cape Town. I have nowhere else to go.'

Forcing himself to ignore her, he ran swiftly down the stairs, expecting the other residents to appear at any moment, while praying she wouldn't follow him in her dressing gown, praying she wouldn't follow him at all.

'Russell!' she screamed, as he let himself out of the main door. 'Russell, please.'

The door slammed, and his footsteps moved away.

'Mum, you have to come in.'

She spun round in shock. 'Oh, Oliver,' she gasped through her sobs. 'I forget you were there.'

'Come on,' he said, keeping his voice gentle as he reached for her in spite of wanting to shout like his father, and shake her back to her senses. 'It'll be all right.'

'But how can it?' she asked pathetically as he drew her inside. 'Will you talk to him, Oliver? Will you make him let me come home?'

'I'll try,' he said, knowing already that it would be a waste of time. When his father's mind was made up about something, that was the way it stayed, and it was definitely made up over this.

'You are such a good boy,' she said, resting her head on his shoulder. He was as tall as his father, and almost the same build; he looked like his father, too, with his deep-set brown eyes and mop of silky dark hair. In fact, he reminded her so much of Russ at twenty-one that sometimes when she looked at him she almost felt young again. Perhaps it was why she loved him so much. She loved Charlie too, her adorable, brilliant, serious older son, who was more like her, at least in looks, with his fair hair, green eyes and delicate skin. They were so different, her boys, and so much a part of her that she knew she would be unable to carry on without them. She wouldn't even want to try.

Needing a drink she went back across the sitting room, and around the breakfast bar into the kitchen. 'What are you doing here?' she asked, searching for the bottle she'd hidden somewhere, she just couldn't remember where. 'When did you come?'

'Oh Mum,' he groaned, angry with her for already forgetting how he'd practically run in through the door less than half an hour ago, desperate for the bathroom, but not forgetting to give her a big hug first. It was while he was drying his hands that his father had turned up, and knowing very well what had prompted the visit he'd decided to stay out of the firing line until the worst of it was over. He'd found, over the last few years, when the drinking had become so much worse, that it was the best way when his parents started laying into each other. 'I got here just before Dad, don't you remember?' he said.

'Yes, yes, of course,' she mumbled, dashing a hand to her head. 'I'm sorry, my mind is all over the place this morning.' Finally finding the vodka in the bin she dropped to her knees, took a glass from a cupboard, quickly filled it, then went to run the tap, making out she was filling her glass with water. After downing the drink in one, she took a deep breath, wiped a hand across her face and turned back to find Oliver standing at the breakfast bar, watching her.

'That's better,' she declared cheerily.

'Mum.'

Her face started to crumple. 'Please don't tell Dad,' she whispered shakily.

Seeing how defeated and vulnerable she looked, he was tempted to go and pull her into an embrace. At the same time he didn't want her sobbing all over him the way she did when drunk, ranting on and on about his father, and how she couldn't live without him, so he turned away to go and pick up the glass and empty bottle she'd left next to the sofa.

'What am I going to do with my life if I am all alone?' she said sadly.

'You're not alone,' he reminded her, unable to keep the edge from his voice. He hated it when she went all self-pitying, as though no one in the world cared about her when it patently wasn't true. 'You've got me and Charlie and all your friends and charities. You know how much you enjoy the fund-raising . . .'

'Oh, *chéri*, it cannot make up for your father. Nothing can ever do that.'

Unable to stop himself, he said, 'Then for Christ's sake quit drinking.'

'I am trying, you know that, but . . .'

'No I don't.'

'. . . it is because your father says he no longer loves me that makes me want to drink.'

'It's not his fault, so stop trying to make out it is. You're the only one who's responsible for the way you are. We all know that, because we've all been to AlAnon to help us deal with *you*.'

Appearing shocked, and concerned, she came to put a finger over his lips. 'Sssh, ssh,' she whispered tenderly. 'Please don't be angry with me.'

'I'm not angry, I'm just . . .'

'Afraid, I know, I understand. How much did you hear just now?'

'How much do you think? All of it.'

'Oh dear. So now you think that Charlie is Daddy's favourite . . .'

'That's not what he said,' he growled, pushing her away. 'Why do you always do that?'

'Do what?' she cried, seeming genuinely perplexed.

'Try to make me think that I mean less to Dad.'

'But that isn't true. He loves you both equally.'

Reminded yet again of how impossible it was to talk to her, he decided the only sensible thing to do now was make her some coffee. Actually, he had a powerful hangover himself thanks to all the booze he'd downed at a party last night about a mile from here, but he didn't imagine it was anything like as bad as hers. Or did they get easier the more you drank?

Thinking about all the mates he'd left dossing about whoever's flat it was on Pembroke Road, he could only wish he was still with them, sleeping it off, dragging themselves out for a hearty breakfast, rather than stumbling his way around the minefield of his parents' marriage. He wouldn't even know what his mother had done last night if he hadn't been dumb enough to check his phone when he'd woken up. The first message had been from her, though he'd hardly been able to make out a word of what she was saying; the second had been from Charlie asking him if he knew what their mother had done to Angie Dickson's car. Before Oliver had a chance to call back, Charlie had rung.

'You have to go and make sure Mum's all right,' his brother had insisted. 'She's not answering her phone, so I don't even know if she managed to get home after what she did.'

Well, apparently she had, and more or less in one piece, though he shuddered to think of the state she'd left Angie Dickson's car in. It was no wonder his father was so furious. But yelling and screaming at her, throwing her out of the house – OK, she'd left of her own free will in the first place, but not letting her back – telling her he wanted a divorce . . . Jesus Christ, she'd always been fragile, his father knew that, so what was he trying to do, send her right off the edge?

With a jolt he asked himself the question again. Was that what was happening to his mother? Was she really losing her mind, or was it the drink that was making her so irrational and violent and so goddamned pathetic?

Why couldn't she just get her bloody act together and be more like other people's mothers?

'I am not sorry that I damaged that woman's car,' she said, as he started to fill the kettle. 'She deserve it for what she is doing to me.'

'But she's not doing anything to you.'

'She is sleeping with your father . . .'

'No, she isn't. I'm living there, remember, so I would know.'

'They are hiding it from you. He is very good at that. He always was, it is why my life has been so hard.'

Giving up the argument, he said, 'What was that about threatening to go public? What's he lying about and pretending he doesn't know?'

Sylvie's expression lost focus as her eyes drifted away.

'Mum?' he growled, suspecting she'd already forgotten what she'd said, never mind what it meant.

'It doesn't matter,' she said, going to stare out of the window. There was no sign of Russ now, only strangers coming and going, and traffic crossing the suspension bridge. 'I will go public if I have to,' she said, turning back to Oliver, 'and then everyone will know what your father is really like, because what he does he only ever does for himself. He cares nothing for others. Tell him that when you see him, Oliver. Tell him I know everything,' and grabbing the vodka bottle she took herself off to her bedroom and closed the door.

After leaving his wife's flat Russ Lomax strode up over Sion Hill towards the Downs, his expression as grim as the misgivings in his heart, his impatience as biting as the wind. Though he hadn't expected any good to come from confronting Sylvie with the outrageous, *criminal* act of taking a sharp object to his associate Angie's car, he'd hardly been able to ignore it. Angie truly had been terrified, though perhaps more by the threats Sylvie had screamed from the street below Angie's flat, than by what Sylvie had done to the Renault. It was fortunate, and amazing, that no one had called the police.

If it happened again, he'd meant what he'd said, he'd damned well do it himself.

Getting into his car, he started the engine and after waiting for the phone to connect with the hands-free he called up Angie's number as he began to drive.

'Hi, is everything all right?' she asked when she answered.

'I'd hardly put it like that,' he retorted stiffly. 'The important thing is, are you OK?'

'Yes, I'm fine. I'm just sorry it happened.'

'You have nothing to apologise for. You must let me pay for the car to be repaired.'

'Oh, there's no need . . .'

'Of course there is. Are you at home now? I'd like to see the damage for myself.'

'Actually, I'm at Clyde Court,' she replied. Clyde Court was the large, rambling old place he called home, set comfortably in the rolling countryside of the southern foothills of the Cotswolds. It was also from here, or more precisely the converted stables opposite the house, that he ran his business.

'Are you on your way here now?' Angie asked.

'I am.'

'And is she . . . Is she coming with you?'

Keeping the irritation from his voice he said, 'She isn't. Have you seen Oliver since you arrived?'

'No, but I haven't been into the house. There's a crisis going on here . . .'

'What sort of crisis?'

'Nothing we can't handle, and it's over now anyway. We'll expect you in half an hour?'

'Slightly longer. I've got a couple more errands to run before I start heading back.'

'It's Sunday,' she reminded him.

'I know, but when did we ever allow a little thing like a day of rest to keep us from the grind? Can you get in touch with Paul Granger to let him know that I won't be at the meeting this afternoon?'

'OK. Can I ask why?'

He'd rather she didn't, but since the suddenness of the decision required an explanation he said, 'He can handle it without me and I need to catch up after losing this morning. Is Oliver's car there?'

'Hang on, I'll have a look.' A moment later she was back on the line saying, 'No sign of it.'

Which meant his son still wasn't home after staying out all night. 'OK, I'll try his mobile,' and abruptly ringing off, he drove on to the lights at the bottom of Bridge Valley Road before connecting to Oliver.

'It's Dad,' he said into the voicemail. 'I know you're old enough to come and go as you please, but a little respect wouldn't go amiss. In other words I'd appreciate you telling me if you're intending to stay out all night. Call me when you get this message.'

As the lights changed he accelerated on to the Portway where the towering cliffs of the Avon Gorge rose majestically either side of him, and the slick, brown sludge of the river was snaking its way to the estuary at Avonmouth. Within minutes he found himself at a complete standstill thanks to an accident, or roadworks, he had no idea which. Annoyed with himself for coming this way, since it was a ludicrous route to have taken anyway, he inhaled several deep breaths in an effort to ease some of his tension.

Damn Sylvie. Damn, damn, damn her. He detested the way she made him feel every time he saw her – strung out with guilt, anger, regret and even something he really didn't want to feel about the mother of his children, disgust. What about love? Maybe, some, but certainly not of the kind he'd felt when he'd married her twenty-five years ago. The overriding, insatiable passion they'd shared then had long since died. Now, apart from gratitude for the home she'd created and admiration for how bravely she'd fought her cancer, the warmest feeling he could muster towards her was pity – and a kind of grief, he guessed. Yes, definitely grief for the loss of the woman she used to be.

She was right, her drinking had become worse following the death of her father, though she'd had wine or champagne with every meal, sometimes even breakfast, for as long as he'd known her. And many were the occasions when he'd had to usher her out of a reception, or dinner, or some sort of charity banquet before she disgraced herself. Maybe if he'd been around more when the boys were growing up she wouldn't have been forced to seek refuge from her loneliness in a bottle, at least that was what she often threw at him. And maybe he was in some way to blame for her drinking, but not the jealousy, never that; because in all the years they'd been together he'd never once given her cause to doubt him.

She wouldn't agree with that, of course. What she would

say was that he was pathologically incapable of keeping himself zipped up – and his answer to that, but only to himself, was if he'd thought he could get away with it then in more recent years he probably wouldn't even have tried to hold back. It wasn't as if opportunities hadn't come his way, because plenty had. This wasn't him being boastful, it was simply a truth occurring fleetingly to him, if at all.

Viagra?

Where the hell had that come from?

He wouldn't even try to guess, because fathoming his wife and the way her mind worked had turned into as pointless a task as trying to make her see things the way most normal people did. She simply wasn't capable of it any more, which was why he knew he should be concerned by her threat to go public with what she knew. Although with Sylvie that could mean almost anything, if she was planning something crazy like telling the world that he knew more than he was admitting to about the girl, Mandie Morgan, he was already sinking with dismay to think of the chaos that would bring down on them all.

As if her addiction wasn't causing them enough already.

Just thank God the boys didn't know about the men she'd started taking home at night; or the way she often didn't make it to the bathroom. He knew it was common for drunks to become incontinent, but what he'd never imagined was it happening to the beautiful young girl he'd married. However, that girl was long gone now; in her place was a stranger, a victim drowning in her own dependence. He'd tried so many times and in so many ways to rescue her, but nothing he did or said ever seemed to make a difference. In the end, it was the cleaning up after her that had finally finished it for him; he never intended to go there again.

'Hey Mrs B,' Oliver said, as his friend's mother opened the front door of the Brents' large Edwardian semi in Redland. 'Is Alfie back yet?'

'In his room,' Janet Brent answered. 'Go on up.'

'Thanks. Oh, is my car still OK on your drive? Do you need me to move it?'

'My love, you're welcome to leave it there all day if you can persuade my son to tidy up his room.'

With a grin, Oliver said, 'Best I go and move it now then?'

Laughing, she closed the door and went back along the hall to the kitchen as Oliver took the wide staircase two at a time, to the second floor. 'Hey,' he said, crashing into Alfie's bedroom and startling his friend so badly that Alfie almost fell off the bed.

'Jesus, man,' Alfie grumbled, picking up the girlie mag he'd leapt to shove out of sight. 'I thought you were my old lady.'

'Like she doesn't know you read that stuff. What time did you get home?'

'About half an hour ago. Where did you rush off to?'

'Oh, I just had something to deal with. Can I use your computer?'

'Sure, help yourself. Did you get laid last night?'

'Did you?'

Alfie threw out his hands. 'Look at me man, what do you think?'

Oliver laughed. Since Alfie was a dead ringer for the most recent *X Factor* winner whose name Oliver had already forgotten, mainly because he never watched the show, Alfie had been getting more than his fair share of action. Not that Oliver was ever short of girls himself, but he never allowed himself to get involved – he didn't need the hassle, especially not while all this was going on with his mother.

'You might want to take a look at Jerome's Facebook page,' Alfie told him, as he settled down at the computer. 'Actually, he could be on his way over here.'

In spite of having been to separate universities these past three years – Leeds in Oliver's case, Nottingham in Alfie's and Manchester in Jerome's – the friendship between the three had remained strong, and now they were all living at home again while they looked for jobs, they'd taken up almost as though they'd never been apart.

'Hey, this is amazing,' Oliver declared as he read Jerome's wall. 'He's only been shortlisted for the job in Durban.'

Yawning, Alfie said, 'Tell me something I don't already know.'

'Lucky bastard,' Oliver muttered as he posted a message asking Jerome if he knew where Durban was. 'Has he ever been to South Africa?' he asked Alfie.

'Not as far as I know. His first interview was in London. Got to widen my own search, 'cos I have to get out of this place. Not Bristol, or yeah, Bristol, but it's more being back here, at home, that's doing my head in.'

'Tell me about it,' Oliver muttered, clicking on to his own page. No big surprise to find that he'd been poked by a couple of girls he'd known at uni, they were regularly in touch, and Cara Jaymes, who was in the sixth form of his old school, Clifton College, had posted some photos of last night's party. A mate, now back living in Reading with his parents, had sent him a link to a job he thought Oliver might be interested in as an analyst for a marketing company based in Blackheath. When Oliver clicked on to find more details he could only wonder what kind of degree his mate thought he'd taken, because for this position he needed either maths or computer science, or better still physics, neither of which, as a media studies grad, he'd come even close to.

Still, it was good of the guy to think of him, so he got back to him saying thanks and they should get together soon, and was just about to click on to his brother's page when he noticed that Thea Cox, a girl he quite liked and who, so all her mates said, had a mega crush on him, had posted on his wall last night.

Didn't realise you had a famous dad.

Going off her in an instant, he reached for his mobile as it started to ring. Seeing who it was, he clicked on saying, 'Hey, is that my famous dad?'

'Very funny,' Russ retorted. 'Did you get my message?'

'Yeah, and sorry, I should have texted last night.'

'Don't forget next time. Where are you now?'

'At Alfie's. Where are you?'

'On my way home. I've just been to see your mother.'

'I know, I was there, but I thought it was best to let the two of you get on with it.'

'So you know what's happened?'

'I do. Is it going to be OK? Does Angie want to go to the police?'

'Thankfully, no. I'll pay for the repairs and we'll just have to hope it doesn't happen again.'

Oliver's expression became strained as he swivelled the chair away from his friend. 'We have to do something about her, Dad. We can't let her just go on you know . . .'

'I wish I knew what to tell you, son, but we've been to the meetings together, so you know as well as I do that until she's ready to help herself there's not much we can do.'

'So why don't you let her come home for a while? At least then we'd know where she is and what she's doing.' Did his dad know about the blokes his mum was picking up in bars and taking back to her flat at night? If not, Oliver didn't want to be the one to tell him.

With a sigh, Russ said, 'It's true, we would, but letting her come back to Clyde Court isn't the answer. She needs professional help, at a clinic where people know how to handle her sort of problems. Much as I'd like to, I'm afraid I can't force her to do that.'

'But you can let her come back.'

Sighing again, Russ said, 'Look, I realise this is your mother we're talking about, but she's also my wife. The way I deal with what's happening between us has to be between me and her.'

'So what you're actually saying is that you don't really care what happens to her?'

'No, Oliver, that isn't what I'm saying at all, and you know it. Now let's drop this till you get home, shall we? Can I expect to see you today?'

'I don't know. What's going on?'

'I'll probably be in the office until about four. Angie and Graham are already there finalising a pitch we're making in London tomorrow.'

'So you work Sundays now, too?'

'That's what happens when you work for yourself, I thought you'd at least learned that by now.'

Stung, Oliver said, 'So really there's not a lot of point me coming home, if no one's going to be there.'

'I shall be fifty yards away, in the stable block, and with any luck I'll be through around four. If you can make it, I have some news for you.'

Oliver was immediately wary. 'What sort of news?'

'It looks as though we're going to get the commission for another series of *Living Houses*. If we do, Paul Granger's keen to have you on board again.'

Oliver's scowl didn't lift. 'But he'll pay me this time, right?'

'Oliver, in your position you should be thankful to be getting some experience . . .'

'I'm twenty-one, I have a 2/1 in Media Studies, I need to earn a living and my father is telling me to work for free. Way to go, Dad.'

'If you don't want the job there are plenty out there who do . . .'

'Not for nothing, they don't.'

'I haven't said you won't be paid, I'm just saying that it hasn't been discussed and you shouldn't make it a condition. Now, this conversation has to be over. Try to be home by five.'

After ringing off Oliver turned to Alfie.

'So?' Alfie said.

'So?'

'What's the deal?'

'You mean with my dad? Don't let's even go there.'

Alfie grinned. 'Seems Thea's impressed with him, even if you aren't. I went on your Facebook page.'

Groaning as he rolled his eyes, Oliver said, 'What the hell's she on about, famous? He gave up all the reporting and news-reading crap over ten years ago.'

'I'll lay money it's her mother who's getting the hots. You know what women are like about celebs, and even if he's not one now, what counts is that he was once.'

Oliver laughed. 'He'd go mental if he heard you call him a celeb. He hates all that stuff.'

Alfie shrugged. 'If it's going to work for you . . . What the hell?' he exclaimed as Jerome suddenly burst into the room. 'Didn't any of you guys ever hear about knocking?'

'Knock, knock,' Jerome cried breathlessly. 'Oliver, man,

let me at the computer. We can't miss this. What's the time?'

Alfie glanced at the clock. 'Eleven thirty-one, precise enough for you?'

'Shit, it's already started. Come on, Oliver, let me in.'

'What's happening?' Oliver grumbled, vacating the chair.

'Lisa Amos is filming someone having a Brazilian at half eleven and if anyone can guess who it is, we get to go with her at Lisa's twenty-first the Saturday after next.'

Oliver and Alfie looked at one another. 'What the hell's he talking about?' Alfie wanted to know.

'God knows,' Oliver answered.

'Here it is!' Jerome shouted, sitting back as a slightly blurry image came up on the screen.

Oliver and Alfie came to peer over his shoulder. 'What's a Brazilian?' Alfie murmured.

'It's a girl thing, to do with waxing,' Jerome explained.

'Exactly what are we looking at?' Oliver demanded.

Jerome didn't seem entirely sure, until the webcam pulled back and the shot gained focus.

'Oh my God,' Alfie murmured, his eyes starting to bulge. 'Is that what I think it is?'

Jerome was grinning and nodding. 'Pussy,' he declared, with great satisfaction. 'Any idea who it belongs to?'

Alfie and Oliver were mute.

'Come on you guys, you've got to fill me in if you know, because it's the only way . . . Shit, what are? Someone's only covering it up.'

The three of them watched, mesmerised, as two delicate hands patted a long white strip over one half of the anonymous girl's genitals.

'Are you ready?' a female voice asked off camera.

'Ready,' Jerome whispered.

'She's not talking to you, you idiot,' Alfie told him. 'Oh my God, what the?' Instinctively they all three clasped their hands to their groins. 'Tell me that didn't just happen,' Alfie muttered.

'I think it did,' Oliver responded. 'Look, no hair on one side.'

'Seriously mental,' Jerome added. 'Shit man, I have so

got to find out who she is. It's my only chance of getting some action.' He looked at Oliver. 'Do you recognise her?'

Oliver was incredulous. 'Yeah, like this is how I always identify women.'

'I'm guessing it's a friend of Lisa's,' Alfie said helpfully. 'I mean, if she's going to the party.'

'She's a babe,' Jerome declared. 'You can tell, can't you, you don't even have to see her face.'

Alfie and Oliver exploded with laughter. 'Sure, she's a babe,' Oliver agreed, 'and because we're such great mates of yours, we're going to put ourselves on a mission to find out exactly who she is, and when we do, Jerome, my friend, she'll be all yours.'

Chapter Four

'Hey, Mum, it's me,' Lauren cried into the phone. 'Did you remember to pick up my car?'

Juggling her mobile as she unloaded her shopping trolley on to the conveyor belt, Emma said, 'I've just been and the problem's fixed, so it'll be waiting when you get back from London. Is everything OK with you?'

'Yeah, cool. Got a ton of revising to do. Where are you?'

'At the supermarket, about to check out, so I ought to go.'

'OK. Did you speak to Granny Berry today? She rang me trying to get hold of you.'

'Yes, we had a long chat earlier. She wanted to know if I'm going to be in town at all before your performance exam, because she's got some paintings going into an exhibition. I told her I wouldn't miss it.'

'Too right we won't. Is Alfonso coming over from Italy?'

'I believe so. Right, it's me next so I have to go. I'll call you later.' As she rang off she heard the sounds of a commotion further along the store and looked up to find out what it was.

The young girl at the till in front of her was on her feet. 'That is so amazing, isn't it?' she declared, beaming all over her face.

'What is it?' Emma said, trying to work out what was happening.

'It's one of them golden angels,' the girl explained. 'She's just paid that old lady's bill. Oh God, look at the old lady's face. She's so thrilled she's crying.'

Recognising Mrs Dempster who lived on the same street as her, Emma found herself clapping and laughing along with everyone else. 'So where's the angel?' she wondered.

'No idea,' the checkout girl replied. 'Been and gone, I expect. Apparently they never hang around. She's such a dear old soul, Mrs D. She's my friend's gran. It couldn't have happened to a nicer person.'

Though she'd only spoken to Mrs Dempster on one occasion, when they'd spent a few minutes standing in the freezing cold outside Emma's house wondering when the new gates were going to be fitted, Emma had no problem believing that the old lady was well liked simply from the kindliness of her smile, and the gentleness of her rheumy grey eyes. 'I wonder what made them choose her?' she said.

The girl shrugged as she sat back down and continued to scan the groceries through. 'No one has a clue. We don't even know they're coming until they're here. They just turn up, pick someone at random, pay the bill, in cash, and go.'

'So they've been to this store before?'

'Only once, about a month ago. They chose some really grumpy old sod that time. He was at the checkout next to mine, and you should have heard him carrying on. He kept telling the woman, angel, whatever, to bugger off and mind her own business, he even tried to hit her with his stick. Then he finally got what was going on and you should have seen him. Honest to God, I nearly cried myself, it was so lovely seeing all the misery melting off his scabby old face. He turned out to have a bit of a lovely smile, and he even had teeth, which none of us expected. I reckon it was the first time anyone had done something nice for him in so long he'd forgotten it ever happened.'

Picturing the scene, Emma found herself wishing she'd thought of doing something like this when she'd had the money, even if on a smaller scale. Alas, she was in no position to do it now. 'So how long has it been happening?' she asked.

'About a year, I suppose. Sometimes they don't come for ages, then just when you think it's all over you get a great flurry of them turning up. The Lidl over by my auntie's had six of them in the week before Christmas, so you can imagine what a fantastic present that must have been for the lucky ones. I just wish someone would drop in and pay my bill is all I can say, but I don't suppose us what works here are going to get a look-in. Right, looks like we're done, so unless the angel comes back that'll be fifty-eight thirty-three, please.'

Relieved that she'd managed to keep the bill below sixty after shelling out ninety-two pounds for Lauren's car, Emma handed the money over and after taking her change and receipt wheeled her trolley out to the car park. It was already pitch dark outside, and so cold that the rain started to freeze in tiny icicles on the fur around her hood. How lucky she was to have her own transport, because she'd caught the bus to the garage earlier without checking first if the car was ready. If it hadn't been she'd be in the queue now with at least a dozen others, having to heft her shopping home on a Green Line.

Sorry that she didn't have the courage to offer someone a lift, she continued on to Lauren's Peugeot, loaded in her bags, and was just returning her trolley when she spotted Mrs Dempster amongst those in the pensioners' transport queue. Not allowing herself a moment's hesitation, she quickly went up to her, saying, 'Hello, do you remember me? I live on the same street as you, at number forty.'

'Of course I do, dear,' the old lady smiled, her words coming out of her blue lips in ragged puffs of white air. 'Emma isn't it, and your lovely daughter, Lauren.'

'That's right. Can I give you a lift? I'm going straight home.'

'Oh my goodness me, this is my lucky day,' Mrs Dempster chuckled delightedly. 'If you're sure it's no trouble . . .'

'Absolutely not. It would be my pleasure. Here, let me take your bags.'

A few minutes later, bundled into the front of the small car with the heater going full pelt and the wipers slicing back and forth, Emma steered them out into the traffic where nothing was going anywhere fast. 'I'm afraid we've hit the rush hour,' she commented with a sigh.

'Oh well, I don't suppose there's any avoiding it. I hope you're not in a hurry.'

'No no, not at all, it'll just be nice to get home and into the warm.'

'Oh, that it will. I nearly never left the house today it was so bitter out, but I'm glad I did now, because if I hadn't the angels would have missed me. Did you see what happened?'

'It was lovely,' Emma smiled.

Mrs D was beaming. 'There's a thing, isn't it?' she sighed happily. 'I don't never win nothing, me, and then suddenly this woman comes out of the blue, and I'm being chosen to have everything in my trolley paid for. I hardly knew what to say. That's like giving me *seventy quid*. Can you imagine having that much you can just hand it over to a stranger? I can't wait to tell our Alan, he'll be tickled to death, he will.'

'Alan's your son?'

'That's right. He lives up Gloucester way, but he knows about these angels, because he was reading it in the paper when he came down with his family at Christmas. He reckoned it could be a sort of marketing thing that some rich person's going to end up making a fortune out of, and I suppose he could be right, but you could hardly begrudge them that if they're being so generous with everyone, could you?'

'I suppose not,' Emma agreed. 'I'd love to know who's behind it, wouldn't you?'

'Oh yes, especially after today, just so's I could say thank you. Actually, I've already decided what I'm going to do with my little windfall. In fact, it couldn't have come at a better time, because our Amy – that's my youngest grand-daughter – is going to be twenty-one in March. I can get her something a bit special now. She'll like that. We should all have something special when we turn twenty-one, don't you think?'

Resisting the urge to squeeze this dear old lady's hand, Emma found herself thinking of her mother and how she'd probably do the same, and put Lauren and Harry's two children at the top of her list of beneficiaries should she happen to enjoy an unexpected bonus. Phyllis was definitely a lot better in a grandmother's role than she'd ever been as a mother.

'I can't help wondering how random these selections really are,' Emma said to Polly on the phone later. 'Do you reckon whoever's behind it is in touch with social services, or Age Concern, or someone who can point them in the right direction?'

'Absolutely no idea,' Polly replied, 'except if you go back over the list of winners I don't think you'll find everyone is really hard up or about to be thrown out on the streets. There was one woman a few months ago who turned out to be the managing director of a garden centre. To her credit, she doubled the amount she'd saved on her grocery bill and donated something like two hundred quids' worth of plants and stuff to a local care home. Which just goes to show, what goes around, comes around. At least some of the time. Oh, hang on, that must be the five fifty easyJet from Geneva going over.'

Grimacing and laughing, Emma said, 'And Billy Fudge, who happens to be on board, is going to be late for the award ceremony he's attending on behalf of his wife who's raised thousands for a cancer charity, but whose terminal illness has kept her at home.'

'Blimey, I didn't realise the poor woman's condition had got that serious,' Polly quipped. 'Should we drive out to the airport to pick him up?'

'No, because then we'd have to collect the Willoughby family, who are returning nine days earlier than expected from their ten-day ski trip, because their house has burned down.'

'Oh God, does anyone on this plane have a happy story?'

'Luckily, there's Fabien, who has just landed the lead role in a feature film all being shot in Bath.'

'Much better. And speaking of jobs, how did things go today?'

Giving in to the urge to refill her wine glass, even though she'd had a large one already, Emma said, 'Great interviews at two agencies, so now I wait to see what they can set up. Actually, one of them suggested I go on a catering course, which was extremely helpful.'

'What a cheek. Had she bothered to acquaint herself with your history?'

'God knows, but maybe what she was saying was that it would help to have some official qualifications. How are things your end?'

'Well, not too bad. In fact, I might have had a visit from an angel myself today. Not at the supermarket, but here, at home – and he didn't drop in, he was at the end of the phone. He's quite a new client actually, his little boy, Taylor, joined us back in October. I've never actually met Daddy because it's always Granny who brings Taylor in, but I know he's some kind of businessman with a company based in the centre of Bristol.'

'What about Mummy?'

'All I can tell you is that Taylor's daddy – Alistair Wood's his name – is listed as a single parent, so whether Mummy died or ran off into the blue beyond I've no idea. Anyway, I got this call around lunchtime today from said Mr Wood saying how sorry he was to hear that the nursery has bumped up against some difficulties and perhaps we could meet to discuss them?'

Emma was blinking. 'So is he offering to help in some way?'

'I'm not sure. I know I should have asked, but I was so taken aback that I didn't think to ask anything until after he'd rung off.'

'When are you seeing him?'

'He's coming here at seven o'clock next Tuesday. Oh, hang on, Melissa's shouting something . . . She wants to know where to get hold of Lauren tonight. Apparently she's not answering her mobile.'

'She's rehearsing with Donna,' Emma told her, 'so I expect they've got their phones turned off.'

After relaying the answer Polly returned to the line with, 'Is she coming home this weekend?'

'As far as I know I'm picking her up from the train on Saturday morning.'

'OK, I'll pass it on when we've finished. They're probably trying to sort out what party, or wine bar, or nightclub they're going to. So, where were we?'

'Mr Wood.'

'That's right, but actually, moving on from there, something . . .' she paused as another plane roared over Emma's back garden, 'something occurred to me this morning that might be of some interest to you.'

'Go on,' Emma prompted, emptying half a carton of tomato soup into a pan to start heating it up.

'Well, a couple of years back there was this series of articles in the local paper about the lives of ordinary Bristolians. It was a young girl who wrote them, I forget her name, but they were really good, kind of relevant and funny, even tragic sometimes. Something happened to her, I can't remember what it was now, but she ended up moving away. Anyway, the point is, she was going round interviewing people at a time when things weren't nearly as dire as they are now and there were still stories to be told. So think how many must be out there now.'

'So what are you suggesting, that I go round knocking on people's doors asking if they'll tell me their saddest stories?'

'Not exactly, or not at first, anyway. What I'm saying is why don't you get hold of someone at one of the local papers or magazines and offer to write a similar series, on spec, but if they run them they have to pay.'

Emma was cautiously liking the sound of this. 'I'd have to go in with a sample story,' she pointed out, 'or how will they know I can write? How do *I* know, when I've hardly done any since I left uni, or not of the creative or journalistic variety.'

'I have every confidence in you, and even though I say it myself, I think I could be a pretty interesting start. If I tell you the story of what happened to Jack, and how I got myself back together, only to be floored again by this recession . . . Well, I can think of worse options to get going on.'

'So can I,' Emma agreed, starting to run with it. 'I'll need to think it over some more, but in principle it could be a great idea. I could do the interviews in between looking for a full-time job, and if I do manage to start work, I might even be able to carry them on in my spare time. Polly, you're amazing. I really think you might have come up with something here.'

'Delighted to be of service. We can get together at the weekend to make a start, if you like.'

'Absolutely. I might even splash out on a couple of steaks if you'd like to come for dinner.'

'In that case, I'll bring the wine. Or can we possibly stretch to dinner at the pub?'

Emma baulked. 'I guess if it's just the two of us . . .'

'The girls are bound to be going out,' Polly reminded her, 'though at some point I'll have to get round to telling Melissa I won't be able to go on funding her social life the way I used to – or her wardrobe.'

Already hearing the explosion, Emma said, teasingly, 'Unless Mr Wood has a plan.'

'Oh, don't get my hopes up, please, but wouldn't it be wonderful if he has?'

'Fantastic, and I'm staying optimistic so you should too. Now, I have to go, I'm afraid. Someone's been trying to get through for the past ten minutes so I ought to find out who it is.'

After clicking off and picking up again she barely had time to say hello before an irritable voice came down the line saying, 'About time too, I've been trying to get hold of you for the past half an hour. Who the hell have you been talking to?'

Tempted to slam the phone straight back down again, Emma somehow managed to keep her tone smooth as she said, 'Hello Will, what can I do for you?'

With a grunting sound as he tried to get past his umbrage he said, 'Lauren tells me there was a problem with her car. It's still under warranty, Emma, so why didn't you take it into a Peugeot garage?'

'As a matter of fact I did,' Emma retorted through her teeth, 'and it turned out that the fault wasn't covered. Does that satisfy your query? Good, I'll ring off now then and next time you call . . .'

'Just a minute, I haven't finished yet. I don't want my daughter thinking I'm landing you with bills that ought to be mine, so if you can let me know the cost of the repair . . .'

'It doesn't matter.'

'I want to know.'

Remembering that she really did need the money, she was fleetingly tempted to double the amount. In the end she said, 'It was just under a hundred quid.'

'OK, I'll send a cheque to cover it.'

Still wishing she could tell him where to stuff it, she said, 'Do you have the address?'

'As a matter of fact you haven't seen fit to give it to me yet, so now might be a good time.'

'I'll text it,' she told him and was about to ring off when he said, 'So how are you settling in down . . . What the hell is that?'

After waiting for the plane to go over she replied mildly, 'The four ten from Corfu.'

There was a brief moment before he said, aghast, 'You're living on a flight path?'

'We weren't so far from one in Chiswick,' she snapped irritably.

'It was never anything like that.'

'Well it is now. So, if you've finished I'd like to have my dinner . . .'

'Why are you always so tetchy?'

'Oh, let me think about that.'

Sighing loudly, he said, 'You know, bitterness isn't attractive.'

Wanting to knife him, she said, 'Nor are cheating, lying and stealing, but it doesn't seem to have done you much harm, does it?'

'Oh, for God's sake, I can't talk to you.'

'You were never invited to,' and before he could say any more she banged the phone down so hard that the back came off the handset and broke.

Damn you, Will Scott, she seethed to herself as she picked up the pieces. She really, really didn't need to be forking out for a new phone right now, much less did she need his preposterous, false-hearted attempts at cosy little chats. Why didn't he get that she wanted no more to do with him? Which part of get lost, drop dead, disappear down a slimy plughole did he not understand?

Just thank God Lauren was getting older, thereby reducing the need for contact, or she might never be done with the thieving, sponging, double-crossing toad, and how much she loathed him. Had she really loved him once? How could that have happened? The truth was, she'd been so swept away by his charm and his looks and the way everything always seemed possible for him, that it had taken years for her to see how worthless and shallow he really was. OK, she was still being harsh, because they had been happy once, blissfully in fact, and if she dug through all the crap of the past few years she'd emerge into pastures full of wonderful memories, especially after Lauren had been born. And even today she was – albeit grudgingly – prepared to admit that he had some good qualities, though the only one she could think of right now was the generous allowance he paid Lauren each month which she, Emma, would never have been able to manage herself.

Deciding, for the sake of her own sanity, to put the last few minutes behind her or she'd be planning her ex-husband's hasty dispatch until gone midnight, she carried her meagre dinner into the sitting room and turned on the TV. A quick catch-up with the news, maybe an episode of *Corrie*, then she'd return to her computer to see if she could conjure some enthusiasm or inspiration from the hundreds of jobs she'd already pored over at least a dozen times. There was always the chance, she supposed, that some little quirk of imagination would kick in to show her why she was just the right person for the position of construction site manager, or even a personal banking advisor – ha, ha, or lol as Lauren would say.

Polly's suggestion was definitely feeling like a pretty good one, provided she possessed the skills to make a go of it, of course, and she was also going to give more thought to something she'd discussed with Berry earlier. She'd started her first little empire with nothing more than a sandwich round, so maybe she could pull it off again. There was a business park a couple of miles down the road, so perhaps she'd take a drive down there tomorrow to get the lie of the land. It had to be worth a try, anything did, if only to light a spark of optimism in the gloomy little backwater that her world now seemed to be.

'Mum! Hey, it's me,' Lauren cried into the phone. 'Have you been trying to get hold of me?'

Forcing herself awake, Emma said groggily, 'What time is it?'

'Just after half ten. Sorry, were you asleep?'

Emma's expression turned wry as she looked around. 'At the kitchen table in front of the computer,' she admitted, wincing as she stretched her neck, 'so you did me a favour. Is everything OK? Where are you?'

'At Granny Berry's. She's decided to fly back from Italy tomorrow instead of next week, so I've come round to turn up the heating. Anyway, I'm ringing because we've just posted some new stuff on YouTube. I've emailed you the links already. There's one of me and Donna on our guitars doing Suzanne Vega's "Marlene on the Wall", which is one of Granny's favourites, so I've emailed her too. Then there's a couple of Skye and Matilda doing their Brahms violin concerto in D minor, and they're both absolutely brilliant. And wait till you hear Salina Buck singing *"Ritorna vincitor!"*, you know, from *Aida*. Mum, she is totally awesome. She is so going to blow us all away when we do our performance exams.'

Smiling as she clicked on to the website, Emma said, 'Did Melissa get hold of you? I think she must have been trying while you were recording.'

'Oh yeah, I called her back about ten minutes ago. She wants me to pick up some strings for her guitar at the shop on King's Road, which is fine. She also wanted to talk about what we're doing at the weekend, but the thing is, Mum, I've got a ton of work to do, plus Dad's offering to pay me to babysit for him and Jem on Saturday night, so if it's all right with you, I thought I'd skip this weekend.'

Having feared this would happen, though not in the least prepared to face it so soon, Emma heard her voice shake slightly as she said, 'That's OK. I know how busy you are.'

'Oh, you do mind, don't you? I knew you would. It's OK, I'll come home like we planned.'

'No, no, no. I understand how much revision you have and if you've already promised Dad . . .'

'Oh, Mum, I feel really terrible now. Is it awful being there on your own?'

'Of course not. I'm so busy I hardly notice most of the time. And Polly's coming over on Saturday. We're going to work on a new project together.'

'Sounds interesting. Are you going to tell me what it is?'

'It can wait. Is someone there with you? I thought I heard voices.'

'Uh, it's just the telly. Hang on.' There were some muffled sounds as she presumably searched for the remote control, then she came back on the line saying, 'So the car's OK and Dad says he's going to reimburse you for the repair.'

'That's right.'

'Cool.' Lauren started to laugh.

Puzzled, Emma said, 'What's funny?'

'Nothing. No, it's just . . . Oh my God, stop . . . Sorry, Mum, it's . . . Actually, I should ring off. Are you sure you don't mind about the weekend?'

'Of course not.' What else could she say? Lauren was eighteen now, had a life of her own and a punishing set of exams ahead of her. 'Actually, before you go, have you heard about these golden angels?'

'These what? Oh God, Mum, I'm really, really sorry . . . We'll speak in the morning, OK?' and she was gone.

Thrown, Emma rang off too and sat staring at the computer where Salina Buck, one of Lauren's outstandingly gifted friends, was poised ready to sing. Not quite ready to hear it yet, Emma got to her feet and went to put on the kettle. It was so unlike Lauren to be abrupt that she still couldn't quite get a handle on it. Maybe she should call back to make sure everything was OK, except she certainly hadn't sounded as though anything was wrong. She'd seemed in quite high spirits, which was fine, excellent in fact, because why would she want her daughter to be any other way?

Picking up her mobile she sent Lauren a text. *Are you sure no one's there with you?*

She didn't get a reply until early the next morning. *At Donna's. Everyone's here. Love you speak later.*

'You know your trouble, you worry too much,' Berry told her when they spoke on the phone later in the day. 'I'm sure there's absolutely nothing going on with Lauren, other than the usual mayhem of being eighteen, talented and as popular as she is pretty. In fact, considering all she's been going through lately, moving house, her appalling work-load, I'd say it's a bit of a miracle she's coping so well. Of course, she gets it from me. I've never been easily fazed either, whereas you, my darling, are your mother all over.'

Emma flinched. 'Beryl, that was just mean,' she accused.

'Beryl? Who is this person?'

'The one who thinks she's funny telling me I'm like a woman who can't stand me.'

'Oh, you do so exaggerate.'

Emma didn't think so. 'Anyway, the important thing is, you're not worried about Lauren.'

'Absolutely not. I admit I haven't actually laid eyes on her since before Christmas, but from speaking to her almost daily I'd say the child is *en pleine forme*, as they say in Italy.'

'That's French.'

'But it means the same thing. In fact, if there's a teensy little problem at all, it's that she's worried about you, being down there all on your own in a house that I fear is too *piccolo* for me to get through the door.'

Emma gave a cry of protest. 'I know she didn't say that – and it's not that small, nor are you that large. You just can't bring yourself to be anywhere but Chelsea when you're in this country, so be honest.'

'At my age, and after all the travelling I've done, I know where I want to be, so why put myself through the torment of going anywhere else? Now, I want to hear that you're coming to London for my exhibition. Oh yes, you already agreed, didn't you? Must be getting Alzheimer's. I shall pay for your rail ticket, of course, *and* the dinner we shall have afterwards. I'd let you choose the restaurant if I didn't think you'd put me on a budget, so it's probably best to leave that to me.'

'Berry, you're being too generous . . .'

'No, what I actually am is a very selfish sixty-something who very much likes to have things her own way.'

Emma had to smile, since her extremely unselfish grandmother was a very lively, and actually still quite glamorous, eighty-two and three quarters.

'I really wouldn't want my little masterpieces to be part of an exhibition if you didn't come to see it,' Berry ran on. 'And having my darling Lauren around makes me happier than hashish, so you see it's all about me really, and if it's all about me, I think it's only fair that I should pay. So I shall ask Lauren to go on to the website when she pops round later, and book your ticket. Are you feeling sufficiently bullied yet, or shall I go on?'

Laughing, Emma said, 'You know very well I'd rather miss my own wedding than one of your shows, but . . .'

'Hang on, I'm not sure that's quite the right answer.'

Still laughing, Emma waved to Mrs Dempster as she passed the window, saying, 'I just want you to know that one of these days I'm going to pay you back for everything . . .'

'I thought I'd made myself clear. I'm doing all this for me, not you, so shall we move on? Or back, actually, because I rang your mother earlier, to invite her to the show, and we ended up having quite a long chat.'

The light in Emma's eyes dimmed. 'Do I want to know about this?' she asked sourly.

'I'm not sure, but she was keen to hear about how well you're settling in down there in Wales . . .'

'Berry, I'm in North Somerset – or Bristol, according to the postcode.'

'I knew it was somewhere in the west. Anyway, it brings me on to the question of why she doesn't have your address.'

'What do you mean? I sent her an email at the same time as I emailed everyone else.'

'Well, you know what she's like. She probably didn't appreciate being one of the crowd. Anyway, she has it now, because I gave it to her.'

'Frankly, I'm amazed she wants it.'

'Emma.'

Emma stayed silent.

'It's true, your mother does have a funny way of showing her feelings at times, but you have to believe me when I tell you I know she has them.'

'You and I have had this conversation so often over the years that it's bewildering to me that we're having it again.'

'OK, then we shall change the subject. Phyllis, be gone. What news on the job front?'

Coming to detest that question, Emma emptied her luke-warm coffee into the sink as she said, 'Nothing's new, apart from a couple of ideas I'm playing with, one of which we discussed yesterday. The other is something Polly suggested, which I'm also quite keen on.'

'Excellent, and if you need a little boost to help get you launched you know where to come. Now, I'm wondering who this belongs to,' she ran on. 'I know it's not mine, and it can't be Lauren's because she texted me earlier.'

'What is it?'

'A mobile phone I've just found down the side of the sofa.'

'Well, if it's not yours or Lauren's it must belong to one of her friends. Actually, I thought someone was there with her last night. Is there anything to identify it?'

'No, the battery seems to be dead and there's nothing on the casing. Oh well, I'm sure we'll find out when its owner realises it's missing. So, am I free to go now? Is your mind at rest about Lauren?'

'More or less, unless you happen to know if she's got a new boyfriend she's decided not to tell me about.'

'If she has then she hasn't told me either, but looking the way she does and being as lovely as she is, I think we have to assume there's always going to be someone. She is on the pill, I take it? At her age, she must be.'

'Yes, she's on the pill, but she only went on quite recently, I think because all her friends are on it, if only to be prepared.'

'Mm, sounds wise. You know I was rather fond of Parker. It's a shame she went off him.'

'I think he'd agree with you on that, because he keeps texting wanting to see her.'

'Poor love is probably totally heartbroken, and I fear he won't be the only one to suffer such a fate at our darling girl's hands.'

'Not that we're biased,' Emma responded drily.

'Not at all,' Berry agreed.

Twenty minutes later, after making the bed and cleaning round the bathroom, Emma was back in front of her computer trying not to read too much into an unexpected message, and failing. *Just wanted to recommend a charming little book called* The Guernsey Literary and Potato Peel Pie Society. *If you haven't already read it, I think you'll enjoy it.*

Once again he hadn't signed his name, but it was obviously from Philip Leesom and she could only wonder, since she hadn't read the book, if it might contain some sort of allusive message for her to decipher or respond to, perhaps in a similar way. How bizarre, and even romantic, it could be to use passages from favourite books as billets-doux, and what an exciting challenge it would be trying to find the right one to recommend next. However, even if she was right, and she almost certainly wasn't, there was simply no way she could enter into any sort of flirtation with one of Lauren's teachers.

It was funny, but she'd never have imagined herself to be his type. There again, she'd never imagined everyone's heart-throb, Will Scott, would single her out when they were at uni, but he had and had even gone on to marry her. And if ever there was a warning not to be taken in by looks and charm, that was most definitely it. She could already feel herself backing away, as well she might if she didn't want to end up making a complete fool of herself. Philip Leesom had kindly recommended a book that he'd enjoyed, and she, sad little person that she was, was sitting here behaving as though he was planning a major seduction. She really, desperately needed to get out more. She might even need to sign up to a dating website after all.

Faint with relief that he had no idea what effect he was having on her, she sent a quick return message saying *Thanks. Really sweet of you. Will look forward to it.* She almost added *and will report back* but stopped herself just in time. She simply wasn't going to encourage this, if indeed there was anything to encourage, so just a pleasant, slightly patronising response was undoubtedly the best way to go.

She was now facing the dilemma of whether or not to go on to Amazon to order the book. She decided it could wait. She wasn't short of reading material right now, and in any case her card was still maxed out, so if she did find herself intrigued enough to read it she would borrow it from the library – if they hadn't already closed it down by then.

Making a note to herself to join any campaign there might be locally to keep the libraries open, she clicked on to her next message and moments later was staring at the screen in overjoyed disbelief. (Probably another overreaction, but she wasn't going to give herself a hard time over this one.) One of the agencies she'd visited yesterday had only emailed to let her know that the perfect job had just come in for her: an Events Organiser at a leading West Country hotel with a salary of up to forty thousand per annum.

Grabbing the phone as it rang, she almost gushed as she said hello.

'Mrs Scott? It's Helen here, from Jobs4U. Have you seen my email?'

'Yes, just,' Emma cried. 'What amazing timing. Are you able to set up an interview?'

'Of course, I just needed to be sure you're interested before I get in touch with them, and to find out if there are any dates that won't work for you.'

'I can make it any time,' Emma assured her, wincing at the thought of Lauren's performance exam and Berry's exhibition. But they were both still a couple of weeks away, and they'd be in the evenings anyway, so there surely wouldn't be a clash. 'Do you know when they want someone to start?' she asked.

'I think they're looking at the beginning of March, which is perhaps not quite as soon as you'd like, but they'll have a lot of people to interview so they obviously want to give themselves time to be sure they have the right person.'

Emma's hopes hit the floor. The competition was going to be like first auditions for *Britain's Got Talent*. And they'd all be *young*.

'I have no doubt they're going to be completely blown away by you,' Helen breezed on loyally. 'I've already sent through your CV and they should let me know later today, or tomorrow, when they'd like to see you.'

When, not if – how sweet of her.

'With your background and experience,' Helen continued, 'I really think you're in with a very good chance.'

'What about my age?'

'Oh, but that can't come into it.'

'Maybe not, but it does. They might not want a woman either.'

'Please try to have confidence in yourself, but if you do sense any sort of discrimination you must let me know.'

'Of course. So I'll wait to hear from you?'

'Lovely. I have your mobile number, just in case, and with any luck we'll be speaking again before the end of the day.'

As she put down the phone Emma had no idea whether she wanted to jump for joy or run away and hide. This job had to be hers, please, please, please God, it just had to be.

Chapter Five

Though Russ's first reaction was to gasp in shock, he found himself unable not to laugh as Angie's cry of euphoria tipped her over the back of her chair and sent her crashing to the floor.

Being the closest, Graham, her fellow associate, dashed to the rescue. 'Are you OK?' he choked, hardly able to contain his own mirth.

Russ was on his feet ready to lend more assistance, but when Angie's beet-red, freckled face peered up over the edge of the desk with a mortified grin, he relaxed again.

'And for my encore . . .' she said boldly.

Bursting into more laughter, Russell sank back in his chair and watched her carefully restoring her dignity as she retook her seat in the most exaggeratedly ladylike fashion she could manage.

'So,' Graham announced, returning to his desk, 'I guess we'll long remember the moment we heard we'd won a commission for *West Country Towns*. Just didn't expect you to go quite so over the top, Angie.'

'Yeah, yeah, very funny,' she muttered, flinging a pen in his direction. 'This is my first big deal, remember, so I reckon I'm entitled to get a bit carried away.'

'Exactly so,' Russ confirmed, deciding they could probably break out a bottle of champagne, even if it was still only four o'clock. With Carleen and Percy Sharland in one of the editing rooms to help them drink it, and Paul Granger and Oliver about to return from a recce, there would be no shortage of takers. It was just a pity that Toyah, their office manager, wasn't around to join in, but she'd left an hour ago to go and collect her poorly six-year-old from school and take her home.

'Oh God, I am so loving this job,' Angie gushed, as the bottle came out of the fridge in the kitchen area of their open-plan office suite. 'Please don't sack me when my probation period's up next month, or I'm afraid I'll just have to shoot myself.'

'With the hours you're putting in,' Russ responded, as he removed the foil, 'and the kind of energy you put into the pitch on Monday, I don't think we'll be handing you the gun just yet.'

With a grin that made his lopsided features almost handsome, Graham said, 'You were totally awesome, Ange, amazing, no one would ever have believed it was your first pitch, so this commission is definitely down to you.'

'Oh, and like all the research and writing up and everything else you guys did had nothing to do with it?'

'It was a team effort,' Russ informed them, standing aside for Graham to take some glasses from a cupboard over the microwave, 'mostly led by you two, which gives me great faith in being able to keep this company afloat while so many of our competitors are going under.' It was going to be a near thing, every commission was vital now, and this was the first good news they'd had in weeks.

Graham said, 'By my reckoning, once this deal's been signed, and I just know it will be, we'll have no less than four projects at various stages of production, which really ain't bad when you consider the state of the world we're in.'

Glancing up at the sound of a car driving across the gravelled forecourt, Russ said, 'But it's no excuse to become complacent. We still need to be pulling in as many projects and producers as we can to help get their ideas to the screen, if we're going to weather this storm.'

Receiving no argument with that, he began filling half a dozen glasses with a fairly decent Laurent Perrier, while Angie skipped off along the narrow corridor that led to the largest editing-cum-meeting room to dig out Carleen and Percy. The pair were putting together a rough cut of a documentary on the current use of coal mines, a joint commission from BBC Wales and the Discovery Channel that Russ and his team had won for them back in September. Now all Russ had to do was executive-produce the project, which meant making sure they stayed on budget, their scripts were both entertaining and informative and the finished product was of the required quality. Not an enormous task when the producers knew their game and conducted themselves in a professional manner – an out-and-out nightmare when they got caught up on their own egos or found themselves unequal to his exacting standards. Fortunately that didn't happen too often, but whenever it did he and Toyah made a note not to work with that producer or production company again.

Times were such that they might not be able to be so fussy in the future. Now, only four out of the eight desks in the office were in constant use, and the three edit suites and two meetings rooms were empty more often than they were full. Still, at least they remained operational, and with ambitious and dynamic young associates like Graham and Angie, he was going to remain confident that they'd stay that way. Angie, considering her tender age (twenty-two) and relative inexperience (actually none that had ever been paid), was probably one of the most impressive finds he'd made in a long time. Her attention to detail, quick thinking and spectacular imagination were becoming as integral to proceedings as Graham's unerring ability to spot a winner, and Russ's own input which oversaw and put together the whole thing.

So it was a great relief to him that Angie hadn't abandoned ship in fright after Sylvie's outrageous behaviour, or taken offence at being accused of an affair with a man who was old enough to be her father, and her new boss to boot. The entire episode had been intensely embarrassing for them both, and he could see how uncomfortable Angie still was whenever she happened to answer the phone to Sylvie. He also knew, through Graham, that Angie hadn't slept alone in her flat since the night Sylvie had let rip outside. Apparently a girlfriend had moved into her spare room to keep her company until everything had been sorted out and all the drama had died down.

Russ couldn't even begin to imagine when that happy day might dawn, but something had to be done to draw it closer. His alcoholic wife attacking an innocent young girl simply for working at his office was so far from acceptable that he shuddered to think what Sylvie might do were she ever to find out about the woman he really was involved with. Fortunately, no one, but no one, knew about him and Fiona, and for her sake, perhaps more than anyone else's, he intended to keep it that way.

'Hey, looks like I turned up just in time,' Paul Granger declared as he came hastily through the door to escape the rainstorm outside. 'Am I to assume from this that you've had some good news?'

'Only the best,' Graham informed him, standing back to avoid the freezing spray as Granger shrugged off his coat. 'The budget we asked for and presenter of our choice.'

'I don't believe it!' Granger cried, turning to Russ. 'That's quite something. I only wish I was producing.' Though Granger wasn't employed by Russ's company, officially, he'd produced and directed so many programmes and training videos for them over the years that the two men had come to view one another more as partners than mere colleagues.

'Frankly, I wish you were too,' Russ told him, 'but Guy Fitch has his strong points, and the idea was his, plus the contacts are all his . . .'

'Was he there for the pitch?'

'Sure, but he was clever enough to let Angie take over. She's got a gift for it, we've discovered, so we're damned lucky to have her.'

'I heard that,' she said, beaming as she came back into the office. 'Hey Paul, how did the recce go?'

Rolling his eyes, Granger said, 'Champagne first, and congratulations to all . . . Carleen, love of my life,' he cried as a willowy brunette with intense green eyes and a low-cut top followed Angie through the door. 'Oh God, husband in tow, how are you doing, Perce?'

Laughing, Percy came to shake Granger's hand, while Russ finished pouring the champagne and Graham and Angie passed around glasses.

'To Clyde Court Productions and all who sail in her,' Graham declared, saluting them all.

'Hear, hear,' everyone echoed.

As they drank, the sound of the rain battering the vaulted ceiling of the old stable block seemed to seal them into a safe and private place that felt like an exclusive refuge from a bad, bad world outside. This sense of security made Russ feel connected to his team in a way that reminded him that not everything had to be about family.

Turning to Granger he said, 'I'm almost afraid to ask, but where is my son?'

Granger's large, bearded face broke into a smile. 'Don't worry, he's done you proud this afternoon, he was right on it with the National Trust gits – guys – and he didn't mention a word to me about being paid.'

Not entirely reassured, Russ said, 'But you told him he will be, and how much?'

'Sure and he fell silent.'

After waiting for the laughter to die down, Russ said, 'So, he knows he's not going to get rich any time soon. Did he come back with you?'

'Yep, but he's gone over to the house. He wants to check his email, he said, in case some proper jobs have come up.'

Russ's face darkened. 'Tell me he didn't use those words.'

'He didn't use those words.'

Knowing Oliver almost certainly had, Russ decided not to spoil the celebration by leaving right now, but his son had better still be in the house when he got there because grown man or not, he clearly still had a few lessons to learn.

'No, Jerome, I haven't worked out who the ruddy pussy belongs to yet,' Oliver was saying into his mobile, as he opened the fridge door to take out a Coke. 'Will you cut me a break for five minutes and stop going on about it?'

'It's all right for you, man, you've got Thea and all those other babes . . .'

'Jerome, Thea and I are not an item . . . Oh, shit!' he cried as a spray of Coke cascaded over the kitchen that had probably just been cleaned, and had supposedly won awards when it was first designed, thanks to its shape and glossy black units and surfaces.

'Are you still there?' Jerome demanded.

'Course I am, but listen . . .'

'I am. I thought Thea was interested in your dad?'

'You are such an asshole at times, do you know that? Don't you get anything?'

'That's my point, man, I'm getting none, so if you can tell me who she is, the one who had the Brazilian . . .'

'I have to ring off now . . .'

'Don't do that. I need to win this . . .'

'For Christ's sake, Jerome, no one's ever going to work out who the pussy belongs to, it's all a great big tease, you've got to see that.'

'But they made a promise, and you've seen more of them than I have, so who would you reasonably match that one up with?'

Laughing, in spite of himself, Oliver said, 'I'll look at it again, OK, and if I come up with anything . . .'

'Tell me you didn't just say that. How can anything *not come up*?'

Laughing again, Oliver said, 'Mate, I've got your best interests at heart. I just want you to remember me when you're down there in Durban raking in the mega-millions and looking for the best ad agency in the world, because that's where I'll be.'

'You so have my business,' Jerome assured him. 'Now, getting back to . . .'

'Jerome, I have to go. My dad's just come in,' and without giving his friend a chance to speak again he clicked off the line and quickly scooped a cloth from the sink to start cleaning up the Coke.

'What's happened here?' Russ wanted to know as he realised what Oliver was doing.

'It was an accident, OK? I flipped the tab and it went everywhere. Now I'm cleaning it up. No need to get in a sweat.'

Not rising to the belligerence, Russ went to pull a stool from under the breakfast bar and sat down heavily. This room with its octagonal shape and wall of windows looking out over the garden and acres of billowing countryside beyond was, quite literally, the very heart of the house. The entrance hall seemed to embrace it with huge double doors – never closed – opening into it, and the sitting room, grand as it was, couldn't quite muster the same comfort or space.

'So what happened with Paul this afternoon?' Russ asked, starting to peel a clementine.

Oliver shrugged. 'I think it all went well,' he answered, still sponging down the American fridge.

'I'm not talking about the meeting, I'm talking about what he's going to pay you. Are you happy with it?'

Oliver didn't even bother to turn round. 'Yeah, sure, minimum wage is what I went to uni for. Great, bring it on.'

Russ did not reply.

Oliver was used to his father's intimidation by silence, so he carried on with what he was doing, refusing to be cowed.

More silence.

More mopping.

Longer silence.

Careful mopping.

'Oliver.'

Wishing he felt as though he'd won while somehow knowing he hadn't, Oliver turned around.

'I want to help you, you understand that, don't you?' Russ said.

Oliver nodded, because yeah, he guessed he did, it was just that they had different views on help.

'My contacts in the advertising world are limited, I've already told you that . . .'

'We don't have to go through this again, Dad.'

'Would you rather not work with Paul?'

'No, it's cool.'

'So what's the problem?'

'There isn't one.'

Another Dad silence.

Oliver sipped from what was left in the can.

'Do you have any interviews lined up?' Russ asked.

'Not right now, but I'm on it.'

Russ nodded slowly. 'I hope you've come to realise what screwing up your internship with McCanns has cost you.'

Oliver's face tightened with anger and embarrassment. 'That wasn't my fault,' he cried. 'I didn't ask that stupid woman to come on to me . . .'

'Maybe not, but you could have backed away . . .'

'Like she gave me a chance. Anyway, yeah, if it satisfies you, I do realise what it's cost me, OK? I could probably have a job there right now, working my way up, but I haven't, because I gave some senior exec what she was begging for.'

Not entirely unsympathetic to the situation his son had found himself in, nor impressed either, Russ decided to let the matter go, already half-regretting even bringing it up. He'd seen the woman and though she was easily old enough to be Oliver's mother, there weren't many lads his age, or any other, who'd have been able to turn her down. 'There is someone I've been thinking about who might be able to help,' he said deliberately. 'He's not actually in advertising, but . . .'

'I can do this, Dad. OK?'

Russ's eyes narrowed.

'Why are you looking at me like that?' Oliver demanded. 'I told you, I can do it.'

'Frankly, I'd find that easier to believe if I saw some energy going into the search.'

Oliver's eyes turned flinty. 'You don't know what I'm doing, or who I'm talking to.'

'Then tell me. If nothing else it might put my mind at rest.'

'Jesus Christ,' Oliver seethed, throwing out his arms. 'Why do you always have to do this?'

'Do what?'

'Make an issue out of everything?'

'My son's future happens to be a very big issue for me, I just wish I could believe it was one for him too.'

Oliver flushed with fury. 'I don't have to stick around here putting up with this shit,' he growled.

'Don't go any further than that door,' Russ warned him quietly.

Spinning round, Oliver shouted, 'When do you get off treating me like a kid? I'm twenty-one . . .'

'I'm perfectly aware of how old you are, and when you start acting your age I'm sure I won't have any problem . . .'

'Wrong! You always have a problem with me. Just because I'm not like Charlie, top of everything, always going out of his way to make Daddy proud . . .'

'Stop being ridiculous,' Russ interrupted. 'You're totally different characters, and I for one am glad of it. But *you*, young man, have got to start facing up to the fact that we don't get anything in this life unless we work for it, and the work doesn't stop when university is over. In fact, it's just the beginning, because this is where the really hard part comes in, and so far I'm not seeing you grasping that.'

Furious, Oliver shouted, 'I don't want to spend the next six months working as a fucking gofer on those shit little dramas that no one ever watches anyway. It'll screw up everything. I won't be free for interviews, or for other temp jobs that'd be ten times more relevant . . .'

'If you could show me some evidence of these jobs, maybe I'd have more sympathy. Until then you can try to show a little more respect for me and the producer who's good enough to offer you a position that a thousand grads out there would give their eye teeth for.'

'Then let them have it, because no way do I want it, and just because you're my dad doesn't mean I have to do it.'

Russ's eyes were boring into his. 'As long as you're living in this house and I'm picking up all your bills, you'll do as you're told . . . Get back here now!'

'No way. I'm done listening to your crap, OK? I don't need your money, or your help. So tell Paul, thanks but no thanks, I can take care of myself.'

As the front door slammed Russ was sorely tempted to go after him, if only to stop his son driving while in a temper. However, it was probably best to let things simmer down in their own time, because Oliver's frustration had been building for a while. He'd needed to let rip, and they also needed some time out from each other – at least Oliver clearly needed some from him, and this blow-up might turn out to be exactly the kick up the pants that would motivate his extremely bright but overindulged and mixed-up younger son towards the battle zones of the future.

Taking out his mobile as it rang, Russ groaned aloud to see Sylvie's name on the screen. He might have let the call go through to voicemail were it not for the fact that he needed to speak to her anyway.

'Sylvie,' he said shortly.

'Russell, I want you to know . . . Are you alone? Can you talk?'

'Yes, I'm alone, go ahead.'

'I want you to know that I have not had a drink since last weekend and it is now Thursday. I hope that pleases you.'

'Of course it does,' he told her, knowing she was lying. 'I hope it pleases you too.'

'Yes, but I admit it is hard, especially while I am here on my own. If I was at home, where I should be, and I could show you . . .'

'Sylvie, you have to give up drinking for yourself, not for me.'

'But you keep saying it is what has caused the problems between us, so I am telling myself that if I stop you will give me another chance.'

Closing his eyes as he tried not to drop his head in despair, he said, 'Listen, I need to talk to you about Oliver. I've just had words with him and I think he's probably on his way to you.'

'What was it about?'

'I'm sure he'll tell you, but I don't want you cosseting him and giving him money every time he asks. He has to start coming to terms with the fact that he probably won't get the kind of job he wants right away, so like everyone else, he has to earn a living doing things that he might be overqualified for, or has no interest in.'

'You have been bullying him again.'

'For Christ's sake, someone has to, because I haven't seen any signs of him getting it together at all since he came down.'

'You need to give him more time. This country is going to the dogs; the jobs are not there . . .'

'Maybe not the ones he wants, but there are plenty of others.' *Boy, was his son going to the wrong place if he was on his way to his mother's, because no way in the world was she going to start pushing him.*

'You realise, I am sure,' she said, 'that you are the cause of his problems. He is very upset about us breaking up . . .'

'He's upset about a lot of things, and one of them is most definitely your drinking.'

'But I just told you, I have stopped so there is no need for him to worry now, and if you would let me come home I am sure you will see a very big improvement in him.'

Russ was barely able to disguise his annoyance. 'I'm not letting you use him like this. Five days without alcohol isn't convincing me of anything where you're concerned, and even if it did, I've already told you, we've reached the end. There is no going back for us . . .'

'But there can be if you would let it,' she cried.

'We were talking about Oliver, and I agree, us breaking up probably is having an effect on him. So please keep me in touch with what he's doing if he does come to you, and if you can talk him into taking the job Paul Granger's offered him, then all the better.'

'And what about us? When are we going to talk about us?'

Biting back his frustration he said, 'I have to go now. Please text me when Oliver gets there so I know he's arrived safely.'

'What if he doesn't come straight here?'

'Then I'll find him.'

'Are you still seeing that whore?'

'Have you written a cheque to pay for the damage you did to *my associate's* car?'

'She deserved it . . .'

'She's barely more than a kid, for Christ's sake!'

'That has never stopped you before.'

'Don't be ridiculous. This call is over. Let me know if Oliver turns up,' and before she could say any more he cut the connection.

An hour later, after a helpful chat with Charlie who'd been to see his mother earlier in the week, and who'd promised to keep in close touch with his younger brother over the next few days while Oliver calmed down, Russ was on his way to Fiona's when he found himself recalling, with some discomfort, the threat Sylvie had made the last time he'd seen her. 'If you go now I will tell everyone what I know about you. You are lying, pretending you don't know things when you do . . .'

She hadn't mentioned it again since, and there was a good chance she'd forgotten she'd even said it. However, there was never any telling when the threat might pop back into her mind, or indeed what she might do with it if it did. It wasn't that he had anything to hide, or certainly not where the murdered girl, Mandie Morgan, was concerned – his only connection with her was the fact that he'd interviewed her for the job he'd eventually given to Angie, a couple of hours before she was killed. The trouble was, Sylvie had already, in an inebriated and vengeful state, threatened to tell the police that he hadn't been completely straight with them when they'd questioned him about the interview. She'd even accused him outright of trying to seduce the girl and then not offering her the job because she'd refused to succumb.

His wife was delusional, there was no doubt about that, but she only had to whisper a few well-chosen words in a sympathetic journalist's ear and within minutes it would be headline news: *Russ Lomax Linked to Murder of Mandie Morgan.* It would soon die down, of course, since he'd already told the police everything he knew, and they'd never had any reason to suspect him anyway, since he hadn't been the last person to see her alive. However, he didn't much relish the thought of the tabloid press seizing the opportunity to haul him on to their front pages, because that kind of mud had a habit of sticking, and even being dug up again if at some point it might suit them to say he'd once been linked to a murder inquiry.

These were the kinds of things Sylvie didn't have the common sense to think about when she was drunk, or even, half the time, when she was sober, and no matter how many days she spent on the wagon, if she was indeed even on it, he knew already that it was only a matter of time before she fell off again. Which was why he was now wondering if he should, for his own sake as well as hers, consider giving in to her demands and letting her come home for a while. If he didn't, then there was a good chance she'd end up doing something that no one, least of all him, would be able to put right.

Chapter Six

Dear Emma,
  Wishing You Good Luck in your New Home with love and best wishes your mother, Phyllis

Were she not in such a good mood Emma might have been irritated by the card and its ludicrously perfunctory greeting – not to mention the fact that it had come via the Internet greetings-card company Moonpig, so wasn't even personalised by her mother's own hand. Today, because she'd just found out that she'd been selected for an interview as Events Organiser at the exclusive Avon Valley Manor Hotel, she simply stood the card on the mantelpiece along with the others to let it blend and be forgotten. Nothing was going to bring her down today, especially not the resentment that formed most of the bond she shared with the woman who sent cards as a duty, with words like love inserted as an afterthought.

Hearing her mobile ringing she ran into the kitchen, and seeing it was Lauren she quickly clicked on.

'Mum! I just got your text. This is such brilliant news. I knew they'd choose you. They just had to.'

Laughing, Emma said, 'It's only an interview, remember, not the actual job, but honestly, even getting this far feels fantastic.'

'You so deserve it. They'll be mad if they don't give it to you. Do you have a date and time yet?'

Trying not to panic, Emma told her, 'It's this coming Thursday at two, so I've only got a couple of days to get my act together.'

'You'll be amazing, I know it.'

Loving her for such unquestioning loyalty, Emma said, 'That's it, keep boosting my confidence, I need it. How come you're ringing now? I thought you'd be in lessons.'

'I'm in English but when I told Mr Leesom about your text he said it was OK to come and give you a quick call. He said to tell you he's glad for your good news.'

Embarrassed for him to know her business, Emma said, 'That's very kind of him.'

'He's so cool, isn't he?' Lauren gushed. 'He's like totally different to all the other teachers. Anyway, I ought to go back, I don't want to miss anything. I'll call again tonight, OK?'

Emma was given no time to ponder Philip Leesom's message, since moments after she'd spoken to Lauren the landline livened up with a call from Berry congratulating her on getting this far and assuring her she couldn't fail. By the time their call ended she'd received a text from Polly saying she'd be over to celebrate that evening straight after her meeting with Alistair Wood; and another from her brother Harry who'd made an impromptu visit with his wife on Sunday, saying he'd be rooting for her all the way.

Refraining from emailing her entire contact list with the exciting news just in case it jinxed her chances, she sat down at her computer to have another quick look at the hotel's website before going to collect Mrs Dempster for their prearranged trip to the supermarket. Tomorrow she was taking another elderly neighbour to do his shopping and on Friday she'd invited a few more people in from the cul de sac for a coffee in an effort to get to know them.

Much as she'd missed Lauren at the weekend, and she really had, it hadn't turned out to be as lonely as she'd feared, since she actually hadn't had much time to herself. Saturday morning hadn't started off too well however, when she'd woken to the sound of a slew of bills cascading through the letter box, and after making herself open them she'd started to despair of when, or how, her fortunes were ever going to turn around. Thankfully, an evening at the pub with Polly and the interview they'd done afterwards at Polly's house had helped put her own life in perspective, given the wrenching sadness of Polly's story. Not that Polly ever felt sorry for herself, to the contrary, she was probably the only person Emma knew who could talk about her misfortunes as though they were no more than mishaps. They'd even found themselves rolling around with laughter at some point, though what had triggered it, apart from too much wine and two very black senses of humour, Emma wouldn't be sure until she came to write it all up.

It had been lovely to see her brother on Sunday too, and Jane, her sister-in-law, who'd brought armfuls of house-warming gifts which had included, most generously, a very smart little Nespresso machine and an exquisite Japanese-style coffee set.

No gift from her mother, but no surprise there. Phyllis never had been big on gifts, at least not for her. She was always very generous with Lauren, the musical prodigy, the follower in her sainted grandfather's footsteps. Emma couldn't help softening whenever she thought of her father who, thanks to old footage, photographs too of course, would always be young and cool in her mind: the lean, handsome rocker who'd swept his children off their feet and allowed them to strum and dance and sing along with him and the band. In just about every frame showing her mother, she looked so radiant and happy and in love that it felt almost impossible for Emma to equate her with the woman she knew now. Not that Phyllis had lost her beauty, though it had faded over the years, and she did little to disguise the greying streaks in her once lustrous long hair that she now generally wore in a tight, single plait. But there was a sternness about her, and a remoteness, even a kind of nervousness that made her virtually impossible to approach, as far as Emma was concerned. She didn't seem to have the same effect on Harry or his children, and certainly not on Lauren, who only had to walk into a room to make her grandmother's sad or bad-tempered face light up in a way that seemed to melt away the years. Emma had never brought that look to her face, or not that she could remember.

'You don't even like me, so I don't know why you bother coming here,' she'd yelled at her mother the Christmas before last, when Phyllis had started to compare Emma's hospitality with Harry and Jane's.

'I sometimes wonder myself, the way you carry on,' Phyllis had shot back. 'Always the drama queen. It's high time you stopped feeling sorry for yourself and grew up.'

Emma still wasn't sure how she'd managed to stop herself throwing her mother out at that point, but somehow she had. Really though, Phyllis Stevens had to be the most infuriating person on the planet, and so emotionally detached from her only daughter that Emma wouldn't have felt at all surprised to learn that Phyllis wasn't her real mother. 'You adopted me, didn't you?' she'd shouted at her many times over the years. 'Or maybe you stole me, well it's *time to give me back.*'

'I know you like to think you belong to another family,' her mother would say coolly, 'but I'm afraid this is the one you were born into, and if you think you aren't wanted perhaps you should ask yourself why I work so hard to keep us all together.'

Work, huh, it was her father's royalties that had supported them over the years, much boosted by one of his lesser-known hits being adapted for a commercial back in the eighties. Her mother had only agreed to it because the rest of the band, who'd dispersed and followed different career paths by then, had persuaded her into it. That had been an enjoyable time, when they'd come to visit with their wives and children, talking about the old days and sharing their memories with Alan's kids who were 'so grown up now'. That was more or less the only time Harry and Emma had ever seen their father's old friends; Phyllis had felt it best to break with the past and not give themselves airs and graces just because they were Alan Stevens's family. They needed to be their own people, and she'd rather lead a quiet, ordinary life pottering about her little jobs in the local garden centre or driving the mobile library, or visiting the lonely elderly on Sundays. She took flowers to her husband's grave every birthday, anniversary and public holiday, but always alone. She didn't want the children with her because this was her private time with Alan, she'd inform Berry, who invariably replied that it was selfish and inconsiderate to leave them behind. Berry had regularly taken them herself of course, never failing to make the visit part of a fun day out, which was what, she'd vigorously claim, their father would have wanted.

If Phyllis had ever been involved with another man since the awful accident that had made her a young widow, then Emma knew nothing about it, and nor did Berry who was confident that ever since that fateful day poor Phyllis had remained as celibate as a cream cracker.

Realising she'd got into thinking about her mother when she'd been determined not to, Emma closed down her computer, grabbed her bag and coat and went off to fetch Mrs Dempster. She'd have plenty of time when she returned to check out the hotel she might soon be working for, and start preparing herself for Thursday. She might even give her mother a call to say thank you for the card.

There again, she might not.

'I can hardly believe it,' Polly was laughing later that evening, 'you get a job interview and I get a new business partner all on the same day. There's no doubt about it, our luck is changing.'

'So what's he proposing?' Emma wanted to know as she struggled to screw the top off a bottle of red wine.

Taking it and doing the honours, Polly said, 'He's going to pay the outstanding rent on the church hall so we can start using it again, and he's also going to cover the staff's wages while we cast a wider net to bring in more clients.'

Emma was astounded.

Polly shrugged. 'That's what he said.'

'And what does he get out of it? Apart from a free nursery for his son, presumably?'

Polly grimaced as she passed back the bottle. 'It's complicated, but in a nutshell he wants a fifty per cent share of the profits once we're back on our feet, which is still going to make things pretty tight for me, unless I can find a way to expand and open more Polly's Playtimes around the region. He says I've already got the brand name, and a good reputation, so once things start stabilising there shouldn't be too much of a problem getting the new nurseries under way.'

Emma was looking seriously impressed. 'I think we need to drink a toast to Mr Wood, don't you?' she said, holding up her glass.

'Absolutely. To Alistair Wood, his adorable son, Taylor, and very elegant grandmother, Beatrice.'

As they clinked glasses, Emma said, 'So what's he actually like, Mr Alistair? Young, old, short, fat?'

Polly's eyes twinkled mischievously. 'If I said George Clooney,' she responded, fanning a hand.

Emma's jaw dropped. 'No way.'

'OK, not quite, but to quote my darling daughter, he actually is pretty fit in a medium-height, fair-haired, blue-eyed sort of way, or they might be green, who knows? He dresses well – a really expensive-looking suit, and I bet his overcoat was cashmere.'

'Age?'

'I'd put him at mid-thirties, maybe a bit older.'

'And what does he actually do?'

'Apparently he runs, might even own, for all I know, a financial services company based in Bristol.'

Emma's eyes nearly popped. 'So he's loaded. He has to be to have stepped in like that. Did you find out what's happened to Mrs Wood?'

'No, it wasn't that sort of meeting. We just talked business and a bit about Taylor and then he left.'

'Didn't you offer him a drink?'

'Of course, but he declined because he was driving. However,' she drew the word out like a drum roll, 'he did say, "perhaps another time".'

Emma nearly smashed her glass as she clapped.

'He was being polite,' Polly laughed, 'so don't let's get carried away.'

'No, let's.'

'Oh, all right then – but actually, he's way too young for me.'

Emma could hardly believe it. 'Are you serious? What's

age got to do with anything?' She wasn't really thinking about Philip Leesom, at least she was trying not to.

'Nothing, really, does it?' Polly replied with a dreamy sigh. 'Would it surprise you to hear that Melissa's already trying to decide where we should go on our first date?'

Emma wanted to cheer. 'Good for her,' she laughed. 'Of course, you know why the girls are so keen for us to meet someone, don't you?'

'I do. So they won't have to worry about us being on our own when they've flown the nest. And they want us to be happy, naturally.' Polly took a sip of her drink as the prospect of their girls going seemed to sober the moment. 'It'll be quite something for you, having a daughter at the Guildhall,' she commented.

'Provided she gets the grades,' Emma responded. 'But she works so hard and it really matters to her to do well. It does to Melissa too.'

'Mm, she doesn't always seem quite as dedicated as Lauren, but I'm sure she'll be fine in the end, unless she manages to get a recording contract, or one of her YouTube postings pays off. We can probably kiss goodbye to exams if that happens. She's looking forward to Lauren coming home this weekend.'

'Mm, me too,' Emma responded, 'but no doubt they'll be off to some nightclub or party so I wonder how much I'll actually see of her.'

'As far as I'm aware they're torn at the moment between meeting up with friends at the Lizard Lounge, or going to a twenty-first birthday down in Cheddar, I think. Or there's some band playing the Colston Hall they're interested in, if they can get tickets. And by the time the weekend comes round I'm sure there'll be half a dozen other options to be considered.' She pulled a face. 'Meanwhile, what do we do, sit here and grow old?'

Chuckling, Emma said, 'Speaking personally, I shall almost certainly be a bag of nerves wondering if I've got the job, because I'll have had my interview by then, and who knows,' her eyes sparkled, 'you might be out on your first date with the dashing Mr Wood.'

Polly laughed. 'Yeah, really.' Then after a pause, 'I think

we ought to see about finding someone for you, though. Someone gorgeous and rich and hopelessly romantic . . .'

Still trying hard not to think of Philip Leesom, Emma said, 'No, no, please don't let's even go there. I don't mind pretending to Lauren that I'm up for meeting someone, but honest to God, all I really want for the next few years is the tranquillity, the utter bliss, of a totally man-free zone.'

Russ was having another of his regular chats with Oliver's voicemail. 'Hi, it's Dad,' he was saying, 'I know you're avoiding me, but I don't want things to stay like this between us, so I'm sorry about what happened on Tuesday. Please call me back when you get this message so we can talk.'

After clicking off the line he turned to Charlie for approval.

'Not bad,' Charlie commented, his normally serious brown eyes showing glints of humour. 'No guarantees he'll ring, because he's definitely in a weird place right now . . . It's like he's angry with you because he can't make you proud of him, so he's telling himself the best thing is not to have anything to do with you, then he won't keep feeling like he's letting you down.'

Both exasperated and concerned, Russ said, 'I've never thought he's letting me down, I hope you told him that. He works hard and he's done well, but I just don't get much sense of him trying to find a job – or understanding that the world isn't sitting back waiting to make Oliver Lomax's dreams come true.'

'That's not what he thinks, and he *is* trying where a job's concerned, he just doesn't always tell you about it.'

'Why the hell not?'

'Because if it doesn't work out you'll think he's a failure. Honest, Dad, you're not giving him enough space. He's got ideas and ambitions and he's definitely not a slouch.'

'I've never said he is, but he has to toughen up, Charlie. Nothing's easy for kids nowadays . . .'

'He knows that. He's living it, for Christ's sake. We all are in our own ways . . .' He looked down as his mobile bleeped. 'It's him,' he said, opening the text.

I know you're with Dad. Tell him I don't need his help. I can sort things out for myself.

After reading it, Russ sighed heavily and passed the phone back.

'Give him some time,' Charlie advised. 'He's OK staying at Alfie's and Mum's for a while and he'll come round in the end, he always does.'

'This is my point,' Russ growled, 'storming off in a sulk is not the kind of behaviour I'd hoped to be seeing in him at this age. I'm sorry to say it, but your mother spoiled him. Of course, I blame myself for letting it happen. I had a better handle on things with you, and look at you, you've got yourself together . . .'

'Dad, don't make comparisons. Oliver and I are totally different, and it doesn't help him one bit to be made to feel as though I'm always coming out on top and he's always second best.'

Annoyed with himself for not seeming able to hit this right, Russ said, 'OK, I get that and I'm sorry, but it doesn't change the fact that I should have insisted on him being a weekly boarder, the way you were, because with how often I was away . . . Well, your mother babied him, she let him get away with things I never would have if I'd been here.'

'There's no point tearing yourself up about it now, what's done is done, and it's not as though he's in trouble or giving you the kind of grief other parents have to go through. So why not just accept that advertising and marketing's his thing, it's what he wants to do, not work with you . . .'

'I'm not saying he has to work with me for ever.'

'I know, but he's feeling the need to prove himself, so let him try.'

Russ looked into his son's kind, intelligent eyes and felt a rush of fatherly love mingle with gratitude and pride. 'You've got enough going on with your exams coming up without having to deal with all this,' he sighed.

Charlie shrugged. 'Well, I kind of got that you weren't managing without me, so I thought I'd better take a couple of days out.'

Russ's eyes shone with humour as he said, 'So how did

you find your mother while you were there? Is she really on the wagon?'

Charlie frowned as he stared down at his empty coffee cup. 'Hard to tell,' he answered. 'I didn't see her actually having a drink, but we all know how good she is at hiding it in tea or coffee, or whatever else she's got in her mug. What really got me was the way she keeps coming out with the weirdest stuff, like you're having two conversations at once, and neither one of them makes much sense. She does it on the phone, and she wasn't any better when I was there.'

Worried too, Russ picked up their cups and went to refill them from the machine. 'I've been thinking about letting her come home for a while,' he admitted, feeling horribly weighted by the words since they were taking him a step closer to committing to the very thing he didn't want to do. 'I don't know how much good it'll do in the long run, but I guess we can't let her go on like this. It's got a lot worse since she moved out.'

Watching his father return to the bar, Charlie said, 'If she weren't my mother I'd tell you to forget it. It's time you had a life without her drunken rampages wearing you down, and the way she accuses you of stuff you've never even thought about doing, never mind done. I bet this time on your own has felt a bit like coming out of prison, you're free to be you, do what you want, speak to whoever you want . . . The trouble is, she is my mother and like you, I can't just ignore the way she is.'

Understanding that perfectly, while appreciating the empathy, Russ said, 'So basically you're agreeing, I should let her come back?'

Charlie pulled a face. 'It has to be your decision.'

'Does Oliver have an opinion on it?'

Charlie sighed. 'I think he's with me in that for her sake he'd rather she was here, but for yours . . . Well, he knows what it's like for you.'

Hating the fact that his boys were having to deal with their parents struggling like this, when they needed to be concentrating on their own futures, Russ said, 'Does she still think I'm having an affair with Angie?'

Charlie shook his head. 'She didn't mention it specifically, but she seems to have convinced herself you're seeing someone – but, as Oliver said, nothing new there.'

No, definitely nothing new there, and feeling thankful all over again that Sylvie knew nothing about Fiona, he was about to offer to buy Charlie some lunch at the pub when the front door opened and Toyah, the office manager, came surging into the kitchen. She was short, sporty-looking, with huge apple cheeks, black-rimmed glasses and raven-coloured hair that was styled in what Sylvie unkindly described as a pudding cut.

'Hey, Charlie,' she said busily. 'Saw your car. How's things?'

'Great, thanks. You?'

'Yeah, cool. Russ, sorry to butt in, but loads going on. First up, I transferred five grand to the GA account, like you said, and everyone was primed for the next round, but then the local news came on and I thought I'd better pull it.'

Baffled, and slightly alarmed, Russ said, 'Go on.'

'Graham's rewinding now ready for you to watch. You'd better come over.'

'This is sounding ominous,' Charlie commented, getting up to follow.

'Is it?' Russ asked Toyah.

Looking awkward, she said, 'Yeah and no. I guess you'll have to decide, but I don't think you're going to like it too much. Or you,' she added to Charlie.

Minutes later Russ and Charlie were standing in front of a large HD monitor in the stable-block offices watching a playback of Sylvie, sitting on the sofa in her Clifton apartment, looking not entirely sober and sounding even less so as she confided her secret to a rapt reporter.

As he listened Russ could feel the heat of embarrassment spreading through him, along with anger and a growing concern for her mental health. Mercifully she wasn't accusing him of hiding something about Mandie Morgan, instead she was ranting on about how he was financing the mysterious golden angels who were swooping on supermarkets paying people's grocery bills.

'But you are not to think he is doing this out of kindness for anyone,' she was almost slurring, 'he is doing it because it will give him good publicity when he is launching a major new programme.'

Charlie glanced at his father, as Russ said, 'She doesn't know what the hell she's talking about.'

'So you see,' Sylvie continued, 'my husband is not the great benefactor everyone thinks is behind the golden angels, he is doing this only for selfish motives and I think it is important for people to know that.'

'Is she going to tell them that it was Granny Lomax's idea?' Charlie demanded. 'And that Dad's using the money she left him to make it happen?'

'No, she doesn't say that,' Graham responded.

Russ signalled for Toyah to switch it off.

'All calls are going through to voicemail at the moment,' Graham informed him, 'but there have already been a few concerning this.'

'I can't work out what she hopes to gain by it,' Toyah commented, glancing at Angie, who shook her head, showing she was equally mystified.

'I don't expect she can either,' Russ told them, 'except the sweet revenge of trying to paint me in a bad light.'

'But how on earth is it going to do that?' Toyah wanted to know. 'I mean, so what if you were doing it for publicity reasons, which you're not, people are still getting their bills paid and that's all they'll care about.'

'Charlie's just pointed out the reason I'm doing it,' Russ declared, 'but you all know it anyway, so I can't take credit for anything. My mother even came up with the name.'

'So how do you want to handle it?' Graham asked. 'The press are obviously going to expect some sort of statement.'

After giving it some thought, Russ turned to Charlie. 'Do you want to take it?' he offered.

Surprised, Charlie said, 'What, you mean speak on your behalf? Sure, I can do that, if you want me to.'

'OK, then let's rough something out that tells Granny's story, and says that we're sorry it's come out, because she always thought that the mystery element of it was part of what people would find so enjoyable.'

'What do you want me to say about Mum?' Charlie asked.

Russ pulled a hand over his chin as he thought. 'If at all possible, don't mention her at all, which I appreciate is going to be difficult, but the last thing we want is to turn this into some sort of public slanging match.'

Chapter Seven

In a hurry to leave for her interview, Emma quickly shut down her computer, checked she'd put the iron away, locked the back door, gave up the search for her gloves and ran into the sitting room to turn off the TV. Having missed the first part of the lunchtime news, she still wasn't any wiser about who was behind the golden angels scheme. She had gathered that the benefactor had been revealed, but since the names probably wouldn't have meant anything to her anyway, she wasn't going to waste any time on it.

Nothing mattered right now, apart from getting this job.

Grabbing her attaché case from the foot of the stairs, an item she hadn't used in almost a year, and that had required rescuing from a coating of cobwebs when she'd retrieved it from a box yet to be unpacked, she zipped it up and jammed it comfortably under her arm. Being of a high-end designer brand it had been easily restored to its former glory and was able, she hoped, to lend her a professional and successful air, in spite of having next to nothing in it. Maybe she should pop in her laptop. Come to think of it, she probably ought to be wowing them with a PowerPoint presentation – it was what people did these days. Oh God, she was so out of date, but it was a bit late to be thinking about it now. How could this not have occurred to her before? However, no one from the agency had mentioned it, so presumably, hopefully, it wasn't necessary. Nor was the iPad she longed to own, though it might have made her seem a little more impressive if she had one.

Deciding to take Lauren's car instead of her older and slightly dented Honda (not her fault, white-van man had pulled out straight in front of her so she hadn't stood a chance), she buttoned up her coat, unhooked the keys and took an enormous, steadying breath to set herself on her way. Fortunately there should be no question of getting lost, since she'd already driven the route twice to be sure of the way, and if there were any hold-ups such as road-works or accidents, that shouldn't be a problem either, because she was allowing an hour for a journey that shouldn't really take much more than twenty minutes.

After settling herself in the driver's seat she turned on the engine, belted up and was about to pull away when she heard a text drop into her inbox. Deciding she ought to read it in case someone from the agency was trying to inform her of a change of plan, she put the car back in neutral and fished the phone from her bag.

It was from Lauren. *Thinking of you. You'll be brilliant. Don't forget to ask about holidays! Remember, we're going to India! Love you xxx*

Smiling to herself, Emma sent a quick *love you* back, and deciding now wasn't the time to fuss herself about India, or Berry's exhibition, or Lauren's performance exam, she put the car back into first and pulled away. It would be awful if she did have to miss Lauren's big night, she was thinking as she drove to the end of the street. She'd abso-lutely hate it, especially when she knew how much it meant to Lauren to have her there. Of course Will would turn up, was there a father alive more convinced that his daughter was going to be even bigger than Norah Jones, or Alicia Keys, or more boastful of the fact? He'd no doubt bring Jemima and their little brood – what a treat it would be for Emma to see them! Berry would certainly make it, so would Phyllis. Harry and Jane would definitely be there, along with all Lauren's friends and probably most of the teachers. Emma was already experiencing tremors of excite-ment and nerves on Lauren's behalf, and ready to burst with pride at the mere thought of her standing up in front of all those people not only to play her flute and guitar solos, but then to provide accompaniment on the piano for Donna while she made her violin sing, and for Emily Brooking who was so gifted on the clarinet that the London

Philharmonic had already approached her. Come what may, Emma had to get herself to London that night, it simply wasn't an option not to be there, and for all she knew there wouldn't be a problem, so she couldn't think why she was getting herself all worked up about it now when she ought to be channelling her entire focus on the personal statement she'd had to submit with her CV.

How excruciating that had been, and remained so, never having had to sing her own praises before. Though she'd read her self-glorification through several times that morning, still cringing in spite of the congratulations she'd received for it from Helen at the agency, for some reason she was totally blanking on it now. Why was she any good? What the heck did she have to offer that would set her apart from everyone else? And whatever great ideas for events, both corporate and private, that she'd managed to come up with this past week had apparently vaporised, along with the reasons why her own business folding wouldn't, shouldn't, impact on the magnificence she had to bring to the Avon Valley Manor Hotel.

It would all come back, she assured herself, as she wove a little too fast through the country lanes. Once she was sitting opposite the three managers who were apparently interviewing her – HR, Catering and General – she would start to sparkle and impress in exactly the captivating manner Berry had assured her she'd have no problem conjuring at will. She better had, because everything, *everything* depended on her getting this job, or that was certainly how it felt, so she wasn't even going to allow herself to consider the fact that she might not.

However, if she wasn't successful, it would only be because she was destined for greater things, and though she couldn't begin to imagine what greater job there might be than this one, she would try to hang on to that cheery little nugget in order to help herself over the crushing, bruising disappointment when it came – if it did.

And it might not.

'I believe they have selected twenty people for interview out of over two hundred applicants,' Helen had told her – and Emma really wished she hadn't.

She was up against *nineteen* other people, all of whom would no doubt have full-on, flashy degrees from hotel schools, top universities or catering colleges, plus years of experience under their belts, references from such prestigious establishments as the Ritz, or the Dorchester, and they probably weren't yet thirty.

Why was she going, again?

Because they had been sufficiently impressed with her application to want to see her.

With so much chaos going round and round in her mind she almost missed a red light and had to pull up so fast that she went into a mini-skid.

No harm done. She could cope with the moron behind who was beeping her, and the bloke crossing the road giving her the evil eye. They were not in her sphere and in less than two minutes they would disappear for ever.

Her mobile was ringing. She could see it was Berry, probably to wish her luck, but dared not answer it, because the lights were turning green and the last thing she needed was to find herself being pulled over by the police.

She had to think about something else. Maybe she should put the radio on, listen to some music, or the news. There might be more about the golden angels. Did she care? Not right now.

Forty minutes later, after an uncomfortable spell in the hotel's plush reception watching two rival candidates (both under thirty) go in ahead of her and come out looking taller and smug, it was her turn to be called into the River Room. It proved to be a rather typical conference suite with an enormous TV on one wall, a long oval table down the centre with a dozen chairs in haphazard arrangement around it and large, sliding glass doors that in better weather would open on to a stately veranda and the (currently winter-torn) gardens beyond. The people sitting at one end of the table were something of a surprise, not for the way they looked, but for how warmly they greeted her. Hamish Gallagher, the general manager, even poured her a coffee himself, which she didn't drink for fear of spilling it, or burning her mouth and dribbling.

Later, she couldn't be sure of how long the interview

went on for, but it certainly felt longer than the time allotted to the two applicants who'd gone in ahead of her, and because it seemed to be going so well, and she'd felt she was being erudite and attentive in equal measure, she even ventured the odd lame joke or two. To her amazement they all laughed, and when she got round to explaining how the economic downturn and a poor choice of husband had done for her business they appeared far more sympathetic than shocked or judgemental.

'All in all,' she said to Polly when she stopped off at her friend's house on her way home to report back, 'I'm not sure it could have gone better, but that's me. God only knows what they think.'

'I bet you blew them away,' Polly declared supportively. 'And that suit really works, by the way. I'm glad you chose it, because red's a great colour on you. It's a bold, confident statement, which is what they'd want from someone who's going to organise their five-star events. Plus, you've got an air about you that would convince anyone to trust you.'

'You make me sound so exciting,' Emma grimaced. 'Anyway, the general manager came across as the kind of man it would be great to work for, which is extremely encouraging when I'm used to being my own boss . . . Where are all the kids, by the way?'

'I've only got five today and they're either asleep or upstairs in the playroom with Jilly. We're moving back into the church hall a week from Monday, isn't that fantastic? Alistair's already paid the outstanding rent, but the vicar's got some other stuff going on there next week, otherwise we'd be in there sooner. Anyway, back to the job, when are they going to let you know?'

Weakened by a bolt of nerves, Emma said, 'Apparently they're hoping to make a decision by the end of next week, so should be in touch soon after that.'

'Oh God,' Polly murmured, seeming to catch the nerves. 'Not long, which is brilliant, but I still don't envy you the wait. Do they still want you to start at the beginning of March?'

'I imagine so. I hope so, because then I won't have to worry about being able to make Berry's show and Lauren's recital. On the other hand, if they want me earlier, I'm hardly in a position to say no.'

'One step at a time,' Polly counselled as she went to answer the phone. 'Help yourself to more tea,' and into the receiver, 'Hello, Polly's Playtime. Yes, this is Polly. Oh, hi, that's right I've been expecting your call.'

After refilling her cup and helping herself to a biscuit, starving now after missing lunch, Emma wandered over to the cluttered bay window that looked across to the quaint old Norman church, a row of miners' cottages made all trendy and desirable in recent years, and the village shop with its Lottery thumb outside on the forecourt and four parking spaces vital to its trade. It was a pity about the busy road running straight through the heart of the community, since it was bordered by two thick yellow lines either side, allowing no one to stop even for a minute, and had turned the coming and going from driveways into a very risky business. Now all the houses were double-glazed, mostly gardenless at the front thanks to the need for hard standings, and people generally felt less involved in their surroundings than they had over the past two centuries when there had been no road at all. Still, there was almost always a good atmosphere at the pub, which had an enormous car park at the back, and the various fetes, sales and children's clubs at the church hall did a lot towards bringing everyone together too.

Noticing a Sainsbury's delivery van pulling into the drive of Orchard House, next to the shop, Emma said, as Polly rang off, 'Did you hear on the news that they've found out who's behind the golden angels?'

'Oh yes, that's right,' Polly replied, going to top up her own tea. 'It's that bloke who used to read the news, ages ago, Russell Lomax. Do you remember him?'

Emma frowned. 'Sort of,' she said, unable to put a face to the name. 'I didn't quite get what his wife was saying about him using it for publicity though, when he seems to have gone out of his way not to be identified.'

'That means you probably haven't heard the latest. Their son was on Radio Bristol about an hour ago explaining that there had been a misunderstanding and that actually, his grandmother had dreamt up the scheme before she died, so she was the one who should be taking all the credit.'

Emma pulled a face.

Polly laughed and threw out her hands. 'I'm just telling you what he said. But that's not all. They had a friend of the wife's on after, Fiona something-or-other, saying that Mrs Lomax hasn't been well lately and that the press would do her a great kindness if they just left her alone.'

Emma's eyebrows rose. 'Come to think of it, she did sound a bit strange during the little I heard,' she commented.

'For strange, read drunk. Apparently she's got a real problem, but they're trying to keep it hush-hush.'

'So is this the end of the angels as we know them?'

'I don't think so. The son said something about it continuing but "the family are not willing to give interviews about it and nor are they looking to be thanked".'

Emma was surprised. 'Well, I suppose that's their right, though I can't see how they're going to stop people thanking them now they know, can you?'

'Not off the top of my head, but I guess that's their problem. Mine is the meeting I've just been summoned to next Wednesday with Alistair's business manager to go over the terms and conditions of our new contract.'

Emma's face broke into a smile. 'It's fantastic that this is going ahead, but do you think you're going to need a lawyer to advise you?'

'I suppose it wouldn't be a bad idea. Or will it look as though I don't trust them?'

Emma pondered. 'Why don't you ask your father-in-law what he thinks?'

'Good idea. I'm going down there on Sunday, so I can talk it over with him then. Now, what are your plans for the weekend? I know Lauren's coming, but she'll be out with the girls on Saturday night so I was wondering if you'd like to join me and my team for a quiz night over in Wrington.'

Emma gave a laugh. 'Can I think about it?' she asked. 'It's just that I'd like to spend some time writing up your interview – which I still haven't got round to yet – and researching other possibilities for my series of articles just in case I do run with it, and I probably ought, because I'll need something to feel positive about if this job doesn't work out.'

Smiling, Polly said, 'It will, I'm sure of it, but it's up to you. You know you're welcome if you do decide to come.'

Hearing the sound of wailing from upstairs, Emma said, 'I'll leave you to it, but we'll talk later, yes?'

'Absolutely. I'm taking Melissa over to the mall this evening, but we should be back around eight. Are you going to be OK backing out on to the road?'

'Don't worry, I reversed in, so I should be fine.'

A few minutes later Emma was in the car, realising she could be going nowhere fast. 'Oh, for heaven's sake,' she murmured crossly as she turned the key again. 'I thought they'd fixed the problem.'

She tried again and to her relief the engine started straight away, so as soon as the traffic cleared she eased down on the accelerator and was about to pull out when her foot slipped off the clutch and the engine stalled. An instant later an Audi came round the bend at such a speed that the collision would have knocked them both straight into the next world if she had managed to get into the road.

So much for a thirty-mile-an-hour limit.

Feeling slightly dizzied by the narrow escape, while thanking whoever was up there for kicking her foot off the pedal, she gave herself a few seconds before attempting to pull out again. If whoever had been driving that car managed to get home in one piece, she was thinking, or without hurting anyone else on the way, then there truly would be some miracles at work today.

And if there were, please could one of them be a message on her answerphone when she got in, letting her know that Hamish Gallagher and his team had been so blown away by her that they'd come to a decision already that they'd like her to start on March 1st.

Russ was staring at a very depressing email from his most prolific producer-cum-partner, Paul Granger, who'd apparently, in the space of fifteen minutes, received rejections for all three of the projects he and Russ had recently submitted to various broadcasters. *It's lucky we managed to get the green light for* Living Houses, Granger had gone on to say, *or yours truly would be staring into the abyss right now.*

Since he knew Granger was in meetings all morning, Russ emailed him apologising for not responding yesterday, which was when Granger had forwarded the rejections, and suggesting they get together at some point over the weekend to discuss the merit of appealing at least one of the decisions.

Knowing they were fortunate not to have run into even more brick walls than this during these times of austerity, Russ reached for his mobile as it started to ring and seeing the coded name for Fiona come up, he immediately clicked on.

'Hi,' he said, 'where are you?'

'Halfway to London. Are you OK to talk?'

'For now. I'm at the office. The others are out, but I'm expecting them back any minute. You got my message?'

'I did. And you got mine? I tried calling you all evening . . .'

'Sorry, I was with Sylvie until late,' (and what a ball that had been). 'So what the hell happened?' he demanded. 'You're the last person I expected to turn up on the news.'

'Russ, I'm sorry, I really am. They called my office out of the blue . . . I didn't even know Sylvie had been interviewed until they told me, and I was between meetings, rushed off my feet, so ended up saying the first thing that came into my head.'

Russ's expression was grim as he said, 'Have you managed to get hold of her this morning? I know she wouldn't take your calls last night.'

'She still won't. I guess she's pretty mad with me.'

'You could say that, but there again, she's mad with the world.' There was no point going into Sylvie's drunken rant about her friend's disloyalty last night, much less her vows of revenge, since it had made about as much sense as the diatribe of tearful self-pity and pleas for understanding that had followed.

'Exactly what did she hope to get out of doing it?' Fiona asked.

With a humourless laugh he said, 'I imagine it was intended to discredit me in some way, or pay me back, or to get some attention . . . Who knows what goes through her mind? It's got so that there's almost no fathoming her at all these days. Or certainly not when she's been on the bottle.'

'So her little spell on the wagon didn't last?'

'If it ever really existed, which I strongly doubt.' Glancing up at the sound of a car arriving, he said, 'We need to talk some more. When are you back this way?'

'I'm aiming for late tonight, but that depends on how today goes. Is tomorrow night any good?'

'Your place? Around nine?'

'Sounds good to me. Come earlier if you can, I've been missing you.'

After promising to try, he ended the call just as Graham and Angie came into the office, but before he could even start to ask how their meeting with a new producer had gone his mobile rang again.

This time it was Sylvie.

Tempted to let it go to voicemail, he decided he probably ought to find out how she'd fared through the night, considering the state he'd left her in, so clicking on he said a curt hello while giving a nod to the others as he turned his back.

'Russ, it is me,' she said croakily. 'I want to tell you that I am very sorry for what I did. It was not a good thing and I feel very foolish now. I hope you will forgive me.'

Having no intention of letting rip in front of an audience, all he could say, very stiffly, was, 'Of course.'

'Thank you, thank you. I told myself you would, but I was afraid you might still be angry.'

'Where are you?' he asked shortly.

'I am at a coffee bar waiting for Oliver. He says he would like to treat me.'

'Did he come back to yours last night?'

'No, he stayed with Alfie, which is a good thing,

because you know, it upsets him very much when we argue.'

Wondering if she had any recollection of Oliver being there before he'd stormed out in disgust, he said, 'It's difficult for me to talk at the moment. Let me call you later.'

'Why?' Her voice was suddenly harsh with suspicion. 'Are you with somebody?'

'I'm at the office.'

'You are lying.'

'Sylvie . . .'

'You are with a woman . . .'

'For God's sake, try to remember you're in a public place.'

'I would be at home, in our house, if you would allow it, but you are very unkind and you have forgotten that I am the mother of your children . . .'

'Please stop this.'

'I know you do not like to hear the truth, but it is for your own good that I say these things.'

'I'm going to ring off now.'

'No! I am not finished with what . . .'

With a flick of his thumb he cut the connection, and knowing she'd call back, he turned the phone off. The great and frustrating irony of this madness was that he'd spent God only knew how long last night trying to persuade her to come home with him, only for her to refuse. She presumably had no recollection of that either, nor would she have any way of knowing how relieved he'd felt when he'd walked out of there alone – and guilty now for not trying harder to remind her that it was what she wanted, apart from when she apparently didn't.

He'd do a better job of it next time, he told himself bleakly.

Lauren was gazing out of the train window, absently watching the countryside speeding by, lost in ecstatic anticipation of what lay ahead. Never, in her wildest dreams, had she imagined that something so amazing could happen, but it was definitely going to, as long as she managed to get Melissa on her side, and she knew she wouldn't have a problem with that. She'd already texted

103

her warning her that there was a change of plan, and why, and Melissa had immediately texted back to say, *OMG, totally amazing. Got something to tell you too. You know you can trust me.*

She really could trust Melissa, every bit as much as she could Donna, and the same would go for her, if ever either of them needed her to keep something secret for them. Of course Donna knew everything about what was happening, because she was a part of it, which was utterly brilliant, and it was a real shame she couldn't come this weekend.

Remembering the mobile phone Granny Berry had found down her sofa, she felt her heart twist with relief and panic all over again. She could have had so much explaining to do about that if the battery hadn't gone flat. Luckily it had, and so now everyone could breathe again. Donna had been in a worse state than anyone until it had finally turned up, which was so sweet of her, because it really wasn't her fault that the phone had been lost.

Taking her precious journal from her bag Lauren opened it to the last entry, and felt delicious frissons of excitement thrilling all the way through her as she read it. By the time she'd finished she was breathless and flushed and so exhilarated she wanted to laugh, or call Donna, or do something utterly rash, she just couldn't think what. Keeping a journal was one of the best things ever, especially when she had so much amazing stuff to write in it. She'd started off shyly at first, but now she never held back, putting down every tiny little detail of what was happening to her, and Donna, with an explicitness that made them tremble and laugh and feel shocked at themselves all over again every time they read it.

After noting the date, she began to describe how she was feeling right now, drawing on lines from her favourite poets and lyricists, even setting some of it to music in her head. What an incredible ballad it would make, full of hope and anticipation, heavy with innuendo and hidden promise.

She was still writing in her neat, girlish hand when the

train finally pulled into Temple Meads station – ten minutes later than scheduled, which had allowed her ten more minutes to record everything that was making her so unbelievably happy. Of course, she should have been studying really, but she was pretty well up on the Romantics by now, mainly thanks to Mr Leesom who was so absolutely amazingly brilliant the way he read and explained some of the most beautiful poetry ever written. She needed to finish her essay this weekend though, then perhaps her mum would go through and correct it, because she was fantastic at editing essays into shape no matter what they were about.

Quickly packing her journal away, she grabbed her bag, laptop and guitar case ready to jump down on to the platform, then almost dropped them in the struggle to get to her mobile as it started to ring.

'Hey Mum, I'm here,' she cried cheerily. 'The train's a bit late.'

'I know,' Emma responded drily. 'I'm at the front of the station in the short-term parking.'

'Be there in less than two,' Lauren promised, and ringing off she hastily joined the crowds surging towards the exit.

'Hi, Mum,' she beamed, throwing her bag into the boot of her own car and getting into the passenger side. 'Sorry I'm late.'

'No problem,' Emma assured her, giving her a hug. Then, laughing as Lauren kept hold of her in a more bruising embrace, 'It's lovely to see you too. Do you want to drive, or shall I?'

'You can now you're there,' Lauren replied, finally letting her go. 'Is it still going all right?'

'It seems to be. I'll put some petrol in for you on the way back, because I've used it a couple of times this week.'

'Oh, no worries. Or actually, I'd better make sure I've got some because I'm the designated driver tonight.'

Starting up the engine, Emma felt a surge of contentment as her world tilted back on kilter. She'd missed Lauren far more than she was going to admit, at least to Lauren. 'So have you decided where you're going yet?' she asked. 'The last I heard it was between a club and a party and a concert.'

Turning to look out of the window, Lauren said, 'Oh, probably a club, I think, unless it's changed again.'

'How many of you are going?'

'Uh, four. Me, Melissa, Lucy and Charlotte.'

Emma frowned. 'I remember Lucy, but have I met Charlotte?'

'I expect so, at some point. She goes to the same school as Melissa and Lucy. She's really cool. Oh, who's this?' she exclaimed as her mobile bleeped with a text. 'Just Donna,' she murmured, taking a moment to read it. 'I'll give her a ring when we get home. So, any news about the job?'

Groaning as her insides turned over, Emma said, 'No. I told you, they're not getting back to anyone until some-time next week. In the meantime, I'm trying to forget all about it.'

Lauren cast her a comically knowing look. 'I bet you're doing really well at that,' she teased.

Narrowing her eyes as she tried not to laugh, Emma steered the car out on to the main Bath road to head towards home.

'You know, you're definitely going to get it,' Lauren informed her decisively. 'I've got this feeling and I'll bet anything I'm not wrong.' She laughed delightedly, as the sheer joy of being alive came over her in fabulous waves. 'You know, I can hardly believe it's been nearly two whole weeks since I last saw you,' she declared. 'It seems ages. I've really missed you.'

Loving how uninhibited she was with her feelings, Emma said, 'The house has been very quiet without you, apart from all the pensioner rave-ups and raucous get-togethers with Polly, of course. I take it you've heard about her new business partner.'

Lauren had. 'Melissa says he's really fit for a bloke his age. Have you seen him?'

'Not yet, but between us I think Polly's quite keen. Being Polly though, she thinks she's not good enough for him, which is . . .'

'. . . like only totally insane,' Lauren protested. 'She's gorgeous. Anyone would be lucky to have her.'

'Exactly what I said.'

'So do you reckon something might come of it?'

Catching the thread quickly, Emma said, 'If you're fishing for Melissa then my answer is, they've only met once so I think we might be getting a bit ahead of ourselves.'

'And if I'm not fishing for Melissa?'

'The answer's the same. You're an unstoppable pair of matchmakers, you two.'

'And we know how to get results, so watch out!' Lauren warned.

Though Emma glanced at her in amusement, she decided to let the subject drop, since she didn't want to flatten Lauren's spirits by warning her off playing Cupid for her mother. It was hardly important, anyway. 'So how much homework do you have this weekend?' she asked.

Lauren sighed as she shook out her hair. 'Absolutely tons,' she replied, 'which is why it's good I'm the driver tonight, because I so can't be dealing with a hangover tomorrow. I've got to finish this essay about the Romantics by Monday or Mr Leesom will do his nut.'

Unable to imagine Mr Leesom doing anything so undignified, Emma said, 'Do I get to have a look?'

'Are you kidding? I'm counting on you to edit it, because I swear I'm up to seven thousand words already and it's only supposed to be five. Anyway, are you going out tonight?'

Moving seamlessly with the change of subject, Emma said, 'I've been thinking about it, but I'm still not sure. If I don't, I could always be your chauffeur.'

Lauren bounced round in her seat to face her. 'Mum, you are so the best mum in the whole wide world, but I am absolutely not going to let you do that. You've got to have a life. Where are you thinking of going?'

Emma grimaced. 'To a quiz night at a pub in Wrington?'

Lauren laughed. 'Well at least it's not karaoke.'

'God help me,' Emma muttered. 'You're the only one with musical gifts in this family. You know, the trouble is, inside I still feel the same age as you, so I keep thinking I should be going to wine bars and clubs, dancing and meeting fellas . . .'

'Mum, this is me you're talking to.'

With a cry of laughter Emma said, 'Time to grow up?'

'Just a bit.' Then, regarding her suspiciously, 'Was that you just asking if you could come out with us tonight? I really love you, Mum, but please tell me I'm wrong.'

Braking to avoid the car in front, Emma confirmed, 'You're definitely wrong! No, we'll leave it as it is, you do the clubbing and partying and I'll do the Mum thing and quizzing. Now, we need to stop off at the supermarket, I'm afraid. Is there anything in particular you'd like me to pick up?'

'Um . . . definitely some Magnums, and bacon for breakfast tomorrow.'

'You don't care about my weight, do you?'

'Nor should you. You're totally gorgeous . . . Oh, I just remembered, I need some more deodorant and toothpaste and mousse for my hair. Don't worry, I've got money. Dad gave me some during the week, so I can easily pay. Not urgent though, because I haven't totally run out yet.'

'It's all right, I can pay for it,' Emma assured her. 'So how did you get on babysitting last weekend? You've never mentioned it.'

Taking out her mobile again, Lauren said, 'Oh, it was cool. No big deal, you know, the kids are sweet and Dad was, well, you know, Dad. I saw him on Wednesday too, when he gave me the money.' She suddenly bounced round in her seat again. 'Oh my God, wouldn't it be cool if one of those golden angel people picked up our bill today? I think I might come in with you, just in case.'

Laughing, Emma said, 'We know who's behind it now. It came out during the week. I'm not sure you'll have heard of him – Russell Lomax? He used to read the news quite a long time ago.'

Lauren was wrinkling her nose. 'Not ringing a bell,' she decided. 'Anyway, good luck to him if that's what he's doing, because as far as I'm concerned it's totally sick.'

Reminding herself that sick was yesterday's fab, or

brilliant, or amazing, Emma pulled bravely into Sainsbury's car park – as though she could afford to shop here all the time – and parked alongside a VW Golf which might, she decided, be her next car *if* she got the job.

And she probably would.

Chapter Eight

Much later in the day Emma was curled up on the sofa with her laptop resting on the arm as she read the all-important essay Lauren had finally finished and emailed across from her own computer. Though it was overwritten and a bit repetitive in places, she could actually feel Lauren's passion behind the points and knew that whoever marked this, and it would almost certainly be Philip Leesom, wouldn't fail to feel it too.

However, it had to be cut down to length, and as editing was an exercise Emma enjoyed, given her own love of the material she was working with it didn't take long to complete it. Of course, she was biased, but after reading it through again, she couldn't imagine anyone in Lauren's class being able to deliver a more evocative and in many ways more sensuous piece. Her daughter had an ear for poetry that was probably unsurprising, considering her gift for music. *The masters' words clearly sing off the page for you, much as adagios and allegros sing from your flute.* Emma remembered Philip Leesom noting that at the end of an essay Lauren had written a while back on the perceived influence of Keats's works on Shelley.

It wasn't hard to imagine Philip Leesom instilling passion for the Romantics in his students when he cut such a romantic figure himself. He was so unlike the rosy-nosed, pockmarked and plump Mr Fredericks, who'd taught A-level English at Emma's school, that it could make her laugh to draw the comparison – and cringe to think of anyone developing a crush on the miserable old goat. How she'd enjoy sitting at the back of Philip Leesom's class listening to the hypnotic cadence of his soft Irish voice as he recited and reflected; interacted and inspired. She could almost hear his zeal, feel his physical responses, see the burning light in his eyes as he cried, *Mock on, mock on, Voltaire, Rousseau, Mock on, mock on, tis all in vain.* Or whispered thoughtfully, tenderly: *Was it a vision, or a waking dream? Fled is that music: do I wake or sleep?*

Amused at the thought of the thrills he no doubt sent spiralling out around the room, driving all those poor teenage girls and their supercharged hormones to wild distraction, Emma set her computer aside and stretched out her aching legs.

She felt both glad and disappointed, she realised, that she hadn't received any more emails from him since the one recommending the book whose long title had slipped her memory for the moment. As pleasing as it was to dream, she really didn't need the complication of a romance, or a crush, while she was busy trying to get her life together, and she could certainly do without the bruising experience of rejection or ridicule when she found out she'd got it all wrong anyway.

All she wanted now was to rest her head against the sofa and listen for a while as Lauren began to play her flute again. There had been a lot of stop-start in the past half an hour, suggesting that many text messages were flying back and forth between Lauren and her friends, which was fine, but Emma sincerely hoped she was going to hear a full rendition of either 'Summertime', Lauren's chosen jazz piece for her performance exam, or Debussy's 'Syrinx', the classical piece, before she went back tomorrow.

An hour later, realising she'd managed to drop off for a while, Emma yawned pleasurably. Pulling her computer back on to her lap, she emailed across the edited version of Lauren's essay and was about to pop upstairs to find out why everything had gone quiet, when Polly rang.

'So have you changed your mind about tonight?' Polly wanted to know. 'Are you coming with us?'

Realising how churlish she'd sound if she didn't, Emma stifled her reluctance and said, 'OK, why not? Shall I pick you up, or will you come here?'

111

'Tell you what, I'm told Lauren's coming here at seven, so why don't you get her to drop you and I'll take over from there?'

'Seven? That's early for her.'

'I think they're all getting together at Lucy's house, in town, before they go out,' Polly explained. 'Is it good to have her home?'

Melting into a smile, Emma said, 'It's wonderful, but don't tell her I said so or it might sound like pressure.'

'And we can't have that, can we? Oh, before I go: we talked about this before Christmas, but haven't mentioned it since, are you up for joining our book club?'

'Absolutely,' Emma assured her. 'Just tell me what's on your reading list at the moment and I'll do my best to catch up.'

'Actually, you're going to love it, because I know it's one of your favourites: *The Book Thief.*'

'I'm in heaven already,' Emma told her, and after ringing off she went out into the hall, listening and trying to make out whether Lauren was on the phone, or singing. Realising it was the latter, she took herself upstairs to find Lauren up to her neck in a bubble bath, eyes closed, iPod plugged into her ears and towel wrapped around her hair, as she struggled with the vocals of a song she clearly didn't know too well.

'Mum!' she cried delightedly, as Emma came to sit on the edge of the bath. 'How was the essay? Oh God, don't tell me, terrible.'

'The reverse. I've sent it back minus about two thousand words, so I hope you'll find it flows a little more smoothly than before.'

'You are so brilliant. Thank you so much.'

'We ought to go over why I've made the changes at some point, so you'll know why . . .'

'Oh, Mum, not now, please. I'm feeling like I really need to chill out for a while, so . . .'

'It's OK, we can do it tomorrow.'

'Cool, thanks. So have you decided to go out?'

Before she could answer Lauren was grabbing her phone to read the latest text that had just bleeped in, so leaving

112

her to it, Emma went back downstairs to start sorting out what they could have to eat before they left.

Why, she was wondering, was she feeling such little enthusiasm for the quiz night? Probably because it was so bitterly cold outside, and it was so snug and warm in this house. She grimaced to think of what Lauren would say if she suggested they stay in for the evening, just the two of them, the way they had the last time she was here. Knowing what agonies of choice it would put Lauren through if she did, when she was so looking forward to seeing her friends tonight, and when she'd hate to feel she was letting her lonely mother down, Emma banished the thought from her mind and got on with making some tea.

'Are you OK?' Oliver asked, going into his mother's bedroom to find her sitting on the edge of the bed staring down at her hands.

Without looking up she said, 'Yes, I'm fine. How are you?'

He knelt in front of her, took her hands in his and tried to catch her eye. 'I'm going out now,' he reminded her. 'I'm going to a party, remember?'

She smiled distantly and cupped a hand round his face. 'You will have a marvellous time,' she told him.

Uneasy without quite knowing why, he said, 'What are you going to do?'

It was a while before she answered, and seeing the tears filling her eyes, he tried to swallow his annoyance as he wrapped her in his arms. Why did she have to start feeling sorry for herself and getting in a state now, when he was on his way out? She always did this and it was doing his head in. Still, at least there was no whiff of alcohol about her, though he guessed that would probably only last for as long as it took him to get down to the street.

'I thought I'd go to see your father,' she murmured tearfully.

Since he liked that better than the idea of her sitting here on her own, he said, 'Yeah, why don't you? He told you the other night that he thinks you should go home again and it's what you want, isn't it?'

Nodding bleakly, she replied, 'Yes, it is, but I am not sure . . .'

'But Mum, you keep saying . . .'

'I know, I know.'

He rose to his feet. 'If you're going to drive, you won't have a drink will you?' he said, making it more of a command than a request.

Looking up, she smiled tenderly. 'OK, I promise.'

'Good.' He hesitated, trying to work out if there was something else he should say before leaving. 'I'll be off then, all right?' he said in the end.

'Is Charlie going with you?'

'No, Charlie's gone back to London.'

She blinked forlornly at her hands. 'Yes, of course,' she whispered. 'I think it would be very nice if we could all be a family together tomorrow, the way we used to be sometimes, on Sundays.'

'Yeah, OK,' he murmured, knowing it wasn't going to happen, but deciding it was probably best to humour her or he'd never get away.

'Are you coming back here tonight?' she wanted to know.

'No, I already told you, it's an all-nighter, so I probably won't see you until late tomorrow.'

Looking down at her hands again, she began twisting her wedding band, not to take it off, but as though remembering all that it meant to her and feeling the sadness of what was happening now.

'If it goes well with Dad tonight you'll probably stay there,' he said, trying to sound upbeat. 'Maybe you should take a few things with you, just in case.'

She nodded.

'So you'll go?'

'I'm not sure. Maybe . . .'

'Do it, Mum.'

Standing up, she put her arms around him and held him close. He could feel her body, so slight and frail, and hated the way it was shaking. 'Have a lovely party,' she told him huskily. 'Is a special girl going to be there?'

'Who knows?' he answered dismissively. 'What's special, anyway?'

Sylvie smiled as she looked into his eyes. 'You are,' she told him softly.

'Yeah, you too,' he replied, wishing with all his heart that there was something he could do to make her better.

Taking his arm, she walked into the sitting room with him and over to the door. 'I'll see you tomorrow then,' she said, as he reached for his coat.

'OK. Don't go hitting the bottle now, will you?'

Putting a finger on his lips, she said, 'I am the parent here.'

Then behave like one he wanted to reply, but didn't. 'Love you.' He planted a kiss on her cheek.

'Love you too,' she whispered, and handing him his car keys she stood aside, clearing the way for him to leave.

Moments later he was down in the street, hunched into his coat as he walked to where his car was parked. He felt sure if he turned round he'd find her watching him from the window, ready to wave, but he kept on going, afraid that if he did look round and she wasn't there it would mean she'd already gone to pour herself a drink.

He didn't want to know about that – if he did he might feel he had to go back.

For a while he debated whether or not he should text his dad to let him know she was thinking of coming over. If his dad knew, he might call and tell her she should. However, in the end he decided they had to work it out for themselves, and angry with how bad he was feeling for not giving her a wave, and for leaving her on her own, he pressed on in defiance, rounded the corner and got into his car.

'There you are,' Lauren declared, drifting like a ballerina into her mother's bedroom and starting to twirl. 'So what do you think?'

Dutifully looking up from the clear polish she was painting on her nails, Emma felt a conflicting rush of warmth and alarm to see how beautiful – and yet brazen – her daughter was managing to look. The gold-sequinned satin dress decorated with swirling lace panels was coquettishly, perhaps even outrageously, revealing, Emma thought, and the full length of her lovely long legs, (at least she was wearing tights) was on eye-popping display. Plus, the shoe-string straps of the dress didn't appear to be quite strong enough to continue holding up Lauren's generous young breasts for long. Emma just knew that if her father could see her he'd hit the ceiling, and might even try to stop her going out unless she changed into something a little more modest, such as a habit, or a sack. However, Emma was more of a realist than Will. Not that she liked to see Lauren flaunting her sexuality like this, particularly when she was barely old enough to understand how powerful it could be, but she, Emma, was well aware that this was how most girls of Lauren's age put themselves together these days. Lauren wouldn't be alone in her almost burlesque-style fashion statement, or in the towering heels that were elevating her way above her mother, or the copious layers of make-up that she really didn't need, but Emma wasn't going to be the one to tell her that. What would set Lauren apart, as it always did, was the glorious mane of honey-blonde hair that bobbed and cascaded in flurries of long loose curls around her shoulders and halfway down her back. It made her seem almost ethereal, like a dream.

This was how her mother saw her, of course; any red-blooded male would have a rather different reaction.

However, Emma trusted Lauren, because fun-loving and flirtatious as she could be, and wilful at times, she was neither stupid nor reckless. So there was no need to worry about her getting drunk and forgetting herself this evening, because she always took her election as designated driver extremely seriously. Nor was Lauren likely to throw herself away on some yob who might fancy his chances, just because she was there and looking available. What concerned Emma the most – her friends too who had girls the same age who dressed the same way – was the thought of someone much older using his more sophisticated seduction skills on their overconfident but still very naive young daughters, and of the possible consequences.

'You're taking a long time over this,' Lauren chided.

'You look lovely,' Emma assured her, 'but I hope you're wearing a coat.'

Lauren pulled a face. 'I won't need one. I've got the car,' she protested.

'That may be so, but I'm afraid you're not leaving here without one. It's freezing out there, and if you have to queue to get into a club, or walk a long way from where you park . . . Where are you going, by the way? Has it been decided yet?'

Mussing her hair in the mirror, Lauren said, 'The Bristol Ram, I think, and then the Lounge Lizard. There's talk of going on to this twenty-first birthday after, but I don't know yet.'

'So what time should I expect you home?'

'I guess, late.'

Emma cocked an eyebrow. 'Helpful.'

'Just don't wait up, OK? Now, are you ready? I'm taking you to Polly's, aren't I?'

Looking down at some of her favourite books piled on the bed, Emma sighed heavily as she felt their pull. 'I believe you are,' she said. Then, looking up again, 'Goodness, not another text,' she cried, as Lauren's phone bleeped once more. 'That thing's hardly stopped all day.'

'I know,' Lauren replied, her eyes sparkling with delight as she turned to leave, 'it's just we're trying to work everything out.'

Failing to see what could be so complicated about ferrying a few girls to a wine bar and then a club, Emma began blowing on her nails as she picked up her bag and started downstairs. For all she knew it was Donna who kept texting about something that was going on in London, which actually seemed more likely, considering how much both she and Lauren were involved in there.

'OK, I'm ready,' Lauren declared, coming down after her.

'Have you got your coat?' Emma called from the kitchen.

'Yeah, yeah, I'll go and start the car.'

As Lauren opened the front door Emma came into the hall and gave a look of surprise when she saw what Lauren was holding. 'What on earth do you need that for?' she demanded, indicating the flute case.

'Oh, no reason,' Lauren replied airily. 'I mean, I'm just

going to play a couple of things for Melissa, because she asked if I would. That's all.'

'Well, make sure you leave it at Polly's when you go out. We don't want anyone trying to break into the car to steal it.'

'It'll be fine, honestly,' Lauren assured her. 'Now, I hope you're wearing a coat because it's freezing out there.'

Laughing, Emma tweaked her nose, and wrapping up warmly in a thick, downy jacket and luxurious pink cashmere scarf – a Christmas gift from Berry – she collected her bag and keys and followed Lauren out to the car.

'Do you know what?' Lauren asked, as she drove them to the end of the street.

'I expect you're going to tell me.'

'I really, really, really, really love you. That's what.'

Startled and pleased, Emma said, 'The same to you with twice as many reallys.'

'The same to you with four times as many reallys and a cherry on top.'

Catching her euphoria, Emma entered into the little game they used to play when Lauren was small, adding four more cherries, a box of Smarties and a double KitKat.

And so it went on, all the way to Polly's, by which time they were laughing so hard at the swimming trunks Lauren had just piled on top of all the other outlandish suggestions they'd come up with that tears were rolling down Emma's cheeks.

'I'm going to have to do my make-up again,' Lauren wailed as Melissa came to let them in.

'What's happened?' Melissa demanded, her delicate doll-like features creased with concern.

'My mother, that's what,' Lauren informed her. 'She's been making me laugh.'

Relaxing, Melissa flicked her springy dark curls over one shoulder as she leaned in to give Emma a kiss.

'She's on cloud nine tonight,' Emma warned, 'so I'm relying on you to make sure she doesn't go floating away.'

'I'm not drinking, remember?' Lauren said from halfway up the stairs, 'so I'll be fine.'

Emma eyed her meaningfully.

Tilting her head, Lauren treated her to such a dazzling smile that Emma started to laugh again.

'What?' Lauren said, innocently.

'Nothing,' Emma replied. It would seem mawkish to admit that an image of Lauren aged two, sitting in the bath, and grinning at her just like that, had suddenly appeared from nowhere. 'Don't be too late,' she instructed, going on through to join Polly. 'And Melissa, please make sure she leaves her flute here before you go out.'

Fiona's immaculate eyebrows rose playfully as she watched Russ walking from his car across the floodlit forecourt of her substantial country house towards the door. She was a slender yet curvaceous woman in her mid forties, with luxuriant auburn hair, a sumptuous mouth, and sea-green eyes that could switch from shrewd to seductive in a heart-beat. As head of a rapidly diversifying construction company that she'd inherited from her self-made father, she had risen to become one of the West Country's most prominent busi-nesswomen, with projects spread over five counties and growing. She also had two homes: a harbourside penthouse in Marbella, and this rural idyll in Gloucestershire.

'Earlier than nine, but not as early as I'd hoped,' she murmured, drawing him into the warm as he kissed her.

'It's been a busy day,' he responded, shrugging off his coat. 'And Charlie called as I was about to leave.'

'Is he all right?' she asked, leading him from the stately entrance hall into the drawing room where an enormous log fire was roaring in the hearth, and casting flickering shadows around the antique furnishings and oak-panelled walls.

'I think so,' he replied, closing the door. 'Worried about his mother, of course, but nothing new there.'

She made no response as she went to pour two generous measures of Scotch into a pair of matching hand-cut tumblers.

Taking one, he met her eyes for a moment, allowing himself to enjoy the unravelling of his tension, then after touching his glass to hers he turned to go and stand in front of the fire. Their affair, and he supposed that was what it should be called, hadn't begun until after Sylvie had moved out, but the attraction between them had been smouldering for considerably longer, and boy, had it been hard to resist at times. When they had finally got together, the heat, the tearing of clothes, the sheer force with which they'd made love to each other had left its mark on them both for days. It was still the same for them, that raw, unbridled desire appeasing its hunger in ways that took them on many erotic journeys to full satisfaction. Until this week he'd been looking forward to finding out how many more routes there were to explore, but with the way things were, he guessed he wasn't going to find out now.

'You need to relax,' she told him softly.

She was right, he did, if only he could.

Going to the sofa she sat into the plush velvet cushions, crossing her legs in the slow, seductive way he loved, but though he felt the bite of desire, he forced himself to look away, focusing on his drink again. It was only fair that he should tell her what was on his mind before they became distracted by other things. God knew, though, he'd like nothing more than to go and sit with her now and lose himself in the excesses of passion they so enjoyed.

'I'm going to take Sylvie back,' he announced, keeping his eyes on his Scotch as though the real truth might be drowning in there. Even as he heard the words, he could feel himself trying to reject them.

It was a moment or two before she asked, 'Is that wise?'

No, was the answer, but what he said was, 'I believe, and Charlie agrees, that if she's with me we'll stand a better chance of persuading her to get the help she needs.' It wasn't as though they hadn't tried before, but just because they'd failed on numerous occasions didn't mean they should give up altogether.

Fiona nodded slowly. Her hair was glinting in the firelight, the warm flush on her skin making it harder than ever to stand aloof from her. As soon as she understood why, when he left in the morning, he wouldn't be coming back, he would go to her.

Chances were, she'd rather he left then.

'Have you told her this yet?' she asked.

His laugh was humourless. 'I've tried, and she turned me down. She'll change her mind, of course, when she's sober – it's just finding that time. She'll realise then that I'm serious.'

'Or maybe she won't change her mind.'

He said nothing to that, because he could find nothing to say.

'Have you considered the possibility that as desperate as she might be to come back to you, she knows that if she does, you won't allow her to have a drink? It'll be the alcoholic in her that's resisting you, and you can't fight that monster, Russ, at least not with reason, or kindness, or guilt, or any amount of good intent.'

He nodded and downed the last of his Scotch. It wasn't as though she was telling him something he didn't already know, but what the hell was he to do, entice Sylvie back with the promise of doing nothing to try and come between her and her addiction? She'd never believe it, and he'd never do it.

'Have you spoken to her sister about the way she is?'

He shook his head.

'Didn't their mother have a similar problem?'

'Yes, but she was dry long before she died.'

'I don't know if this problem is hereditary, because I don't know enough about it, but I think you should speak to her sister.'

'And what exactly do you think Olivia can do that I can't?'

'I've no idea, but I can tell you this, you shouldn't be shouldering it alone.'

'I've been to AlAnon, so have the boys . . .'

'Yes, but it's not changing anything, is it? You're still having to live with it, or I should say in fear of it, and frankly it's no life for any of you. Maybe Olivia knows what their mother did to get over it.'

'She went into rehab, and stayed there until she could handle being out again.'

'Then maybe, as her sister, Olivia can get Sylvie to do the same. Is she aware of how much Sylvie drinks?'

'I'm not sure. They haven't seen one another in a while.'

121

'Then you need to tell her.'

'I can do that, but it won't change the fact that Sylvie is still my responsibility.'

Fiona looked incredulous. 'Why? She's a grown woman, Russ. She makes her own decisions and if she wants to screw up her life, it's her choice.'

'She's not capable of making rational decisions while she's under the influence, and anyway, she's the mother of my sons. They care about her, they love her, and even though they probably don't know it, they're looking to me to rescue her from herself.'

Though Fiona's eyes showed understanding, she continued to push. 'They're grown ups too,' she reminded him, sliding an arm along the back of the sofa. 'Do they blame you for the way she is?'

Though he'd have preferred to be distracted by the prominence of her nipples showing through the smooth satin of her blouse, he said, 'I'm not sure. I don't think Charlie does, but Oliver is very mixed up. And let's face it, if she'd been happy, if I'd been there more in the early years, she might not have felt the need to drink the way she does, so you could say that in some way I am to blame.'

Sighing, Fiona shook her head as she replied, 'I have a one-word answer to that, but I don't think you want to hear it.'

The flicker of a smile crossed his lips. 'Probably not,' he agreed, and was about to go and refill his glass when he remembered he might no longer be welcome to stay the night. If he wasn't, he'd better quit drinking now.

Seeming to read his mind, she gestured for him to continue. 'Go ahead,' she said, 'and top mine up while you're at it. If this is going to be goodbye, I see no reason to hold back on anything now, do you?'

'Will someone please shut that idiot up,' Oliver complained, as he drove his friends through the winding country lanes of North Somerset towards the outskirts of Cheddar.

'Yeah, gag him,' Alfie shouted over his shoulder to Rob, who had the misfortune to be sitting next to a desperately rampant Jerome in the back seat.

'You don't even know if it is Kimberley Walsh in the video,' Rob reminded Jerome as he grabbed him in a headlock.

'Let me go, man.' Jerome fought himself free. 'I'm telling you, Sophie Ash told Mark Johnson, who told Nick Jersey, that it's definitely her, and Sophie should know, because she's the one who did the, you know, waxing thing.'

Wincing as he glanced in the rear-view mirror, Oliver said, 'Fifty quid says they're winding you up mate, and if they are, you're going to find yourself in deep trouble if you . . .'

'Come on, you said yourself Kimberley's the type *and* you agreed it looks like hers.'

'I said it could be,' Oliver protested, 'because how would I know what hers looks like when I've never even seen it?'

'I have,' Alfie informed them, 'and I'm telling you, I'm not convinced.'

'Because you've probably never seen it bald,' Jerome pointed out.

As all four of them burst into laughter, Oliver turned up the music – The Streets was one of his favourite bands.

'Is Lara going to be there tonight?' Alfie demanded.

'Who?' Oliver asked.

Alfie gulped a laugh.

'Lara Patel's been coming on to him,' Jerome piped up from the back, 'and she's definitely going to be there. Lara Patel,' he added dreamily. 'Now that is one seriously hot babe.'

'Is anyone not hot to you?' Rob asked, meaning it.

Breaking into more laughter, Alfie began rocking to the music as Oliver drove on down over the hill knowing they were heading in the right direction, but no more than that. 'Does anyone know where this place is?' he shouted over the music.

'Yeah, like that's why you're giving me a lift,' Rob shouted back. 'Lisa's my ex, remember? It's how come we've been invited.'

'And what's the deal?' Alfie wanted to know, lowering the sound. 'We're all staying over, right?'

'It's cool. Her parents are away so she's got the place to herself.'

'So how many are supposed to be there?' Jerome wanted to know.

'Dunno, she never said, but I'm guessing about fifty, or a hundred. Who knows? Who cares?'

'What's the score with weed?' Alfie asked. 'Not that I've got any, but do you reckon someone else will?'

'We won't know till we get there. The big deal is booze.'

'Well, we've got plenty of that,' Jerome grinned, holding up his third can of beer since setting out from Alfie's.

'Christ, you lot are already half smashed,' Oliver grumbled.

'Keep cool. Not far to go now,' Rob assured him, and flipping open another can he passed it over to Oliver. 'Even if you manage to down the whole lot before we get there, you still won't be over the limit,' he assured him.

Raising the can and catching Jerome's eye in the mirror, Oliver said, 'Here's to you mate, and finding the bald one.'

As Alfie and Rob howled with laughter, Jerome insisted, 'You're going to help me though, right? Promises are promises and I *cannot* leave that party without getting some action.'

'Don't worry,' Oliver assured him, starting to get in the mood now, 'we won't send you to Durban a virgin, because we're all going to get some action tonight, you just wait and see.'

Chapter Nine

Sylvie was sitting in her car outside the tall iron gates of Fiona's estate. She'd followed Russ here two, maybe even three hours ago. She didn't know when; she'd lost track of time. She might even have fallen asleep. Sometimes sadness did that to her, robbed her of knowing, closed her down and didn't release her again for a while.

She knew what was going on in inside, because it would be what went on with every woman he met. What a fool she'd been to trust Fiona. She was no different to the *putains* who threw themselves at her husband, just because he was famous – or used to be – and because he was so charming and good-looking and ready to satisfy all their cravings.

She had never been enough for him. Not once, in the entire twenty-five years they'd been married, had she as much as looked at another man – or not in the same way as he looked at other women. She'd never wanted anyone else, and she still didn't. The men she slept with now, she didn't set out for it to happen, and she didn't know their names, but they were kind and fun and always left in the morning without making any fuss. Sometimes she wondered why she needed them, then she remembered they were a substitute for Russ.

She'd left her home for him, her family, her country. It was true, when they'd first come into each other's lives she was already in England, working as an au pair in Kensington, but she'd never come intending to stay. Then she'd met him and from the first time they were together she'd known she would never go back. He'd loved her so much then that he'd had to see her morning, noon and night. He'd wanted her in his bed, his world, the rest of his life. He'd married her less than six months after their first meeting. Their families had been shocked – they'd been so young, yet had felt so mature, as children always did at that age – but eventually everyone had come round.

Her parents had considered him the son they'd never had.

His parents had always seemed baffled by her, but she was sure they'd loved her in the end. She'd definitely loved them, gruff and boringly English though they were.

The boys had brought everyone together and had kept them that way – how could they not? Both families adored the boys. They were the centre of everyone's world.

They still were, but they were starting to live their own lives now, the way they should. Charlie had already gone and Oliver had only returned for a while.

Her heart dissolved in the heat of pain and loss.

If she'd been able she'd have had more children, three, four, six, seven, but after Oliver it had not been possible. Strangely, Russ had seemed sorrier not to have had a daughter than she had. She loved her boys. They were everything to her and she'd have loved more.

Russ was devoted to their boys too, she'd never doubted that, but their innocent affection had never been enough for him, the way it had for her. It had taken her a long time to learn that, but she'd definitely learned it now.

He was in that house with her best friend.

Earlier, she'd tried to call her father, before remembering she couldn't. It was funny how that still happened from time to time. He'd been dead for almost five years and yet in many ways it felt as though he was still there, going about his day in the small, leafy suburb of Paris where she and her sister had grown up. It was hard to believe that place no longer existed, bulldozed to make way for an autoroute. Perhaps it did still exist in another dimension.

She'd like to go to that dimension now. Somewhere, anywhere, as long as her father was there, and her mother, the parents who'd loved her and whom she'd always been able to trust.

Rain trickled down her windscreen like tears, while grief poured into her heart like a storm. There was a bottle on the seat beside her, untouched, unopened. The need for it was clamouring, clawing, promising its guarantee of release. It would dull the pain, throw the cries of longing and despair into a distant, other domain. A domain that echoed with what might have been, with what could never be now.

Her father was dead; Russ had gone, he was inside with her best friend.

Picking up her phone she pressed in his number.

Would he ignore the call when he saw it was her?

Would he dare to answer and lie?

There were six rings before he picked up.

'I know where you are,' she told him, gazing along the black drive towards the house.

Shaking himself awake, Russ rolled away from Fiona as he said, 'What are you doing? Where are you?'

'If you look outside you'll see me.'

Russ got up from the bed, his heart thudding with disbelief as he went to the window and parted the heavy drapes. At the end of the drive two headlights were staring straight at him like the eyes of a predator.

Surely to God, it couldn't be her.

'Sylvie, what are you doing?' he cried.

'I came to see you,' she told him, 'but you were already on your way out, so I followed you here.'

His head was thumping, the world was turning crazy. 'What the hell for?' he shouted. 'What are you trying to prove?'

'My point. And I think I have. Does she think she's the only one?'

Turning from the window, he began snatching up his clothes.

'Let me speak to my friend,' she said.

Ignoring her, he put a hand over the phone as he said to Fiona, 'She's outside.'

Getting up from the bed, Fiona reached for a robe. 'What are you going to do?' she asked.

Right now he had no clear idea, but he couldn't let Sylvie just sit there, gazing through the bars like a preying, or wounded, animal pleading to come in.

'Is she drunk?'

'I don't know, but I think we have to assume she is.' Going back on the line, he said, 'I'm coming out.'

'Why?'

'Why do you think?' he almost yelled. 'I don't know what the hell's got into you. Are you going to start stalking me now, is that what this is about?'

'You have no right to be angry with me . . .'

'I have every damned right.'

'You said you wanted me to come home.'

'But not like this. Couldn't you have rung? For Christ's sake, why am I even having this conversation?' and ending the call he threw the phone on the bed and hauled on his trousers.

'I should call a taxi,' Fiona suggested. 'If she's drunk, we can't let her drive away from here.'

Before he could answer he heard a loud crash outside and whipped back the curtains again. 'Jesus Christ, she's trying to ram down the gates.'

By the time he'd raced downstairs and thrown open the front door she was already driving away.

'I'll have to go after her,' he said, as Fiona joined him at the door.

'But you can't!' she protested. 'You're over the limit.'

His eyes closed in frustration.

'Call her and tell her to go to your place. At least it's not as far.'

Back upstairs, he snatched up his phone and pressed in the number.

No reply.

To her voicemail he said, 'Sylvie, I want you to go to Clyde Court. Do you hear me? Please don't drive back into Bristol tonight. I've been drinking so I'll have to get a taxi, but I'll meet you there.'

*

Oliver was sprawled out on a sofa, a beer in one hand, a spliff in the other and Lara Patel's beautiful dark legs hooked indelicately over his. There were bodies everywhere, writhing to the beat, lolling about the floor, swaying in groups, smooching against walls . . .

Last seen, Jerome was on his way to a bedroom to live his dream with Kimberley Walsh, who'd admitted to being in the video and was prepared to prove it, if Oliver was interested. He might have been, because he'd had enough to drink by then, but he'd promised Jerome, and Kimberley hadn't seemed too bothered about who wished to see proof of her exploit. Nor did Jerome seem very bothered by the fact that Alfie had already been there tonight, and a couple more blokes were probably lined up to take over once he'd finished.

She was a girl, Kimberley Walsh.

A slut, was what Thea had called her, and Oliver couldn't really argue with that.

He had no idea where Thea was now, nor did he care. All she'd been interested in was his mother's appearance on the news a couple of days ago, and why he'd never told her his father was famous.

Who the hell cared that his father *used* to be famous?

What did it have to do with anything, for Christ's sake?

All he wanted was to forget about his effing family for once and have a good time.

He'd been able to tell from the way Thea had rubbed herself against him when they'd danced that things would go his way if he played it right tonight, but though he'd started to, he'd soon found that he was more interested in having another drink and a smoke than he was in getting it on with her. Maybe it was the fawning tone of her questions that had turned him off, or perhaps he'd never really fancied her anyway. He wasn't going to bother analysing it. What was the point? She meant nothing to him.

Resting a hand on Lara's thigh, he took another deep drag of the spliff and let his head roll back against the sofa as he passed it on. Lara turned his face to hers and gazed into his eyes.

'Hey you,' he murmured softly.

'Hey you,' she murmured back.

As they started to kiss he felt the desire for it draining away.

'What's wrong?' she frowned as he stopped.

He put a hand on her face, gazed at her mouth and tried again. This time it worked, and as the kiss deepened and his head started to swim he felt himself rising towards a place he really wanted to be.

Then a swathe of freezing air blew across the room.

They both looked round and peered through the fug to see what was going on over by the door. Some girls had turned up.

'It's Milly Butler and her friends,' Lisa, their hostess, declared. She was wrapped around her boyfriend on a nearby chair and didn't bother getting up, merely waved to the newcomers and told them to help themselves to anything.

Resuming the kiss with Lara, Oliver started using his tongue and raking his fingers through her hair.

'Do you want another drink?' he asked when they paused to take in air.

'Sure,' she replied.

'Another of the same?'

She nodded and swung her legs to the floor to let him get up. He staggered and almost fell on to her.

In the kitchen he found Rob and a few others engaged in heavy debate about something serious, though it didn't sound as though any of them knew exactly what it was. He cracked another beer and dashed some Bacardi into the glass he'd brought with him.

'Hey!' Rob called, pulling him over. 'You know all about this.'

'All about what?'

'The technique they use to transmit images from lunar modules.'

'You've got to be kidding,' Oliver protested.

'No. Nathan here reckons . . .'

'I'm out of here,' Oliver interrupted.

As he made his way back into the main room he saw a

couple of the newcomers chatting to Lara, so leaning over the back of the sofa he put her drink in her hand and went to join Alfie, who was studying a surreal-looking portrait on a wall between two windows.

'Someone you know?' Oliver quipped.

Alfie turned to look at him, too stoned to register who he was straight away. 'Oh, it's you,' he slurred. 'Thought you were with Lara.'

'I am, sort of. How come you're on your own?'

'I'm with the one who looks like Duffy. Forgotten her name . . . She's gone to the loo.'

Feeling his mobile vibrating in his pocket, Oliver fished it out, and seeing it was his mother an angry darkness came over him. He turned it off, but a moment later turned it back on. She was ringing again. 'What?' he barked into it, moving towards an empty corner so no one would hear.

'It's Mum,' she told him.

'I *know*. What is it?'

'I am calling,' she said haltingly, 'because I went to see your father . . . He is with someone else and I am very sorry, Oliver, but I cannot bear to go on like this . . .'

'Mum, for Christ's sake . . .'

'Please listen,' she begged. 'I am so very unhappy. It is too difficult for me this way . . . I love you very much, you know that, don't you?'

His insides were starting to burn hot with fear. 'I'm not listening to any more of this . . .'

'No, don't hang up. I must say goodbye to you and make sure that you know . . .'

'Just stop.' His voice rose. 'If you're saying what I think you are . . .'

'Yes, I am, *chéri*, but don't worry. Everything will be fine. *Ca serait mieux si je partais* . . .'

'Mum, don't do this to me,' he cried, and thrusting his drink at Alfie he began stumbling and crashing over bodies to get out of the room. 'I'm coming, OK, just don't do anything before I get there.'

Lauren was trying very hard not to be upset and angry, she understood that things didn't always go the way they were supposed to, but she just couldn't help feeling crushed by the way tonight had turned out. She'd been so looking forward to it, had bought her dress specially *and* brought her flute. It wouldn't have been so bad if Donna had been there, at least then she'd have had someone to talk to. Donna had really wanted to come, but at the last minute her dad had suddenly said they were spending too much time gadding about in the week, never telling anyone where they were going, and he'd had enough. Donna needed to knuckle down and study this weekend.

Lauren had written in her journal earlier, kind of to keep herself company while she was waiting and still feeling seriously wicked and excited. The book was tucked inside her flute case now, the big padded one that Granny had bought her for Christmas with pockets for sheet music and her thumbport and cleaning rods. Everything had been in a state of readiness, her journal to record all that had happened, her flute to play, and Lauren herself to perform.

What a waste of time it had all turned out to be, and now to make everything worse she was bloody well lost. It was so dark out and the country lanes so similar with their gloomily clustering hedgerows and sharply twisting bends that it was almost impossible to pick out a landmark she might recognise. Was she even in the vicinity of somewhere familiar?

Feeling a shudder of nerves loosening her insides, she took some comfort from the fact that her mum had remembered to fill up the tank with petrol so at least she wouldn't run out, and sooner or later she was bound to come across a village she'd heard of, or, even better, a signpost to a place she knew. It might not bring her out exactly where she wanted to be, but at least she'd stand a better chance of finding her way home if she had some directions to guide her.

She thought about calling Melissa to see if she could help, but what was the point if she couldn't even tell Melissa where she was? Besides, it was one thirty in the morning, so Melissa was either still out clubbing, or maybe even already all tucked up and safe and warm in her bed. What she wouldn't give to be in her own bed! She'd rather be almost anywhere than wandering around out here in the great black beyond, no longer even sure if she was heading in the right direction.

The digital clock on her dashboard was reading 1.34 when, almost by chance, it was so obscured by branches, she spotted a signpost to Lulsgate airport. With a dizzying sigh of relief she indicated to turn left, and after driving up a small, winding hill she found herself descending to a two-way stretch of road that she felt sure looked familiar. Yes, it did, because she remembered passing the oddly petrified tree in front of her when she was on her way out – it looked like a woman's bouffant taking off in the wind. She wasn't sure what it was close to, but at least she knew she'd come this way.

Feeling less tense now, she pressed down on the accelerator to speed things along and was just turning up the music when she realised, to her confusion, that instead of going faster she seemed to be slowing down. She pressed harder on the accelerator, and harder still, but to her alarm the engine was definitely losing power. Trying not to panic she checked the petrol gauge, but of course she wasn't running out, so she kicked the pedal again and again, but instead of surging ahead the car only continued to slow down.

Feeling the presence of real fear closing in on her from the darkness, she steered the car to the side of the road, where it eventually rolled to a stop. She tried starting the engine again, but there was no more than a click as she turned the key. Nothing was happening at all.

'You're supposed to be fixed,' she cried, banging the steering wheel. 'You can't let me down now.'

Rigid and too scared to peer into the darkness around her, she forced herself to wait a couple of minutes, then turned the key again.

The same dull clicks.

She had to call her mother. It didn't matter that she had no clear idea of where she was, somehow they'd work it out, her mother would come and everything would be fine. Taking out her phone she pressed in the number, only to discover when the connection failed that she had no reception.

'No, no, no!' she exclaimed furiously. 'This can't be happening.'

Tearing off her seat belt, she swivelled on to her knees and leaned over to the back seat with her phone. Still no reception. She held it to the passenger window, and out of her own window, but not even one bar charged. Almost as angry as she was afraid, she got out of the car and stormed across to the other side of the road. There had to be a better reception over there.

There wasn't.

She ran up the road a little way, but there was still nothing.

'Oh God,' she sobbed, and shivered. What the hell was she going to do?

Everything was so quiet, and still, and *cold*. No cars were passing at all, there weren't even any planes overhead, much good they would do her even if there were. She could hardly follow one, could she? But at least she'd have an idea where the airport was, if she only had a car that would go.

A rustle in the undergrowth close by shot her with terror. She knew it had to be an animal, but her imagination was managing to conjure far worse.

There was nothing else for it, she'd have to walk, though God knew how when she was wearing five-inch heels and when it was so cold that the countryside tucked into her narrow view was glistening with frost and her teeth were chattering so hard. She didn't even know how far it was, or which direction to take apart from straight ahead, and what if someone had turned the signposts around? She might be out here all night. She could even freeze to death. She definitely would if she didn't have her coat. How she loved her mother in that moment for making her bring it.

Praying there were no psychos out on the prowl, she started – hobbled really, given how much her shoes were hurting – back across the road to fetch her bag and flute from the car. Heavy though it was, she'd have to take her flute, because it had cost way too much money for her to risk leaving it behind.

She was almost halfway there when she heard the sound of a car approaching. Her heart immediately leapt to her throat. Should she flag the driver down or run and hide? It could be a psycho, or it could be rescue. Two huge cones of light flared up over the trees and reached the top of the hill. She started to run, but was suddenly torn about which way to go. She looked at her car, then the one that was approaching. It was so close . . . She had to make herself *run . . .*

Oliver's hands were clenched so tightly to the wheel that his knuckles felt close to cracking. His anger and dread were so fierce it was like thunder in his brain.

He'd stopped a few minutes ago to do what he should have the instant his mother had rung him – call his father, his brother, the police, anyone, but he hadn't been able to get a reception. He didn't even know if he was going the right way. This wasn't his part of town; he'd hardly ever been here before. A sign half a mile back had directed him to the airport, which was better than nothing. At least he knew his way from there.

The music was doing his head in. He leaned over to turn it off and his eyes returned to the road as he flew over the brink of the hill . . .

Jesus Christ Almighty.

He jammed on the brakes, jammed and jammed, but he couldn't come to a stop. It was all happening too fast, yet he was in slow motion. He slammed right into her. She flew up over the bonnet. Her head hit the windscreen so hard that the glass shattered into a web of a million pieces. He couldn't see where he was going. He was still braking like mad. The car hit something else, swerved and finally came to a stop.

His hands were still gripping the wheel, his head was reeling and hanging forward as he tried to catch his breath.

What the hell had just happened? He was having a nightmare, right?

His heart felt like it was having an attack.

He forced his head up. He could see nothing ahead of him – the windscreen was a net of smithereens. He turned to the side and saw only bushes, gnarled and thistly in the glow of his headlights. The only sound was the dull click of the cooling engine.

His breath stopped coming. Then it was there again in harsh, ragged bursts.

He'd hit someone, he was sure of it.

Jesus Christ, he'd just hit someone.

Pushing open the door, he stepped out into the frosty night air and his legs started to buckle beneath him. He took a deep breath and made himself look back along the road. He couldn't see anyone, but there was a car . . . Then he saw something lying next to it.

He started to heave, huge, dry, retching sobs, with nothing coming out.

When it was over he looked down the road again.

It was still there.

He could tell it was a person. Were they all right?

No, you stupid fucking bastard, of course they're not all right.

He started towards them, broke into a run, then stopped suddenly and took a step back.

He didn't know what to do. He wasn't a doctor. He knew nothing about first aid, or emergencies, or anything like that. And he'd been drinking.

But he had to try and help.

Running to the figure crumpled on its side, one arm outstretched, face hidden by a mane of bloodied hair, he threw himself down next to her and tried to make himself think. 'Are you all right?' he urged. 'I'm sorry. I didn't see you. Oh God, please be all right, please, please. Can you hear me? Say something. Anything.'

Through the tangle of her hair he could see that her eyes were closed and her mouth was hanging open.

Terrified, he looked around. Everything was hauntingly still.

He had to get help. 999. An ambulance.

Galvanised, he dashed back to his car and snatched the

phone from the passenger seat, but when he dialled he saw there was still no reception.

This couldn't be happening. It just couldn't. Someone had to come along *now* and give them some help.

Hardly connecting with his own movements, he ran back to her. 'I don't know what to do,' he cried, holding up his phone. 'I can't call for help.'

What the hell do you think she's going to do, you fucking idiot?

'I won't be long,' he told her hurriedly. 'I swear I'm not leaving you.'

He started to run, faster than he ever had in his life. Some way past his own car he came to an abrupt stop. When the ambulance turned up the police would be bound to come too. They'd breathalyse him and there was no way he'd pass. He'd lose his licence, maybe even go to prison for hitting her.

What if he'd killed her?

No, no, no, no. Everything was happening too fast. He was out of control. He had to calm down.

What if he got back in his car and drove away? They might never know it was him. Someone was bound to come along in a minute, they'd find her and call the emergency services. She'd be all right.

He turned around and looked back down the road. She was still lying there, not moving. If she was dead there was nothing anyone could do anyway.

But what if she wasn't?

He'd hit her so hard she had to be.

Feeling his knees turning weak again, he bent double as he started to retch. He had to get out of here before someone came and saw him.

Staggering back to his car, instead of getting in he found himself going straight past it, back to her. He picked up her hand. He had to find a pulse, but his heart was hammering so hard that he had no idea what he was feeling. He put his face down to hers to try and hear her breath.

There was nothing.

He started to cry. If she wasn't breathing, she had to be dead.

'Oh God, oh God,' he sobbed. What should he do?

He stood up, stumbled a few steps and stumbled back again. He was shaking so fiercely he couldn't even hear the silence. He could only feel it, smothering him with its terrible stillness.

He dropped his phone, picked it up and started to walk again. He was going to get out of here, pretend it had never happened. It hadn't been his fault. She'd been in the middle of the road. He hadn't stood a chance.

Remembering his mother, he clenched his hands to his head.

What was he supposed to do?

Get out of here, a voice inside him urged. *Go now before anyone comes.*

He turned back to the girl. 'I don't even know you,' he sobbed. 'It wasn't my fault. I didn't know you were there.'

The terrible echo of his voice retreated like a frightened animal over the empty, frosted fields.

'I have to go, OK?' he said. 'I'm really sorry, but I can't use the phone here, and I don't know how to help you. I promise I'll call someone as soon as I can.'

He ran back to his car, started to get in, but suddenly he was slamming the door and running on down the road. He kept going until his phone showed some bars of connection.

It took three seconds to dial 999. It took forever to explain what had happened and who he was.

'It doesn't matter who I am,' he raged. 'I'm trying to tell you, she needs help. You have to send an ambulance.'

'We will, sir, but you have to tell us where you are.'

He didn't know.

'It's OK,' the operator said soothingly, 'we're going to work it out. I just need you to stay on the line.'

'Why?' he shouted. 'It doesn't have anything to do with me. I just saw what happened . . .'

'But we need a location, and your phone can give it to us, so please don't ring off.'

He couldn't decide what to do. How the hell could he get out of this and still help her? He had to make himself think. They had his number now, so they'd find him anyway. And could he really, seriously, just leave her there?

Chapter Ten

Oliver had no idea how much time had gone by. It might have been minutes, hours, even days. He only knew that it felt as though he'd been sitting here, on the side of the road, for most of his life. Nothing seemed to exist beyond the girl lying next to him and the night that belonged to a terrible dream.

A while ago he'd turned her head to make sure she could breathe. Maybe it was already too late for that, but he wasn't going to allow himself to think it, he just couldn't. Every now and again he spoke to her, saying, 'I'm sorry,' or 'I didn't see you,' or 'They're coming. You're going to be all right.' His words grated the stillness, and were shredded with the kind of fear he'd never known in his life.

Was his jacket, wrapped around her leg, doing anything to help? The bone was sticking through the skin, he'd had to do something to try and protect it.

Where the hell was everyone?

A few minutes ago he'd noticed some car headlights approaching in the distance, but then they'd turned off in another direction and disappeared from view.

It was as though they'd been abandoned, him and this girl. They were the only two people in the world.

He wanted to leave her, but he couldn't make himself do it. He kept trying, but it just wouldn't happen. It was as though he was tied to her now, and there would never be any letting go. Their lives had collided, crossed, become enmeshed in a way that couldn't be escaped; even if she didn't make it, she would always be a part of him.

If she came round she'd be afraid, in pain, probably unable to move. He wished he knew what to do.

Yet why should he care? He didn't know her. He'd never even seen her before. She shouldn't have been standing in the road.

Still there was no sound apart from the rustle and cry of night creatures, and the unstoppable voices in his head.

What was happening to his mother?

Fear contracted him again. He should have called her while he could, but he'd forgotten, and now he was back here and unable to leave this girl in spite of the cold and the fear that was gripping him so cruelly.

Ca serait mieux si je partais, she'd said. It would be better if I left.

His eyes closed as more terror sliced through him. She couldn't have meant what he'd thought. She wouldn't do that, she just wouldn't.

If she did it would be his fault for not stopping her.

He couldn't call her now, and he couldn't drive away to get to her.

Maybe she'd meant she was going to be with Aunt Olivia in Cape Town.

He wished he was in Cape Town. Or still at the party, or at his mother's – or *at home with his father*. . .

He started to cry, helplessly, self-pityingly.

'They won't be long now,' he told her, dashing away his tears. He had to hold it together for her. 'They'll take care of you, make sure you're all right.'

He was holding her hand, squeezing it hard as though trying to push his own life into her. She was cold, but so was he.

He tensed at the distant wail of an animal screeching into the night. He looked around, terrified, frozen, hardly able to move. Then he recognised the sound, and as relief and fear pumped more adrenalin into his veins he dropped her hand and shot to his feet.

'They're here,' he told her, his voice mangled by a sob. 'They're coming. Can you hear them? You're going to be OK.'

*

Bob Tillman was at the wheel of the response vehicle; Clive Andrews was next to him, keeping his eyes peeled for some sign of what they were looking for. They should be close now, he thought, and after they rounded a bend, tore along a straight stretch, lights flashing, siren screaming, he finally spotted a car up ahead slewed into a ditch. 'OK, what's this?' he said.

Hitting the brakes, Bob Tillman slowed as they approached a VW Polo with a shattered windscreen; then, seeing a young lad frantically waving, Clive Andrews started to get out of the car.

'It's all right, son,' he shouted, running towards him. 'Where's the victim?'

'She's here,' the boy shouted back, pointing.

'Is she still alive?'

'I – I think so.'

Seeing the girl lying crumpled next to a second car, Andrews immediately instructed Tillman to call out a chopper and go to seal off the road. The girl had to be got to hospital faster than fast, and the last thing they needed was some poor unsuspecting sod ploughing into the scene and making things worse than they already were.

'Are you a relative?' Andrews was asking as he brushed past the lad to get to the girl. 'What happened here?'

'She was in the middle of the road,' Oliver cried. 'I didn't even see her.'

'It's OK,' Andrews said, putting a firm hand on the boy's shoulder. That was all he could give him for now – the girl was his priority. 'Oh Jesus Christ,' he murmured to himself, as he knelt down beside her. He hated it when it was kids the same age as his own. One day, it might turn out to be one of his.

'I turned her head so she could breathe,' Oliver told him.

'Good, you did good,' Andrews assured him, without knowing if it was true. It would be if she was still with them, and Andrews was hoping with all his heart that she was.

Hearing more sirens in the distance, he softened his voice as he laid a hand gently on her head, and said, 'Hello beautiful. Are you going to have a bit of a chat with me now? Can you hear me? I think you can. Open your eyes, there's a love. Let me see how pretty they are.'

Receiving no response, he squeezed her earlobe for a pain reaction.

Nothing.

Stooping closer, he listened for breathing.

If it was there, it was too faint to hear.

Internal bleeding could be affecting her pulses, so no guarantees there.

'We're going to have you nice and safe very soon now,' he told her gently. 'The ambulance is on its way. Can you hear the siren?'

Nineteen minutes was the maximum response time, they'd already used up sixteen and he wasn't sure this girl had many more minutes left in her, if she had any at all.

'Is she alive?' Oliver blurted.

Andrews didn't want to frighten the lad. He needed to reassure himself too. 'I think there's a chance,' he replied, keeping his eyes fixed on the girl. So young, her whole damned life ahead of her. Would he ever get used to this? He had to hope not, because this life-shattering tragedy wasn't something any normal person would ever want to get used to. It churned him up inside so badly that his doctor had told him he was in the wrong job.

'Where's the police car gone?' Oliver asked.

Andrews said, 'We have to close the road.' He wouldn't add that they were obliged to treat this with the same level and resourcing as a murder scene, regardless of whether or not the girl was dead. The lad was clearly spooked enough, he didn't need any more.

'You should go and sit in your car,' he told Oliver. 'You're in shock and there's nothing you can do here.'

'Can you save her?'

'We're going to do our best, but you'll have to help us, sweetheart,' he told the girl. 'You'll have to fight with us, OK? We'll all be here for you, every one of us, so don't you go letting the side down, will you? The ambulance is here now. Can you hear it?' Footsteps were running, the medics were upon them. 'This is Bernie,' he said as a long-time colleague knelt down next to him. 'He's going to take care of everything, OK. Pam's with him. She's one of the best.'

'Good job,' Bernie whispered, pushing past Andrews. 'Chopper's on its way. Any signs?'

Andrews shook his head.

Pam already had the spinal board and collar.

'Pelvic splint?' she asked.

'Absolutely,' Bernie confirmed.

As Bernie began checking for vital signs and talking to the girl the same way Andrews had, Andrews drew back and turned to the boy. 'Come on, son,' he said, 'we need to clear the scene.'

Oliver was about to go with him when Bernie shouted after Pam, 'Oxygen, fast.'

Andrews's hand tightened on Oliver's shoulder.

'Does that mean she's breathing?' Oliver cried desperately.

Andrews didn't answer. He was aware of other vehicles pulling up around them, more police, paramedics, fire brigade, but he was listening to Bernie speaking to the girl.

'It's all right, my old love, it's all right,' Bernie was telling her as Pam set about attaching the oxygen and he started to move the girl's broken body. 'I'll try not to hurt you now.'

As the girl's leg was exposed Andrews's eyes closed. The bone was jutting out of the skin. The splint for that would come later; what mattered now was getting air into her lungs and her body on to the spinal board.

The paramedics descended at speed. One took over the oxygen while the other helped Pam and Bernie to wrap a large red and blue belt around Lauren's hips.

Andrews knew how vital it was to take care when trying to straighten the pelvis. Please God don't let her be bleeding in there anywhere – if she was, chances were they wouldn't be able to save her.

He didn't even want to think about the injuries to her head.

By the time Bob Tillman was back from securing the

road the scene was teeming with people and lights, and the sound of the helicopter approaching was growing louder all the time. Andrews sat the boy in the back of the Polo and told him to wait. He wouldn't mention a breath test yet, but the kid had to know it was going to happen.

By now the girl was tethered to the spinal board and supported by a collar. The oxygen mask was clamped to her face, an IV drip had been inserted into a vein. As the helicopter was waved in to the nearby field, Andrews found himself looking past all the life-saving equipment to her matted, yet beautiful hair. She was someone's daughter, their pride and joy, perhaps even their reason for living.

Why did God do this to people? What good reason could there ever be to punish a parent like this?

'Jackie Dennis is on her way,' Tillman said, coming up behind him.

Andrews simply nodded. The Accident Investigation Unit was always mobilised to an incident such as this, and Inspector Jackie Dennis was nothing if not thorough.

The helimedics were out now, rushing to the girl and transporting her swiftly back to the craft. Once they were all inside, the pilot took the chopper up gently, tentatively, before swooping rapidly away into the night, leaving a remote country scene swarming with police officers, firemen, paramedics and investigators doing their jobs.

'I guess we ought to get on with breathalysing the kid,' Tillman said to Andrews. 'Where is he?'

'In his car.' Andrews spotted a female officer heading his way. 'We found a handbag in the Peugeot,' she told him. 'Indications are the girl's name is Lauren Scott, eighteen, and she lives about four miles from here. She's also got an organ-donor card in her wallet, which the hospital might want to know about.'

Andrews's heart gave a painful kick as though it wanted rid of the information, and all the knock-on effects about to come with it. 'Radio it through,' he told her. Then, 'We're going to need a family liaison officer.'

'I'm a FLO,' Tillman reminded him.

As Andrews looked at him he was ashamed of the relief he felt, knowing he wouldn't have to face the parents himself. He was turning to retrieve the breathalyser kit from the unit car when someone shouted and two uniforms took off down the road, like a pair of stags on a hen night.

It was only a matter of seconds before they caught up with the lad, who, Andrews reckoned, had to be way too traumatised even to know where he was going, much less what he was hoping to prove by running away.

By the time his captors had returned him to the scene and dumped him in the back of a police car, Jackie Dennis had turned up and was unpacking her investigator's kit. Leaving Tillman and the others to fill her in, Andrews stood over the open rear door of the Focus estate and looked down at the lad. How old could he be? Late teens, early twenties? He must be terrified out of his tiny mind.

'Not the smartest move you've ever made,' Andrews told him, 'trying to run like that.'

The boy kept his head down.

'OK, we best get this over with. For your information my name's Clive Andrews, and you are . . .'

'Oliver Lomax,' Oliver mumbled.

'Right, Oliver. I expect you understand . . .'

'I have to make a call,' Oliver interrupted. 'Please, just one . . .'

'All in good time.'

'No, you don't understand. It's my mother. I was on my way there when . . . when all this happened. I think she's going to try and kill herself . . . She might already . . . I have to stop her.'

Jesus Christ, Andrews muttered to himself. 'What makes you say that?' he asked cautiously. He'd come across a lot of excuses before and this one wasn't unique.

'She rang me at the party I was at. She said she wanted to say goodbye, that it was better if she left . . . Please, you have to let me call her.'

Deciding to give the lad the benefit of the doubt, Andrews said, 'OK, give me your mother's address, we'll send someone round there.'

Oliver began to answer, then blanked.

Sensing him starting to panic, Andrews said, 'Just take it nice and slow. What's the house number?'

After jotting the details down, Andrews radioed them through, then standing back for Oliver to get out of the car, he said, 'I'm afraid it's time for us to talk about what happened here tonight, and that has to start with the obvious question: were you driving the car that hit her?'

Oliver's mouth opened, but all that came out was a strangled sob.

'That's your car, the Polo?' Andrews prompted.

Oliver nodded.

Andrews looked down at the form on his clipboard that required flawless completion. 'This is all going to sound very formal now,' he warned, 'but I'm obliged by law to follow procedure to the letter. Do you understand that?'

Oliver's head stayed down as he nodded.

After quickly filling in his own details, Oliver's evident ethnic origin, and brief details of the incident, Andrews asked, 'So, Oliver, when did you last consume alcohol?'

Oliver seemed to shrink away.

'Come on now, let's not make this any more difficult than it already is.'

'Um, I don't know. At the party. What time is it now?'

Andrews checked his watch. 'One fifty-five,' he answered. 'And don't lie, son, I promise it won't help you in the long run.'

Swallowing hard, Oliver said, 'I suppose it was about an hour ago.'

Since they were well past the twenty-minute requirement between last consumption and initial test, Andrews said, 'OK, I want you to provide me with a specimen of breath for a breath test which I am empowered to require under the provisions of the Road Traffic Act 1988.'

Oliver wrapped his arms round his head as Andrews threw his clipboard into the car and produced the device for him to blow into.

'You see this here,' Andrews said, indicating the transparent tube sticking up from the gadget like an aerial.

Oliver glanced up.

'I want you to take a nice deep breath and blow into it as hard as you can for as long as you can.'

Oliver took a step back. His face was chalk-white, his eyes glittering with a terrible fear. 'What if I said no?' he asked shakily.

Andrews cocked an eyebrow. 'It wouldn't be a good idea,' he informed him.

'But what would happen?'

'Well, you could end up with a ban anyway and that would just be for starters, so come on now, don't make this any harder for yourself.'

It didn't surprise Andrews when the boy started to cry, and he might have had some sympathy if a lovely young girl wasn't now fighting for her life – if she hadn't already lost it. 'Come on, pull yourself together,' he said, sharply. 'Just do as you're told and we can get out of here.'

Though the boy was shivering badly, he put enough force behind the breath to create a reading that didn't surprise Andrews when it topped out at sixty-seven. Not quite twice the legal limit, but as near as damn it.

'Did I fail?' Oliver asked wretchedly.

'Yes, son, I'm afraid you did, so now I'm arresting you under Section 5 of the Road Traffic Act 1988 on suspicion of driving a motor vehicle while exceeding the prescribed limit of alcohol in your blood, the prescribed limit being thirty-five micrograms of alcohol in 100 millilitres of breath.'

As he finished he was aware of someone coming to stand behind him, and turning he found Jackie Dennis, a short, serious-looking woman, nodding for him to follow her. Bob Tillman and the female officer stepped forward to usher Oliver to another car.

'I'm sorry to do this to you, Clive,' Jackie Dennis said, keeping her voice low, 'but we both know you're a FLO and I think you're better equipped to handle this than Bob Tillman.'

Andrews felt a cold vacuum opening up inside him. 'Please tell me you're not saying . . . ?'

'You have to go to the parents.'

He could accept that, almost, just as long as the girl . . .
'Tell me she's not dead. I don't want to hear . . .'

Putting a hand on his arm, Jackie Dennis said, 'The family deserves someone with your experience to break the news. Now, let's get into the car for a minute, so we can talk it through before you go.'

Emma had woken several minutes ago, unsure whether it was a dream that had jolted her, or a noise outside. After the initial unease had passed she'd remained curled up in the armchair where she'd dozed off in front of the fire whilst reading. Her sixth sense seemed still to be listening out for whatever might have woken her, but apart from the yowling cry of a cat in the distance, and a car passing, there seemed to be nothing out of the ordinary.

In the end she put her book aside and got up to go and make a hot drink. She'd intended to take it up to bed, but noticing how late it was she decided to continue waiting up for Lauren who, if her high spirits earlier were anything to go by, was probably going to come bursting through the door any minute full of every last detail of what had happened during the evening. Or she'd have worn herself out by now and so be ready to collapse straight into bed with a furry-hot water bottle and a plea not to be woken too early in the morning.

Whichever way was fine by Emma – she was awake enough now for a chat, or happy to carry on reading if Lauren did flake out on her. Sleep was going to be difficult when she'd already had a couple of hours, especially with so much churning round in her mind, the job, what she would do if she didn't get it, how hard Lauren was working to pass her exams, whether she put too much pressure on Lauren to do well, plus a general unease about everything that seemed to be settling over her in dark, uncomfortable waves. She reminded herself of the ungodly hour and remembered something she'd read about it once: this was when logic stood in front of a distorting mirror and paranoia got gleefully to work.

But Lauren really should have been home by now. This was far too late for her to be out without at least ringing to say she'd gone to the party or had decided to stay over with Lucy or Melissa.

Going to check her mobile just in case she'd missed a text or voicemail, she found no messages and couldn't stop her concern deepening. It really wasn't like Lauren to be inconsiderate, though she had to admit that it wasn't actually unheard of, so perhaps she should try ringing her.

Finding herself diverted to Lauren's voicemail she felt a stab of anxiety and annoyance pierce straight through her common sense. Quickly reminding herself that Lauren could simply be out of range, or unable to hear the ringtone over the music, or perhaps even out of battery, she rang off and picked up her drink. Lauren's credit would be fine, because Will took care of her monthly mobile bills, and she'd had enough money on her when she'd left to get a taxi home in case she broke down, or decided to have a drink after all.

If that had happened she'd have called – unless she'd managed to lose her phone.

Why had she taken her flute?

Nothing was quite making sense.

Perhaps she should try Melissa's number to find out where they were.

Did Polly realise that Melissa wasn't home yet, or had Polly tumbled straight into bed after their victorious quiz night, and was she even now lost in dreamland?

Glancing at the time again, Emma felt her head starting to spin with mounting unease.

Two fifty-one in the morning.

Russ couldn't bring himself to go to bed. He'd been back at the house for what seemed like hours, pacing the kitchen waiting for Sylvie to turn up, or at least to call back. He'd tried her mobile countless times, and left half a dozen messages, but she either had her phone turned off, or was simply ignoring him. The other alternative, that she'd been in an accident, or done something stupid like topping herself, was unthinkable, but as the time ticked on it was becoming increasingly difficult to ignore.

Snatching up the phone as it rang he saw it was Fiona and clicked on.

'Still no news?' she asked.

'Nothing. I'm thinking about taking a taxi into town to find out if she has gone back to the flat.'

'OK, call me when you can, and don't worry about your car, I'll have it delivered back to you in the morning.'

Thanking her, he rang off and decided to give it half an hour more and if he still hadn't heard from Sylvie by then, he'd do as he'd said and get a taxi into Bristol to check up on her.

It was almost three thirty now and Emma was so worried that she barely knew what to do. She kept trying to tell herself she was wildly overreacting, that it could be five, even six a.m. before a guilty, giggly and starving Lauren came tiptoeing through the door – at which point Emma felt sure she'd go ballistic and ground her for a month – but until that happened she could hardly even make herself sit down.

She'd tried Melissa about ten minutes ago, but had received no reply from her mobile either, and Lauren's calls were still going straight through to voicemail.

Fast losing the struggle to keep calm and rational, she decided she had to ring Polly. She hated doing it, but what choice did she have? If Melissa wasn't home yet Polly needed to know – or, if Melissa had been in touch to say where she and Lauren were, then she, Emma, needed to know. Grabbing the landline she pressed in Polly's number.

Polly answered groggily on the fourth ring.

'Pol, it's Emma. I'm really sorry to wake you, but Lauren . . .'

'Emma? What time is it? Are you OK?'

'Yes, I'm fine. Well, actually, I'm not. It's half past three and I was wondering if you'd heard from Melissa. I can't get through to Lauren . . .'

'Hang on, hang on,' Polly interrupted. 'Melissa's here as far as I know. She came home about . . .'

'Is Lauren with her?'

'I'm not sure. I didn't actually see her come in. Shall I go and check?'

'Yes, yes please. I'll hold on.'

As she waited Emma tried hard to reassure herself that Lauren was even now grumbling about being woken up, then feeling terrible for forgetting to call her mother . . .

Hearing the sound of a car pulling up outside, she felt hope and relief jar in her chest. It had to be Lauren. Dropping the receiver she ran to open the door, ready to collapse, shout, laugh with relief.

She stopped dead at the sight of a police car.

The terror was so blinding, so paralysing that she couldn't make herself move. Then she heard someone choking and begging and felt herself backing away as the policeman came towards her.

'No, no, no, no, no, no,' she sobbed. 'Please please, not my baby.'

'Mrs Scott?' he said gently. His ageing face was crumpled with sadness, his small blue eyes full of regret.

Falling back against the wall she sank to the floor, shielding herself with her hands. 'Please tell me it's not Lauren,' she begged. 'I'll do anything, just please don't let it be her.'

Dropping to his knees he took her hands in his as he said, 'Is your husband here?'

'No, he . . . Oh God, she's dead. My baby, my baby . . .'

'Mrs Scott, she isn't dead,' he broke in quickly, 'but the accident was serious. You need to come with me.'

Accident, serious . . .

'I'll take you to her.'

Suddenly she was running, grabbing her coat, searching for her keys. The landline was ringing, but she ignored it.

'Is anyone else in the house?' he asked, when she was ready to leave.

She shook her head. 'No, just me. Please take me to her.'

'Of course. Is everything turned off?'

'Yes, no . . . The fire . . .'

Placing his hands on her shoulders, he said, 'Take a nice deep breath. You're in shock . . .'

'Please take me to her. Oh my God, where are you going?' she cried as he turned into the sitting room.

'The fire,' he reminded her.

The phone was still ringing, but she had to get to Lauren as fast as she could.

'Is this yours?' the officer asked, coming back into the hall.

It was her mobile. 'Thanks,' she whispered, almost snatching it.

'I'm Clive Andrews,' he told her. 'You'll probably forget that, but I won't mind telling you again.'

'Where is she?' she asked, following him out of the door.

'They've taken her to the Bristol Royal Infirmary.' Using her keys, he locked up and handed them back.

'She's going to make it, isn't she?' she urged as he led her to the car.

'Everyone's already doing their very best to make sure of it,' he replied.

Terrified by his failure to reassure her, she got into the car and put her head in her hands. She wanted to be sick, her heart was pounding out of her chest, she was shaking so hard it hurt. An accident, she'd been injured, her beautiful, perfect baby . . . Oh God, don't let her die, please, please . . .

'Breathe,' Andrews said, putting a calming hand on her shoulder.

Doing as she was told, she lifted her head and stared sightlessly ahead as he started the engine. Somehow she had to pull herself together, force herself into a place where she could handle this. She had to be strong for Lauren.

'How – what happened?' she finally managed to ask.

Andrews indicated to pull out of the cul de sac. 'An investigation is already under way to determine that,' he told her, 'but . . .'

'Was she in her car? Where did it happen?'

'On a country road between Wells and Cheddar, about four miles from here, and she wasn't actually in her car when the other vehicle went into her.'

Bemused, Emma turned to look at him. 'What do you mean? I don't understand.'

'We're not sure yet why she was in the road, but it seems she left her car and when the other driver came over the hill . . . He would have had no idea she was there.'

'But she wouldn't have been near Wells. She was going into Bristol tonight. Oh my God, it can't be Lauren. You've got the wrong person.' Hope and relief were flaring so wildly in her chest that she almost started to laugh.

Glancing at her uneasily, he said, 'We found a handbag in the car with her wallet . . .'

'Someone must have stolen it.'

'The car was a Peugeot 206 – it's registered to your daughter.'

'Then someone must have stolen the car too.' Realising that didn't answer where Lauren was now, she dropped her head in her hands. 'The girl you found . . . The one we're going to see . . . Does she have long, honey-coloured hair?'

Glancing at her again, he replied, 'Yes, she does.'

'Oh my God,' Emma choked as horror severed her brief cling to hope. 'I don't understand what she was doing there. Didn't you ask her? She must have told you why she was . . .' Her voice was starting to shred. 'She couldn't, could she? Oh please God don't let this be happening, please tell me it isn't. She means everything to me, everything.'

Reaching over to squeeze her hand, Andrews said, 'We'll soon be there,' and terrifying Emma even further he turned on the flashing blue lights and siren as he put his foot down.

Starting as her mobile rang, she looked at it, stupidly expecting it to be Lauren.

'Polly,' she gasped into the phone.

'What's happening?' Polly cried. 'I rang you back, but you didn't answer. What's all that noise?'

'Lauren's been in an accident . . .'

'Oh my God! What happened? Where are you?'

'In a police car on my way to the BRI.'

'Oh, Emma, Emma, what can I do? I'm right behind you, OK? I'm getting in my car right now. And Emma?'

'Yes?'

'Everything's going to be all right. Do you hear me? *Everything is going to be all right.*'

Chapter Eleven

Accident and Emergency was overflowing with casualties, most of them drunk it seemed, though Emma barely noticed. She simply followed Clive Andrews to the desk and felt herself breaking apart inside as he said to the receptionist, 'This is Lauren Scott's mother. I think you're . . .'

'Mrs Scott,' the receptionist said, her eyes so full of pity that Emma wanted to hit her. 'Please come round.'

Horrified by what seemed to be special treatment, Emma followed Andrews through a door marked Staff Only, and into a corridor behind reception where a nurse was already waiting.

'Hello, I'm Jenny . . .'

'Where is she?' Emma choked out. 'Can I see her?'

Sounding reassuring, the nurse said, 'The doctor's going to speak to you, so if you'd like to come with me . . .'

Emma felt herself shrinking away. 'Please don't let him tell me she's dead. I can't . . .'

'Ssh, ssh,' the nurse soothed.

'Come on,' Andrews said, taking her hand gently, 'it's going to be all right.'

'How do you know?' Emma cried. 'You don't know any more than I do.'

It was true, he didn't, because he'd deliberately stayed out of contact on the way here, not wanting her to learn anything via his radio.

'The doctor won't be long,' the nurse promised. 'We've got a special room for family . . .'

'It's OK, Jenny.'

Emma looked up to find a young man dressed in loose green scrubs coming towards her. He appeared tired and worried, but was attempting to smile. 'I'm Lester Grayling,' he told her, 'and you're Mrs Scott?'

Emma nodded dumbly.

'Would Mr Scott be on his way?'

With her heart in her mouth Emma shook her head. If they needed Will to be here it could only be because . . . No, no, please God no.

'OK,' Grayling said, 'let's go and sit down,' and gently taking her arm he led her towards a side room.

Andrews came too, and went to stand next to a sink and kettle, while the nurse closed the door and the doctor drew Emma on to a chair beside him.

'Please,' Emma begged, starting to cry again. 'I don't . . .'

'It's OK,' the doctor said gently. 'Just tell me what you know so far.'

Emma's frightened eyes darted to Andrews. 'I know she's been in an accident,' she said, 'and that . . . I . . . That's all I know.'

Grayling nodded. 'Well, we've carried out a full assessment of her injuries and she is in a critical condition.'

Emma's heart stopped beating. 'But she isn't dead?' she whispered.

Instead of answering directly he said, 'Our findings showed that she has an extensive bleed in her brain and because the specialist centre for head injuries of this severity is at Frenchay Hospital we have urgently transferred her there.'

Emma felt stunned, confused, afraid. 'So, so she isn't here?' she said.

Grayling shook his head. 'She'll be in expert hands over there,' he assured her, 'and Jenny here has already been in touch with the nurse in charge at the neuro centre who will meet you when you get there.'

Emma didn't know what to say. Everything was crashing, echoing inside her head, her voice was being choked back by fear.

'Is there anything you'd like to ask me?' Grayling said.

She could only look at him, then at Andrews as Andrews said, 'Will she be there yet?'

Grayling checked his watch. 'I imagine so.'

157

'Will they be able to save her?' Emma managed.

'They'll certainly be doing their best.'

She wasn't dead, she wasn't dead. It was a lifeline that seemed to be fraying by the second, but at least it was there and she was going to hold on to it with all her might. 'Are they going to operate?' she asked.

'That'll be for the doctors there to decide.'

She looked up as Andrews came to take her hand. 'Come on, we should get you over there,' he said.

As she stood Emma told the doctor, 'She's going to make it, you know.'

Meeting her eyes, he smiled reassuringly.

She nodded her gratitude and turned to go with Andrews. Of course this doctor didn't know what was going to happen really, nor did she, but now she knew that Lauren was still holding on, albeit by a thread, there was absolutely no way in the world she was going to let her go.

Oliver had never been inside a police station in his life, much less locked up in a cell. He was so afraid and bemused that he could hardly take it in. It had all seemed to happen so fast, one minute he'd been driving home, the next he was on the side of the road with a strange girl dying beside him, and the next the police were bringing him here. They'd made him take another breath test when he'd arrived, which he'd failed again, then they'd wanted some blood and DNA and after that the custody sergeant had charged him with the offence of driving while under the influence, except he hadn't put it quite like that. He'd said something about driving a motor vehicle while in excess of some kind of limit, and that he didn't have to say anything, but if he did it could be used against him.

He couldn't remember it all now – it was making his head hurt and knotting up his insides so tightly that he could barely breathe.

They hadn't mentioned the girl or the fact that he'd driven into her. He didn't understand why, when that surely must have been the more serious offence.

Perhaps it was all a nightmare and he was going to wake up any minute.

Where was she now?

Please God, please, please, please, let her be all right.

He wanted to ask Bob Tillman, but Tillman had disappeared a while ago and even if he banged on his cell door for attention, the sound would probably be lost amongst all the other banging and swearing, threats, jeering and pleading clanging about the cells around him. Some of the people in here sounded like animals. It was horrible, sickening to hear.

Before he'd left, Tillman had told him that his mother was fine. Relief had come at him so fast that for a moment he'd seemed to lose his balance. Had his mother been drunk when the police turned up? What were they thinking now, like mother, like son?

But he wasn't like her. He never *never* got into a car after he'd had a drink. His father had pushed the seriousness of it home to him so hard that Oliver had become a joke amongst his friends, because he'd never let them drink and drive either. His father had even made it a condition of paying his and Charlie's uni fees, and of buying their cars. If either of them ever contravened the agreement they would have to pay back every penny their father had shelled out for their education – no matter how long it took – and whether they were charged or not their cars would be taken away.

Oliver never wanted to see a car again in his life.

All he wanted was to know that the girl was all right, that none of this was as terrible as it felt and that somehow, in some way they would both survive it.

He couldn't even begin to imagine how that was going to be possible.

He wanted to cry like a baby, but his hands were clamped tightly to his head as though to hold it all in. It stank in here, the mattress was stained with other people's filth, the toilet had no seat, the window was too high and too thick to provide any sort of view. They'd taken his shoes and belt, his phone, money, everything he'd had in his pockets. He was a prisoner, a criminal, a pathetic no-hoper whose future was ruined before it had even begun.

Hearing keys going into the door he tensed even tighter. He had no idea what was going to happen now, who might be coming in – maybe it would be a rank, mouthy drunk who wouldn't be able to see straight to piss, or lie down without throwing up.

He was a drunk too. It was why he was here.

'OK, young man,' the custody sergeant barked, 'we've got a bit of a lull so you can make your call.'

A lull? Behind the stable of locked doors, trapped, human animals were yelling, spitting, hissing, vomiting, maybe shitting themselves or even dying.

He followed the sergeant into the corridor. The strip lights were blinding and harsh, making the walls gleam like mirrors and the air feel putrid and hot.

He was put in front of a wall phone and told how to contact the duty lawyer. The number was there, chiselled into a plaque.

'Does it have to be a lawyer I call?' he asked.

'Up to you, but just one call,' the sergeant told him and walked back behind his desk.

Oliver stared at the number, then the keypad. He was thinking of his father and how angry and disgusted he would be, disappointed and ashamed. His mother's shock, panic and drunkenness would make everything even worse than it already was. Charlie would try to help, but what could he do?

He started to dial, and kept on dialling until it was time to wait for a ringtone. When it began it stopped almost immediately. 'Oliver?'

His father's voice, sharp and surprised, was so comforting and yet so terrifying that Oliver almost hung up. He bowed his head as though it would prevent him having to confront his shame. 'Dad, I . . . Something's happened . . .'

'What is it? Where are you?'

Squeezing his eyes tightly closed, Oliver forced himself to go on. 'I've . . . I've been arrested and . . . I'm really, really sorry . . . I didn't mean . . . It wasn't . . . Oh God, Dad . . .' He was suddenly sobbing so hard that no more words would come.

'It's OK, son, it's OK,' his father said firmly. 'Pull yourself together now and start by telling me where you are.'

After taking several breaths Oliver finally managed to

say, 'I'm at a police station. They've arrested me for drinking and driving and I'm . . .'

In a terrible voice his father said, 'Oliver, please tell me you didn't just say that.'

Clutching an arm round his head Oliver said, 'Dad, I'm sorry. It wasn't . . . I swear, I wouldn't have . . .'

'I'm not bailing you out of this, you know that don't you?'

Trying to brace himself, Oliver stammered out, 'Dad, I ran someone over . . . I think I might have . . .'

There was an awful silence before his father said, 'You need to tell me where you are, *right now.*'

Oliver looked around. 'I'm in a police station. I don't know which one . . .'

'Put someone on who does.'

Looking at the custody sergeant, Oliver was about to ask when the sergeant came towards him and took the phone. After giving the address of the station – *Knowle West*, one of the most dangerous areas in Bristol – the sergeant passed the phone back to Oliver and walked away.

'Are you there?' his father barked.

'Yes, I'm here.'

'OK, I'm going to call Jolyon Crane now. You remember Jolyon, don't you?'

Oliver's heart was thudding with dread. 'Yes,' he said. Jolyon Crane wasn't only his father's friend, he was a really big lawyer. If he needed someone that important then this was as bad as he feared.

'If Jolyon can't come himself, he'll send someone who can,' his father was saying. 'You'll need to tell them every-thing that happened, and I mean everything, do you hear me?'

'Yes,' Oliver replied.

'Do you have any idea how badly injured the person is?'

'No, but I think it's serious. It was a girl . . . She . . . she was unconscious . . . Oh Dad, I'm sorry,' he choked, breaking down again. 'I didn't see her . . .'

'All right, son, all right,' his father said briskly. 'I'm on my way.'

*

By the time Emma and Andrews had arrived at Frenchay Hospital Lauren had already been taken into surgery. They'd been given little information then, because there had been almost none to give, apart from the surgeon's decision, following a CT scan, to operate right away. After that they'd been brought here, to this waiting room, with its dull but comfy chairs, twin casement windows with tight, opaque nets and notices advertising the services of nurses, charities and God.

The last time Emma had looked at her watch it had been a quarter to six. It shocked her now to see that it was almost seven. Maybe she'd dozed off, or more likely she'd fallen into a stupor where time had no more meaning than the whispering, waking world going on outside this room.

Why was everything taking so long? Was it good or bad that they were still operating on Lauren more than two hours after they'd begun? Merely to think of her precious girl undergoing something as drastic and *invasive* as brain surgery made her own head reel and cower from the images that kept flashing in front of her. She must stop tormenting herself, shut it all down completely, and go on telling herself that it didn't matter how they saved Lauren, just as long as they did.

Clive Andrews was sitting quietly in one corner, next to a pile of blankets. His arms were folded over his chest, his legs stretched out in front of him and crossed at the ankles. His eyes were staring at nothing, unless she moved, when he instantly became alert again.

He must be exhausted. She wondered when his shift might end and how she would cope when it did. She'd come to see him as her link to Lauren, so if he went there would be nothing left to hold on to – apart from Polly, who was here too, sitting quietly beside her, half dozing, but also seeming tuned in to Emma's every move. She'd caught up with them not long after they'd arrived, and wasn't going to leave, she'd said, until Emma did.

Emma wanted to go now, this minute, and take Lauren with her. She wanted it all to be a nightmare that she could wake up from to find Lauren safe and fast asleep in her bed; or coming sheepishly in through the front door, having forgotten to let her mother know she was staying out all night.

Will was on his way; so was Berry. She'd called them herself, about an hour ago, having delayed in the hope of being able to tell them that though it was serious Lauren was going to pull through. In the end, Clive Andrews and Polly had persuaded her that as her father Will must be told. Emma kept thinking about her mother and wondering whether she should call her, but she hadn't yet, and wasn't sure that she could. If only all she had to tell her about was a compound fracture, some internal bruising and scratches to Lauren's face, but these injuries were so minor in comparison to the trauma Lauren's brain had suffered that they weren't even being attended to yet.

'Would you like some more tea?' Polly asked, as Emma suddenly got to her feet.

'No thanks,' Emma answered. She didn't know where she was going, or what she wanted to do, except she'd found herself unable to stay sitting any longer.

'Would you?' Polly asked Clive Andrews.

He shook his head. 'I'm good, thanks,' he said.

Emma looked at him. Oddly, he reminded her of her brother, though she couldn't think why when they were nothing alike. Perhaps it was his kindness – Harry was always kind. Should she have rung him? He'd be upset that she hadn't, but what could he do? 'Thank you for waiting,' she said to Andrews, trying and failing to smile. 'I expect you should have left a long time ago.'

With a gruffness she was coming to know – maybe that was how he and Harry were alike – he said, 'I've called my missus, she won't be expecting me until there's been some news.'

Feeling his words punch at her heart, Emma looked away. Her hands clenched and unclenched, her temper rose and fell. 'I don't understand what she was doing on that road,' she said for the seventh, eighth, ninth time since Andrews had told her where the accident had happened. It didn't make any sense when Lauren had been going into Bristol for the evening, with Melissa, and as far as Emma knew coming straight home from there. The road where the accident had happened was in completely the opposite direction.

'I'll have another chat with Melissa when I get home,' Polly assured her again.

Polly's first call to Melissa had elicited only a denial of knowing anything at all about where Lauren had been, followed by cries of shock and tears for her friend when Polly had told her how serious Lauren's injuries were. Her second call hadn't got her much further.

'She must be able to throw some light on it,' Emma insisted.

'This is the trouble with kids,' Andrews ventured, 'they don't tell us everything.'

Emma wanted to say that Lauren wasn't like that, but how could she when she was unable to offer any kind of an explanation as to how Lauren had come to be on a country road in the middle of nowhere, and *out of her car* in the dead of night. Why on earth would she have stopped in such a remote spot and got out of her car? Andrews had said no one else was with her, and a first inspection had shown no flat tyres, so maybe the stalling problem had recurred.

'If there was something wrong with the car,' she said shakily, 'I don't understand why she didn't call me. I'd have gone to get her.'

'It could be that she tried and couldn't get a signal,' Andrews suggested.

It made sense, but it was awful to think of Lauren stranded and alone in the depths of a countryside she barely knew, and unable to make contact with anyone.

Far worse was thinking of where she was now.

'The car that hit her,' she said, feeling horribly light-headed. 'Where's the driver? Did you see him or her? Were they injured too?' Why hadn't she thought of this before? It seemed odd that it was only coming to her now.

'It was a young lad in his early twenties,' Andrews told her. 'He was breathalysed and taken to the station.'

Emma's eyes turned glassy as she registered the words. 'He'd been drinking,' she said incredulously. 'He was over the limit?'

Andrews nodded. 'I'm afraid so.'

She was speechless, had no idea how to articulate her fury. 'Then he shouldn't even have been on the road,' she cried savagely.

Andrews didn't deny it.

Unable to bear the hatred rising up in her, she clapped her hands to her head and began sobbing with a terrible despair.

Coming to embrace her, Polly urged, 'Don't think about him now. Lauren's all that matters. We have to use all our energy to will her to pull through.'

'Yes, of course,' Emma whispered, nodding her gratitude. 'That's absolutely what we have to do.'

Russ watched Jolyon Crane come out of the police station into the murky post-dawn drizzle over Knowle West. He was a tall, striking man in his mid-fifties with an air of authority about him that could be either intimidating or reassuring, depending whose side he was on, and most wanted him on theirs.

'Thanks for coming,' Russ said, as they shook hands. 'How is he?'

'Bearing up, but as scared as you'd expect. He'll be out in a minute, he's just collecting his things. Before he comes, though, I think there's something you should know.'

As a grip of dread clenched Russ's insides, he watched a sorry-looking bride limping her way out of the station to a waiting car.

'The reason Oliver was driving last night,' Jolyon began, 'was because his mother rang him and what she said led him to think that she was about to commit suicide.'

Russ's face tightened in shock; a beat later his eyes were burning with fury. 'Are you saying he was on his way to, what? Rescue her?'

Jolyon nodded. 'It looks that way. The point is, this could, to some degree, help in his defence.'

'Well, that's just great,' Russ tried not to shout, 'when if it weren't for her he wouldn't bloody well need a defence. Does she know yet what she's done?'

Jolyon tightened the scarf at his neck. 'I'm not sure. Oliver tells me the police went to check on her after he'd explained why he was driving, but whether they told her what had happened, I've no idea.'

Still fuming, Russ said, 'So my son, thanks to his drunken mother, has put an innocent young girl in hospital and his own future . . .'

'Here he is,' Jolyon broke in quickly. 'Go easy on him now, this has been a huge shock.'

Turning around, Russ peered through the dull, grey light. As Oliver came out from behind a police van, he felt such a fierceness to his love and despair to his anger that all he could do was clasp his son in his arms and hold him tight as Oliver tried stoically not to break down.

'I'm sorry, Dad, I'm sorry, I'm sorry,' he said shakily. 'I know I shouldn't have . . .'

'You're damned right you shouldn't,' Russ growled, 'but Jolyon's explained what made you . . . For Christ's sake, why didn't you just call me?'

'I didn't think. I got the call and I . . . It was like I had to get to her . . .'

'But drinking and driving, son. You could have rung anyone . . .'

'I know. I wish I had. Oh God, Dad, what's going to happen? Is she all right? Have you heard yet if she's still alive?'

Russ turned to Jolyon.

'All I've managed to find out so far,' Jolyon answered, 'is that they've transferred her to the neuro centre at Frenchay.'

'Jesus Christ,' Russ muttered, the cold clammy hand of fear closing around his gut.

Oliver's face was grey. He looked about to pass out. 'I swear I didn't see her,' he said hoarsely. 'One minute the road was empty, the next . . .' His breath caught, and Russ took hold of his shoulders.

'He's still in shock,' Jolyon murmured. 'Come on, let's get him somewhere warm,' and taking Oliver by the arm he started to steer him across the road. 'Where's your car?' he asked Russ.

'I came by taxi,' Russ replied. 'Can you fit us all in yours?'

'Sure. It's right over there,' and using the remote to unlock a large BMW, Jolyon went to open the rear door for Oliver to get in.

'I take it he's on police bail,' Russ said, as Jolyon started the engine.

Jolyon nodded. 'Once they've had the results of the blood test we'll get a date for the magistrates' hearing.'

'What happens in the meantime?'

Jolyon glanced in the mirror as he steered the car away from the kerb. Catching a glimpse of Oliver's frightened eyes, he tempered his response by saying, 'To all intents and purposes life goes on as normal.'

Already aware it could probably never be that again, Russ said, 'Presumably there'll be some kind of investigation . . .'

'It's already under way,' Jolyon confirmed.

Turning to look at his son, Russ decided not to press any more questions on him for now. The boy was drooping with exhaustion and clearly terrified enough without having to deal with the full horror of what he could be facing in the weeks, months to come.

Twenty minutes later they were at Jolyon's office in the centre of town, and since Oliver had gone to one of the bathrooms to freshen up Russ braced himself for the bottom line. 'What's the worst we could be looking at?' he asked, taking the piping hot coffee Jolyon was passing him.

Going to pour another for himself, Jolyon said, 'I think we need to take this one step at a time. So far he's been charged with driving under the influence . . .'

'That's a given, but whatever happens to the girl, it's going to impact in a big way.'

Unable to deny it, Jolyon went to sit at his desk.

'I know you're hedging,' Russ said, 'but I need you to give this to me straight.'

Jolyon's shrewd eyes came to his. 'If she doesn't pull through,' he replied, 'they'll charge him with causing death by dangerous driving.'

Though not surprised, Russ felt the horror of it starting to crush him. 'And the maximum penalty for that?'

As Jolyon was about to answer Oliver appeared in the doorway, so he merely took a sip of his coffee.

'I heard the question,' Oliver said raggedly.

Jolyon's eyes went to Russ, seeking guidance, while Russ regarded his son, trying to weigh up just how much more he could take. In the end he said, 'He needs to hear it too.'

'It would be a custodial sentence of up to five, maybe more years,' Jolyon said, looking at Oliver, 'but I . . .'

'Oh God,' Oliver gasped, dropping his head in his hands.

Going to him, Russ held him up as Jolyon went on, 'There's a long way to go before we have to start facing anything like that, and we're going to do everything we can to make sure we don't. So now, why don't you go home and at least try to get some sleep. It's been a rough night all round. As soon as there's any news the police will know, and if it changes anything we can be sure they'll be in touch.'

Chapter Twelve

Emma was pacing, wringing her hands and wanting to scream in frustration. 'Can we go and ask someone what's happening?' she pleaded. 'They must have some news by now?'

'I'll go,' Andrews said, getting to his feet.

As the door closed behind him, Emma sank back into her chair and bent over her knees. 'She's going to be all right,' she said determinedly. 'I can feel it. She'll get through this, I know she will.' Her eyes went desperately to Polly. 'She's young and strong and has so much to live for. It just wouldn't be right for her to go now.'

Sitting down beside her, Polly said, 'Of course it wouldn't, and she won't.'

They both looked up as the door opened, and Emma's heart contracted to see that Andrews wasn't alone. Then, recognising the man behind him, tall, fair-haired and haggard with shock, she felt so overwhelmed by the reason he'd driven full speed from London to be here that she could say nothing to greet him.

'Hello, Will,' Polly said softly.

His eyes seemed angry and dazed. 'Why are they still operating?' he demanded, as though Emma should know. 'They told me she's still under.'

'They're doing everything they can,' Emma replied, keeping her voice as steady as she could.

'But why is it taking so long?'

'I don't know. It just is.'

'Neurosurgery is extremely complex,' Andrews said quietly.

Will turned to glare at him. 'We need some answers,' he barked.

'We'll get them,' Emma broke in angrily. Then, forcing herself to be calm, 'Will, please don't make this any worse . . .'

'*Me*, don't make it any worse,' he cried heatedly. 'It was *you* she was staying with. *You* who should have been taking care of her. What the hell was she doing out at that time of night?'

'She's eighteen . . .'

'Will, this is pointless,' Polly interrupted, 'and you're really not . . .'

'This has nothing to do with you,' he snapped. 'I want to know why she was out at that hour, and . . .'

'What difference does it make now, *why* she was out,' Emma shouted. 'She's fighting for her life, and us fighting in here isn't helping one bit.'

Seeming to realise the sense of that, he put his face in his hands and tried to calm down. 'I'm sorry,' he said in the end. 'I just . . . Christ, I can't even think straight.'

'None of us can,' Emma told him, 'but we have to try to for Lauren's sake, if not for our own.'

Nodding acceptance of that, he dragged a hand through his hair and turned to Andrews. 'Sorry,' he said roughly.

Andrews merely nodded.

'Can I get you some tea?' Polly offered.

He looked as though he had no idea what tea was. Then, shaking his head, he insisted, 'I want to know how it happened. Where she was, who hit her, what's being done about it . . .'

Andrews said, 'Instead of putting Lauren's mother through it all again, why don't you come with me and I'll tell you what I know.'

Will's eyes went to Emma, accusingly, desperately, then saying no more he turned to follow Andrews out of the room.

Only minutes after they'd gone Emma heard voices outside, and a terrible pounding started in her chest as she waited for a doctor to come into the room, but it was a nurse who opened the door to show Berry in.

'Oh my dear,' Berry murmured, wrapping Emma in a crushing embrace. She was neither tall, nor fat, simply ample and in her own ageing way quite enchanting. This morning, however, with not a scrap of make-up to cover the lines on her face, nor the hint of a hairbrush having gone through her bright silvery mop, she looked tired and lacklustre. 'The nurse told me they're still operating,' she said. 'That's good, it means she's fighting.'

Emma nodded as she fought back more tears. 'Thanks for coming,' she said, resting her head on her grandmother's shoulder.

'Oh Emma, of course I would come. Our girl means more to me than my own life, you know that.' She glanced at Polly and managed a smile. 'I'm so glad you're here. At least Emma hasn't been alone.'

'Will's arrived,' Emma told her.

'Yes, I saw him with the policeman. They said I could go and join them . . . Oh my goodness,' she slurred, putting a hand to her head.

'Oh Berry, sit down,' Emma cried, taking her to a chair. 'The shock, the drive . . . Will should have brought you.'

'He offered,' Berry said breathlessly, 'but I thought I might need my car. I'm sorry, I'll be fine in a minute, just a little dizzy spell.'

'I'll get you some water,' Polly said.

Taking Emma's hands, Berry said, 'I stopped on the way to call your mother. I realised you might not have and she'd want to know.'

Emma's face was more strained than ever.

'She's on her way,' Berry told her gently.

Emma seemed surprised.

'You didn't imagine she wouldn't come?' Berry sounded genuinely amazed.

Before Emma could respond the door opened and a tall, lean man with sunken cheeks and birdlike eyes came into the room. His scrubs left no doubt about who he was. 'Mrs Scott?' he said, looking at Emma.

Emma was no longer breathing.

'I'm Nigel Farraday,' he told her, shaking her hand, 'the

surgeon in charge of your daughter's case. I'm sorry I haven't been in to speak to you before, but I'm afraid there hasn't been an opportunity until now. The nurse has gone to fetch your husband – Lauren's father. Shall we sit down?'

Moving as though not in touch with her limbs, or even her mind, Lauren perched on the edge of a chair and didn't take her eyes off the surgeon, even when Will came in with Clive Andrews.

After introducing himself again, Farraday gestured for Will to join Emma, then sitting down too, he waited for a nurse to usher the others from the room before he said,

'I'm sure the first thing you'll want to know is that your daughter has survived the operation . . .'

Relief came so fast at Emma that she started to sob and couldn't make herself stop. Will was rocking back and forth, seeming to want to shake the surgeon's hand, put an arm round Emma, get up, do something, anything to demonstrate his own relief.

'Thank you,' he said jaggedly. 'Thank you.'

'Thank you, thank you,' Emma echoed.

Farraday's expression remained grave. 'That's the good news,' he said. 'The rest is, well, I'm afraid the procedure she's just been through has been extremely tough on her. It was necessary in order to remove a large clot which was applying pressure to the brain stem. There's still a lot of bruising and swelling, and she remains in a very critical condition.'

Emma was barely taking it all in, she couldn't yet, because she didn't know how to deal with it. 'Where is she?' she faltered. 'Can we see her?'

'They'll be bringing her up soon,' he answered, 'and once the lines have been set you'll . . .'

'Lines?' Will interrupted.

'The nurses will explain what they're for, but basically it's the intubation she's going to need to make up her life-support system.'

Emma's eyes widened. *Life support?* 'She's going to make it though, isn't she?' she insisted.

Farraday's eyes softened as they met hers. 'We certainly

hope so,' he told her, 'but I'm afraid these next few days will be critical.'

Russ was too tired and far too stressed to be able to deal with Sylvie rationally for the moment – if there was indeed anything rational about what had happened, and frankly if there was, he couldn't see it.

After leaving Jolyon he'd brought Oliver home, prepared them both some food which neither of them had had the stomach to eat, and had then sent Oliver off to take a bath and try to get some sleep. Meanwhile, he, Russ, decided to ignore all the messages on his machine and call Fiona to thank her for having his car delivered back.

'I wish there was something I could do,' she said, after he'd brought her up to speed with what had happened so far.

'Thanks,' he responded, 'but seems like we're pretty much in the lap of the gods now, and a damned good surgeon.'

'At least you have Jolyon on the case. You can't get any better.'

'True, but he's not a magician. Oliver was over the limit, the girl is critically injured, might even die, so what defence does he have? Worst-case scenario, Oliver's on his way to prison.'

'You really think it'll come to that?'

'Right now I'm failing to see how it can be avoided, and though he won't admit it, I don't think Jolyon can either.'

With a tightness in her voice, she said, 'I'm sorry, but it's your wife who should be taking the rap for this, not your son.'

'Tell me about it,' he replied, 'but sadly we can't change the way it is. I suppose I ought to check up on her as I still haven't heard from her since she drove off last night.'

'The police went round there though, so you know she didn't carry out the threat she made to Oliver.'

'Not then, but who knows what she might have done since.'

With a groan of sympathy she said, 'This is so hard on you . . .'

'If you're going to feel sorry for anyone, make it Oliver, or better still the girl and her family.'

'Don't worry, they're all in my thoughts. Do you know her name yet?'

'You obviously didn't hear the eleven o'clock news. Lauren Scott. Apparently she's out of surgery, but still fighting for her life.'

After ringing off, he stood staring down at the answering machine knowing already who all the messages were from, because they'd come through to his mobile too while he and Oliver were on their way home. The only surprise was that it had taken this long for the press to start clamouring for statements. Any time now a gaggle of them would be gathering outside his gates, possibly even attempting to climb walls to try and get a shot of him, or Oliver. This was the real downside of a fame that had expired a dozen years ago, but was now being resurrected for the purposes of sensationalism, another dimension to the story.

Since Charlie clearly hadn't heard the news, or he'd have been in touch by now, he pressed his elder son's number into his mobile and went to pour himself a coffee while waiting for the connection. Finding himself diverted to voicemail, he swore under his breath, and left a message for Charlie to call the instant he could.

He wondered if anyone from the press had contacted Sylvie yet. If they had she'd surely have rung him, probably in a panic, so it seemed likely that she wasn't answering the phone to them either. It would only be a matter of time though, and if she didn't already know about the accident he probably shouldn't let her learn about it from a reporter. Not that he felt he owed her any favours, but if she was drunk when she found out there was no telling how she might react.

Coming reluctantly to the conclusion that he had to break things to her in person, he was about to go and check on Oliver before driving back into town when his mobile rang, and seeing it was Charlie he immediately clicked on.

'Dad, Oliver just told me,' Charlie cried in a rush. 'This is terrible. We have to do something. I'm coming home . . .'

'Charlie! Stop!' Russell barked. 'There's nothing you can

do, at least not for the moment, so please stay where you are. You can't miss these exams . . .'

'But Dad . . .'

'No buts, son. You heard what I said, now please, I've got enough to be dealing with without worrying about you too.'

'OK, I get that, but what about Mum? Does she know? Have you spoken to her?'

'I'm about to go over there. Has she rung you today?'

'She left a message earlier saying . . . I don't know, she was rambling on about finding you with her friend Fiona . . .'

'What time did she call?'

'Uh – I guess it must have been after eight o'clock, because Freddy, one of my flatmates, left a message then asking if I was in because he'd lost his keys. And her message was later than that. I haven't rung her back, I'm afraid. Do you think I should?'

'No. I'll deal with it from here. Just be there for Oliver if he wants to talk again, but most importantly, stay focused on getting through those exams. Everything else you can leave to me.'

It hardly looked like Lauren. For a moment, when she'd first seen her, Emma had dared to hope they had the wrong person. It was her hands that had crushed the doubt: the polish on her nails was the colour Lauren had painted on last night. Her head was swathed in so many bandages it was almost twice its size, the tender skin around her eyes was bruised black and swollen, her cheeks and lips were badly cut and grazed. Sutures stood out against her deathly pale skin like tiny wings. So many tubes were running into her nose, mouth, neck and arms that it was impossible to remember what they were all for. The doctor had told them, when they'd finally been allowed to see her. Nigel Farraday himself had explained in as simple language as he could what was happening to her.

Though he hadn't actually put it this way, it was clear she was being kept alive by these tubes and the battery of machines that were making her breathe, or monitoring her heart, or keeping a check on her intracranial pressure. Drugs and fluids were flowing into her, a sats probe, which Emma thought had something to do with measuring oxygen, was attached to her finger, and a number of catheters were providing drains and infusions and possibly something else Emma might have forgotten for now.

Her leg was in a temporary splint. Nothing more would be done about it until Nigel Farraday gave the go-ahead to the orthopaedic surgeon. The brain always comes first, Emma had been told, but when the time was right Lauren would have to undergo more surgery to repair her leg.

Emma knew she could ask Mr Farraday to go through things with her again, if necessary, and maybe in the coming hours or days she would need him to, but right now all she wanted was to sit with her angel and will her with all her heart not to let go.

'Keep talking to her,' Nigel Farraday had said. 'I can't promise that she's able to hear you, but if she can I'm sure it'll be a great comfort to her.'

So between them Emma and Will were keeping up a flow of soothing words, never taking their eyes from Lauren's face in case there was the tiniest flicker of an eyelid or a murmur of response. Many hours had passed now and the only sounds they'd heard were the heavy sucking and puffing of the ventilator and bleeping of the monitors; the only movements came from the wave forms on the screens and the attendant nurse who was never more than a few feet away.

The lights were low; the other bed in this small section of the ward was empty. Somewhere at a distance, perhaps in another world, the wail of sirens came and went. It was warm, so warm that Emma could feel sweat trickling between her breasts and down her back. She found herself wondering what had happened to Lauren's clothes, that beautiful gold dress that had been so exquisitely shocking. Had they been forced to cut it from her? Had they shaved off her hair to get to her skull? They must have.

'. . . And when we get you out of here,' Will was saying, 'we're going to throw you a great big party and invite all your friends. They're all ringing up to find out how you are. Donna, Selina, Melissa, Lucy . . . and they send their love. They'll be coming to see you when you're strong enough to have visitors. For now it'll be just me and Mum . . .'

'And Granny,' Emma came in. 'She was here earlier, I expect you heard her, didn't you. She's in the waiting room now with Polly and Berry. Uncle Harry and Aunt Jane have popped out to find a coffee shop to pick up some drinks for us all. They're very worried about you too and came as soon as they heard. Dad and I are going to spend the night here, so we'll be close at hand if you want to speak to us. They won't let us stay by the bed all that time, in case we wear you out.'

'I know you're listening,' Will resumed, his voice starting to falter, 'and I expect you want to tell us to shut up, but until you actually say it, I'm afraid it's not going to happen. We're just going to keep on going . . .'

Emma wished he'd go away. She wanted Lauren all to herself, to do what only a mother could, reconnect to her child in a way that didn't need tubes or syringes or anything tangible. As Lauren's mother she could reach her through the unbreakable bond they shared, the bond that would never allow them to be anything but a part of one another. Through it she could transfer all her energy and willpower, her love, her courage and every ounce of determination she possessed for Lauren to use as her own. These things would need no words or even touch to be transmitted, but would simply flow straight from her into Lauren, as vitally and as restoratively as any medicine, or air, or surgeon's skill.

'Mr and Mrs Scott?' someone said softly behind them.

It was Anna, the large, sweet-faced Polish nurse who'd been assigned to Lauren.

'I think you both need to take little break now,' she said kindly. 'I will stay with her. Doctor will be coming back shortly.'

Though Emma found it almost impossible to tear herself away, she was willing to do whatever she was told if she thought it would help Lauren, so pressing a kiss to her fingers and touching them gently to Lauren's bloodied cheek, she started to step away. It was a moment before she realised what was happening, but as Anna's strong arms caught her, she swiftly came to again.

'You are exhausted,' Anna told her. 'And I expect you have not eaten for all of the day.'

'I'm fine,' Emma whispered. 'Sorry, I . . . I . . .'

'Come on,' Will said, putting an arm around her. 'Lean on me.'

Emma moved away. She didn't want to get close to him, or depend on him in any way, because she knew from experience how unreliable he was. All that had ever been constant about him was his love for Lauren, and belief that he was destined to become the father of a truly great musician, but even that hadn't been enough to persuade him to keep their family together – or to make him offer his beloved daughter a weekday home in London.

He was here now though, which was what really mattered, certainly as far as Lauren was concerned, and Emma guessed it mattered to her too, because she simply wouldn't have been able to bear it if he'd allowed anything to prevent him from coming.

Outside the waiting-room door Will took Emma's arm and held her back. 'We need to talk,' he said in a growl. 'I need some answers.'

Deciding not to get into whatever he was talking about, she pulled her arm away and continued on through the door.

'Something's not right about this,' he hissed from behind her.

Emma stiffened. *Had he actually just said that? Had those words really passed his lips? What the hell was supposed to be right about it?*

Realising all she could do was ignore him, she walked on into the room and allowed Berry's ready embrace to enfold her in wave after wave of trust, loyalty and years of just being there when she was needed. Over Berry's shoulder she saw her mother watching, embarrassed, anxious, seeming lost, even afraid.

Not knowing what to say to anyone, Emma turned to her brother whose strong arms were already opening to hold her, but as she moved towards him an alarm suddenly sounded outside.

With terror slicing her very soul, Emma barged past Will to the doors of the ICU. Through the windows she could see nurses and intensivists running in Lauren's direction. 'What is it?' she cried. 'What's happening? *What's happening?*'

'Clear the way,' someone shouted, as the doors flew open.

Seconds later Lauren was rushed past.

'Oh my God, no! *Nooooo!*' Emma screamed, going after them.

'Please wait there,' someone said sharply.

Anna the nurse put an arm around her.

'What is it? Where are they taking her?' Emma demanded, wild-eyed with fear.

'For another CT scan,' Anna answered. 'She has experienced a surge in intracranial pressure.'

'What does that mean?'

Anna's pale blue eyes were full of compassion as she said, 'I'm afraid we'll have to wait and see.'

Chapter Thirteen

Russ had no idea how Jolyon had got hold of the information about the girl last night; all he knew was that at the time Jolyon had called he'd wished he hadn't. Being told that she'd been rushed back into surgery had been almost as bad as hearing that it had happened to one of his own – in some ways he couldn't help wondering if that might have been easier. Less guilt, blame, shame – a full due of sympathy for Oliver that he would never get now, even though in some small way he deserved it. At least to Russ's mind he did, from the rest of the world – and the judicial system – he was hardly likely to get it.

According to the news this morning the girl, Lauren, had come through the night, but the twenty-four-hour watch continued, and if she'd made any contact with anyone at all since the surgery it hadn't yet been reported. But the fact that the drunk driver who'd struck down this beautiful, gifted girl with a dazzling future ahead of her belonged to the family behind the golden angels was now widely known. One local headline had already labelled Oliver the 'demon son of an angel', and Russ could only imagine that worse was to come.

When he'd turned up at Sylvie's apartment last evening he'd been in such a rage that perhaps it was no bad thing that she'd refused to let him in. He needed to break this to her in a way that was going to leave her in no doubt of the part she had played in this tragedy, and he couldn't do that if they were shouting and she was drunk.

Before leaving he'd rung Connie Wilkes, one of Sylvie's old secretaries who lived close by, to ask her to come and stay the night at the flat to make sure Sylvie didn't overdo

180

the booze, or turn on the news before he returned today. The latter wouldn't be a difficult task, since Sylvie had little interest in the world beyond herself these days. The former, however, was likely to have proved much more of a challenge.

One look at his wife as the redoubtable Connie let him into the apartment was enough to suggest that Connie might have had some success. Dishevelled and red-eyed though Sylvie was, and not yet dressed, he'd seen her looking a great deal worse at ten in the morning – and in spite of the way she bristled when she saw him, she didn't seem entirely surprised that he was there.

'I told you,' she said to Connie, 'that if it was my husband you must not let him in. He has no right to be here when all he does is shout at me, and I do not want to see him now he is sleeping with another woman.'

As she reached for a tissue to blot more tears from her eyes, Russ turned to Connie.

'Thanks very much for staying,' he said warmly. 'I'm sorry to have called on you at such short notice . . .'

'It wasn't a problem,' Connie assured him, picking up her purse. After giving Sylvie a hug and promising to drop in again later, she followed Russ to the door, where he unhooked her coat.

Keeping her voice low as she slipped her arms into the sleeves, she said, 'How's Oliver?'

Tensing at the question, but reminding himself that she wasn't only genuinely kind, but discreet, he said, 'Frankly, not great.'

Looking deeply sorry, she squeezed his hand as she said, 'You know where I am. If there's anything I can do you only have to pick up the phone.'

'Thank you,' he said, touched by the offer. 'I'll call you later and settle up for last night.'

Her eyes widened in protest. 'I don't need paying,' she told him. 'You've always been good to me, you and Sylvie, so I'm more than happy to be there for you in any way I can.'

Remembering how she'd lost a grandchild to meningitis, and her daughter a year later to suicide, seemed to make his own problems fade a little. At least Oliver was healthy and safe and had, eventually, some chance of rebuilding his life. That could never happen for Connie's daughter and grandson – and it might not for Lauren Scott, either.

After seeing Connie out he turned back to the kitchen where Sylvie was still seated at the breakfast bar, a wad of ragged Kleenex clutched in one hand, the neck of her dressing gown bunched in the other.

'I have nothing to say to you,' she informed him tearfully.

'Good, because for the moment I'm the one who needs to do the talking.'

Appearing unnerved by his tone she started to get up, but catching her arm he sat her back down again.

'You are being very rough with me,' she protested, 'and it is I who should be upset, not you. You have not the right . . .'

'Just listen,' he said quietly. 'You need to hear what I'm about to tell you.'

'I do not want to. You are having an affair with my friend . . .'

Slamming a hand on the table he watched her jump, then keeping his voice low, he said, 'Something very serious has happened and I'm afraid you do need to hear it.'

As she paled he realised his mistake.

'The boys are fine,' he told her quickly. 'At least Charlie is, but on Saturday night when you rang Oliver threatening to commit suicide . . .'

'That was not what I said, and anyway, I told the police when they came here . . .'

'I'm not interested in what you told them, Sylvie, because by then the real damage had already been done.'

Her expression darkened with confusion and suspicion.

'Oliver thought you were going to kill yourself,' he continued, 'so being a son who loves his mother he jumped in his car to get to you. On the way he had an accident and as a result a young girl is now in intensive care fighting for her life.'

Sylvie's eyes began to dilate with horror.

'Oliver was arrested for drink-driving, and now we are waiting to see what happens to the girl to find out the full extent of what he's to be charged with. Either way, he is likely to go to prison for this.'

Sylvie was becoming agitated, not knowing which way to turn, or how to escape this. She was trying not to look at the wine rack, but the need was too great. 'I – I don't believe you,' she rasped.

Turning her back to face him, he said, 'Do you really think I'd make up something like this?'

'I don't know . . . I can't . . .' She tried to get up, but knowing where she wanted to go he held her firm.

'This,' he told her, 'is what your drinking has done. It's *you*, Sylvie, and that demon inside you, who are responsible for ruining the lives of two young people, and one of them is your own son.'

Tears filled her eyes as she shook her head back and forth. 'But it is not my fault . . .'

'It is absolutely your fault. If you hadn't made that call . . .'

'I wouldn't have if you had not been with Fiona . . .'

'Don't worry, I accept my role in this, but if you think that in any way exonerates you then think again. What you did, that selfish, drunken, *cruel* act of calling your own son to frighten him by suggesting you were about to end your life is now going to cost him his freedom. Think about that, Sylvie . . .'

'I cannot listen to this,' she sobbed. 'It was not my fault. If you had not thrown me out . . .'

'You can cast as much blame on me as you like, but you're not getting out of your own responsibility.'

'Stop it, just stop,' she cried, blocking her ears. 'You do not understand how hard this is for me . . .'

Thumping the table again, he said, 'This is no longer about *you*. It's about our son and a young girl who might yet die from her injuries. Try to think of what her family must be going through now, and if you can't do that surely to God you can think about Oliver.'

'I always think about Oliver, which is more than I can say for you, because for you it is always Charlie . . .'

'For Christ's sake, you haven't even asked how Oliver is yet.'

'Because you have not given me the chance . . .'

'You've had every chance, but it hasn't even occurred to you how much he might be suffering after the trauma he went through. How stricken he is with fear and guilt and shame for what's happened to the girl. You're only thinking about yourself, and that's not who you used to be. Our boys always came first for you . . .'

'They still do . . .'

'No, *that's* what comes first now,' he shouted, pointing to the wine rack. 'Nothing matters more to you than that . . .'

'It is you who made me this way. If you had been a good husband my life would not be ruined . . .'

'Get dressed,' he snapped, stepping back. 'You're coming with me.'

'I am not going anywhere with you. You are frightening me . . .'

'I swear I'll do a lot more than that if you don't put yourself in the shower right now and make yourself presentable.'

'No! You are trying to take me to a clinic, but I will not go and you cannot make me.'

'Believe me, if I could you'd already be there and this wouldn't have happened. No, you're coming with me to see Oliver. You're going to confront what you've done to your own son, and if that doesn't change your mind about getting some help then I swear to God you will no longer be a part of our lives.'

Emma was sitting with Lauren, hardly noticing what was going on around them – nurses and intensivists coming and going, consultants visiting other patients, a new casualty being admitted. She wasn't even connecting with the sounds of the ventilator or monitors. She was only seeing her daughter behind the web of life-giving tubes, her face as white as the bandages wrapped like a turban around her head, her eyes unmoving beneath their bruised lids, her lips as colourless as the hose parting them.

After the horror and panic of the surge of pressure in

her brain yesterday, Emma had lived in mortal terror of leaving her again. It was only when she'd all but collapsed over the bed in exhaustion last night that her mother had come to help Will walk her to the waiting room, refusing to listen to her pleas to let her stay. With her energy so low she'd been unable to fight them, but when she'd woken a few hours later it was with a renewed terror that Lauren had slipped away in the night because she, Emma, hadn't been there to hold on to her.

Thank God it hadn't happened, but Emma knew Lauren was a long way from being out of danger yet, because Yuri Nelson, the consultant in charge of her case, had spoken to her and Will about the dangers of further surgery should a similar surge in intracranial pressure occur.

'How likely is it to happen again?' Will had asked dully.

Speaking frankly, but gently, Nelson said, 'At this stage it's very hard to tell, but we're all staying hopeful that it won't.'

'Is her brain – is it damaged?' Emma faltered. 'I mean, will it be lasting?'

'It's still very early days,' Nelson replied, 'and once again we're all staying hopeful of a good recovery.'

Emma knew there would be one. She wasn't even going to countenance the possibility of there not being one. Lauren was simply going to lie quietly for a while, regrouping her energy, recovering from the shock and the surgery, while her heart continued to pulse blood through her veins and send oxygen into her brain the way it always had. At the same time, she, Emma, would be transmitting all her maternal strength and love into the very fibre of Lauren's soul, resulting in a pure, ceaseless flow of vital energy. Nothing was going to stop this; no one would even be allowed to try.

'Emma, why don't you get cup of tea?' Anna said softly as she came to check Lauren's levels.

Emma barely looked up as she shook her head. In her mind she was talking to Lauren, and didn't want to be interrupted.

Will had left the bedside a few minutes ago, maybe to go to the bathroom, or perhaps to use the phone. His other family would be wondering about him, and about Lauren too, of course, because the children knew her and loved her. Emma didn't know how Jemima felt about Lauren, nor did she wish to.

Polly had taken Berry and Phyllis to Emma's house last night so they could get some sleep, while Harry had booked into a B & B nearby and Jane had driven home to see to the children. Polly had returned just after eight this morning with coffee and pastries. Though Emma and Will had managed the coffee neither of them had found the stomach for food, and Emma had detected no return of her appetite yet.

'You must have something, sweetie,' Berry had insisted when she and Phyllis had arrived around ten. 'It's the only way you can keep up your strength.'

Her mother had looked on, seeming smaller, somehow less than her usual self, yet her hand as she'd put it on Emma's arm had felt firm. 'We'll get through this,' she'd said in a tone that seemed to brook no denial. However, when Emma had met her eyes she'd looked away, whether because she didn't believe her own words, or because she found it too hard to connect with Emma the way Emma could with Lauren, only she knew.

They'd left again now – her mother was driving Berry back to London to pick up the insulin Berry, in her panic, had forgotten to bring with her yesterday.

'We'll be back by late afternoon,' her mother had assured her.

Emma couldn't remember now if she'd responded. It hadn't occurred to her until long after they'd gone that the hospital would probably have provided Berry with some insulin. It didn't matter though, they'd be back soon enough, and meanwhile Emma could sit here with Lauren wondering if her mother would sit with her if she was fighting for her life. She felt a pang of loneliness and resentment as she found it hard to imagine.

'What were you doing on that road?' she whispered to Lauren. 'I don't understand why you were there, all alone.'

'Clive Andrews is here,' Will said, breaking into her quiet

communication with Lauren. 'He's come to update us on the investigation.'

It took a moment for Emma to register the words, then sitting back she pushed her hands through her hair, feeling every muscle in her body protest at their first movement in more than an hour. Did it matter now, she wondered, how the accident had happened, why Lauren had been on that road when she had? It wouldn't change anything. Lauren would still be lying here, lost in a world between this one and the next. Knowing why wasn't going to bring her back. And yet she needed to know what had taken Lauren out on to that country road when she'd told Emma she was going into town.

Sending a silent message to her letting her know she wouldn't be far away, she rose awkwardly to her feet and followed Will back to the waiting room. This morning, during the early hours, another family whose son had suffered a brain haemorrhage had joined them, but there was no sign of them now. She thought maybe the boy had already been moved to another ward, but she couldn't be sure. She hoped he hadn't died. Please God let him still be alive.

'Hello Clive,' she said, attempting a smile as she shook Andrews's hand. They'd agreed on first-name terms before he'd left last night, and she felt vaguely surprised now by how easily it had come.

'You look exhausted,' he told her. 'You really have to get some sleep.'

'I've had a few hours,' she assured him. 'I hope you did too. Yesterday was a very long day for you.'

The raise of his eyebrows told her that his own hardship was the least of his concerns. 'How's Lauren today?' he asked.

'I told you,' Will said, 'there's been no change.'

Annoyed that Will hadn't realised Andrews was showing her his consideration by asking again, Emma said, 'She's still sedated and they don't have any plans to try waking her up today.' How was she able to speak those words so calmly when they were breaking her apart inside?

'I see,' Andrews murmured. 'Well, I have no doubt that on some level she knows you're here.'

'I like to think so. Shall we sit down? Have you seen my brother? I thought he was in here.'

'He went outside to make some phone calls,' Will informed her.

Relieved that Harry hadn't gone far, Emma settled down on one of the softly cushioned chairs and felt her head swim as a wave of tiredness came over her.

'Are you all right?' Will asked.

'Yes, yes, I'm fine,' and patting the nearby chair for him to sit down too, she fixed Clive Andrews with her sore, red-rimmed eyes.

Taking an adjacent seat, Andrews said, 'Most of the work at the scene has been completed now, and both cars have been removed to a garage in South Bristol for analysis.' He stopped, his eyes on Emma.

She was staring through the nets at the window, speckled with rain on the outside, but what she was seeing was a remote country road where traffic was once again flowing as though nothing had happened there to change anyone's life. One minute total devastation, the next nothing at all to show that lives had been ruined.

'Emma?'

She turned to Andrews. 'Sorry,' she said, realising he was waiting for her attention. 'Why was she there?'

He shook his head regretfully.

'Did you find her flute?' she asked, and felt vaguely surprised because this was the first time she'd thought of it.

He nodded.

'The cars are being analysed,' Will said, bringing them back on track. 'What do you expect to find? I thought we knew how it happened. A drunk driver came speeding out of nowhere and slammed right into her.'

Flinching, Emma turned her head away. She couldn't allow herself to imagine the violence of that impact, or feel it, and yet she never stopped seeing and feeling it.

Still watching her, Andrews said, 'What we didn't know straight away was why your daughter was parked at the side of the road and out of her car.'

Emma's eyes came back to his.

'When one of the investigation team tried to start the engine it didn't respond,' he informed her, 'so the early indications are that she had broken down.'

'Well, I think we'd managed to work that much out,' Will said tightly. 'Why the hell else would she be in the middle of nowhere and not in the car?'

'Will, for heaven's sake,' Emma growled.

'It's all right,' Andrews told her. 'I know that seemed the obvious answer, but it had to be looked into. So, in the event that this case comes to trial . . .'

Will's eyes bulged with shock. 'Well of course it's going to bloody trial,' he cried. 'How can it not?'

'If the driver pleads guilty . . .'

'It makes no difference what he pleads. He's going to prison and the Lomax family are going to pay with every red cent they possess.'

'The who?' Emma asked, confused.

'You haven't seen the news,' Will told her. 'The kid who did this is Russell Lomax's son. You'll remember him from . . .'

'Yes, I know who he is,' she interrupted, trying to think why she'd heard Russell Lomax's name recently. It didn't come to her, and it didn't feel as though it mattered anyway.

'If anyone thinks they're going to get that kid out of what's coming to him by insinuating my girl was at fault for being in the road . . .'

'I think we're getting ahead of ourselves,' Andrews interrupted. 'I can't imagine anyone would try to blame Lauren for what happened.'

'How could they when that kid was *drunk*, which means he had no goddamned business being on the road anyway. He was already committing an offence, while my girl was probably scared out of her wits . . .'

'Why didn't she call?' Emma mumbled, her heart breaking at the thought of Lauren stranded on an unlit road in the dead of night with a car she couldn't make start. *And what had she been doing there?*

'The mobile-phone reception is very poor in that area,' Andrews informed her, 'and we know now from her phone that in fact she did try to call.'

'Oh God,' Emma choked, burying her face in her hands. How much worse was this going to get? Did she need to know any more of the details?

Sounding close to tears himself, Will said accusingly, 'I thought you got the car fixed. I sent you a cheque for a hundred quid. Please don't tell me you used it for yourself and didn't . . .'

The sudden bang of Emma's fist in his face shocked even her.

'What the fuck?' he spluttered, holding his nose.

'Don't ever dare to insinuate that I would put myself before my daughter,' she seethed. 'That car was repaired, it was working fine . . .'

'Well, obviously it wasn't . . .'

'And that's my fault? You bought it, so now I have to ask where it came from. What sort of dodgy deal did you do . . .'

'OK, OK.' Andrews was stepping forward to prevent any more punches being thrown. 'We're not achieving anything this way, so let's try to calm it down.'

Embarrassed by the outburst, Emma turned away. If only she could make Will go, he wasn't helping anything, or anyone, and yet, furious as she was with him, she understood that his anger was coming from fear and impotence and a desperate longing to make some sense of it all.

'You see, what gets me,' Will ranted on, 'is *why* Lauren was out that late in the first place. I would never allow it, but *you*,' he said to Emma, 'are so fixated on yourself and all your *problems*'

'Will, just shut up,' she cut in tightly.

'Well why was she there? Did you know where she was going when she went out? Who did she go with?'

'I only know what she told me,' Emma retorted, hating him for making her admit that Lauren might not have been truthful with her. 'You seem to be forgetting how old she is. She doesn't have to tell me everything . . .'

'Yes she does . . .'

'What's going on in here?' Harry demanded, as he came in the door. 'I can hear your voices down the corridor.'

'Will is trying to make me responsible for what's happened,' Emma explained, feeling suddenly stronger at the sight of her brother's familiar face. 'The fact that Lauren and I wouldn't even be living in this area, if he hadn't stolen all our money and walked out on us, seems to have escaped him.'

'The fuck did I steal your money. I was the one who worked his ass off, day in day out . . .'

'OK, Will, let's cool it,' Harry cut in, putting a hand out to stop Will coming any closer. 'We seem to be losing the plot here, because this isn't about why you two broke up, or why you, Ems, live here, it's about my niece, your daughter and what Clive here has come to tell us. I saw him downstairs, so I know about the car. Have we moved on from there?'

Feeling her heart thudding with stress and fatigue, Emma leaned against him as she said, 'Not really.' Then, looking shamefacedly at Andrews, 'I'm sorry. I don't know what you must think of us . . .'

Holding up a hand to stop her, Andrews said, 'You're under a lot of strain here, both of you, and letting off some steam isn't a bad thing, but all that really matters is Lauren. I know you haven't lost sight of that . . .'

Will scowled. 'Don't even think it. I want the name of the garage you took the car to,' he told Emma. 'I'm going to be suing them too.'

'Will, please just stop,' Emma groaned.

'What? We just sit there and let them get away with this?'

'No one's saying that,' Harry reminded him, 'and maybe in the end that is the way we want to go, but for now, at least, we should be focusing on Lauren.'

Will's eyes remained fierce. 'Are you trying to say I'm not?' he challenged, looking as though he might take a swing.

'Of course not,' Harry said gently. 'I know how much she means to you. She does to all of us . . . Oh Christ, Will,' he choked as Will suddenly started to break down.

'Take my heart, take my brain, take anything,' Will sobbed, as Harry caught hold of him, 'just let her live. Please,' he said to Andrews, as though Andrews could make it happen. 'I don't want to lose her. She's my baby. She means everything to me.'

'They're doing everything they can,' Emma reminded him, feeling herself detaching from his anguish as though it might in some way encroach on hers. She needed to keep herself separate, totally focused on Lauren in order to help her. Whatever anyone else felt had nothing to do with them.

'I know that, *I know*,' he cried, 'but are we in the right hospital? Do we know we're getting the best attention?'

Going very still Emma looked at him, and then at Andrews. 'Are we?' she asked.

Without any hesitation Andrews replied, 'This is one of the best neuro centres in the country. Check it out on the Internet if you like, but I'm telling you, I have a daughter the same age as Lauren and if she was where Lauren is now, this is exactly where I'd want her to be. What's more, in Farraday's world, he's about the best you can get.'

Emma's eyes returned to Will.

'I'm not saying I don't believe you,' Will said, 'but he can't object to a second opinion.'

'I'm sure he won't,' Andrews told him.

There was a long, awful silence during which none of them seemed to know what to say next. Doubting Lauren's treatment had thrown them into a new void of despair. In the end Will said to Emma, 'We've got to find out why she was out there, on her own, in a place she didn't know, at that time of night.'

To Andrews Emma said, 'The only person who might be able to tell us is her friend Melissa, but her mother's tried and Melissa keeps saying she doesn't know.'

Andrews was in no position to comment on that, but he looked as sceptical as the rest of them. Melissa was one of Lauren's best friends, and best friends always knew.

Chapter Fourteen

Melissa was lying on her bed surrounded by the cuddly toys she'd collected and treasured over the years. Until this weekend she'd thought she'd started to outgrow them, had even stored most of them in the back of a cupboard, but now she was clutching them to her, trying to draw comfort from their softness as she sobbed and pleaded with God to make Lauren all right. She hadn't been able to go to school this morning and she knew Donna hadn't gone either. They'd been texting each other, or speaking on the phone, ever since they'd found out about the accident, sharing their horror and grief, and trying to work out the best thing to do.

We can't tell, Donna kept saying in her texts, *we just can't. If we do it'll be like we don't think she's coming back and she is, because she has to.*

Reading those words caused yet more grief and panic to rise up from Melissa's heart, making her choke and gasp in utter despair. She kept feeling as though it was all her fault, even though she knew it wasn't. Except she'd given Lauren an alibi for Saturday, and if she hadn't Lauren wouldn't be where she was now. She wanted to go and see her, to tell her everything was going to be all right, but she was terrified of confronting how badly she was hurt. She would go though, later, or tomorrow, or as soon as she was allowed to. For now it was only family, and every time Melissa thought of Emma she felt like screaming out, because she just couldn't stand how awful this must be for her.

The local news was on now, but she had the sound turned down on her small TV because she didn't want to listen to them saying again that Lauren was still in an induced coma. She knew that if anything changed her mother would be bound to hear and come to tell her straight away. She was living in dread of hearing her mother's footsteps on the stairs, but she was longing for them too in case the news was good.

The nursery had moved back over to the church hall this morning, and Jilly and another helper were taking care of the children while Polly drove back and forth between the hospital and Emma's house. She'd come home about half an hour ago and had been on the phone ever since. Melissa wanted to go to her, to see if there was anything she could do, but she knew what her mother would say, so she stayed where she was, unable to face any more questions about what she did or didn't know.

Clicking on her mobile as it started to ring she said, 'Hi, are you OK?'

Donna's voice was tearful. 'I don't know, not really. I just can't stop thinking about her.'

'I know, it's the same for me. It was on the news again just now, but I didn't listen. Anyway, I think it was really only about the boy who was driving, because they showed his dad getting into a car with a woman who I suppose was his mum. I don't know.'

'Have you seen Lauren's mum yet?'

'No, she's still at the hospital. My mum's been taking things in for her. Lauren's dad's still there, and her uncle Harry. I wish they'd let me see her, she might speak to me.'

'That's what I was thinking,' Donna confided. 'Do you think they'll let you see her without anyone else there?'

Not sure whether she wanted that to happen or not, Melissa said, 'I wish you were here. It's horrible having to deal with this on my own.' It was Donna's and Lauren's secret, not hers, she shouldn't have to be going through this at all.

'I know, but I'm definitely coming at the weekend. My parents are going to drive me down.'

Hearing a knock on her bedroom door, Melissa said, 'I have to go,' and stuffing the phone back under a teddy bear she watched her mother coming into the room.

Polly's face was drawn and pallid, her eyes heavy and raw. 'How are you feeling now?' she asked, coming to sit on the edge of the bed.

'I don't know really,' Melissa answered shakily. 'I just wish it hadn't happened.'

'I know,' Polly soothed, stroking damp tendrils of hair away from Melissa's face. 'Emma just rang, apparently they're going to leave her sedated for now.'

Melissa looked confused. 'What does that mean?'

'I'm not really sure, except Emma's going to come home later to shower and try to get some sleep.'

'So Lauren's going to be left on her own?'

'No, Will's gone to his hotel now to try and rest. He'll go back to the hospital this evening and stay through the night.'

Melissa turned her head to one side. Everything was so awful she hardly knew what to say.

Taking Melissa's hand, Polly watched her for a while, feeling the sheer horror of how it would be if she was on the verge of losing her precious daughter, the way Emma was with Lauren. The very thought of it was breaking her, twisting her, doing things that were so painful that she tried to shut her mind down.

When Melissa's eyes finally came back to her, Polly said, 'Why won't you tell me where Lauren was before the accident?'

Melissa immediately turned away. 'I told you, I can't,' she replied.

'But darling, this is nonsense. Lauren's fighting for her life . . .'

'And knowing where she was on Saturday isn't going to make a difference, I promise you.'

'It might to Emma. If she could understand why Lauren wasn't with you when . . .'

'Oh Mum, please don't keep asking, it's just making everything ten times worse.'

'But how? I don't understand why you think you have to keep this secret . . .'

'Because it's what she'd want, I know it, and Donna agrees, so please don't keep trying to make me.'

195

Stifling a sigh, Polly said, 'Look, it seems fairly obvious to me that it has something to do with a boy . . .'

'Why do you say that? You don't know.'

'OK, so tell me I'm wrong.'

'You're trying to trap me now and it's not fair. I haven't done anything wrong . . .'

'No one's saying you have, but all this secrecy, Melissa. And what's the story with the flute? She told her mother she was going to play it for you, but she didn't even bring it into the house.'

'I don't know why she said that, or why she had it,' Melissa cried truthfully. 'All I know is that I made her a promise, and I have to keep it. If I don't it would be like saying I don't think she'll get better, so is that what you want?'

'No, of course not, but you surely understand why her parents want to know what took her out to that road in the middle of the night. If she hadn't been there this wouldn't have happened . . .'

'I know, but it did and none of us can change that, so please stop keeping on at me. I'm really upset about everything and I just want to be left on my own now.'

'I spoke to Donna's mother twenty minutes ago . . .'

'Why?'

'Why do you think? Oh, Melissa, are you sure you fully understand what's going on? Your best friend could die . . .'

'Don't say that!' Melissa sobbed, clasping her hands to her ears. 'She's not going to die. I won't let her, do you hear me? She's going to be all right.'

Getting to her feet, Polly said, 'These questions won't go away, Melissa, I hope you realise that. You're going to have to answer them sooner or later, so I want you to start thinking about how much extra heartbreak you're causing by holding back, when as far as I can see there's absolutely no reason to.'

As her mother reached the door Melissa said, 'Have you considered that I might be trying to spare Emma any more heartbreak? What she doesn't know, she doesn't have to worry about.'

Polly's eyes held firmly to hers. 'Why don't you let me be the judge of that?' she responded.

For a moment Melissa was tempted, but in the end she only shook her head. 'You'll tell Emma,' she said, 'and I'm really sorry, but Lauren really, really wouldn't want her mum to know.'

Russ was standing with his back against Oliver's bedroom door, his arms folded, his head throbbing with anxiety as he watched Oliver move away from his desk and slump down in the window seat to stare blindly out at the fields behind the house. It was a dull, dank day, with no wind to stir the trees or sunlight to enliven the landscape. It was as though the whole world had paused and was holding its breath, not sure if it could dare to breathe again.

Though the computer on Oliver's desk was switched on, whatever he had been looking at before Russ came in had been closed down hurriedly the instant Russ had opened the door. Now, the only image on the screen was a design of jagged pieces floating and swirling across the surface, bumping into the sides and corners, sinking in on themselves, then beginning again.

'I understand you're angry,' Russ said in the end, 'and I don't blame you, but your mother wants to see you, so . . .'

'I don't care.' Oliver didn't turn round; he kept his eyes on the fields, his shoulders squared against his father as though he could somehow block out the reasons either of them were there. 'I've got nothing to say to her,' he went on roughly. 'Or I have, but she wouldn't want to hear it.'

Suspecting she probably wouldn't, Russ said, 'Maybe she needs to.'

Though Oliver's head moved to one side, he said nothing.

'I didn't think she'd come here,' Russ admitted. 'Right up to the last minute, I felt sure she was going to back out . . .'

'She should have, because I don't want to see her. If it weren't for her it wouldn't have happened.'

'That may be true, but I'm sure you don't believe she did it deliberately.'

'It hardly matters whether she did or didn't, the fact is

I might have killed someone and if it turns out I have, it'll be her fault, every bit as much as mine, but I'm the one who'll have to pay.'

'She will too, in her own way.'

'Like hell she will. All she'll do is get drunk and pretend it never happened. For Christ's sake, she's ruined my fucking life.'

Unable to dispute the likelihood of that, Russ continued standing where he was. He was searching for a way to reach his son, to find some words that would offer hope, or comfort, or some sort of rationale he could hold on to, but there wasn't much rhyme or reason to what was happening to Oliver now.

Feeling the door moving behind him he was tempted to carry on blocking it, but in the end he stood aside, allowing it to open.

Sylvie's eyes were anxious and beseeching as she looked up at him.

'I'm sorry,' he said. 'He doesn't want to see you.'

Flinching, she said, so Oliver could hear, 'Please, Oliver, don't be angry with me. I want to try and make this up to you . . .'

'Make her go away,' Oliver growled. 'I told you, I've got nothing to say to her.'

Realising he'd made a mistake in forcing Sylvie to come here, that he should at least have discussed it with Oliver first, Russ eased her back on to the landing.

'What shall I do?' she asked tearfully. 'You said that I should speak to him . . .'

'I was wrong. I thought it might help, but I can see now that it won't, not while he's feeling like this.'

'So how can I make him feel better?'

Sighing as he dashed a hand through his hair, he said, 'You can't, no one can, apart from the girl – and even if she makes it God only knows what kind of state she might be in.'

Covering her face with her hands, she muttered, 'Maybe it would have been better if I had killed myself . . .'

Marching her away from the door he said, furiously, 'You don't have the luxury of being able to talk like that any more. Your son is suffering in there, and all you can think about is yourself and how hard this is for you?'

'But I am thinking of him . . .'

'Then prove it. Check yourself into any clinic and start drying out.'

Shrinking from him, she said, 'You make it sound so easy, but it is very hard to do what you are saying.'

'And how hard do you think all this is for Oliver?'

'I know it is difficult, but I know you, you will make it all right for him. You have friends in the police, right at the top. If you ask them, they will make it go away . . .'

'Are you out of your mind?' he cried savagely. 'There's no making something like this go away, not for anyone. A girl is dying – for all we know, she's already dead. Either way, your son is going to pay with his licence, his conscience, even his freedom. How does that make you feel, Sylvie? Are you proud of what you've done? Has it sunk in yet what all this really means, or are you, even now, so desperate for a drink that you can't take it in?'

'It is you who gives me the need for a drink. I am afraid of you when you are like this.'

His eyes flashed. 'Your excuses sicken me,' he told her harshly.

'What are you doing?' she demanded as he started back along the landing.

Turning round, he said, 'I'm going to check on Oliver, then you and I are going to get on the phone and find a clinic that's able to take you today.'

'No, no, we must talk about this some more. I need to . . .'

'There's nothing left to discuss,' and pushing open the door to Oliver's room he closed it on her cries of protest.

'Why don't you knock?' Oliver snapped, quickly closing down his computer again.

'I'm sorry, I should have,' Russ apologised. 'I just wanted to make sure you're all right.'

'Of course I am, why wouldn't I be?'

Watching him walking back to the window, a man and yet still a boy, Russ said, 'I got it wrong about bringing your mother here, I can see that now. I thought . . . I guess

I was hoping to use you to make her see sense, and you've already got enough to be dealing with.'

Oliver shrugged and kept his back turned.

After a lengthy silence, during which he was overcome as much by helplessness as frustration, Russ said, 'Now may not be the best time, but at some point we'll have to work out how we go forward from here.'

'We can't go forward, until we know what's going to happen to . . . to . . .' As his voice started to falter Russ went to put a hand on his shoulder.

Oliver's attempt to shrug him off was only half-hearted. 'I keep seeing her face,' he whispered hoarsely. 'I mean when she hit the car, but that doesn't make sense, because I know I didn't see her then. It all happened too fast.'

Understanding that the clarity of her image had probably come from the news, Russ said, 'I know it's going to be impossible to put any of it out of your mind, but you have to try . . .'

'OK, you tell me how!'

'Well, to begin with, shutting yourself away up here isn't going to help . . .'

'So what do you want me to do, pretend it hasn't happened? I'm sorry, I can't do that.'

'Of course not, but right now there's nothing you can do to change things, and the job's still open with Paul Granger so maybe you should take it.'

'And be grateful?'

Ignoring the bitterness, Russ said, 'And throw yourself into it to help pass the time until we have a better idea of what's going to happen.'

'You mean with her . . .'

'I mean with you. Whichever way things go with Lauren Scott now, you will still be facing charges, so maybe the way you conduct yourself during this time could count in your favour if you're seen to be doing the right thing.'

'And that would be working for you?'

'Oliver, don't make this even harder than it already is. I'm trying to help you, for God's sake.'

Dropping his head in his hands, Oliver pushed his fingers into his hair and wrenched it by the roots. 'I should have rung you from the party,' he seethed angrily. 'I know that now. All my mates, everyone keeps emailing and asking why the hell I took off the way I did. Some of the things they're saying . . . They're really going for me. Not that I blame them, I know it was my fault, but I didn't set out for it to happen.'

'Of course you didn't, and they know that.'

'Some of them might, but I've started getting hate mail even from people I don't know. They're saying I've always been arrogant and too full of myself . . . Someone even tried to say I used to go out with Lauren Scott and this is what I've done to get my own back because she chucked me. Can you believe that? I'd never even heard of her before Saturday, and how the hell was I supposed to know she was going to be on that road, when I've never spoken to her before in my life?'

'People can get very mixed up and misinformed at times like this. Quite often there's no point trying to reason with them. Many of them really don't know what they're talking about. They just jump on a bandwagon and think they have the authority to say whatever they like, whenever they like, as if they're the only ones who have right on their side.'

Oliver's head went down. 'It's the worst thing about Facebook,' he said. 'Everyone's putting stuff on my wall . . . You should see some of it.'

Guessing he'd probably rather not, Russ said, 'It might be a good idea to stay away from it for a while. Just keep a low profile, stay out of town and get some work experience under your belt with Paul.'

Oliver nodded, then looked up at the sound of something crashing outside.

Russ's eyes closed as he murmured, 'Please don't let that be what I think it is.'

As he turned to the window overlooking the forecourt, Oliver came up behind him and cried disgustedly, 'God, just look at her. She's taking your car.'

Able to see that, as well as the dent in Angie's newly sprayed Renault, Russ took off out of the room and down the stairs, but by the time he reached the forecourt Sylvie was already speeding through the gates at the end of the drive. He supposed he should feel thankful that she'd bothered to open them.

'What are you going to do?' Oliver asked, as he joined him.

Having no clear idea of what could be done, since this was obviously another attempt to escape a clinic, Russ simply shook his head and put an arm round Oliver's shoulders.

Chapter Fifteen

Clive Andrews was sitting outside the neurology unit in a marked police car when Jackie Dennis, the inspector in charge of the Scott/Lomax investigation, called his mobile.

'Clive,' she said, when he answered. 'I hope this is a good time.'

'Depends,' he responded drily. 'What can I do for you, Inspector?'

'It's about Lauren Scott. Are you with the family at the moment?'

'Not exactly. I'm waiting to drive Emma Scott home for the night.'

'I see. How's the girl?'

'Hanging on in there, but exactly what she's hanging on to is hard to say.'

Sounding suitably sombre, Dennis said, 'This can't be easy for the family. Everything I've heard or read about the girl these past couple of days tells me what a bright young lady she was.'

'Is,' Andrews said stiffly.

'Sorry, of course.'

OK, there was a chance Lauren Scott might not be that person any more, but as they didn't know anything for certain yet, Andrews was going to believe there was hope.

'So, before I get into updating you from my end,' Dennis continued, 'has anyone from the family come up with any sort of explanation yet about where Lauren might have been before the accident?'

'No. I don't think any of them know.'

'Mm, that's what I thought, and there's nothing on her Facebook page about what she was doing on Saturday night, apart from going out with her friend Melissa, which we know didn't happen. There are dozens of messages turning up from other friends, wishing her well. They're very moving. She was – *is* – a popular girl.'

Appreciating the correction, Andrews said, 'What about the mobile phone? Any leads there?'

'I'm coming to it. First though, has there been any sign of a boyfriend either calling Mrs Scott to find out how his girlfriend is, or turning up at the hospital?'

'Not that I'm aware of. No one's even mentioned that she has one.'

'And her relationship status on Facebook is single, if that means anything. Being as pretty as she is . . .'

'Excuse me interrupting, but I'm wondering why it's relevant? We know who committed the crime on Saturday night, so why the investigation into Lauren's movements?'

'Procedure, and the fact that we don't want the defence digging up something that might help get their lad off that we don't already know about. *Plus* all the secrecy surrounding where she was before Lomax hit her is cause for suspicion of a second, possibly unrelated crime.'

Andrews had to concede that was true. 'So where are you going with it?'

'Several places, one of which is an address just outside Glastonbury which we found in a text to her mobile, received Saturday afternoon, along with directions of how to get there.'

Andrews wasn't sure why he felt surprised; after all, he was hardly familiar with Lauren's friends or activities. 'So what is this place?' he prompted. 'Have any of the locals been to check it out?'

'They have, and apparently it's an old millworker's cottage belonging to a Mr and Mrs Ian and Rachel Osmond of Kew, London. They use it as a weekend retreat, so they weren't in residence when our chaps turned up earlier. But we managed to get hold of Mrs Osmond at her shop in Chiswick, and she informed us that she and her husband were in Suffolk at the weekend, visiting her parents.'

'So could she throw any light on why Lauren might be visiting her cottage?'

'No. In fact, she claims never to have heard of Lauren. We're still waiting to speak to Mr Osmond.'

'You've obviously tried the number the text came from?'

'Of course, but we just keep getting bumped through to a recorded message. It doesn't correspond with either of the mobile numbers Mrs Osmond gave us for herself and her husband, but that doesn't tell us much, because if it's his he wouldn't be the first cheating bastard to own a phone his wife knows nothing about.'

Remembering that Jackie Dennis was one such wife, now ex, Andrews said, 'So without even seeing or speaking to this guy, you're thinking he and Lauren might be involved?'

'Aren't you?'

He had to admit, he was. 'Does the in-laws' alibi check out?' he asked.

'It's in progress, and we're waiting to hear back from O2 with details of who the unidentified number is registered to. Meanwhile, I'd like you to ask the Scotts if either of them knows the Osmonds, or if the mystery number is familiar to them. I'll text it to you when we've finished this call. We also need a DNA sample from them both to try and establish if anyone else could have been in the car on Saturday besides Lauren.'

'Is there a suggestion someone might have been?'

'Not yet, we're still waiting on forensics, but they can't tell us much until they're able to eliminate the obvious candidates such as parents and friends, which reminds me, someone still needs to talk to Melissa Hunter.'

Spotting Emma looking for his car, Andrews started to get out as he said, 'I need to ring off now. I'll get back to you once I've spoken to the Scotts.'

Twenty minutes later, having expected to be at least halfway home by now, Emma was back in the ITU waiting room, feeling utterly drained, and not a little unnerved by what Clive Andrews had just told her and Will.

'So neither of you know the Osmonds?' Andrews asked, fixing them both with his shrewd, but kindly eyes.

Emma shook her head.

'Never heard of them,' Will said croakily.

'Apparently Rachel Osmond works in Chiswick,' Andrews offered. 'Isn't that where you used to live?'

'Yes, but . . .' Emma couldn't think what she wanted to say. She longed for this all just to go away, no more questions, no more shocks, no more hospitals or life support, just her and Lauren safe and together the way they'd always been. This place was alien, wrong, they shouldn't be here at all.

'Chiswick's a big place,' Will said.

'Of course, but I'm wondering if they might be the parents of one of Lauren's friends.'

'I don't know anyone by that name,' Emma told him. 'Have you asked any of her friends, or someone at the school?'

'It's in hand,' Andrews assured her.

'Do you know what this woman does in Chiswick?' Will demanded.

'I know she has a shop. I can find out what kind it is.'

'What about her husband, what does he do?'

'I don't think that's been established yet, but I'm sure we'll know more by tomorrow.' Taking out his mobile, he showed them the text from Jackie Dennis containing the unidentified number. 'Does it mean anything to either of you?' he asked.

Will looked at it and shrugged. 'I've no idea. Why? Whose is it?'

'That's what we're trying to find out. It's where the message came from giving directions of how to get to the place near Glastonbury which the Osmonds apparently own. Do you happen to know anyone who lives down that way?'

Again Emma shook her head. Right now she could barely even remember where Glastonbury was, or if she'd ever visited, though of course Lauren had been to a couple of the festivals.

Will said, 'So you think she went there before the accident to . . . to what? Meet someone?'

'It seems the most logical reason,' Andrews replied. 'Or perhaps she was giving someone a lift there.'

206

'Like who?'

'I've no idea, I'm simply putting forward possibilities.'

'I don't understand why it matters,' Emma said, feeling as though the words were coming from a far distant place. She was too tired to do this, yet how could she not? 'Whatever her reason was for going there, she wasn't doing anything wrong, so why are you trying to make it sound as though she was?'

Andrews was registering her pain and understanding her confusion. 'I'm afraid it's because we don't know what she was doing that we have to ask all these questions,' he explained gently. 'But at least we know she hadn't been drinking.'

Will's eyes widened. 'How do you know that?' he demanded.

Colouring slightly, Andrews said, 'It's normal procedure to carry out a blood test on someone in Lauren's position.'

'And if she had been drinking, what then? Would it make the kid who hit her less culpable?'

'No, but as it's not an issue perhaps we should return to the point of this discussion, which is to try to establish the reason Lauren went down into Somerset that night . . .'

'Why?' Will broke in belligerently. 'Surely you can't think she was up to no good. If you knew her you'd know it's insane even to consider it.'

Only too aware that parents almost never knew as much as they thought they did about their teenage offspring, Andrews said, 'It's very difficult to know what to think at the moment, but clearly there are some issues, queries, that need to be addressed.'

Will's whole body seemed to stiffen. 'Are you trying to say she was having some sort of affair with this Osmond bloke?' he growled. 'Is that what you're getting at here, because if you are . . .'

Unable to bear it, Emma said, 'Will, just stop . . .'

'The hell I will,' he cried, 'because I for one won't have my daughter slandered that way, and even if she was having an affair, it's *not a crime*. She's eighteen, for God's sake, she can come and go as she pleases, so why are you

. . . Actually I know what you're leading up to here. You're trying to make out she's to blame for what's happened to her.'

'Absolutely no one thinks she's to blame for that,' Andrews assured him. 'We know exactly how the accident happened, and no one, not even the Lomax family, is trying to contest it.'

'But they will . . .'

'I doubt it . . .'

'. . . it only happened two days ago, and they've already got one of the city's top lawyers working for them, so how the hell do you know where this will go?'

'Will, can we please just hear what Clive is trying to tell us,' Emma said sharply.

Flipping a hand to show his impatience, Will sat back with a tight expression and angry eyes as Andrews prepared to continue.

'I'm sorry to say,' he began, 'that the mystery behind Lauren's movements during the hours leading up to the accident is giving rise to suspicion. And the investigators would be failing in their duty if they didn't try to find out what was going on, just in case it turns out to be something the defence can use to achieve a lesser sentence. Or in case Lauren was involved in some kind of illegal activity.'

Feeling her head starting to spin as Will leapt to his feet, Emma tried to stay detached from his anger, but it wasn't possible when in her own exhausted way she was as appalled and offended by the suggestion as he was.

'I get what's going on here,' Will raged. 'It's taken me a while to catch up, but the Lomax boy's family are putting on pressure, aren't they? They'll have contacts in the police force at the highest level . . .'

'I can assure you nothing of the sort is going on,' Andrews interrupted.

'But you're all corrupt, the whole bloody lot of you. I bet I won't have to go very deep to find out that your top chap is a Freemason buddy of Russell Lomax . . .'

'Will, this isn't helping.'

'So what are we supposed to do, just sit here and let

them get that boy off the hook by staining our daughter's name?'

'Mr Scott, that really is not happening,' Andrews told him firmly. 'No one is trying to deny that Oliver Lomax was driving the car that hit Lauren . . .'

'Good, then let's focus on him a bit more, shall we?' Will snapped. 'Let's leave my girl, who's probably brain-damaged thanks to him . . .'

'Don't say that,' Emma cried, burying her face in her hands.

'. . . to carry on fighting for her life while we find out where *he* was before the accident, what *he* was up to. Did you test him for drugs? I bet you didn't . . .'

'I wasn't there when he was taken to the station,' Andrews broke in, 'but I'm sure the drugs test was carried out.'

'But the charge was for drink-driving?'

'Yes.'

'What difference does it make whether it was drink or drugs?' Emma exclaimed. 'He was still driving the car, and Lauren's still where she is, so for God's sake, can we stop wasting time and energy on petty detail and concentrate on getting her through this?'

Seeming to lose it altogether, Will shouted, 'And how highly do you rate her chances of survival, may I ask? Exactly what are you telling yourself in that pathetic little world of denial you live in? Without those machines she'd be dead, you do realise that, don't you? She can't breathe on her own, or eat, or even think . . .'

'Stop, stop, stop,' Emma sobbed, covering her ears. 'You're her father, for God's sake. What's the matter with you? Do you want her to die? Is that what you're saying?'

'Of course I don't want her to fucking die, but I don't want her to be brain-damaged either . . .'

'Mr and Mrs Scott,' an intensivist barked, coming in the door. 'Whatever's going on in here, you have to keep your voices down. Otherwise, please take it outside.'

Shamed by the reprimand, Emma said, 'I'm very sorry. We didn't mean . . . Is Lauren all right?'

'She's the same, but I'm afraid we really can't have you causing this sort of disturbance.'

'Of course not,' Will said gruffly. 'I'm sorry, it was my fault. I just can't seem . . . I . . .' His eyes went to Emma. 'I'm sorry,' he whispered, and dropping his head in his hands he slumped down in a chair while Andrews offered a further apology to the intensivist, with an assurance there would be no further disruption.

'Are you sure you want to stay here tonight?' Emma asked Will when the intensivist had gone. 'What I'm saying is, I don't mind . . .'

'Of course I'll stay,' he interrupted. 'You need to go home and get some proper rest. I'll call if anything happens.'

Emma glanced at Andrews, then back to Will. She was afraid of what she wanted to say, but knew she couldn't leave until she had. 'Please don't tell her that it's OK to let go,' she whispered brokenly. 'She's fighting, Will, I know she is, and she needs to know we're both with her, so please don't let her think that you're giving up.'

Will lifted his head. His face was ashen, his eyes wet with tears. 'I have to do what I think is right,' he told her, 'not for me, for her . . .'

'Will, please . . . I can't let you stay here if you're going to . . .'

'I'm not going to do anything,' he broke in roughly, 'except sit with her and read her a few stories. Tomorrow though, or as soon as we can, we have to talk to the doctor and find out exactly what he thinks her chances are.'

'You know what keeps bothering me,' Emma said, staring absently out at the passing landscape as Andrews drove her home, 'is why she took her flute. She told me she was going to play for Melissa, but I went into Melissa's house with her and she left it in the car.' She took a breath. 'I suppose she could have gone back for it after Polly and I left, but . . . I don't know, it's just something that keeps bothering me.'

Unable even to attempt an explanation, Andrews replied, 'Someone's going to be talking to Melissa in the next day or two, so perhaps she'll be able to throw some light on it.'

Knowing from a conversation she'd had with Polly earlier how unlikely that was, Emma sighed and closed her eyes. 'I might need to talk to her friends myself,' she said wearily. How was it possible to feel so tired, and yet so wired at the same time? 'At the moment they don't seem to be opening up,' she went on, 'but Polly's convinced Melissa knows something. I think she's more or less admitted it, she just doesn't want to break Lauren's confidence.' She ached and shuddered inwardly. 'I dread to think what it might be.'

Slowing as they reached the end of the M32 to merge round Cabot Circus, Andrews said, 'Inspector Dennis was asking me earlier about a boyfriend. Do you know if she has one?'

Emma shook her head. 'Not currently – at least I don't think so, but I'm beginning to wonder now how much I really know.' Her eyes remained closed as she tried to connect lies, deceit, secrecy with the daughter she knew and loved.

'For what it's worth I'm told her relationship status on Facebook is single,' Andrews said, 'and I'm guessing there aren't any texts of a romantic nature on her mobile or Jackie Dennis would have mentioned it.'

'Actually,' Emma said, experiencing a disturbing mix of alarm and doubt, 'an ex-boyfriend has been in touch a few times lately, wanting to see her. His name's Parker Jenkins. I can't imagine why she'd have driven to Glastonbury to see him, and pretended to me she was going out with Melissa, unless maybe he found some way of tricking her into going.' Her head was thumping with the stress of so many scenarios, all of which seemed to peter into nonsense.

Easing off the accelerator as he headed into the underpass, Andrews said, 'It's sounding like a long shot, but it's probably worth checking to find out if he sent the text, or has any connection to the Osmonds. Do you have a number for him, or an address?'

'No, but I'm sure Donna does, and it'll be in Lauren's phone, of course, unless she's erased it. Maybe it'll match the one Inspector Dennis sent you.'

'We'll find out.' And clicking on his earpiece as his mobile rang he listened for a few moments, then said, 'OK, I'll pass it on. Thanks.' To Emma he said, 'That was Jackie Dennis. Apparently someone with the Met has spoken to Ian Osmond and he's saying the same as his wife, that he's never even heard of Lauren.'

Feeling her head throbbing even harder, Emma pressed her fingers to her temples as she tried to think. 'So why did she have their address?'

'I've no idea, but Jackie Dennis is arranging to go up to London to speak to the Osmonds herself. At the moment we only have their word that they don't know Lauren, but there's obviously some connection and we need to find out what it is.'

'Do you know what I'm thinking?' Emma said, feeling dizzier than ever. 'That maybe they run some kind of cult, and somehow or other Lauren's got mixed up with it. Except how could I not know, I'd surely have picked up on something?'

'You'd have thought so, but in my own experience with teenagers – I have two of my own and of course dealings with a lot more from all walks – I've often found that the answers, or signs, are there to be seen, but we're looking the wrong way.'

Emma turned to him. 'I don't know if I can handle oblique right now,' she said.

Grimacing, he replied, 'And I'm already regretting saying it, because the last thing you need is more confusion being heaped on top of what already exists. Your theory about a cult could hold up. We'll know more after Jackie's made her inquiries.' Then, changing the subject, 'Would you like to stop somewhere like a supermarket before I drop you off?'

Shaking her head she turned to gaze sightlessly ahead, trying to process this new information with its new angles and puzzles, and hardly registering the way other drivers were slowing as they clocked the police car coming up behind them. Nothing about her surroundings seemed quite real; it was as though everything had slipped out of focus and was moving in a strangely separate world.

Familiar streets and buildings went by like apparitions from a distant past, hazed as though caught in a dream. She closed her eyes and opened them again and felt a swirling light-headedness coming over her.

'Not long now,' Andrews told her, as she buried her face in her hands, 'another ten, fifteen minutes and we'll be there.'

'I'm dreading going home without her,' she confessed shakily.

'Of course,' he said gently, 'but someone's there to meet you, so you won't be alone.'

She nodded. 'Both grandmothers and my brother,' she said, as though he didn't already know that. 'Polly might be there too.'

Realising how crowded the small house would probably feel, and yet empty without Lauren, she started to wonder if it was where she really wanted to go, but where else was there, apart from back to Lauren? She felt a bite of panic at the thought of what Will might be saying to her. She couldn't bear the idea that he was even considering letting her go. If God had meant her to die, He'd have taken her at the scene of the accident, so He obviously wasn't ready for her yet. And if He'd let her live just so they could say goodbye, why allow her to survive both operations? She wasn't meant to leave them now. She was going to get through this, no matter how long it took. Emma knew that in her heart as surely as she knew that Lauren was hers. So why didn't Will?

Should she tell Andrews to turn round? She oughtn't to have left Lauren alone with her father, not while he was thinking this way. 'I need to call Will,' she said, taking out her mobile.

Before she could find his number the phone rang, and seeing Will's name come up her heart turned inside out with fear. 'What is it?' she gasped, already shaking as she clicked on. 'Has something happened? Is she all right?'

'Everything's the same,' he told her, 'I just wanted to say sorry about the stupid things I said before you left. You're right, she's definitely going to make it, we've just got to let her do it in her own time.'

As tears scalded her eyes Emma said, 'I don't think it'll be long now, I really don't.'

'I hope not,' he whispered. 'Anyway, I just wanted to say that so you wouldn't worry. I'd best get back there now, we're in the middle of a story.'

'Which one?'

'*Pooh Goes Visiting and Pooh and Piglet Nearly Catch a Woozle.*'

Laughing through a sob, Emma said, 'Don't tell me you've memorised it.'

'No, I went out to buy it earlier. She always loved Pooh the most when she was little, so I thought I'd start with that and later we might move on to Brer Rabbit, if I can find him, or perhaps some Aesop's Fables.'

Knowing he'd selected the favourites from his own childhood, which indeed he'd shared with Lauren during hers, Emma said, 'She's still got her own copies, somewhere. I'll look them out if you like, and bring them in.'

'That'd be good, thanks. I'll see you tomorrow then.'

'OK, send her my love, won't you?'

'Of course.'

After ringing off, Emma sat holding the phone, staring down at it as though the past was captured right there, showing her younger self standing at Lauren's bedroom door listening to Will reading her stories, and smiling proudly every time Lauren joined in with the words, or asked what something meant, or giggled at the naughtiness of one of the baddies.

Will had always been a champion reader of stories.

'Again, again,' Lauren would cry every time he tried to finish.

'It's time for you to go to sleep,' he'd tell her.

'But I'm not tired and Pooh really wants me to help him find some honey.' Or, 'Please can we have some more of *What Katy Did*?' Or, 'I promise I will go fast asleep the very minute you finish reading *Gulliver's Travels*.'

How Emma had laughed to herself at that, the cunning little minx.

'But that'll take me all night,' Will had protested.

'I know,' she'd grinned and then yelped with laughter as Will tickled her and reached for another book.

He'd never been able to say no to her; the discipline had been left to Emma, not that Lauren had ever needed much, but there had been times when she'd had to be reminded of her manners, or sent to bed early for being cheeky, or grounded for clobbering another girl with her recorder, aged nine. There had been plenty of instances over the years when Emma had had to take a firm hand, but never once had it been for lying. In fact, she couldn't think of a single occasion when she'd doubted Lauren's honesty, which had to be why learning of Saturday night's deception was proving so hard to take.

Who on earth were the Osmonds, who were claiming no knowledge of Lauren? How did she know them? What kind of role were they playing in her life?

'Here we are,' Andrews announced, pulling up outside the house and turning off the engine.

Emma couldn't move, could barely even catch her breath as she sat staring at all the flowers, cards, soft toys, attached to the railings either side of her gate. She hadn't been prepared for this, it hadn't even occurred to her that it might happen and she could feel herself starting to panic. This was a scene from TV or the newspapers, something that happened to other people, not to them. They'd become the targets of publicity, curiosity, pity, victims of a crime, a family in the grip of a tragedy. She thought fleetingly of how much worse it must be for the parents whose children had been stolen or murdered, but Lauren was so close to death that at any moment she could become one of them.

It wasn't going to happen. She simply wouldn't let it.

Getting out of the car, Andrews came round to open the passenger door and gave her a hand to step out.

'Is it awful to wish someone would take it all away?' Emma whispered.

'No, of course not.'

'It would hurt people's feelings though, and Lauren would never want that.'

'Emma,' Harry said, coming out of the door to greet her.

215

Seeing her brother heightened her emotions, but she was glad he was there. The strength of his arms enfolding her and the love she knew he had for Lauren were what she needed right now. What she needed most of all, however, was a call from Will telling her that Lauren had come round. That wasn't going to happen, though, while they still had her sedated.

The next big fear would be when they withdrew the sedation. Would she wake up, or would she. . . ?'

She couldn't think about it now.

'Thanks for bringing her,' Harry was saying to Andrews. 'Will you come in?'

'No, it's OK,' Andrews replied. 'I just need to remind you,' he said to Emma, 'to drop into the station on the way to the hospital tomorrow so they can take a sample of your DNA.'

Emma nodded. 'Which station?' she asked.

'I'll write it down. Actually, better still, I'll pick you up at nine and take you there myself.'

As he returned to his car, Emma told Harry, 'He's being so kind. I don't know what we'd do without him, but at the same time I wish we'd never met him.'

'Come on, my sweetheart,' Berry said, appearing at the door. 'We've been waiting for you. Mum's putting the kettle on and it's nice and warm inside.'

Emma had been home for almost an hour now, drinking tea, trying to make conversation, but her mind couldn't settle on what anyone was saying, or even on what she was thinking. Everything was feeling wrong about being here, from the affection and attentiveness of her family, who might as well have been strangers, to what seemed a curious, cold-hearted lack of change in the fabric of the place. Yet what did she expect, that the windows would be smashed, the furniture ripped and doors torn off? A physical manifestation of the grief and dread it was now harbouring in its shell? How could it, or anyone, or anything remain impervious to what was happening? What kind of world just carried on turning as though it had done nothing to shatter dreams or lives, to break hearts and devastate the brilliance of a young girl's future?

That wouldn't happen. Somehow Lauren would get back on track and everything would be the same again. They just needed to have faith.

Time had lost all meaning. Her efforts to try and stay positive had begun faltering the moment she'd come through the door; now they seemed to have vanished altogether. She knew that fatigue was blackening her thoughts and stealing her strength, but knowing it did nothing to fight it. A week, a month, even a year could have passed since Clive Andrews had first come here; now nothing would go back together the way it should, and probably never would again.

Everyone – Berry, her mother, Harry – was talking in whispers and moving carefully around her, as though the normal tone of a voice or unexpected touch of an arm might startle her and make her take flight. She was torn between resentment and gratitude, wanting them here, but wishing they would go, as if their absence could somehow undo what had been done. She could feel her mother's eyes watching her, and Berry's kindness softening the tension between them that might not even be there. Harry was mostly silent, unable to express his feelings, but showing them in the shadows around his eyes and taut paleness of his skin. These three people, whom she loved in different, and – in her mother's case – problematic, ways, were the core of her family. They were who she'd have left if Lauren didn't come home.

Getting abruptly up from her chair, she said, 'I'm going to take a shower.'

'Let me run it for you,' Berry said, getting up too.

'No, really there's no need.'

'You should try to eat something,' her mother said, turning from the window where she'd been staring out at the night, watching planes going over, or perhaps sending silent messages to Lauren via the stars.

Emma didn't bother to say she wasn't hungry, her mother would know without being told.

'Is there anything I can do?' Harry offered.

'It's OK, I can manage,' she replied.

They were treating her like an invalid and she didn't blame them, because she felt like one, but she didn't want it to become about her when the only one who mattered was Lauren.

Understanding that taking care of her was the only way they had of taking care of Lauren, she told herself to accept their concern, and allow them to help her, just not tonight. She needed to be alone now to try to lose herself in the oblivion of sleep, with a phone next to her pillow in case Will rang.

Half an hour later, after showering and washing her hair, she was standing in the doorway of Lauren's room staring at all the things that made it Lauren's: the guitar in its case; the electronic keyboard, piles of sheet music, jeans and belt abandoned across the back of a chair; trainers askew and unlaced in the middle of a rug; the muddle of make-up, hair clips and brushes on the dressing table; the wardrobe with clothes hanging from the doors; the boxes of books and posters yet to be unpacked; the bag she'd brought home with her on Saturday when she'd seemed so full of excitement and ready to conquer the world.

What had she been hiding in her mind then? What kind of secrets had made her eyes glow so brightly and her laughter bubble up as pure as a spring? How did she know the Osmonds? What promises or temptations had they put her way to make her so joyous and dress the way she had to go out?

Why were they saying they didn't know her when they surely must?

Why had she taken her flute?

Hearing someone coming up the stairs, she dragged her hands through her wet hair and sat down heavily on the edge of the bed.

'I wasn't sure whether to tidy it up or leave it as it is,' her mother said, coming into the room.

Staring absently at the small desk where Lauren's laptop and schoolbooks were piled, Emma replied, 'You made the right decision.' This way it was ready for Lauren to step back into, just as she would have on Saturday had the Osmonds not tempted her to Glastonbury, and the Lomax boy hadn't got drunk and with the arrogance of young men of his age and background thought he could get away with driving his car.

Will was right, Oliver Lomax had to pay for what he'd done.

'There's obviously not enough room for us all to stay here tonight,' her mother said, 'so Harry has booked a couple of rooms at the pub. We thought you should decide who you wanted to stay with you.'

Feeling a wave of resentment creeping over her, Emma buried her face in her hands. Why should she have to choose between them, decide whose feelings she was going to hurt, when they were perfectly capable of sorting it out themselves?

'I'll understand if you want it to be Berry or Harry,' her mother said.

Emma's head came up. 'Just as long as it's not you? Is that what you're saying?'

Phyllis's face paled.

'It would be far too awkward for you to deal with me on your own while I'm in an emotional state, wouldn't it?' Emma accused, getting to her feet. 'Well, don't worry, I'm not asking you to.'

'Emma, you misunderstood,' Phyllis began as Emma brushed past her.

'No I didn't. I know how you feel about me, I've always known, so please don't let's start pretending now.' As she opened her bedroom door she turned back. 'I don't mind who stays, Harry or Berry, tell them they can decide between them,' and closing the door behind her she fell back against it, letting herself sink helplessly to the floor. Never before in her life had she felt this wretched, and being horrible to her mother had just made it a hundred times worse, in spite of the fact that Phyllis probably couldn't give a damn anyway. She was only here out of duty; it had nothing to do with love or support or sympathy, at least not for her own daughter. Where her granddaughter was concerned it was a different story, because there had never been any doubt about how much Phyllis loved Lauren.

Chapter Sixteen

It was barely six thirty in the morning, but Oliver was already awake when his mobile rang and seeing it was Charlie he decided to click on. Had it been anyone else, he wouldn't have bothered.

'Were you asleep?' Charlie asked.

'No. What are you doing up so early?'

'I've got my exams today, remember? I thought I'd do some last-minute revising.'

'You won't have a problem. You never do.'

'Says you. Anyway, are you OK?'

'Sure, why wouldn't I be?' Oliver replied, getting out of bed. He was wearing plaid boxers and an old T-shirt that stretched across his chest showing, if he'd cared to look in a mirror, how muscular he was. Mirrors had no interest for him now; all he saw when he looked in one was the ugly face of guilt, a no-hoper staring back at him.

'You sounded pretty bad when we spoke last night,' Charlie informed him.

'Did I?' Cracking open the curtains Oliver saw his father going across the courtyard to the stables. It seemed they were all early risers this morning.

'Oliver, you've got to stop thinking about the girl,' Charlie said firmly. 'You're going to drive yourself crazy if you don't, and there's nothing you can do.'

Tension tightened round Oliver's head. Did his brother seriously think he didn't know that?

'I don't want you to keep worrying,' Charlie went on, 'because I'm on it, OK? As soon as I'm done here I'll be home and we'll work it out.'

Oliver's thoughts were scathing. Exactly what did Charlie think he could do that top doctors, lawyers and their father couldn't? This law degree was going to his head. 'Have you spoken to Mum?' he asked, changing the subject.

'Only briefly, after I rang off from you last night.'

'Was she OK?' He didn't want to care, but he supposed he ought.

'As OK as she ever is. I've come up with a way to work that out too.'

'I thought you were studying to be a lawyer, not a magician.'

'Ha, ha. Did Dad get his car back after she drove off in it?'

'Yeah. It's a bit dented, but driveable.'

'Any news on yours yet?'

Oliver felt himself shrinking inside.

'I guess there probably won't be for a while,' Charlie ran on. 'The forensic stuff takes time. Just remember, you're not banned yet, so you're still free to drive – and to have a life.'

Seeing his freedom as a great mass of light being swallowed by some hideous black cloud on a close horizon, Oliver turned away from the window, as though he could somehow escape it.

'What are you doing today?' Charlie asked.

'Starting work with Paul Granger.'

'Of course, you mentioned it last night. That's good. It'll keep your mind off things.'

'She's got a name,' Oliver snapped.

Charlie drew in his breath.

'It's Lauren Scott.'

'I know.'

'Did you go online like I told you? Have you seen her, what she was like?'

'Yeah, I've seen her, but you've got to stop obsessing over this. It's not going to help.'

Oliver's tension clenched again. Didn't Charlie get that everything was way beyond help? Why was he going on like it was possible to turn back the clock, or bring Lauren

Scott round, or do away with the charges that were going to pile up whether she pulled through or not? His life, his future, everything was ruined and there was no escaping it.

And what kind of mess was hers in now?

'I guess I should go,' Charlie said. 'I'll call again tonight, OK?'

'Sure. Good luck with the exams.'

After ringing off Oliver went to slump down at his computer, but knowing he'd only go on tormenting himself with everything he could find about Lauren Scott, he decided to put the TV on instead. No better really, because his first stop was the local news just in case they mentioned her. They didn't, mainly because everyone was talking about the creep who'd been arrested for murdering the girl from Thornbury.

The Box channel should give him some decent background sounds while he showered, no classical flute stuff, or piano, or jazz-type singing – the kind of funk Lauren Scott went in for (it seemed she could do it all).

Not now, thanks to him.

He wondered if his dad had heard about the arrest of Mandie Morgan's killer yet. If he had, he'd be relieved, like everyone else – no one wanted a psycho on the loose – but in his dad's case he'd actually met the girl only hours before the lowlife had offed her. He'd even been interviewed by the police; everyone in the office had, while his mother – his *sick* mother – had got it into her head for a while that his father was in some way involved. She'd let it drop, thank God, probably because she'd washed it away with a few dozen gallons of vodka-laced vino by now, but there was never any knowing when it might be regurgitated, and since he, Oliver, was making a quality job of heaping shame on the family all on his own, they really didn't need any help from her.

So, hooray for the cops, they'd finally nailed the sicko neighbour who everyone was saying they'd always thought was weird.

They'd nailed him too and he didn't have to worry what

they might be saying about him, he already knew. It had
been in the papers, on the news and was pouring into his
email and plastering his Facebook page every minute of
the day.

Wilkie, as he and Charlie usually called Connie Wilkes,
their mother's old secretary, was staying with their mother
now, no doubt following strict instructions from their father
not to let her charge behind the wheel of a car. It was a
sorry irony, Charlie had said last night, that she, who rack-
eted about in her Merc under the influence all the time,
had managed to escape the law, while he, Oliver, had only
done it once – and then to save her – and now look where
he was. As far as Oliver was concerned, there was no sorry
irony about it; it was serious, fucking bad luck that he'd
no way deserved, and if there was any effing justice in the
world his mother would be sobering up fast and
taking the rap for him, not sneaking about her own flat
taking crafty swigs from her secret stash of booze.

Once he'd showered and not bothered to shave, he pulled
on a clean pair of jeans and an old Chelsea T-shirt, covered
it with a thick, baggy sweatshirt and tied a black wool scarf
around his neck before going across to the stables to see
his father. No way was he looking at his emails and
Facebook today; he'd had enough of all the crap that had
been turning up since early Sunday; real shitty hate-mail
stuff calling him anything from a waste of skin, to the scum
of the earth, to a raving psycho. A few had even sent links
to suicide sites recommending he did himself and everyone
else a favour.

Maybe he would.

He'd had no idea until now that this was how people
who got done for drinking and driving were treated by
strangers. He hadn't even been to court yet, but to them
he was obviously guilty, the breath tests said so, and who
gave a shit about backup blood tests, let's hang him anyway,
cretin shouldn't even have been on the road. Plus, even
worse, like a million times worse, he'd caused grave physical injury (and they didn't always put it like that, morons)
to a 'beautiful, innocent young girl' (that was the general
description of her, and having seen and read what he had,

he wouldn't argue with it). Of course some of his new correspondents, maybe even all of them, would be friends of Lauren's – actually he knew some were, because they said so. If it was their intention to make him loathe and despise himself any more than he already did, then they were failing, because he was already so far down in the pits that it just wasn't possible to go any further. Even his own friends didn't seem to hold him in any greater esteem than he did himself, and who could blame them? Although Alfie and Jerome had written on his wall that they'd support him no matter what he'd done, and maybe his 'anonymous accusers, how brave are you?' ought to get over themselves and find out all the facts before 'you start shouting your mouths off'. Oliver knew that if he'd allow it they'd broadcast to the world the reason why he'd been driving that night, but furious as he was with his mother, and as much as she probably deserved to be outed, he just didn't want everyone knowing what a pitiful wreck she was.

'Hey,' his father said, looking up from his computer as Oliver came in. 'What are you doing about so early?'

Closing the door as the wind tried to rush in, Oliver said, 'Couldn't sleep, so thought I'd make a start on some of the research stuff for Paul.'

Russ nodded approval. 'Have you had breakfast?'

'Not hungry.'

'Well, starving's not an option, I'm afraid, so I'll make you some when I've finished here. Meanwhile, there's fresh coffee in the machine.'

Going to help himself, Oliver said, 'I can make my own breakfast.'

'I know, and you will tomorrow. Mine too. Today can be my turn.'

'So what are you doing?' Oliver asked, coming to look over his shoulder.

'Reworking a pitch that Angie and Graham are presenting to the Beeb this afternoon. It's more or less there, but it could do with being a bit punchier.'

'Aren't you going with them?'

'No, I've got too much to do here. Paul's coming at ten

to start going through an order of shoot for the new series. You should be in on that too.'

Oliver shrugged, and went to sit at the desk he'd used the last time he'd worked for his father. It was at the back of the large room, about as far from his father's desk as it was possible to get.

Russ watched him put down his coffee and turn on the computer. 'I was thinking it might be a good idea for you to drive us to the garage later,' he said.

Oliver immediately baulked.

'My car's going in for repair and they're lending me another which you won't be insured for, so . . .'

'I know where you're going with this, and I don't think it's a good idea.'

'You have to get back behind the wheel sometime, son.'

'Why? They're going to take my licence, aren't they? I'm going to be banned for at least three years, and if I end up in prison . . .'

'It might not come to that, so don't let's start making assumptions.'

'So what, we start kidding ourselves instead?'

'We haven't had the blood-test results yet. If they come back negative . . .'

'Oh Dad, get real. I was over the limit, OK? And even if they did come back negative, Lauren Scott's still where she is, and I'm the one who put her there. No blood-test result's going to change that, is it?'

After waiting a moment for the tension to ebb, Russ said, 'It was an accident, Oliver. You didn't do it intention-ally . . .'

'I know that. I'm just saying, we can't change the facts, so what's the point in trying to make out we can?'

'My point is only this: it could be a while before you lose your licence – if it does come to that – so I think you'd be helping yourself if you started to drive again. Let it go too long and your confidence won't . . .'

'I don't ever want to drive again, OK? Not ever.'

'Oliver, I understand . . .'

'No you don't.' Oliver's temper was flaring. 'You've never hit someone with your car. You haven't seen them go up over your bonnet and smash into your windscreen. You haven't sat with them on the side of the road willing them to live. You haven't been where I am now, knowing you're the lowest of the low, hating yourself so much you might as well be dead. You don't get the kind of emails I do, or texts, telling you you're the worst form of human life. So please don't tell me you understand, Dad, because you really, really, don't.'

Russ continued to watch him, as, pale-faced and frightened, he turned his attention to the screen and began banging something into the keyboard. He couldn't argue, because Oliver was right, he had never been in his position, but that didn't mean he couldn't feel his son's angst probably even more deeply than he'd ever feel his own, because that he could deal with. Turning things around for Oliver, giving him back his hope, confidence, self-esteem and dreams of a future was slipping so fast out of his grip that there seemed to be almost nothing left.

Going to sit at the empty desk next to Oliver's, he said, 'We need some proper help, son. Some professional advice on how to handle post-traumatic stress, which is what I think you're suffering from. And maybe they can advise me of the best way to help you.'

Oliver kept his head down.

'All I want,' Russ said softly, 'is to do the best for you. It's all I've ever wanted.'

'I know,' Oliver replied hoarsely.

Resisting the urge to hug him as though he was still a child, Russ said, 'No matter what people are putting in emails and texts, you and I both know that you are a decent, worthwhile human being at heart who really cares about what's happened, and who would do anything possible to make up for it.'

Oliver tried to nod.

'We'll find a way,' Russ told him. 'I don't know how yet, but we'll find one, I promise.'

During the night, finding herself awake after only a few hours of sleep, Emma had crept quietly past Lauren's room where Berry was sleeping, to go downstairs to her computer.

Seeing so many emails from her own and Lauren's friends, all of them presumably wanting to express how sorry and worried they were, had instantly made her regret going online. It was making it too real and there was a part of her that still wasn't ready to catch up with that, so she'd left them unread and clicked on to Lauren's Facebook page to find it crammed with so much love and grief that her own seemed to be swept up into the tide of it.

You are absolutely the very best friend in the world. I love you so much, Lauren. I can't bear to be without you. If you don't come back I'll never play the piano or guitar or sing again, because I only want to do it with you. So you see, you have to come back. Great big hug to you my darling. Coming to see you at the weekend. We've got loads to catch up on, so you'd better be awake. Donna.

As soon as they let me I'm coming to see you. I can't stop thinking about you. I've known you all my life and you've been the best friend ever, even though we don't live close to one another, or go to the same school. No one means as much to me as you do. Don't worry about anything, I'll always be there for you. Melissa xxxx

We're here for you my darling, we'll never let you go. Skye and Matilda.

This can't happen to you. You're definitely coming back to us. Hold on, babe, love you, love you, love you, Salina.

We're trying to get the performance exams delayed to wait for you. Wouldn't be the same without you. Pippa.

I owe everything to you. I've got friends now and a life, because you talked to me when no one else would. Please, please, come back. Jessica.

I can't believe this has happened. I lit a candle for you and I just know that you'll find it and come back to us. Anna.

I can't stop crying. This is so awful. I'm thinking about you all the time. School's so quiet. Everyone really misses you. Alex.

We want you to be reading this very soon so you'll know how special you are to us. Be brave, be strong. We're playing three flute adagios in your honour in class today, Mrs Maddison.

The inspirational music teacher who Lauren adored.

'A damsel with a dulcimer, In a vision once I saw, It was an

Abyssinian maid, And on her dulcimer she played . . . Weave a circle round him thrice, And close your eyes with holy dread, For he on honey-dew hath fed, And drunk the milk of Paradise.' Your mischievous recital of this had us all laughing with delight less than a week ago. We now hold that memory as preciously as we hold our hopes that you will be back amongst us very soon. Sleep lightly, be well, Philip Leesom.

Emma had noticed that he'd sent an email to her too, as had several other teachers and the head, who'd written on Lauren's Facebook page:

It's always been such a delight having you at this school. Along with everyone else I've developed a deep and genuine fondness for you, Lauren. We're all very proud to know you, and are very much looking forward to the day you're able to return to us. Mr Gibbs.

So many postings, plenty from friends she'd never heard of, perhaps strangers to Lauren too, but every one of them as tender and caring as the last. There were others that included anger towards 'the monster who did this to you' and a few even swore revenge. Emma felt fractured into so many pieces and each seemed to feel differently to the next – while one part of her raved with anger at the injustice of it all, another wanted to be gentle and at peace, thinking only of Lauren. There were others, huge parts of her, that struggled with a terrible fear of what the future might hold, while yet more fragments of her shattered self tried to control a consuming hatred of the boy who'd done this. Only in the last few hours had she seemed to start connecting with that, but like all the other broken pieces, after its moments of stark intensity it fell back soundlessly into the shadows.

The only mentions on Facebook about where Lauren had been on Saturday night had come from those wanting to know why she'd been in a strange place on her own when they'd thought she was clubbing with her mates in Bristol; or from others banally wondering where the actual road was. Maybe it wasn't banal, though, because they might be wanting to travel all that way to put flowers on the spot.

Emma hoped they wouldn't – it was a gesture she

associated with bereavement, and, thank God, they weren't there yet.

They would never get there; she couldn't allow it.

There wasn't a single mention of the Osmonds, nor a message that might conceivably have been from them. Nor was there any word from Parker Jenkins. Did that mean anything? Maybe he'd sent an email instead.

'Jackie Dennis is going to London this morning,' Clive Andrews told her as they drove to the police station for her to give her DNA, with Berry in the back of the car. Harry and her mother had turned up at eight thirty, and were staying at the house while the police searched Lauren's room for heaven only knew what, and took away whatever they needed. What kind of criminal activity did they think Lauren had been involved in? Emma couldn't begin to imagine, and wouldn't, because then she'd have to start facing the fact that her daughter wasn't who she thought she was.

'Jackie's arranged to talk to both Osmonds,' Andrews went on, 'and the Jenkins boy, so maybe we'll know more later.'

'What about Donna?' Emma asked. 'Is she going to see her?'

'I believe so. She's definitely going to the school, and yours truly is going to have a chat with your friend's daughter today, Melissa.'

Emma nodded and turned to look out of the window.

The session at the police station was over now, and Clive Andrews had just dropped Emma and Berry next to the hospital's Accident Centre so they could walk through to the ICU.

'I could wish this wasn't quite such a gloomy place,' Berry murmured as they went in through the North Entrance. A long, low-ceilinged corridor stretched out like endless arms either side of them, neon-lit and scuffed with age. Swing doors, some security-coded, some not, led to various wards and units; paintings and photographs lined the walls, and medical staff, porters, and administrators moved busily about their tasks.

'It was used by the Americans during the war,' Emma told her, standing aside as a mentally impaired young man loped awkwardly past them with a man who was probably a nurse.

'Really? As some sort of barracks?' Berry asked.

'No, as a hospital.' It seemed odd to be having this conversation, but it was OK too.

'How do you know?'

'I read it online during the night.'

'Mm, I thought you were up. Did you manage to sleep at all?'

'Yes, for a while.'

Berry said no more, simply linked Emma's arm as they followed a couple of porters along the eternal walkway until they reached the waiting room outside Intensive Care.

'I'll just check to see if Will's in here first,' Emma said, pushing open the door.

To her surprise the room was crowded with strangers, some of them children – except she realised after a moment that they weren't strangers, because the woman who was standing up awkwardly to greet her was Will's wife, Jemima. The children must be Will's other family.

'Emma, I'm so sorry about what's happened,' Jemima said, seeming genuinely to mean it, which of course she would. She was even taller than Emma remembered, too tall, and as blonde as her Scandinavian origins could make her. Her sloe eyes looked tired, but no less arresting for that and even without make-up she could only be described as a beauty.

'I didn't know you were going to be here,' Emma said, feeling uncomfortable and angry and wishing she was able to send them away.

Colouring slightly, Jemima said, 'We came to . . . Well, to see Lauren, obviously, and to lend Will some moral support. He's taken this very hard. Of course, I'm sure you have too.'

Emma wondered what she was supposed to say to that. She knew what she'd like to say, but even if she had the nerve she never would in front of the children. They were watching her, all four of them with wide, worried eyes,

231

apparently picking up on the tension and not knowing what to do. The little boy was breathtaking, and the little girl was so similar to Lauren at that age, with her golden curls and brilliant golden eyes, that it made Emma's heart ache. She could imagine three-year-old Chloe having a big crush on her glamorous stepsister. The twelve-year-old-twins were the image of each other, and must resemble their father since they were dark-haired and sallow-skinned, quite unlike their mother. One of them said, 'Hello, I'm Cecile.'

'Hello,' Emma replied, impressed by her good manners. 'It's nice to meet you.' It wasn't, but it was hardly the child's fault this was happening.

'And I'm Robin,' the boy told her.

Emma gave him a smile.

'Are you Lauren's mum?' Cecile asked.

'Yes, I am. I've come to see her. Is Will in with her?' she asked Jemima.

'Yes, he's been going in and out all night. I think they're saying that we'll have to start keeping to regular visiting hours from now on.'

Flinching at the 'we', and hating being told by Jemima that the rules were soon to be imposed, Emma turned to Berry. 'I should go in now,' she said. 'Will you be all right out here?'

'Actually, I'll go and give Harry and your mother a call, find out what time they expect to get here.'

Saying no more to Jemima, Emma followed Berry out of the room, and after exchanging a wordless but eloquent look, they parted company. As Emma went to buzz for entry into the ward Will came out, so catching the door she made to move past him.

'Emma,' he said, stopping her.

'I want to see Lauren,' she told him.

'The doctors are with her.'

Emma let the door go and lifted her eyes to his; tears were stinging them even as her blood boiled. 'You could have told me Jemima was going to be here,' she said tightly.

'I'm sorry. I guess . . .'

'Don't you think it's a bit much for Lauren, having so many visitors during the night?'

232

'The kids only went in once, and very quietly. Jem's been in a couple of times, but just to say hello and tell her to get well. No one hassled her, or did anything to wear her out.'

Finding her throat too tight to say more, Emma put a hand to her mouth, pretending to stifle a cough. It was absurd, she knew, and she already hated herself for it, but for a brief moment she'd felt unable to bear the thought of Lauren coming round and seeing Jemima, and not her. All that mattered was that Lauren should wake up; it really didn't matter who was there.

'Apparently the orthopaedic surgeon's doing his nut about not being able to operate on the leg yet,' Will told her. 'They're going to pin it this morning.'

Emma tried to take it in. 'That's good,' she said. 'If they're doing that, they must think . . . They must have decided it's worth doing.' No matter the kind of straw, small, strong, weak or even broken, just please keep giving her something to cling to.

'That's what I told myself,' Will agreed.

Emma stood aside as a nurse came out of the ward.

'You need to clear the way,' the nurse told them. 'We're about to bring a patient through.'

'Sorry,' they apologised in unison, and because there was nowhere else to go, Emma found herself following Will back into the waiting room.

'Are you OK?' Jemima asked softly as soon as she saw Will. Little Dirk was on her lap now, while Chloe snuggled up against her. The big bad lady, Lauren's mummy, must have scared them, Emma thought, because it looked as though they'd been crying.

'I'm fine, just tired,' he sighed. 'How are you two?' he asked the twins.

'We're OK,' Cecile answered. 'How's Lauren? Can we see her again?'

'Not now. The doctors are with her.'

'Are they going to make her better?' Chloe asked.

'They're trying to.'

'I want her to wake up,' she said, her chin starting to wobble.

'I know, sweetheart,' Jemima soothed. 'We all do, but we have to be patient.'

Unable to be a part of this 'other family' scene, Emma said to Will, 'Don't forget the police want a sample of your DNA,' and without saying goodbye to Jemima or the children she left the room.

She found Berry a few minutes later, in an open concourse between two red-brick wards. Taking her arm, she said, 'The doctors are with Lauren, so let's go and find a cup of tea.'

'Did she have a good night?' Berry asked, as they followed signs to a WRVS coffee shop.

'I don't know, with all that coming and going.'

Berry clucked her disapproval. 'It was a very poor show, inviting Jemima and the children here without telling you,' she commented. 'What was he thinking?'

'About himself, as usual, and them, I guess. They consider Lauren family, which of course she is, so the children were bound to be worried. Who knows, maybe hearing them has helped her in some way.'

'Well that would certainly be welcome. I know Lauren's very fond of them.'

Emma's insides ached as she almost smiled. 'She is of everyone,' she reminded Berry, 'but you're right, they matter a lot to her. Will says they're setting her leg this morning. And it seems we're going to be told at some point that we have to start keeping to visiting hours.'

'Which are?'

'I don't know yet. We'll find out. What did Mum and Harry have to say?'

'Apparently the police have taken Lauren's computer, as we expected.'

Wishing she'd thought to go through it herself first, Emma asked, 'Did they take anything else?'

'Not that Harry mentioned. They were just leaving when I spoke to them, so they should be here in about an hour.' Pushing open the coffee-shop door, Berry said, 'Am I allowed to ask what happened between you and Mum last night?'

Feeling a pang of guilt flare up from her conscience,

Emma replied, 'I was probably a bit shorter with her than I should have been.'

'About?'

'She said she wouldn't mind if I'd rather have you or Harry stay with me than her. In other words, the last thing either of us wants is to be left on our own together, especially at such an emotional time.'

Joining the end of a short queue, Berry said, 'I think you misread her at times, you know.'

Emma couldn't stop herself bristling. 'I think I read her far more clearly than she'd like, which is half the problem. Anyway, let's please not talk about her. The day is off to a bad enough start as it is, thanks to Will, and the police, and having to be in this place. I haven't even seen Lauren yet, which is making me feel awful.'

'I know, but look at it this way, there could be some good news waiting for us when we get back to the ward.'

Emma caught the thread of optimism, dared to hold it for a moment, and smiled. 'What will you have?' she offered as they approached the counter.

A few minutes later, with a stainless-steel teapot and two white china mugs between them, they sat staring at the biscuits they'd chosen, seeming to have run out of words.

In the end, Emma said, 'Am I imagining things, or did you say before we left the house that there's something you want to tell me?'

Berry waved a dismissive hand. 'Oh that, it's nothing,' she answered, picking up her mug.

'Come on, what is it?' Emma coaxed.

'No, really, it's not relevant any more.' She glanced out of the window and as her face seemed to fall, Emma turned to find out what was wrong.

'Oh God,' she murmured, her insides churning with all kinds of emotions as she saw Will walking by carrying his handsome little son with one arm, and the other arm around Jemima who was holding cute little Chloe. The twins were straggling on behind, and when the girl caught Emma's eye she blushed to the roots of her hair. She must have called out to her mother, because the next instant Will and

Jemima were turning round. Spotting Emma and Berry, Will said something to his wife and came into the cafe, still carrying his son.

'Hello Berry,' he said, when he reached the table.

'Hello Will,' she replied.

'How are you?'

'Oh, you know. How are you?'

'I guess the same.' To Emma he said, 'I'm going back to London today.'

'Of course,' she replied bitterly. 'You have other priorities, I understand that.'

He flushed. 'I'm going to get more clothes. Jem forgot to bring them last night.'

'Oh, dear.'

'When I come back,' he went on, carefully removing his son's little hand from his mouth, 'we should talk. There are things . . .'

'Exactly when are you coming back?' she interrupted.

'Tomorrow, probably. I've been up most of the night, so I ought not to do a drive up and back in one day. If there's any change, will you let me know?'

'Of course.' Her eyes went down as she picked up her mug.

'Are you sure?'

Surprised, she looked up at him. 'I wouldn't keep it from you. I understand you're her father.'

An awkward silence followed as Berry gazed down at her tea and Emma turned to look at his little family outside.

'I know what you're thinking,' he told her.

Her eyebrows rose as she turned back. 'Really?'

'You're thinking that having Dirk and Chloe makes this easier for me.'

'You have Jemima too, let's not forget her.'

'Lauren means every bit as much to me as she does to you.'

'I don't think that's possible, because to me she's everything.'

'It's not a contest,' Berry came in gently. 'This isn't easy for either of you, and the best way you can help each other, and Lauren, is to try to put your differences aside during this difficult time.'

Knowing Berry was right, and annoyed with herself all over again for becoming angry and bitter with Will, Emma said, 'I'll try to remember to look out those books for you.'

Will seemed baffled.

'The children's books you wanted to read to Lauren.'

'Oh yes, thanks. I'd appreciate it.'

After he'd gone, Emma said, 'I know he loves her, I'd never doubt it for a minute, but I can't help asking myself, how can he bring himself to leave before the doctor's finished his rounds?'

'Maybe he has finished,' Berry replied.

Emma's eyes went to hers. 'And already spoken to Will who said nothing to me?'

Looking dismayed, Berry said, 'Why don't we go and find out?'

'The orthopaedic surgeon will come to talk to you when he's finished,' Nigel Farraday was telling them at the nurses' station ten minutes later, 'but essentially I've agreed that he can operate if there's no change in Lauren's condition by the end of the week.'

Emma's eyes were watching him hungrily, trying to find any tiny morsel of hope he might be offering. 'Will that be good, if there's no change?' she asked.

Farraday's smile was faint. 'That very much depends on the nature of the change. If it means she's woken up, then of course it would be good.'

'But if she hasn't?'

His eyes were solemn. 'Let's just say we'd prefer it if she did.'

'Do you think she will?'

He glanced briefly to Berry before he said, 'Mrs Scott, I don't believe I've misled you about the severity of your daughter's injuries . . .'

'No, no, I understand that they're serious, but there *is* a chance she'll wake up, isn't there? I mean, when you stop sedating her.' Her nails were biting into her hands; blood was pulsing through her ears.

Farraday's eyes went down for a moment. 'I'm sorry,' he said, 'I thought someone had told you, she's no longer being sedated.'

Emma's heart jarred. 'So she's . . . she's in an actual coma?' she whispered.

'It would appear so,' he replied sombrely.

'Oh God,' Emma choked, taking a step back as though to avoid the words.

Farraday's registrar put a steadying arm on her shoulder, while Berry, beaten by the news, stared at the nurses' station as though she'd lost a sense of where she was.

No more than ten yards away Lauren lay inert on her bed, still attached to her tubes, surrounded by monitors and showing no voluntary signs of life as two doctors and a nurse worked on her leg.

To Farraday, Emma said shakily, 'Isn't there anything you can do to bring her round? There must be something, surely.'

'If there were, believe me we'd . . .' He turned as an alarm sounded.

Emma's heart leapt to her throat.

Nurses and intensivists started running.

Emma turned to run too, but Farraday's registrar caught her.

'It's OK,' he said gently.

Emma didn't understand, how could it be OK when an alarm was sounding? Then she realised he was telling her that it wasn't Lauren, and she almost collapsed with relief. It wasn't that she was wishing harm to anyone else but she had no idea if Lauren could survive another crisis.

Ushering her and Berry out of the unit, Farraday and his team came into the waiting room with them.

After exchanging a few words with the registrar, who was looking at his watch, Farraday turned to Emma, taking a moment to bring himself back to Lauren's case. 'Unless there are any unexpected occurrences,' he said, 'we should start weaning her off the ventilator tomorrow or Thursday.'

Emma could only stare at him, confused, trying to piece

it together. Repairing the leg, taking her off the ventilator
. . . 'What . . . what does that mean exactly?' she finally
managed.

'It means we'll find out if she's capable of breathing on
her own.'

'And if . . . if she isn't?'

He smiled reassuringly. 'If she isn't we'll perform a
tracheotomy, but let's try to remain positive. Now, if you'll
excuse me, I'm already late for theatre.'

After the door closed behind him Emma turned her
bewildered eyes to Berry. As she started to speak her mobile
rang, and seeing it was Will she clicked on.

'Is Farraday still with her?' he asked.

'No, he's just left.'

'So what did he say?'

'Did someone tell you she's in an actual coma and you
didn't pass it on?' Emma asked accusingly.

'What? I don't know what you're talking about.'

'Farraday just told me that they've stopped sedating her,
but she still hasn't come round.'

'Oh Jesus,' he murmured. 'So what does that mean?'

'It means she's in a coma,' she tried not to shout.

There was only silence at the other end.

'They're talking about taking her off the ventilator to see
if she can breathe on her own.'

'When?'

'Tomorrow or Thursday.'

'And if she can't breathe on her own they'll put her back
on it, right?'

'I don't know, he said something about a trach . . .' She
looked at Berry.

'Tracheotomy,' Berry supplied.

'What the hell's that?' he demanded.

'I don't know, I didn't get a chance to ask.'

'OK, we need some proper answers. See if you can find
the consultant, Yuri Nelson, and call me back.'

Unable to stop herself, she said, 'It would help, you
know, if you were still here.'

'I was waiting for that.'

'Well, don't you think you should be?'

'Yes, but I happen to have a business to run, and I also need fresh clothes.'

'For God's sake, Jemima can handle the business, and you could have *bought* clothes. There are shops down the road and she needs you here.'

'That's funny, because you keep giving me the impression you'd rather I was a thousand miles away.'

'What I'd rather is that none of this was happening, but it is, and I really don't appreciate being ordered about . . .'

'OK, OK, talk to who you want. I'll find out my own answers when I get back,' and the line went dead.

After clicking off Emma bit down on her temper as she said to Berry, 'He's right, we have to find Yuri Nelson, but I'm scared to, in case his answers aren't what I want to hear.'

'That's perfectly understandable,' Berry assured her. 'We're all afraid . . .'

'But I'm her mother. I need to deal with the facts . . .' Breaking off, she put her head back and blinked away the tears. 'He seemed quite positive about her breathing on her own, didn't he?' she said. 'And if she can, it has to be a start, doesn't it?'

Reaching for her hand, Berry said, 'Yes, of course.'

Wishing Berry had sounded as convinced as she'd needed to hear, Emma turned away, feeling increasingly alone in her belief that Lauren was going to make it. She wanted to go to Lauren right now and push everyone aside as she connected with her daughter in a way that only she could. She needed Lauren to listen and understand that she could do this; she could pull back from whatever brink she was balancing on, and return to the world as the beautiful, happy-go-lucky girl she'd always been. There was no reason for her not to; everyone loved her and she had so much to live for. She wasn't going to be in a coma for years, or left brain-damaged, she simply wasn't.

You need to read your messages, she told Lauren in her mind. *You'll know then how much you mean to us all, and how desperately we want you back.*

It was only as she let the intensity go that she found herself wondering about the lies Lauren had told last Saturday. What had been making her so happy, and yet had to be hidden from her mother? Whatever it was, it couldn't be as important as her survival, because nothing, but nothing, could ever be as important as that.

Chapter Seventeen

Inspector Jackie Dennis wasn't easily impressed, but the rambling old fancy manse in Kew that the Osmonds called home could have knocked her inspector's cap off, if she'd been wearing one. Not that she ever allowed wealth or status to sidetrack or even intimidate her, far from it, because in her long experience she'd often found that the richer, or more aristocratic people were, the nastier they could be. And currently Mrs Osmond wasn't exactly coming across as nice. Her husband, on the other hand, appeared a little less hostile, though he was letting his cold fish of a fifty-something wife do most of the talking.

'As I told you on the phone,' Rachel Osmond was running on in a bored sort of way, 'we have never heard of this girl, much less sent her our address by text. So I really don't know why you've bothered coming all this way to ask the question again.'

Jackie Dennis only looked at her.

'Well?' Rachel Osmond prompted.

'Something I'm curious about,' Jackie Dennis said, 'is, when I take into consideration the size and splendour of this house . . . Well, what I don't quite get is the minuscule one up, two down in Somerset.' It might not be relevant, but there again, it might.

Rachel Osmond's eyes, and tone, were withering. 'Forgive me for asking, Inspector, but is there a law against owning a small residence in Somerset?'

Dennis gave an amiable shake of her head. 'Not as far as I know,' she conceded, 'I was just wondering, that's all.'

'Actually,' Ian Osmond came in with a reproving glance at his wife, 'it was bought by my father-in-law for his children's old nanny in her retirement, which she then left to her former charges in her will.'

Dennis jotted down the information, and said, 'So, if neither of you texted the address to Lauren Scott, can you perhaps shed some light on who might have?'

Ian Osmond glanced at his wife again as he said, 'We've asked one another that several times since your calls, and I'm afraid we have no idea.'

'Perhaps another member of the family?' Dennis suggested.

With mounting impatience, Mrs Osmond said, 'Our daughter is married to a US senator and living in the States, and our son is with the Foreign Office, currently stationed in Cairo, so I rather doubt either of them has ever heard of your girl either.'

Dennis was bristling. 'Can I remind you that Lauren Scott's life is hanging by a thread? Would it be too much to show a little respect, even if you don't know her?'

Rachel Osmond flushed deeply.

'I apologise,' Ian said gruffly. 'Of course it's a terrible thing to have happened to someone of her age – of any age, in fact.'

It wasn't much, but better than nothing, Dennis decided, and moved on. 'Is there a neighbour down that way who might have a key?' she asked.

'There's the cleaner, of course,' Rachel Osmond replied, 'maybe you should talk to her.'

'Yes, thank you, she saw our officers at the house yesterday morning and was very helpful. I was thinking more of a friend from around those parts, or from around here, or anywhere in fact, who you might let use the place once in a while?'

'There isn't anyone,' Rachel Osmond said sharply.

'I see,' Dennis responded. At this point she might have put down, or even picked up her cup of tea, had she been offered one, but she hadn't. So instead she made do with a bit of a scribble in her notebook, and when she abruptly looked up again she caught an interesting exchange of glances between her hosts.

'I should get that,' Mrs Osmond stated as the phone

started to ring, and without excusing herself she left the room.

'So,' Jackie Dennis said, turning her attention back to the man of the house, 'how often do you actually visit this cottage?'

'Actually, hardly at all,' he replied, fiddling with his tie. 'My wife and her brother have been talking for years about selling it, but they've never quite got round to it. Busy lives, you know.'

Dennis nodded her understanding. 'What exactly is it that you do?' she enquired.

His face seemed to twitch. 'I work in the City,' he said shortly.

'As?'

'A banker.'

'Oh dear,' she sympathised, mentally giving him a point for balls, since it took some these days to admit to being one of the bandits who'd brought the country to its knees. Even harder to admit to if, like him, you were still sitting in a multimillion-quid mansion, and raking in the bonuses, while the innocent lesser folk lost their jobs and homes. Let them eat cake, just not from my table. 'And your wife, what does she do?'

'She designs and manufactures interior dressings such as wallpaper and fabrics.'

'You mean a bit like the Chancellor's family?'

Stiffening, he said, 'Something like that, yes.'

She smiled and nodded. 'Can you remind me again where you were on Saturday night?' she threw at him.

It seemed to hit him on the nose – a blink and a twitch – but by the time he answered he was managing to sound more weary than startled. 'As I said on the phone, we were visiting my parents-in-law in Suffolk.'

'So nowhere near Somerset?'

'No.'

He didn't seem to be lying, but blowing the cover off these types when they banded together often required something nuclear. 'Aren't you in the least bit curious to know how your address could have ended up on Lauren Scott's phone?' she asked bluntly.

His grizzled eyebrows rose. 'I can only assume someone sent it to the wrong number,' he responded coolly.

'And yet she was in Somerset that night, so it would seem she'd followed the directions . . .'

'Do you know if she actually went into the house?' he interrupted.

'Not yet, we're waiting on forensics to tell us that. Do you know if she did?'

He regarded her askance. 'How on earth could I when I wasn't there, and have no idea who she is?'

Coming back into the room, Mrs Osmond said, 'I'm very sorry, Inspector, but something urgent's come up that I have to attend to.'

Wondering whose wallpaper was hanging off, or sofa covers didn't fit, Dennis tucked away her notebook and got to her feet. 'I think we're about done here anyway,' she said. 'Thank you for your time. You've been most . . . helpful.'

Mrs Osmond cast a dubious look at her husband. 'I'll see you out,' she said, leading the way.

'If anything else should come to mind,' Dennis said, handing her a card at the door, 'feel free to call me any time.'

Taking it, Mrs Osmond replied, 'I'm sorry you've had a wasted journey, but I did tell you on the phone that we have no idea who this girl is.'

'And they really don't seem to care much either,' Dennis told Clive Andrews when she rang from the car to appraise him of the visit.

'So do you think they're telling the truth?' he asked.

'Actually, I don't, at least not entirely, but their alibis are borne out by the in-laws, and no one at Lauren's school seems to know who they are, nor does anyone from around the Scotts' old neighbourhood. It's going to be interesting finding out whether Lauren went into the cottage, because if we can place her there, they really will have some explaining to do.'

'I take it no news on that yet?'

'No, you know what forensics are like, overworked, underpaid and like to tell you all about it. And this isn't a murder, so we're hardly a priority. In fact, we really don't know what it is. Any hunches coming up for you yet?'

'Not really. Did you manage to get an ID on the number the text was sent from?'

'I've got someone chasing the phone company. I don't know what's taking them so long, because we should have had something by now. Again, I suppose we're low priority. What news on Lauren?'

'I'm guessing she's hanging in there, because I haven't heard from Emma Scott since I dropped her at the hospital this morning.'

'OK, let's presume then that it's good. If we lose her, you realise this'll have to go to CID, because something's definitely being covered up here?'

'Of course.'

'So, how close are you to Melissa Hunter's place now?'

'I'm ready to go and knock on the door as soon as you give me the word.'

'Great. I reckon I'm about twenty to thirty minutes from Donna Corrigan's place. I take it Melissa's mother is expecting you?'

'Affirmative.'

'Same goes for Donna's mother, so I'll give you a call when I get there,' and ringing off she began programming the satnav to take her to Hammersmith where, unless Mrs Corrigan had spilled the beans, young Donna was about to receive a surprise visit from the police at the very same time as young Melissa down there in North Somerset received one too. Dennis had decided to do it this way to make sure neither girl had a chance to get on the phone for a tip-off session before the other one was questioned.

Forty minutes later, after battling the usual snarl of London traffic made worse by rain, Jackie Dennis was sitting on a very comfy sofa in the Corrigans' conservatory with a welcome cup of tea and plate of biscuits on the table in front of her, and an extremely edgy, though stunning, ash-blonde teenager perched on an opposite chair. Together, Dennis was thinking, Donna Corrigan and Lauren Scott must have presented a vision to take anyone's breath away.

When she added in their musical talents and the air of rampant femininity this girl exuded, no doubt shared by Lauren until less than a week ago, Dennis could only contemplate the injustice of beauty allocation: some girls seemed to have it all, while others were woefully overlooked.

'Is Lauren going to be all right?' Donna asked nervously. 'She is, isn't she?'

'Everyone's certainly hoping so,' Dennis assured her, putting her cup down. 'It was a very serious accident though, and if she does come through her injuries are likely to take a long time to heal.' *If they ever do,* she considered adding, but decided that Donna was pale enough already.

'I wish there was something I could do,' she said brokenly. 'I mean, if it was a kidney or something, I could let her have one of mine, couldn't I?'

Touched by such generosity, perhaps naivety, Dennis said, 'If it was a match, probably you could, but as it is, the only way you can help her really is to tell us why she wasn't out with Melissa on Saturday night, when there's quite a bit of chat on her Facebook page to say that was where she was going.'

Donna's eyes immediately went down. 'I don't know why she changed her mind,' she answered softly. 'She didn't text me or anything, so I only knew what had happened when Melissa's mum called mine to tell her on Sunday morning.' She used a finger to dab a tear from the corner of one eye and continued to stare down at her lap.

'You're her best friend, Donna, and she didn't tell you where she was going, or why?'

Still not looking up, Donna shook her head.

'Is that usual? Do you normally have secrets from one another?'

'No, hardly ever. I mean, not that I know of.'

After wondering whether to shock her into looking up, Dennis chose to let things ride for the moment, simply saying, 'So who do you think she might have told?'

'I don't know.'

'Melissa?'

'Maybe. I mean, I don't think so, because if Melissa knew I'm sure she'd have told me by now and she hasn't.'

Dennis feigned a look of surprise. 'Is there a chance Melissa's keeping a secret from you too?'

Donna took a breath to answer, but only ended up shaking her head. 'I don't know,' she whispered. 'I was here all weekend. I'm not . . . I can't tell you what happened down there.'

'So what *can* you tell me, Donna? I mean, there must be something going round in your mind about all this. You've surely got some sort of theory about why she showed up at Melissa's house, but didn't end up going out with her, so why don't you share it?'

Donna swallowed noisily. 'I – I can't. I mean, I don't have one.'

'Now *that*, I'm afraid, is a lie.'

At last the girl's eyes came out of her lap. Her face was turning crimson. 'I – I don't understand.'

With a friendly smile, Dennis said, 'You're an intelligent girl, you have an imagination, so it stands to reason you must have some sort of theory. All I'm asking is that you tell me what it is.'

Donna only looked at her.

Dennis stared back, but after a few moments the girl's head went down again.

'You understand that I'm a police officer, don't you?' Dennis said firmly. 'Lying to me, or covering up for someone who's been involved in committing an offence . . .'

'She hasn't,' Donna cried, 'she'd never do anything wrong, so you shouldn't be treating her as though she's a criminal, because she isn't.'

'You can't have it both ways, Donna. If you know she didn't do anything wrong, you must know what she was doing, or at least who she was with?'

'I just . . . I just know she wouldn't.'

'Then what do you have to worry about?'

'I'm not worried.'

'Really?'

'Well, I am about her, obviously, but I know she hasn't done anything wrong.'

Dennis took another sip of her tea. 'Do you know Ian and Rachel Osmond?' she asked.

Donna frowned. 'Who?'

Dennis repeated the names.

'I've never heard of them. Who are they?'

'Lauren received a text on Saturday evening giving her their address in Glastonbury and directions of how to get there.'

Donna's colour vanished altogether.

'You do know them, don't you?' Dennis said, watching her closely. 'So who are they? And what are they to Lauren?'

'I swear, I've never heard of them,' Donna insisted. 'That's the honest truth. I really can't tell you who they are.'

'Can't or won't?'

'Can't. Honest to God, this is the first time I've ever heard their name.'

Unsure of whether she was being truthful or not, Dennis said, 'Why would Lauren have taken her flute on Saturday night?'

Donna's colour rose again. 'I – I don't know,' she stumbled. She put a hand to her mouth, stifling a sob. 'Like I said, she never told me where she was going.'

'OK. Then tell me about Parker Jenkins.'

Donna's eyes widened with surprise. 'You mean Lauren's ex? What about him?'

'Well, he's been pestering her, hasn't he, wanting to get together to talk, trying to persuade her to go out with him again.'

'Well, yes, but I wouldn't say pestering, exactly, and anyway he knows she's not interested.'

'Is he upset about that?'

'I don't know. I mean, he was, but . . .' She shrugged as her answer trailed off.

'Do you know him very well?'

'I guess so. He lives about four streets from here and we went to the same primary school.'

'So you introduced him to Lauren?'

'No, she went to the same school. She knew him from there.'

'Do you know when he was last in touch with her?'

'Not really. I think she said it was a couple of weeks ago, but she didn't text him back.'

'So does she have another boyfriend now?'

A swathe of painful colour came rushing back to Donna's cheeks. 'No, neither of us do at the moment. We've got our A levels coming up. We're having to work really hard, so we don't have time for anything else.'

'Except Lauren had time to drive into Somerset on Saturday night, apparently on her own, though we can't actually be sure of that. Was someone with her?'

'No! I mean, I don't know.'

'Which is it? No, or you don't know?'

'I don't know. I already told you I thought she was going out with Melissa . . .'

'And Melissa's already told her mother that she's keeping a secret for Lauren because it's what Lauren would want, and apparently you agree with her. That sounds very much to me like you both know a lot more than you're telling.'

'No! I only know that Melissa asked me if she should keep the secret and I said yes, because if she didn't it would be like we thought Lauren wasn't coming back.'

'She might not, Donna, so what then?'

The girl's eyes flooded with tears. 'I don't know, and I don't understand why you're questioning me like this when the only person who's done anything wrong is the one who got drunk and drove his car into her. He's the one you should be talking to, not me.'

Dennis feigned surprise. 'You think he knows why Lauren was in the middle of the road when he came up over the hill?'

Seeming to crumple, Donna said, 'No, I'm just saying, he's the one who's committed a crime, so you should all of you, everyone, go and talk to him and leave Lauren alone.'

After a frustrating half an hour further along the street with Parker Jenkins whose broken heart seemed to be well on the mend if the new girlfriend he'd mentioned was genuine, Jackie Dennis was now back in her car heading towards the M4. 'Hi, it's me,' she told Clive Andrews when he answered his mobile. 'So how did it go with Melissa?'

'I didn't manage to get any more out of her than her mother did,' he replied, sounding weary and exasperated. 'She knows something, obviously, she's not actually denying that, but no way is she going to give it up. How about Donna, any more communicative?'

'No. She's not even really admitting to being in on the secret, but I'm not swallowing that. She knows as much as Melissa, that's for sure, but whatever it is, like you said, no way are they giving it up.'

'Of course it could all be totally irrelevant.'

'It could, but there again it might not. Did you get anywhere mentioning the Osmonds to Melissa?'

'Another blank. Apparently she's never heard of them.'

'Did you believe her?'

'She sounded pretty convincing, but not knowing her, I've no idea how good a liar she is.'

'Mm, I'm left feeling pretty much the same way about Donna. I couldn't get anything out of the ex-boyfriend either, apart from how he's really sorry about what happened to Lauren, and he really hopes she gets better, but he's over her now – he's met someone else apparently – and surprise, surprise, he's never heard of the Osmonds either.'

'So what next?' Clive asked.

'Good question. Without any actual evidence of a crime I guess we've gone as far as we can for now, because we have no powers to seize phones or computers, apart from Lauren's of course, much less to shake the girls up with a trip to the station. So, what can I say apart from thanks for coming on board today? I'd hoped, with you being that bit closer to the Scotts and what's happening with them, it might have persuaded Melissa to open up.'

'I hoped so too, and I ladled it on, believe me, but her loyalty's firmly with Lauren, misguided though it might be, and right at this moment I can't see a way to change it.'

'OK, I'll catch up with you tomorrow. Let me know if there's any change in Lauren,' and after ringing off she clicked the controls on her steering wheel to take an incoming call.

'Hey ma'am,' the voice of one of her sergeants came cheerily down the line. 'It's Chester.'

'What's up?' she asked.

'Two things. First, the CPS is sniffing around wanting to know more about the Scott–Lomax case.'

'What? Why? Does he know something we don't?'

'No idea. I'll have to leave that with you.'

'OK, go on. Second?'

'Second, we've had some interesting news from the labs where Lomax's blood's been tested.'

'Oh?' she said curiously. 'Not the results, surely. I wasn't expecting them for at least another month.'

'Not the results, no.'

'Christ, don't tell me, he's got Aids.'

'Not even warm. Are you sitting comfortably? You're going to like this, but probably not a lot.'

It was Wednesday evening, just after eight. As soon as he'd finished his exams Charlie had driven straight to Gloucestershire, arriving not long after Oliver's closest mates, Alfie and Jerome, had turned up. With Russ in Bristol at some TV awards do, they had the place to themselves; nevertheless Charlie had decided to hold their strategy meeting in Oliver's room.

'I haven't had as much time as I'd have liked on this,' he was telling them, pushing his glasses up his nose as he took out the papers he'd brought with him, 'but I've been looking into it and honest to God, there's more case law around drinking and driving than practically anything else. It's a minefield, but the good news is, we've got a few ways we can go.'

'I thought you had a lawyer,' Jerome said drily to Oliver.

Turning his gaze from the dark night outside, Oliver shifted on the window seat as he said, 'I have . . .'

'And Jolyon's definitely one of the best,' Charlie jumped in. 'But he's like mentally busy, so I thought if we did some of the groundwork for him, we could take it to him when we're done and with any luck your defence will be all wrapped up.'

'And you'll have a job,' Alfie quipped.

'There is no defence,' Oliver reminded him. 'I was breath-alysed, and . . .'

'I know all that,' Charlie interrupted, 'but that's not where it begins and ends. There's all sorts of mitigation we can bring into play, what the law calls "special reasons", or "mistakes in police procedure", "duress of circumstances", "medical issues", there's loads. We've just got to work out which will suit us best. I've made a list, and at the top, for the moment anyway, I've got "spiked or laced drinks". This is where you come in, Alfie and Jerome, because if you were to say that you'd spiked his drinks at the party, chances are he can't be found guilty, because he wouldn't have known he was over the limit.'

Alfie definitely appeared impressed as he looked from Charlie to Oliver, and then to Jerome. 'I'm up for it,' he said. 'Anything to help get him out of this.'

'Sure,' Jerome agreed. 'It's just, are we going to find ourselves up on some sort of rap then?'

'No,' Charlie assured him, 'because you had no idea he was going to get in a car.'

'We can't ask them to lie,' Oliver protested.

'Oh for Christ's sake,' Charlie cried impatiently, 'do you want to make this go away, or don't you?'

'Of course I do, I just don't like the idea of my friends having to lie like that.'

'What difference does it make?' Alfie protested. 'All we've got to say is that we poured a couple of vodkas into your beer, and job done.'

'What if someone comes forward and says it's not true?'

'They won't,' Charlie told him. 'Why would they? Anyway, how would they know?'

Realising they probably couldn't, Oliver said, 'You mentioned there are other ways, so what are they?'

Charlie looked at Alfie and Jerome. 'We're OK with the first one as it stands?' he said.

They both nodded.

'Right, keeping that on the list, the next option could be for Oliver to say he wasn't driving when the accident happened.'

Oliver looked stunned. 'How the hell can I do that, when I was right there?' he expostulated. 'The car doesn't drive itself . . .'

'Did anyone actually see it happen?' Charlie challenged. 'As far as I'm aware there were no witnesses.'

'No, but it's my car, for God's sake, and everyone saw me leave the party *on my own*. Anyway, who the hell am I going to say was driving when no one else was at the scene?'

'You can say that the driver legged it. It'll be your word against the police's, and they've got no way of proving you were actually at the wheel when the car hit the girl.'

Flinching, Oliver said, 'Please tell me you're not about to ask one of my friends to say he was driving, because no way . . .'

'That's not where I'm going,' Charlie cut in. 'All you have to do is say it wasn't you, it was someone else, but you're not prepared to give his name.'

Alfie and Jerome were looking as doubtful as Oliver. 'I don't get how that would fly?' Jerome queried.

'It won't,' Oliver told him, 'because no one's going to believe it.'

'It doesn't matter,' Charlie declared, 'the point is, they can't *prove* you were at the wheel, and if they can't prove it, they don't have a case.'

Alfie still wasn't convinced. 'If it was that easy, wouldn't everyone be doing it?' he asked.

'Lots do, and they get away with it.'

'I can't see Jolyon going for it,' Oliver stated.

'Maybe he won't, I'm just putting it forward as an option. We can always throw it out, but for now we'll leave it on the table. Next is what they call the hip-flask defence. This is when someone has a drink *after* the event and prior to being breathalysed. Sure, you'll be positive, but the point is, you were sober when the accident happened, and then had a drink to calm yourself down.'

'I was in the middle of nowhere so where was I supposed to get this drink?' Oliver demanded.

'It was already in the car, vodka, beer, cider, it could be anything . . .'

'And they have the car now, so they'll know there was nothing . . .'

'True, but you could have tossed the bottle over a hedge. OK, they can go searching for it, and they've probably already combed the area, so perhaps this option is a non-starter, but I had to run it past you.'

'This is frigging amazing,' Jerome commented. 'I had no idea about any of this.'

'Why would you, when you've never needed to?' Charlie replied. 'So, next up we have mistakes in police procedure. We'll have to go through the police reports with a fine-tooth comb to check this out, but you'd be amazed to know how often they miss out one little thing, or don't use the correct wording, and if they do, the case just collapses. But since we can't know about that until we see the reports, we'll put it aside as a possible, and move on to the next. *This* is the one where I think we've got it cracked. In fact, it can't fail, provided you, Oliver, are prepared to go with it.'

'Anything that gets him off the hook, man,' Alfie said, glancing at Oliver, who was staring out of the window again.

'This is a kind of mix between "special reasons" and "duress of circumstances",' Charlie informed them, really warming to his theme now. 'Where are my notes? Right here. First up, we say you were responding to an emergency, which you were, and that already constitutes a "special reason". But listen to this, I've written it down somewhere, ah here it is, so I'll read it out: "In a situation where an individual fears serious harm to him or herself, or to anyone else, this *may* amount to a legal defence, and *may* avoid not only a ban, but also a conviction *and* criminal record."'

He looked up triumphantly and had the pleasure of being regarded with gobsmacked awe. Even Oliver had turned to look at him, though his expression was harder to gauge.

'That is it, you've got it,' Alfie told him. 'Oliver, did you hear that, man? This isn't only about avoiding a driving ban, this gets you off the hook completely, for everything.'

'All we have to do,' Charlie continued, 'is get Mum to admit that she made the call. I mean, they can easily trace the fact that she rang you that night, but what the trace won't tell us is that she was the one who actually made the call, or what she said. For that, we're going to need her to come clean.'

'I told the police,' Oliver said, daring to get excited, 'and they sent someone round that night to check up on her. That's surely got to count for something.'

'It's a slam dunk!' Jerome declared, high-fiving Alfie. 'This is going away, Oliver. The future's looking bright, my friend. Where are the beers?'

As he and Alfie charged off downstairs to fetch some, Oliver sat looking across the room at his brother. 'Do you think Mum will admit it?' he asked, trying to get his hopes back under control, while wondering, considering the state Lauren Scott was in, if he had any right to hope at all.

'She has to,' Charlie assured him. 'No two ways. Just don't start telling me that you want to protect her . . .'

'Of course I do, we all do, but I'm not going to let her problems screw up my life.'

'That's what I want to hear. It'll be tough on her, obviously, having to go public with her issues, but the way I see it, once she does, she won't have any choice but to go into rehab.'

Though Oliver didn't imagine it would turn out to be quite as simple as that, he had to admit that his brother had really done him proud with all this, and if they could prevail upon their mother . . .

Much later that night he was alone in his room, staring at Lauren Scott's face on his computer screen. For once it was a still image of her laughing at the camera. Usually he watched her on YouTube, either playing her flute, strumming her guitar, sometimes singing moody songs, or even reciting poetry. She danced a lot too, crazily, gracefully, flirtatiously . . . She wasn't like anyone else he'd ever known; she seemed so alive, so driven and passionate, and he couldn't bear to think he was the one who'd brought it all to an end. Moreover, it seemed cruel, unjustified somehow, that he was starting to see a way to help himself now, when what he really wanted, more than anything, was to find a way to help her.

*

Lauren's smiling face was filling the computer screen in Donna's bedroom. Donna was staring at it, barely able to contain her tears. She wanted her friend back so much she could hardly bear it.

'*That moment of naturalness was the crystallising feather-touch,*' Lauren recited from *Middlemarch* in a whispery chant. '*It shook flirtation into love.*'

'We all love you,' Donna wept.

The visit from the police had upset her so much, especially when she'd been asked why Lauren had taken her flute.

She knew why, but she could never, *never* tell anyone. It wasn't only Lauren she was trying to save, but herself – and him. He'd begged her to keep their secret, and what choice did she have?

Chapter Eighteen

'Emma? Am I interrupting?'

Emma looked up from her computer, feeling a gritty strain in her eyes after weeping over so many emails. It was eight fifteen in the morning. She'd be leaving around nine to go to the hospital. With Frenchay being across the other side of the city she'd decided to pack a lunch to take with her, and wondered if she should add something for Will, who'd returned from London yesterday and was now staying with friends near Bath. Harry had gone home last night, he had a family and job to attend to, but he'd promised to come again at the weekend with Jane; they'd probably bring the children too. Lauren was very close to her cousins. Rather than let her mother or Berry stay alone at a hotel, Emma had given up her own bed last night and made another on the sofa. Her mother and Berry had argued, of course, but Emma had won and had ended up sleeping surprisingly well.

'I wanted to have a quiet word while Berry's in the bathroom,' her mother said, closing the kitchen door behind her.

Dragging her hands over her face, then pushing them into her hair, Emma said, 'OK. What is it?'

'It's Berry. She won't tell you this herself, so I've decided I should do it for her.'

Emma's heart contracted. She couldn't take any more bad news, please, she just couldn't. 'She's all right, isn't she?' she said, making it a command more than a question. 'Oh God, her art show. She needs to be there . . .'

'No, no, it's not that,' Phyllis interrupted. 'She's already pulled out of it. It's Alfonso. He's had a fall and they think it might have been caused by a stroke.'

'Oh no,' Emma murmured, sorry, of course, but more relieved to know that Berry was all right. 'When did it happen?'

'She got the call late on Monday. She was going to tell you on Tuesday morning, but then decided not to, because she thinks you need her here. She's very torn, Emma . . .'

'Oh God, of course she is. Poor thing. She has to go to him. I'll tell her as soon as she comes down. Meantime, I'll see if I can get her a flight.'

Phyllis's smile was grateful. 'She'll probably put up a fight, but I think she needs to go, if only to reassure herself that it's not as serious as she fears.'

As she opened up a website to check the flights, Emma suddenly realised this would leave her and her mother alone together, a situation Phyllis, for sure, wouldn't welcome. 'I expect you've got quite a lot of commitments you need to attend to as well,' she said, trying to keep her tone light, 'so if you want to go too . . .'

'No, I don't,' Phyllis interrupted quietly. 'If it's . . . If it's all right with you, I'd like to stay. There might be things I can do.'

Not sure whether she was more surprised or relieved since she really didn't want to be on her own, Emma simply said, 'Thanks, that would be good.'

Phyllis hesitated a moment. 'I'll . . . I'll go and tell Berry then, shall I?'

Emma nodded, but still didn't look up. 'Please tell her no arguments. She's known Alfonso for over twenty years, he's always been good to her, so her place is with him now.'

As Phyllis left the kitchen, Emma tried to put aside the emotions that were rising up from as far back as her childhood and threatening to engulf her. Her mother staying here wasn't proving easy to deal with, though thankfully she was finding it easier to control herself this morning than she had for a while; possibly because she'd finally had something approaching a decent night's sleep. Or, more likely, because they were going to start weaning Lauren off the ventilator today. At last they were doing something, and though Emma was terrified of finding that Lauren couldn't breathe on her own, at least giving her the chance felt like progress.

She went back to her emails, some of which had been sent from people she hadn't heard from in years: families they'd met on various holidays when Lauren was still a toddler; teachers from Lauren's primary school; girls Lauren had been at Brownies with; a couple whose dog they'd looked after one summer, after which Lauren had begged not to give it back. There were over two hundred messages piled up in her inbox and with the exception of perhaps four or five, every one of them was expressing love and support for her and Lauren. She felt profoundly touched by them all, especially the long, emotional outpouring from Donna telling Emma what a brilliant mum she was and how much Lauren loved her, so she was bound to come back. She ended her message with a promise to be there at the weekend. *If they're still only allowing family in*, she'd said, *it doesn't matter. I just want to be near her and if I can, hold her hand.*

The headmaster was asking if it was possible to send a recording of the school choir singing whatever Emma thought appropriate. *A few are suggesting 'Someone Like You', by Adele, one of Lauren's current favourites. Salina would like to sing 'J'ai Perdu Mon Eurydice' with the school orchestra accompanying her. I've had many requests, everyone wants to do something, but I will be guided by you. Please know that my thoughts are with you, and if there is anything I can help with, anything at all, you know where I am. Henry Gibbs.*

Moved by his kindness, as well as the students' need to be in touch with Lauren, Emma sent a message back letting Mr Gibbs know that no electronic devices were permitted in the ICU so she'd be unable to play the music, but she would be sure to read the email out to Lauren for now. *Please make the recordings anyway,* she finished, *because I know Lauren will very much want to hear them when she comes round.*

Buoyed by her own positivity, she clicked on to Philip Leesom's message next. *My dear Emma, to say I was shocked by the news of Lauren's accident doesn't do justice to the terrible emotions it triggered for me, and for everyone who knows her. You don't need me to tell you what a special daughter you have, you of all people know only too well. She lights up everyone's world, and I can't believe it will be long before she is doing so again. My thoughts are constantly with you both, and if you are reading aloud to her, which I'm sure you are, I'd like humbly to suggest that you might add 'The Love Song of J. Alfred Prufrock' to the list. As you know, she is very fond of this poem, though it is a lengthy work, so if you would like, I'd be happy to highlight some passages which I believe to be amongst her favourites.*

It was a gracious and heartfelt message that warmed Emma in a way little else had these past five days. She wrote back thanking him for the suggestion and saying she would greatly appreciate his selection, which she'd be sure to read to Lauren over the weekend.

As the landline rang, she turned to reach for it, still half focused on her emails. Expecting it to be Will she said, 'Hi, are you going to be there this morning?'

There was a short pause before the caller said, 'Sorry? Am I speaking to Emma Scott?'

Immediately tensing in case it was a doctor, she said, 'Yes. Who's this please?' *Don't let it be the hospital with bad news, please, please.*

'It's Hamish Gallagher here,' he told her.

She knew the name, but how? Intensivist? Anaesthetist? Registrar?

'I'm the general manager at Avon Valley,' he explained.

'Oh gosh, yes, hello.' Her mind was suddenly whirling, trying to pick up pieces of her life from before all this had happened. The job! Of course. She'd totally forgotten.

'I hope I'm not calling too early,' he said, 'but I'm going into a meeting shortly that I expect to be in for most of the day.'

'No, no, it's fine,' she assured him. 'What can I do for you?' *Was that the right question? Why was he calling? What was she going to say if he told her she had got the job? She couldn't take it, it wouldn't be possible, but how was she going to afford to live if she didn't?*

'To be frank, Mrs Scott, Emma,' he began, 'I'd hoped to be offering you the position of Events Organiser this morning, but I'm afraid, owing to the unfortunate economic times we find ourselves in, that the hotel is not experiencing its usual flow of business, which means that the job we interviewed you for . . .'

'No longer exists,' Emma finished for him, feeling crushed in spite of knowing she'd have had to turn it down anyway. It would have been nice to be wanted, to receive some good news for a change. 'It's OK, I understand.'

'If you'll allow me to finish,' he said politely. 'The job we interviewed you for was a full-time position, but if you are able to join us on a part-time, or even a freelance basis, we would very much like you to become a member of the team.'

Emma felt shocked. This wasn't what she'd expected at all, and considering her circumstances it could be perfect – couldn't it? She wasn't sure. She needed to think. 'Do you . . . Is it necessary for me to give an answer now?' she asked.

'Not at all. I realise this might not be ideal, but . . .'

'Actually, there's something I should tell you,' she interrupted. 'The only reason I might not be able to take it is because last weekend my daughter, Lauren . . .' She took a breath. 'She was in . . . was in an accident and we don't know yet . . . It was quite serious. She's in a coma . . .'

'Oh my dear, my dear,' Hamish Gallagher murmured softly. 'I read about it of course, but I had no idea she was your daughter. I'm so sorry to hear this. What a dreadful thing for you to be going through, I very much hope it all turns out the way you want it to. Please take some time to think about this, and if you'd like to discuss it further to see if there is a way we can make it work to suit us all, I will be happy to do so.'

An hour later, while driving to the hospital, Emma was relating the conversation to Polly via her Bluetooth. 'Can you believe that?' she almost laughed through yet more tears. 'I hardly knew what to say. It's so kind and *human* that it made me realise if I can't be my own boss any longer, then he's absolutely the type of employer I want to have.'

'He sounds a dream,' Polly agreed, 'and the freelance thing could turn out to be perfect.'

'True – or a nightmare. If a big event comes in and we're

in the middle of it, I won't just be able to abandon ship if something happens with Lauren, except I'll have to.'

'Well, like he said, he's open to discussion. So, tell him what your reservations are, and if, in the end, you both think you're taking too big a risk, at least you'll have been open and honest with him, which is the most he could ask for.'

'You're right. I'll decide next week. He's given me till then to make up my mind and the great thing is, it's given me something else to think about. Believe me, I had no idea how much I've needed it. Everything's been crowding in on me . . . There's Lauren, obviously, and everything that's happening there, but there's also my family . . . I love them, really I do, but knowing that Mum's driving Berry to Heathrow this morning, and not coming back until early tomorrow . . . Actually, I'm starting to feel as though I can breathe more freely, which I'm taking as a good sign when Lauren's going to be given the chance to do so today.'

'It's a fantastic sign,' Polly agreed.

Emma smiled. 'OK, so enough about me, what do you think about what's happening to me?'

Polly gave a cry of laughter. 'Oh, Emma, you don't know how wonderful it is to hear you make a joke.'

Wryly, Emma said, 'It's feeling pretty strange, but at least I can do it. So now come on, what's been going on with you? Is the nursery back in the church hall? How's it working out with your new boss, sorry, *partner*, Alistair Wood? Oh my God,' she ran on, feeling her insides starting to churn, 'how's Melissa? What happened when she talked to the police?'

Polly sighed. 'To be honest, I'm not really sure,' she confessed. 'She's eighteen, so I wasn't allowed to be there, but from what Clive Andrews – and Melissa – said about it after, she didn't tell him anything different to what she'd told me.'

Baffled, and still not really knowing whether or not to care when she couldn't see how it would change anything, Emma said, 'So she knows where Lauren was – or who she was with – but she's not prepared to break the confidence?'

'I think that more or less sums it up.'

'Does she know these Osmond people?'

'She says not.'

Emma shook her head in confusion. 'What on earth are they hiding? What can be so bad that Melissa won't give it up even now?'

'Believe me, I've been racking my brains . . . Melissa's insistent that it isn't anything criminal, but what worries me is that it might be, and she and Donna don't realise it.'

Fighting down her unease, Emma said, 'I think the real criminal of the hour is the boy who drove into her. Surely that should be enough?'

'I agree, and Clive Andrews gave me the impression that he's not thrilled about the way the investigators are going for this. He says it's a waste of police time when they don't have any evidence of a crime, but on the other hand if these Osmond people are up to no good with girls of Lauren's age I guess it ought to be exposed.'

'I wish I knew how Lauren knows them. Are they associated with the school in any way?'

'Not that I've heard. I'll call Donna's mother and ask her, maybe she knows. I got the impression from Clive Andrews, though, that they're struggling to make a connection. Have you spoken to Will about them? Maybe they're someone he knows.'

'He says not, but I'll ask him again. I should go now, I've just arrived at the hospital and I expect I'm going to have a nightmare trying to park.'

'Are you staying all day? Maybe I could come over and keep you company later.'

'That would be lovely. You never know, by the time you get here, Lauren might be breathing on her own.'

'Oh God, I hope so. Good luck with it. I'll be thinking of you. Call if you need to.'

'Thanks,' Lauren responded with a shaky smile.

Now she was here her nerves were starting to get the better of her, and she really could have done without this problem of trying to find somewhere to park. She just wanted to get to Lauren now and be told exactly what they intended to do and when.

After finally finding a space at the top end of the site, she decided to take heart from the sudden burst of sunshine that had broken through the cloud, and was just locking her car when her mobile rang. Seeing it was a number she didn't recognise, her heart skipped a beat as she clicked on. 'Hello, this is Emma Scott.'

'Mrs Scott,' an unfamiliar voice said at the other end. 'It's Liam Grant speaking, Mr Farraday's registrar.'

Emma's chest had become very tight. 'Is . . . Is everything OK?' she asked.

'I'm sorry to tell you that Lauren has experienced another surge in intracranial pressure.'

No! No, no, no, Emma cried inwardly, clapping a hand over her mouth.

'As a result of the CT scan, Mr Farraday has decided to operate again. We thought you'd want to know that Lauren is being prepared for theatre now.'

Emma's mouth widened in a silent scream. It was all she could do to keep herself upright. 'I'm here,' she managed, stumbling out of the car park. 'I'll be there in a few minutes. Please tell her . . . Please tell her I'm coming.'

It was the middle of the afternoon by now. Will and Emma were seated either side of Lauren's bed, whispering to her softly, telling her how brave she'd been to come through yet more surgery, and not to worry because everything was going to be fine. As yet they had no idea what had caused the sudden surge in pressure, or how serious Nigel Farraday was considering it to be. All they knew for certain was that she was still with them, and that the plans to start weaning her off the ventilator had, at least for the time being, been abandoned. Mr Farraday would be coming to speak to them as soon as he'd completed the scheduled operation that had had to be postponed because of Lauren's emergency.

Emma glanced anxiously at Will as he stood up and went to the window. He couldn't see out; no one could see in. Blurred figures moved past and footsteps clipped along, out of sync with the bleep and hiss of Lauren's life support. Sharon, this morning's duty ICU nurse, was close by keeping watch on the monitors, and making notes every five minutes or so on her clipboard. What was she seeing, Emma wondered. Was everything happening the way it should, or was Farraday going to be disappointed, even alarmed by her recordings?

She wouldn't ask in front of Will. Already very much on edge, he needed no further cause for anxiety.

'Hey, sweetheart,' she whispered, putting a hand on Lauren's. Lauren's skin was warm and soft, her fingers were slightly bent, her nails as perfect as they'd been last Saturday. Her broken leg was covered, while the other was bare to mid-thigh: the expanse of tender, flawless flesh was virtually unmarked by the trauma. Her head was swathed in new bandages, white and crisp; no sign of blood, no indication of anything that was going on beneath the bulky turban. Emma wondered again if all her lovely hair had gone, or if they'd only shaved part of it away. It didn't matter, nothing did, as long as the pressure had been relieved inside her skull and the immediate danger had passed. She looked at the bruised eyelids, as delicate as a butterfly's wings, and longed to catch a tiny fluttering of life. Lauren's shapely lips were as colourless as the skin on her face, with a few tiny cuts seeming almost black against the paleness. 'Are you going to squeeze my hand?' Emma asked softly. 'I'd love it if you did.'

'You're not giving her a chance to come round from the anaesthetic,' Will told her irritably.

He was right, of course, but what was the harm in trying?

Checking his watch, Will returned to the bed and sat down again. 'All this waiting,' he complained in a whisper. 'We need to know what keeps causing this, what they're doing to stop it happening again.'

She didn't answer, afraid it would descend into an argument, and she wouldn't allow that in front of Lauren.

By the time another hour had passed she couldn't bear Will's agitation any longer. She was sure she knew what he was thinking, but wasn't prepared to ask or listen to him rant, or spout words no one needed to hear. He'd gone out a while ago, to use the bathroom he'd said, but she suspected he'd been on the phone to Jemima, releasing his pent-up emotions. If she was right, it hadn't done him any good, because he still couldn't stop tapping his foot, or sighing.

Finally, the main doors to the unit opened, and glancing out of Lauren's cubicle Emma saw a young woman heading their way.

'Hello, I'm Claudia Buckley, Mr Farraday's PA,' she said with a smile. She didn't look at Lauren, Emma noticed, realising she minded about that. 'Mr Farraday's asked me to take you to his office.'

Feeling sick with nerves and wishing she could just scoop Lauren up and run away with her, Emma rose unsteadily to her feet. 'Won't be long,' she whispered to Lauren. 'We're just going to have a chat with the doctor, then we'll be back.'

Detesting Will for simply turning away, she felt momentarily tempted to tell him to go and talk to Farraday alone while she stayed with Lauren. However, there was nothing to be gained from that. She needed to hear what the surgeon had to say, though God knew she'd like to put it off for ever, unless it was good news, of course. That she could deal with, even if it was only that they were going to continue with their plans to remove the ventilator.

Claudia Buckley led them to the very end of the main hospital corridor with all its nightingale wards spread out along one side, like barracks, and various units and pharmacies opening off the other. Finally they reached the neuro-centre reception. Mr Farraday's office was tucked in amongst a cluster of other offices at the back, presumably all set aside for surgeons and their administrative staff.

'Mr and Mrs Scott,' he said, getting to his feet as his PA opened the door. 'Thank you for coming. I thought it would be easier to talk away from the ward.' After thanking Claudia, he indicated two chairs at the guest side of his desk, one large leather wing-back and a less grand upright. Emma found herself in the wing-back, and felt suddenly trapped between Will and the window. There was almost no room to move in here, so little space for a surgeon who performed such vital work, and slightly depressing too with its dusty tomes and need of fresh paint.

Farraday's expression was grave as he folded his hands

on the desk and looked from one of them to the other. 'As you've no doubt ascertained for yourselves,' he began, 'the emergency procedure carried out on Lauren earlier has once again reduced the pressure on her brain, which has returned her to the position she was in before.'

Emma swallowed dryly and was aware of Will's fists tightening on his knees.

Farraday continued gently, 'I had hoped that this conversation wouldn't prove necessary, but I'm sorry to tell you that the outlook for your daughter is becoming increasingly less optimistic.'

Emma's heart folded in on itself. She sat back, unable to breathe.

'It's highly likely,' Farraday pressed on, 'that if Lauren does come out of the coma she will suffer from some long-term neuro disabilities, either physical, intellectual, or a combination of both. In other words, her quality of life could be greatly reduced.'

Emma was reeling; this was the wrecking ball she'd sensed heading towards her for over a week, the ball she'd tried desperately to ignore, and now here it was smashing her whole life to pieces.

Will sat rigidly, seeming ready to break apart.

'Should something like this happen again,' Farraday continued, his grey eyes full of compassion, 'I need to know if it's your wish for us to prolong her life at all costs?'

'Yes, yes, absolutely,' Emma jumped in.

'No, it's not our wish,' Will told him roughly. 'We can't allow her to . . .'

'Stop!' Emma was filled with panic. 'What are you talking about?' she shouted, rounding on Will. 'We're being asked to take a decision on whether or not to let her go . . .'

'I know what we're being asked, and I'm saying that for Lauren's sake we have to allow nature to take its course.'

Emma could hardly believe what she was hearing. 'No! Never!' she cried, leaping to her feet. 'Do you hear me? I am *never* going to give up on my daughter. She's still alive – if nature had meant to take her it would have done by now.'

'That's the point,' Will argued heatedly, 'it's trying, and medical science is preventing it.'

'No, *she's* preventing it, I know she is. She's hanging on and if you give her the chance she'll show you that she can come through this.'

'But in what kind of state? The doctor's just told you what's going to happen; she's brain-damaged, damaged, Emma, to a point that even if she lives she's never going to be the same again.'

'Don't you dare say that!' Emma wept, tears streaking down her face. 'You don't know for certain; nobody does.'

'You surely to God don't think the doctor's making it up? He's the expert, he knows what he's talking about and the impact she suffered . . .'

'I am not having this conversation,' she raged. 'My daughter is still alive and as long as she is I will *never* give up on her.

'It's not only your decision, she's my daughter too and I'm not prepared to subject her to the kind of life she'd hate if she was given the choice. Think of who she is, Emma, what she's like, and then ask yourself if you really, truly believe she'll ever be that girl again.'

'Of course I believe it. Have you never heard of miracle recoveries, and when did you ever know someone who was more of a miracle? She can do this, Will. She'll come back to us . . . Won't she?' she said desperately to Farraday. 'There is a chance, isn't there? You're not telling us that there's no hope at all.'

'What I'm saying,' he replied gently, 'is that if we have to operate again her quality of life will most probably be greatly reduced, if it isn't already.'

Emma was trying to back away, but the chair wouldn't allow it.

'I understand this has come as a terrible blow to you both,' Farraday continued, 'so I think you should take some time to think things through and try to discuss the situation rationally, always keeping in mind what's best for Lauren.'

'I'm her mother, do you really think I don't know what's best for her?'

'Keeping her alive as a vegetable isn't what she'd want,' Will seethed through his teeth. 'And think of what it's going to mean for you if she is that badly damaged. Your own life will virtually be over; you'll have to devote all your time to taking care of her . . .'

'And you think I wouldn't do that for my own baby?' Emma was close to hysteria. 'I gave birth to her, I've raised her and I'm damned well going to give her the chance to prove you wrong . . .'

'This isn't about *you*, it's about her . . .'

'Don't you dare throw that at me. Everything I do, everything I am is about Lauren. Her life is a thousand times more precious to me than my own, and I just hope to God that she never finds out that you, her own father, were prepared to let her die . . .'

Trying to calm things down, Farraday said, 'It might not come to that . . .'

'But the point is,' Will raged on, 'it might and chances are it *will*.'

'You don't know that,' Emma almost screamed.

'She's not going to have the brain capacity to understand anything, let alone why she's in the state she is,' Will cried savagely. 'She's gone, Emma, she's not . . .' his breath caught, 'she's not . . .' As he started to break down Emma felt so fractured, so helpless that she hardly knew where she was. 'She's gone,' he whispered wretchedly, 'you have to make yourself accept that.'

Turning to Farraday, Emma said desperately, 'I'm begging you, please don't let her go. She's hardly had the chance to win this fight . . .'

'She's already lost it!' Will shouted angrily.

'No!' Emma seethed, banging her fists into him.

Catching them, he said, 'Why won't you listen? What is the point of putting us through any more of this when we're never going to have the Lauren we know again?'

'Lauren is still Lauren, no matter how sick or damaged she is, and I don't care whether she can play the flute, sing, dance or even walk down the street, she will always be my daughter and I will *never* give up on her.'

Will looked helplessly at Farraday. 'Who has the legal right here?' he asked.

'It belongs to both parents,' Farraday replied.

'But if we don't agree, you can't let her go?' Emma insisted.

Farraday shook his head. 'If it's your wish, Mrs Scott, to prolong life at all costs, then that is what we'll do.'

Going to the door Will tore it open, then turned back, his face quivering with grief and outrage. 'I'm going to fight you on this, Emma,' he snarled. 'I am not going to stand by and let you put my daughter through the hell of a living death . . .'

'You're not thinking about Lauren,' she yelled, 'you're only thinking about yourself, and how this is disrupting your other life with your other family. Well go back to them, Will. Run to them now and forget about us, because we don't need you here.'

Devastation was written all over him as he glared back at her.

'You've got your other children,' Emma sobbed, collapsing against the desk. 'Lauren is all I have . . .'

Coming round to help her up, Farraday glanced at Will, but Will didn't move.

'I know she can make it,' Emma gasped as Farraday eased her to her feet. 'OK, she might not be exactly the same as before, but between us, Lauren and I are going to fight for her life, and if *you*,' she shouted at Will, 'even begin to fight for her death then I'm warning you now, one day you will have to look her in the eye and explain to her why you did it.'

'I'm only thinking of what she would want if she was here now, and able to speak for herself,' he shouted back. 'She wouldn't be as afraid of death as you are if she understood the alternative – and if she knew what you were thinking she'd hate you for forcing her to carry on, just because you're so terrified of being on your own. Well you are on your own, Emma, and so sad and wrapped up in your own self-pity that you've come to a point where you'd rather turn your own daughter into a vegetable and live through her that way than have to face up to who you really are.'

'You're such a fool,' she choked. 'You can't even see that it's you who's terrified, not me, because of how it would impact on your life and your image to have a daughter who's not quite as perfect as the one you have now. Well, don't you worry, you can carry on with your other family, while I go on loving Lauren and wanting her however she might be . . .'

'Then do it – *do it*– and in five, ten years from now when you're worn out and sick to your soul of watching your daughter suffer, or sitting by her bed wiping up her drool, don't ever forget that you were the one who put her there,' and without even saying goodbye to Farraday, Will turned on his heel and left.

Chapter Nineteen

Jolyon Crane was looking both amused and impressed as Charlie finished presenting the defence he'd put together for Oliver with a triumphant flourish. 'Well, you've certainly been doing your homework,' he declared amiably. 'I'm not sure when I last had so much case law thrown at me with such enthusiasm, but it was all relevant and apparently carefully researched.'

Charlie's youthful shoulders expanded with pride.

Russ glanced at Oliver, who'd said virtually nothing since they'd arrived at Jolyon's office. He knew only too well how much hope his son had invested in Charlie's findings. God knew, he'd weighed in with every ounce of his own, but he also knew that no matter how logical and irrefutable Charlie was managing to make this sound, the idea that they might get the charges dismissed altogether was nothing short of delusional.

'I should tell you, Charlie,' Jolyon continued, 'that special reasons and duress are certainly the line of defence we're intending to take. If we can make it work, there's a chance we could get the drink-drive charge thrown out at the magistrates' hearing. This depends quite a lot on your mother, of course, and whether she's prepared to admit that she was threatening suicide when she rang you, Oliver, and I don't believe those actual words were used, were they?'

Oliver blanched slightly as he shook his head.

'There's also going to be the question of why you didn't call your father, or a neighbour, someone who was close by who could have reacted more promptly – thereby saving yourself the necessity of driving under the influence.'

'I thought,' Charlie said before Oliver could speak, 'that

we could explain how things are with our mother, her refusal to admit she has a problem, her erratic behaviour and the fact that Oliver wouldn't have had a number for anyone who lives near her. Dad was in Gloucestershire at the time, and couldn't have gone anyway because he'd had a drink . . .' He grimaced. 'We're starting to sound like a family of alcoholics, so I guess we'll have to phrase it more carefully than I'm managing right now, but the point is, Oliver thought Mum was going to do something stupid, he panicked, leapt into his car without thinking, which is all perfectly true, no one's making anything up here . . . And actually, he did stop at one point to try and call Dad but he couldn't get a reception. That's got to count in his favour, surely?'

Jolyon didn't disagree. 'Except there's no record of the call, and even . . .'

'Because it didn't go through, but it's still on his mobile, so the time that he tried is recorded, isn't it?' Charlie turned to Oliver.

'I don't know,' Oliver admitted. 'I'll have to check. Do failed calls register?' he asked.

Not knowing the answer, Charlie turned back to Jolyon. 'We'll find out,' he said. 'Anyway, I think we can go on to describe what a toll Mum's drinking has taken on the family, not least in trying to keep her problem out of the public eye. For her sake, you understand, not ours. We can also bring up how she helped run the golden angel project, which everyone knows about, and which shows that she has a good side. And she's definitely not a bad mother, just a sad example of someone who's lost their way through drink and depression and who's got us all, me, Dad and Oliver, so that none of us are thinking straight.'

As he listened Russ could only feel thankful that neither Charlie, nor Oliver, had been around when he'd called in at Sylvie's at the weekend. He'd found her as drunk as he'd ever seen her, with Connie trying desperately to wrest the bottle from her hands, while some fellow drunk she must have picked up the night before skulked about in the background grabbing his clothes and making good his escape. Sylvie's abusive language, as she'd warned Russ and Connie to stay away from her, had been as chilling to hear as her appalling physical state was to see. If it got any worse she really was going to kill herself, and probably not intentionally.

The strain on Connie was too much, he'd realised. At her age she shouldn't have to be struggling with the demons unleashed by Sylvie's addiction. She'd insisted she could cope, but it was obvious to Russ that she couldn't, which was why he'd sent her home with instructions to try and get the good night's sleep she'd clearly lost. He'd stayed with Sylvie himself after that, never letting her out of his sight, even standing over her when she went to the bathroom. He knew how skilled she was at hiding her poison, and he hadn't been prepared to allow her another drop no matter how viciously she excoriated him, nor how violently she tried to attack him. The bruises he'd come away with on Sunday were, thankfully, not visible, but he suspected her own would be by now, given how heavily she had fallen against the furniture as she'd staggered about the place, eventually crashing into the bath when he'd tried to put her in it after she'd thrown up all over him. What a blessed relief it had been when she'd finally passed out.

Connie was with her again now, and had promised to call Paul Granger if she needed any backup.

'Tell me, have you spoken to your mother yet about how she can help?' Jolyon was asking Oliver.

Coming in, Russ said, 'I decided that we should run it past you before we approached her, to make sure we're off on the right foot and that her input will make a difference.'

Jolyon nodded understanding, and asked bluntly, 'Considering the way she is, do you think you can persuade her to speak in your defence?' He was looking at Oliver again, but this time it was Charlie who answered.

'She doesn't have a choice,' he stated baldly. 'But actually, yes, when she realises how important it is to Oliver, I think we can rely on her to step up to the plate because he's always been her favourite.'

Dismayed by this ludicrous favouritism thing, Russ simply let it go unchallenged; now wasn't the time to get into it.

Not appearing as confident as his brother, Oliver said, 'The trouble is, what Mum says one day she's either forgotten the next, or has changed her mind about completely, or she comes up with something totally irrelevant because she's got something else going on in her head.'

Jolyon looked at Russ. 'Given her condition,' he said, 'we could be wiser to ask for a sworn affidavit rather than have her appear in court.'

Russ nodded. 'I was thinking the same thing. Presumably it would carry more weight if she was undergoing rehab when she makes her statement, which would explain why it's not possible for her to appear in person?'

'It would certainly help,' Jolyon agreed. To Oliver he said, 'You understand that this is only the drink-drive aspect of the case, but as you haven't actually been charged with dangerous driving or anything related yet we'll stay with the drink-drive for the moment, because a couple of things have come to light since late last week and one of them is relevant to this charge. I'm told that the labs have, I quote, temporarily mislaid the samples of blood you provided.'

Oliver's heart jumped.

'You're not serious,' Charlie cried, astonished. He turned to his father. 'This is like totally major.'

'An excellent legal term,' Jolyon commented wryly.

Oliver was trying to keep up. 'Does that mean . . . ? What *does* it mean?' he asked.

'Well, first of all,' Jolyon replied, 'some fortuitous ineptitude is clearly at work, but more importantly, if it doesn't turn up there might not be a drink-drive charge to answer to at all.'

Oliver could only stare at him. It couldn't be this easy, it just couldn't, and even if it was, it wouldn't be fair. Lauren Scott was still where she was; how was everything going to be all right for her?

'Good old police,' Charlie was laughing, 'can always rely on them to cock it up.'

Jolyon raised a sardonic eyebrow. 'The problem is,' he said, 'if they do find themselves unable to press charges for the drink-driving offence, then they're likely to come down even harder on the dangerous driving, particularly given the girl's condition. Which brings me to the other piece of information that arrived in my email this morning: apparently Lauren Scott suffered some sort of relapse at the end of last week, and there is talk now of not intervening to save her if it happens again.'

Oliver's heart caught with horror. 'No,' he protested, 'they can't do that. She's going to make it, she has to . . .'

Jolyon's hand went up. 'I understand what this means to you, son,' he said, 'but I'm afraid it's all down to her parents. I don't know if they've made up their minds about anything yet, obviously it's an enormous decision to come to . . .'

'And what happens if she has another relapse in the interim?' Russ wanted to know.

'I presume the medics will act to save her life until they're instructed not to.'

Oliver's eyes were wild. His face had turned deathly white. 'They have to,' he growled urgently.

'Does this mean,' Charlie began hesitantly, 'are we actually saying here that she's already brain-dead?'

'No,' Oliver cried, refusing to believe it. 'She can't be, it's just not possible.'

Regarding him closely, Jolyon said, 'I'm not in touch with her doctors, only an administrator at the hospital, so I'm not sure what the official line is, but I think we can probably assume that her condition is extremely grave or they wouldn't be talking to the parents about the possibility of non-resuscitation.'

'In which case,' Russ said, before Oliver could object again, 'we'll be looking at a charge of causing death by dangerous driving, which won't only incur a ban regardless of the drink-drive charge, but a custodial sentence?'

'That is certainly the worst-case scenario,' Jolyon agreed, 'but happily we're not there yet. I'm still waiting on more information from the police investigation and frankly, with the way things are going, anything could happen between now and when this case finally comes to court.'

'Whatever happens,' Oliver broke in hotly, 'I'm not going to say I wasn't drunk, because I was.'

'Oliver,' Russ said quietly.

'No one's asking you to lie,' Jolyon assured him.

'But you're going to try and get me off on some kind of technicality, when we all know that I'm responsible for what happened. Do you reckon that's fair? What's it going to do to help her?'

Flicking a quick glance at Russ, Jolyon said, 'But it's not in our power to help her, Oliver. You must understand that. You're our concern. We have to do what we can to help you.'

Oliver's face was stricken, his eyes burning bright with emotion as he accepted the words and looked away.

After a moment's awkward silence, Charlie said, 'OK, so next move. Do we go ahead and talk to Mum?'

'Why not?' Jolyon replied, tearing his gaze from Oliver. 'If you're able to get her onside it can only help.'

'And an affidavit will do it? Won't it have to be notarised?'

'It will, and I can do that for you. I'll need to be there when she makes her statement, unless she's prepared to come here to the office and swear under oath that whatever you concoct between you is true and wasn't given under duress.'

As Russ got to his feet he was tempted to declare, *she'll do it if I have to put her in a mangle and wring it out of her*, but deciding the humour was likely to misfire, he kept it to himself and waited until his sons had left the room before saying to Jolyon, 'Oliver's becoming fixated on the girl. He's online morning, noon and night watching videos of her, reading everything he can find about her. Do you think I need to be worried?'

Jolyon gave it some thought and still appeared uncertain when he answered. 'It often goes one of two ways in these situations,' he said, 'total denial, in that the driver won't allow him or herself to know or feel anything about the victim at all; or a terrible racking of conscience that makes it virtually impossible to stop thinking or worrying about them. And now we have Facebook, and YouTube, all kinds of new media providing a false sort of connection that I can see might easily turn into an obsession. Whether that's happening here . . .' He sighed as he shook his head in dismay. 'The girl is very close to Oliver's age, and I'd say that being the kind of young man he is, he's probably feeling the responsibility as acutely as it's possible to feel it. Which, though tough on him, should serve him well when it comes to court, because showing no remorse would definitely work against him.'

Russ's irony was weighted by despair. 'Oh, he's full of that,' he assured Jolyon. 'To the point that what's starting to worry me now is what the heck's going to happen to him if she doesn't pull through.'

'How was Lauren today?' Polly asked, as Emma searched for a corkscrew. They were in Emma's kitchen which, thanks to her mother, was as clean as a new pin.

'Still managing without the ventilator,' Emma replied, looking haunted and wrecked by tiredness. 'They took her off yesterday; you know that, don't you?'

Polly smiled sadly as she nodded.

'It's good that she's breathing on her own,' Emma continued, 'but she still hasn't come round.' The dark night beyond the window started to fill with the sound of a plane going over, but neither of them attempted to guess where it might have come from, or who could be on board; it had no meaning now.

After it had passed and quiet was resumed, Emma said, 'I felt tempted to tell her why her father hasn't been to see her since last Thursday, but if she can hear me . . .' She bowed her head. 'Hurting him through her would be an awful thing to do. Do you know, when I texted to tell him she was breathing on her own he sent a message back saying it would only be good news if she'd woken up.'

Flinching at such brutality, Polly said, 'Does he have any intention of coming to see her?'

'Personally, I'd like it to be never after the things he said,' Emma replied, a wave of resentment washing through her at the mere thought of Will showing his face again.

Knowing how viciously he'd lashed out at Emma during their talk with the surgeon, and how divided they were over keeping Lauren alive, Polly said, 'My guess is he's too embarrassed to face either you or Farraday again after behaving the way he did.'

Reaching for glasses, Emma said, 'I got the impression Mr Farraday's seen a lot worse. I suppose when you're dealing with matters of life and death the way he is every day, his news doesn't always bring out the best in people.' She smiled wanly. 'That was more or less what he said after Will had gone, that people often behave out of character, or irrationally, at times of grief and stress. I'm not sure it is out of character for Will these days, but I didn't say so. What mattered more was how kind he was when he told me not to be rushed into a decision and reminded me that it will only be an issue if she experiences another surge, or some other complication.'

'Does he think it's likely that she will?'

Emma sighed shakily. 'I don't think he knows, but he says there's no conscious aspect . . .' Her voice trailed off as fear and exhaustion tried to overwhelm her again. 'He's happy to talk to me any time I feel the need, but I want to leave it for a while, because I'm sure the upshot of any further conversation now will only be a repeat of what he told me on Thursday, and I really don't need to hear it again.'

Understanding that, Polly took the glass Emma was offering and looked carefully into her eyes as she said, 'Here's to you and how brave you're being.'

Emma tried to smile. 'To Lauren,' she whispered, but before taking a sip she put her glass down again. 'I'm sorry, but to think that this, alcohol, is what's responsible for putting her where she is . . . I wonder if I'm ever going to be able to drink again. Am I repeating myself? How many times have I already said that?'

'You're completely shattered,' Polly told her. 'You should be getting some sleep, not standing here talking to me.'

'But I need to talk to someone . . .' She broke off as her mobile bleeped with a text, and going to fish it out of her coat pocket she opened up a message from Will. *How was she today? Are you still with her?*

Suppressing the urge to ignore him, or send back something he wouldn't want to read, she quickly tapped in *The same* and clicked off. 'I see no reason to expand,' she told Polly after showing her the texts. 'If he wants to know how she is, he should be here.'

'Of course he should. He's doing this to punish you for not seeing things his way. He's not thinking about Lauren at all.'

'According to him, he's thinking about nothing else, while all I'm thinking about is myself. I had an email from him yesterday explaining why he's decided to stay away – have I already told you this?'

Polly shook her head.

'He's saying that he's not prepared to go on pretending Lauren can hear us, or kidding himself that she's coming back, when as far as he's concerned Nigel Farraday made it perfectly clear that she isn't. I think his actual words were: *What you're doing, Emma, is beyond cruel and selfish, and if you can't see that then I'm almost as sorry for you as I am for Lauren.*'

Polly's eyes were full of pity. 'This is so hard for you,' she murmured sympathetically.

Unable to deny it, Emma simply shrugged and went ahead into the sitting room, where she slumped down on the sofa and let her head fall back.

'Where's your mother?' Polly asked, going to the armchair.

'At the hospital. She'll be with Lauren till the end of visiting hours, then she'll come back here. I only left because I was afraid I'd fall asleep at the wheel if I stayed any longer, but if I don't talk to someone I'll be awake again in the early hours, driving myself crazy, frightening my mother who doesn't have a clue how to handle me, and why would she when she's never even tried before, but let's not go *there* now. What I need is someone who'll tell me what they think even . . . even if it's not what I want to hear.' Her eyes were so desperate that Polly almost went to hug her.

'If you're asking,' Polly said softly, 'what I'd do in your position, then all I can tell you is that I'm absolutely sure it would be the same as you're doing now.'

As a spark of warmth flickered inside Emma, she said, 'Even if the doctors were telling you that all the chances have gone?'

'Doctors have been known to get it wrong, and *you* are her mother. I think your feelings, your instincts are every bit as important as medical science. Maybe even more so.'

Emma seemed to crumple with relief. 'That's what I keep telling myself, but I can't make up my mind if I'm delusional, or in denial, and you know what Will thinks . . .'

'He's entitled to his opinion, but I don't think it should have any bearing on what *you* know in your heart. And if you know, or feel, that there's still a chance, you absolutely have to go with it. If you don't, you'll never forgive yourself.'

'Thank you,' she whispered raggedly.

After allowing a few moments to pass quietly, Polly said, 'I'm interested to know what your mother thinks of your decision.'

Emma's eyes were closed; her head was swimming with tiredness and too many emotions. 'She says she's willing to support whatever decision I take, which means I suppose that she doesn't have the depth of belief that I do, but at the same time she's not prepared to criticise, or stand against me and take Will's side. I think that surprised me, though I'm not sure why when I know she loves Lauren almost as much as I do.'

'So how are the two of you getting along, here on your own?'

Opening her eyes and lifting her head, Emma said, 'OK, I guess, probably because we don't actually see all that much of each other now she's taken over Will's visiting hours at the hospital. Harry came at the weekend with Jane, which seemed to cheer her. You saw them, didn't you? Actually, you cooked dinner for us all. Sorry, my head's all over the place.'

'It must be reassuring to know that Harry and Jane think you're doing the right thing.'

Emma nodded. 'Yes it is, and Berry agrees with me too. I just keep wondering what they'd say if I suddenly decided that Will was right after all – and I have to admit, there's a tiny part of me that's afraid I could be getting this horribly wrong.'

'You wouldn't be human if you didn't have doubts, especially over something so important.'

Putting her face in her hands, Emma combed her fingers back through her hair and took a deep, ragged breath. 'The orthopaedic surgeon is keen to operate on her leg,' she said. 'I think they're scheduling it for sometime in the next few days. All this surgery, so much anaesthetic . . . Still, it has to happen,' she added briskly, as though to buoy herself. 'Tell me what happened when Donna and Melissa went to see her on Sunday. Did you hear them talking to her?'

Polly shook her head in regret. 'No, they wouldn't relax the rule of two visitors at one time, so all I can tell you is that whatever they said to her, they've decided to carry on keeping it to themselves.'

Emma's laugh was mirthless. 'Well, at least that shows they have some faith in her coming round, or why keep the secret? Maybe they wouldn't tell us anyway. I was thinking I'd give Clive Andrews a call tomorrow. I haven't heard from him since last Friday, so maybe something new has happened, though I'm sure he'd have been in touch if it had. Come to think of it, I must contact Hamish Gallagher too, to let him know what I've decided about the job.'

'And what have you decided?'

'That I can't take it, not even on a part-time basis, but I'll ask him to consider me for freelance work at a later stage, once things have settled down a bit.' Would that ever happen, she was wondering. What on earth did the future hold for them? 'Will was asking in his email if there's been anything in the local press about what's happening to the Lomax boy. Have you seen or heard anything?'

Polly shook her head. 'Not recently, but he must be going in front of the magistrates any time now.'

'I'll ask Clive when I speak to him. I'm as keen as Will to know that justice is taking its proper course, and not just focusing on Lauren and where she went that night.'

Jackie Dennis was at her desk, half hidden behind a mountain of paperwork, when Clive Andrews returned her call.

'You wanted to speak to me,' he stated.

'I did. It's about Lauren Scott. Have you seen her mother recently?'

'I spoke to her this morning. I didn't mention anything about Lomax's missing blood, because I was hoping it might have turned up by now.'

'You, me and the CPS,' Dennis answered, trying not to be annoyed. 'I don't know what the bloody hell's going on over in those labs, but I heard yesterday there have been a few mistakes recently, and apparently questions are raining down from on high. Which doesn't help us much, I know, but for the moment I'm afraid it's all I can tell you about that.'

'So no magistrates' hearing in the offing?'

'Not yet, no, and I'm sorry to land you with this, Clive, but I'm afraid the Scotts' case has been relegated to the bottom of my pile, thanks to a lorry decapitating an elderly couple on the M4 on Saturday night, and a father of three who went under a bus on the Fishponds road Sunday afternoon. And that's just for starters; it's been a hell of a weekend, so you're lucky you were off, and frankly I'm considering going off altogether with the way things are. How the hell are we supposed to run an accident investigation unit, or any kind of unit, when they keep forcing all these cuts on us, is what I want to know. It's a bloody nightmare. Everyone who's left is either running scared for their job and pension, or they're so busy looking for some other kind of employment they might as well not be here at all. It's crazy. We can't function like this, no one can. But just you wait, any day now some shifty little git from the Home Office, or the press, is going to be down on us like a ton of bricks over something we've missed, or got wrong, and will they want to hear that we've had our manpower reduced by forty per cent, or that the budgets we're being given barely pay for the sodding petrol to get us to a scene, never mind getting us back again? Will they hell! Are you sorry you rang in yet, because there's plenty more in my spleen that's needing out?'

'I think I'm getting the picture,' Andrews answered wryly. 'It's the same whoever I ring these days, from traffic, to CID, to the Coroner's office, which is understandable, given what we're all having to deal with, but you still haven't told me what you're landing me with.'

Dennis's heart sank. 'You're not going to like it,' she warned, 'but I know I can trust you to handle it discreetly. A journal's come to light. It was found in Lauren's flute bag and it makes for some very, how shall I put it, interesting reading. Made my eyebrows shoot up, anyway.'

'So what does it say?'

'I'm going to let you read it for yourself. I haven't contacted the school yet, you should talk to Emma Scott before we do that.' She began digging through the precarious pile in front of her. 'We finally heard back from the service provider for the mobile phone that sent the mystery text to Lauren. Turns out it's registered to the address in Glastonbury, with its direct debits paid from a bank account in London. The owner's name's escaping me for the moment, but . . . Ah, here we go. Are you sitting comfortably, Clive-o, because once I've explained to you who this is and how they're connected to both the Osmonds and Lauren Scott, you're the one who'll have to decide how to break it to her mother.'

Chapter Twenty

Oliver wasn't counting, why would he, but he guessed, if anyone asked, he'd have to say that the sequence he'd watched most on YouTube of Lauren Scott was one of her dancing, a bit like a ballerina in a cream diaphanous dress and no shoes, twirling, gliding, bending, swooping, until she lost her balance and started to fall around laughing at the end. Someone else burst out laughing too – it must have been whoever was shooting the video, probably her friend Donna, because someone had been playing the piano and Donna always seemed to be in the other videos. On the other hand, it could have been her friend Salina, because all the laughter sounded female. Salina was a quality singer, if you were into all that operatic stuff which Oliver wasn't, but he enjoyed watching the performances anyway, if Lauren was involved.

It was as if by playing the videos, over and over, he was somehow keeping her as alive as she appeared in them. Occasionally when he watched her it was as if she was speaking poetry, or singing in her smoky soul voice, only to him. She had a look in her eyes that could make someone feel as though they were the only person that mattered. And when she played the flute, all romantic and haunting, he'd watch her lips, her fingers, her chest as she breathed, and feel it doing things to him that that kind of music had never done before.

It was like he was getting to know a ghost.

He was blown away by how brilliant she was at just about everything. It was almost impossible to stop watching her. She had a real magnetic quality about her, and she seemed so happy all the time. Everything about her kind of glowed, from her skin, to her smile, to her hair, even her voice seemed to ring with joy which should, by rights, have made her seriously annoying, but somehow it didn't. It just made her seem like the kind of person you wanted to be with, all the time, and that was what made him feel so desolate and empty, he guessed, that he'd never been a part of her world, nor would he ever be now. It was as though he'd lost her, which was crazy, when she'd never been his in the first place, so maybe what he was thinking was that he'd destroyed his chance of ever knowing her, because he was the moron who'd driven his car when drunk and smashed her beautiful, golden life to pieces.

It was no wonder her friends were pointing him to suicide sites and threatening all sorts of violence towards him; he would too if he was one of them. Her friend Donna had posted a video of herself on his Facebook page saying, 'She had everything to look forward to, she loved life and we all love her, but you, you vile drunk, aren't loved by anyone. I hope they lock you up and never let you out again.'

Her friend Melissa had posted another video saying, 'On behalf of all Lauren's friends here in Bristol, I hope someone does the same to you as you did to her, because it's what you deserve. Why should you be out there living a normal life, when she might never know what one is again? We hate you, go away and die.'

He'd only watched those videos once, he'd have to be some sort of weirdo to have gone back for more, but he hadn't forgotten what they'd said, and even wondered at times if he should go away and die. After all, what right did he have to anything, now that he'd taken everything from Lauren?

He wished, more than anything, that he could go to see her. He longed to tell her how sorry he was, and how he would do *anything* to be in her place so she no longer had to be. He felt sick with guilt and horror every time he thought of how he'd almost left her that night. Thank God he hadn't, or she'd have died on the side of the road like an animal, and he'd be to blame.

'Oliver! Are you in there?' his father called from outside the door.

Quickly closing down the screen, Oliver said, 'Yes, what do you want?'

'Can I come in?'

'Sure, why not?'

Pushing open the door, Russ stepped into the room. Finding Oliver already showered and dressed, which he often wasn't first thing in the morning, seemed to smooth some of the flintiness from his eyes. 'Charlie and I are off now,' he said.

Oliver swallowed dryly. 'Do you think I should come?' he asked.

'No. Like I said last night, you should spend the day working with Paul. You don't need to be dealing with your mother right now.'

'I'm not a child.'

'I'm aware of that, but this accident is taking over your life, and you need to let it go for a while. Doing some research for Paul should help focus you elsewhere for a few hours. Most particularly outside yourself.'

Oliver flushed. 'If you were in my position . . .'

'That wasn't a criticism, merely advice. Paul's already here, he's over in the office, and Charlie's happy for you to drive his car if you need to go out today.'

Thrown in so casually, as if Oliver had been behind the wheel a hundred times since the night his and Lauren's lives had collided with such terrible force. *When we collide we come together.* Not one of his favourite songs, but it was in his mind now and he guessed it would probably stay with him all day. 'Thanks,' he said, glad his father wasn't making a big deal about him driving, the way he had the last time.

'I'll see you later then.'

'OK, good luck with Mum.' He was probably wishing it more for his father's and Charlie's sakes than he was for himself. They were desperate to get him off these charges, and obviously he wanted rid of them too, he'd have to be a serious loser if he didn't. It just seemed so unfair to Lauren, though, that he stood a chance of extricating himself from the consequences of that night when she'd never be able to.

He'd have liked to post something on her wall about how sorry he was, but he knew that having his name there would sully the page, for her and everyone else, and he wasn't prepared to do that. He wanted everything about her to stay as pure and lovely as it had been before he'd come along and smashed out all the lights.

'Are you OK?' Phyllis asked, coming into Lauren's room where Emma was sitting on the bed taking books from a box. 'Is there anything I can do?'

'No, I don't think so, thanks,' Emma replied, feeling herself welling up as she looked at Lauren's old copy of *Winnie-the-Pooh and Some Bees*. So many memories came rushing at her that she felt almost dizzied by the images that were too painfully joyful to hold on to for long. She quoted softly from *Winnie-the-Pooh*. 'Can you remember which book that's from?' she asked.

'No, I'm afraid I can't,' Phyllis answered.

Why would she, Emma thought fleetingly, she'd never read the books to her children; Emma couldn't remember her mother reading her any stories at all. 'Me neither,' she said. 'It just came to my mind.' She lifted her head, and seeing how uneasy her mother looked she straightened her shoulders to try and appear more together. 'I told Will I'd dig out some of her old children's books,' she explained. 'I think she'd like to have them read to her, so if he isn't going to do it I will.'

'I'd like to as well, if it's OK,' Phyllis offered.

Emma managed a smile. 'Yes, of course.' She paused. 'I've been thinking, it must be quite a strain on you, spending all those hours sitting next to her, so if you need to go home . . .'

'I'm happy to do it,' Phyllis assured her. Then she added, 'For Lauren, and for you.'

Emma felt a jolt inside. Before she could stop herself, she'd tilted her head to one side and was saying, 'Really? For me?'

Phyllis's cheeks reddened. 'Yes, really,' she said quietly.

Emma didn't know what to say to that, so she looked down at the book again and then held it out to her mother. 'Why don't you start with this one?' she suggested.

Taking it, Phyllis stood looking down at it, keeping it closed. Finally she said, 'I know now probably isn't the time, but perhaps later we could talk about . . . things . . . I mean, you and me and how . . .'

Embarrassed, and annoyed, Emma got to her feet. 'You're right, now isn't a good time,' she said shortly. Had her mother forgotten how often in the past she'd pushed aside Emma's efforts to discuss what was wrong between them? Emma wasn't doing this now to punish her, she was doing it because she genuinely couldn't spare the time today, or the emotion. 'What are you doing this morning?' she asked, sliding the box of books back under the bed.

Forcing herself past the rebuff, Phyllis said, 'Mrs Dempster, from along the road, is coming to help sort out the flowers and cards outside. I got talking to her when I was out there yesterday. She said you've been very kind to her.'

'Not really,' Emma responded, straightening Lauren's pillows and feeling as though the day Mrs Dempster had received a visit from a golden angel had happened years, rather than weeks ago. 'Would you mind asking her if she needs to go to the supermarket?' she said. 'They've cancelled the old people's bus, so she struggles to get there on her own.' Then it came to her who had been behind the golden angel scheme, and she felt her head starting to spin. 'Nothing's ever the way you think, is it?' she said faintly.

Phyllis was watching her closely. 'What is it?' she asked gently.

Emma shook her head. 'It doesn't matter.'

Phyllis turned away, then came back again. 'If you're going to try and keep Lauren alive through your own force of will,' she said, 'you're going to need all the energy you can get, so please let me make you some breakfast.'

Emma's eyes widened as she registered what her mother had said. She turned to look at her.

Phyllis held the look, and Emma felt unsteadied by the determination and emotion in her mother's eyes. 'You can do it,' Phyllis told her, 'and whether you like it or not, I'm going to be here making sure you do.'

*

Twenty minutes later, having eaten most of the bacon sandwich her mother had prepared, Emma was about to leave for the hospital when Clive Andrews arrived.

'I don't want to hold you up,' he said, as she let him in, 'but there's something I need to discuss with you.'

Experiencing an all too familiar churn of fear, Emma showed him into the sitting room, looking curiously, anxiously, at the heavy box that he put down next to the coffee table.

'I picked this up yesterday,' he explained. 'It's from Lauren's car; her flute case, handbag, shoes – and the laptop.' As he said the last he lifted it out to show her.

Looking at the computer with Lauren's name in thick pink pen across the front, along with stickers of her favourite musicians, Emma had to take a moment before she could thank him. Shoes? Why were her shoes there? They must have come off in the accident. What if they were broken? She wasn't sure she could bear to see them.

As he handed the computer to her, she said, 'Was it . . . ? Did it prove useful?'

'If you mean did it yield up any deep, dark secrets,' he replied with a smile, 'then I don't think so.' His face started to colour, as though he was embarrassed by what he'd said and was wishing now that he hadn't. 'The car is ready to come back to you,' he continued. 'I'll give you the address of where it is.'

'We have to collect it?'

'I'm afraid so.'

Taking a quick decision to leave that to Will, she said, 'Please sit down. Would you like a tea or coffee? I was just going to the hospital, but Lauren's leg is being operated on this morning, so I don't really have to be there until they bring her back to the ward.'

'That's very kind,' he responded, 'but I've just had a coffee.' He cleared his throat. 'A few things have happened, relevant to Lauren's case . . .'

Hating the reminder that her daughter was a case now in both a legal and medical sense, Emma heard herself saying, 'She had a good night. I rang the hospital about an hour ago. No more sudden surges in pressure, or drops either – and she's still breathing on her own.'

'That's encouraging,' he said with a smile. 'Ah, Mrs Stevens, how are you?'

'Please call me Phyllis,' she said, coming to shake his hand. 'Can I offer you a drink?'

'Emma already has, but I'm fine, thanks.'

'Apparently a few things have come up,' Emma told her.

Phyllis looked concerned. 'I'll let you have some privacy,' she said, turning to leave.

'No, stay,' Emma insisted. She looked at Clive Andrews again. 'It's good for me to have someone with me when news is being broken,' she explained. 'I'm sure I'm taking it in, but then I can never seem to remember it all later.'

He smiled sympathetically, and waited for Phyllis to sit down. 'Well, to begin with,' he said, 'I'm afraid there's been a bit of a mishap at the labs. It seems, for the moment at least, that the blood samples Oliver Lomax provided have been . . . mislaid.'

Emma became very still. 'What does that mean, exactly?' she asked.

'It means that without the results of his blood test a prosecution for drink-driving is going to be difficult to pursue.

The colour drained from Emma's face.

'Of course, we're still hoping . . .'

Emma wasn't listening. 'So my daughter is in a coma, and might even die, while the boy who put her there walks free? Is that what you're saying? Is it? Are you seriously telling me that because some idiot has lost this blood, it's all over for Oliver Lomax? Well, it's not going to happen. I won't let it, and nor will her father. That boy has to pay for what he's done. He needs to learn that he's not above the law, and that when he gets into a car, drunk, there are consequences to be paid, consequences my daughter is paying . . .' Her voice started to fracture with rising emotion. 'He's got to be taken off the road,' she cried shrilly. 'No one's safe while people like him are around. I'm telling you, he has to be taken off the road and put behind bars.'

'Believe me, I understand how you feel,' Andrews said

gently, 'and I promise you, everyone's looking for these samples, so they might yet turn up . . .'

'His father's behind this!' Emma shouted. 'That newsreader. He's used whatever contacts he has to make that blood disappear.'

'I really don't think that's the case . . .'

'How do you know? They wouldn't tell you.'

'No, but . . .'

'And what about the breath tests? They were positive, weren't they? Can't you use them?'

'Probably not on their own, I'm afraid, but I'm not going to rule it out, because I think prosecutions have gone ahead in the past based only on a breath test. And don't forget, there's still the charge of dangerous driving . . .'

Emma was suddenly beside herself. 'I can't believe this,' she cried, clutching her hands to her head as she shot to her feet. 'That boy gets into his car, knowing he's drunk, not giving a damn about anyone else, and now Lauren, my precious baby, is so badly injured that she's barely able to hold on to her life, never mind fight for it.'

Looking as wretched as he felt, Andrews said, 'Believe me, I'm not in the business of defending Oliver Lomax, but . . . I'm not sure whether or not it'll help you to know the reason he got into his car that night – it was because he thought his mother was about to commit suicide. He'd received a call from her, and was on his way to try and stop her when he . . . when the accident happened.'

Emma's eyes closed as her heart launched a dreadful beat. A strange darkness was coming over her, a weight that was unbearable, a fear that seemed to be sucking her into a terrible abyss.

'Sit down,' her mother told her, coming to her. 'Take a deep breath . . .'

Emma's head was still spinning. Everything felt wrong; nothing was making any sense.

'I'll get some water,' Andrews said.

As he went off to the kitchen he was willing his mobile to ring with news that the samples had been found, but of course it didn't. He felt doubtful that the missing blood would ever reappear. Obviously the Lomax family would be hoping that it wouldn't, and did it seem entirely fair for the boy to pay with a driving ban, even imprisonment, for dashing to his mother's aid? On the other hand, he'd known very well he'd been drinking, and he could always have called the emergency services, but hadn't, and since nothing in the world could justify the price Lauren Scott was already paying for his foolhardy errand of mercy, Andrews's sympathies for the boy could only go so far.

For Lauren, it was a totally different story: his entire heart went out to her, in spite of now knowing how she'd come to be in Lomax's path that night. Since learning the truth, he'd been trying hard to find a way to break it to Emma, and had decided in the end that she really wouldn't want to hear it from him. She needed to read the diary for herself, so he was going to leave it with her and when she was ready they could decide together what should be done.

Something Russ really hadn't counted on finding, when he and Charlie turned up at Sylvie's flat, was a strange man slumped in the bed beside her. Just thank God he'd steered Charlie straight to the kitchen, and that Jolyon wasn't due to join them for another hour – he was going to need every minute of that time to sort out this mess, plus a small miracle to get her compos mentis by then.

Connie, having found herself locked out last night, had been waiting at the door when he and Charlie arrived, still unaware at that point that Sylvie had a guest. The first she'd known of it was when she and Russ had walked into the bedroom, a moment ago, and nearly gagged at the stench that assailed them.

Chances were Sylvie's one-night stand (if it had even got that far) had no idea that his willing conquest occasionally became incontinent when under the influence, and unfortunately for the middle-aged stud this was one of those occasions.

Shaking the poor bloke awake, Russ stood over him, waiting for his eyes to focus, while Connie went to check the state of the bathroom.

As he came round, the befuddled visitor peered at Russ, looked scared, groaned at his aching head, and tried to sit up. Catching the smell, he glanced down and almost leapt from the bed. 'What the fuck?'

'I'm sorry, my friend,' Russ said quietly.

'She's only gone and . . .'

'I know, but you don't need to shout about it. Just . . .'

'Who the hell are you? What the hell's going on here?'

'I'm her husband. Now I want you to put on your clothes and then I'm afraid you'll need to leave by the fire escape.' Although tragic, the scene contained the elements of farce, he thought, with the husband bundling the lover out of the window.

It happened pretty much that way, with Russ tossing a forgotten shoe down into the street after the humiliated, unwashed Romeo had made his unseemly descent.

'I'm so sorry,' Connie whispered as Russ returned to the bed. 'I should have taken my keys . . .'

'I'm the one who should be sorry,' Russ interrupted, turning Sylvie on to her back. She snuffled, moaned, but didn't wake up. 'When you rang to tell me she'd locked you out, I should have got straight in the car.' Faced with the choice of preventing his wife from sinking herself in a vat of vodka last night, or stopping Oliver from going back to his computer to carry on tormenting himself over the girl, he'd chosen Oliver. Bad call, looking at this, but his sons would always come first.

Lifting an empty vodka bottle from under the pillow and placing it on the nightstand, he told Connie, 'You might not want to watch what I'm going to do now.'

Connie said, 'I'll go and fetch some towels.'

As she went into the bathroom Russ took hold of Sylvie's nightgown and ripped it right down the front. It was easier than trying to get it off her in the normal way.

The sight of her body shocked him, even though he'd been forced to bathe her recently. Today, the bruises she'd acquired from all the staggering about and crashing into furniture were livid purple clouds over her fragile bones, and her once pert breasts hung like empty pockets from her frame. The pubic hair that she'd always kept so neat had become a dry, grizzled patch of neglect.

And she stank in the worst ways it was possible to stink.

Next door Connie had turned on the bath; even the sound of fresh water felt cleansing to him. Taking the towels Connie brought back, he began wiping away the worst of the soiling, then sitting Sylvie up he slipped the remnants of her nightdress down over her arms.

'*Qu'est-ce que tu fais*?' Sylvie slurred, barely opening her eyes and unable to hold her head up. 'Who are you? *Laisse-moi.*'

Ignoring her, Russ whipped the sheet out from under her and tossed it on to the pile of dirty towels.

'Can I come in?' Charlie called out, knocking on the door.

'No,' Russ barked, 'your mother's not decent,' and wrapping the duvet round Sylvie in order to protect his clothes, he scooped her up and carried her into the bathroom.

'I want to pee,' she rasped in a parched voice as he set her down on the toilet.

Lifting her up again, he raised the lid, removed the duvet and left her to it.

'What are you doing?' she asked, putting out a hand to stop herself tilting any further towards the wall. 'And what is the smell?'

He didn't answer, merely tested the water and turned the taps to increase the pressure.

Her head fell forward, hanging as if her neck was broken, and for several minutes she didn't attempt to lift it. When she did, he scooped her up again and put her straight into the bath.

After a cry of protest she murmured luxuriously, as the warm water embraced her.

'Would you like me to wash her?' Connie offered from the door.

Yes, he would, very much indeed, but what he said was, 'If you could take care of the laundry, I'll be fine here,' and pressing down on Sylvie's shoulders he dunked her right under the water to wet her hair. Though she spluttered and splashed and choked when he brought her up again, she seemed to enjoy the way he squirted shampoo over her head, like fresh cream over a cake. He was brutal in the way he lathered it.

Five minutes later he pulled the plug from the bath, stood her up and turned the shower on full blast, cold.

She shrieked and tried to leap out, but he held her there, getting wet himself in the struggle, but not caring. He was going to bring her to her senses or bloody well drown her, and right now he didn't much care which proved more successful.

'Let me go! *Let me go!*' she gasped, trying to wrest herself free and step out of the bath. He grabbed her leg and forced it back.

'I hate you. You cannot do this,' she spluttered.

Only just catching her as she staggered, he stood her up again, and resisting the urge to tie her to the taps and simply leave her there, he turned off the water. 'Here, dry yourself,' he snapped, handing her one of the clean towels Connie had brought in.

She was shivering so violently that her next words barely came out. 'I cannot . . . I am . . .'

Realising she needed help stepping over the side of the bath, he took her roughly by the arms, heaved her clear and set her down. 'Get dressed and then come into the sitting room,' he ordered. 'Charlie's here, so you'd better make sure you're decent.'

Looking about to pass out, she grabbed for the wall, missed and fell into him.

'I'll send Connie in to help you,' he told her, and after depositing her on the bed, he gladly escaped the room, only wishing that he could take Charlie and get out.

'What's happening in there?' Charlie asked, as Connie disappeared into the bedroom. He looked and sounded like a much younger, less confident version of himself.

'She didn't have a good night,' Russ answered gruffly, 'but she'll be out once she's dressed.'

'Is she sober?'

Russ sighed. 'Frankly, it's hard to know whether she's more drunk at this point or hung-over, but I guess we'll find out soon enough.'

Charlie seemed to deflate before his eyes.

'It'll be OK,' Russ assured him, coming to squeeze his shoulder. 'I'm just not sure that we'll be able to get through to her this morning.'

'But we have to try,' Charlie insisted. 'It's important for Oliver that we go back with a result, and once we've explained everything, I know she'll want to help him.'

Deciding not to argue, since he had no idea what state Sylvie's conscience was in, if indeed it even still existed, Russ went to put on more coffee. He wanted to tell Charlie how proud he was of him for standing by his brother like this, but was afraid that it might, in some way, put pressure on him to achieve even more than he already had. So he said nothing, simply began psyching himself up for the coming ordeal.

An hour later Jolyon still hadn't arrived, but his secretary had been in touch to let them know he was running late. Russ felt this hardly mattered, as he and Charlie had got nowhere with Sylvie.

At first, after Connie had left, Sylvie had barely seemed to understand where they were, never mind what was being asked of her, and the copious amounts of coffee Russ had forced down her hadn't done much to help.

However, mainly thanks to Charlie and how tender he was being with her, they'd finally reached a point now where she was starting to admit that she remembered calling Oliver that night. 'I call him often,' she said hoarsely. 'He is my son, like you, so I must speak to him.'

'Yes, but we're talking about the night of the accident,' Charlie reminded her. 'You remember the accident, don't you?'

In their puffed red sockets Sylvie's eyes were blank.

'Yes, you do,' Charlie told her. 'It happened the same night that you rang Oliver to tell him that you couldn't go on.'

Sylvie blinked and looked at Russ. 'I remember I followed your father to Fiona's,' she said. 'Is it that night?'

'Yes,' Charlie answered, keeping an arm around her. 'You were very upset . . .'

She was nodding. 'Yes, I was. Your father, he is always unfaithful to me and this time was with my friend. I cannot forgive you, Russ.'

Russ said nothing. He didn't even want to look at her.

'Mum, listen, this isn't about that,' Charlie said, gently turning her face back to his. 'It's about Oliver. He really needs your help. Without it, he's going to end up losing his licence. He might even go to prison.'

Sylvie's eyes moved edgily away from his to start hunting round the room.

Russ knew she was looking for a drink; she'd even begun shaking.

'Did you hear what I said, Mum?'

'Yes,' Sylvie said distractedly.

'When Jolyon comes, he's going to take a statement from you, and we need you to say that you rang Oliver at about one in the morning and told him that you couldn't go on.'

Sylvie's attention was still vague. 'But I did not say that.'

'Yes, you did, or something like it. Basically, you let him think that you were going to commit suicide . . .'

'No, no, no. I cannot have said that . . .'

'You did, but look, the truth is, Mum, you don't really know what you said. In a way it doesn't matter, because all you have to put in your statement is that you were upset that night, or depressed, you'd had a lot to drink and you led Oliver to believe you . . .'

'I am not going to do this,' she interrupted, starting to drum her fingers on the table. 'It is not true, so I cannot.'

'But it is true,' Charlie insisted, covering her hand with his. 'And this is for Oliver. You . . .'

'Please stop harassing me,' she protested, trying to stand up.

Charlie pulled her back down again.

'I want to . . . I need to go to the bathroom.'

Getting to his feet, Russ said, 'I'll come with you.'

She looked frightened, then angry. 'I don't need you to . . .'

'I know what you're up to, you've got a bottle stashed away somewhere . . .'

'If you would let me have a drink I could do as you ask,' she cried. 'It is cruel the way you are doing this to me.'

'You have to be sober to give this statement,' Russ growled, 'so sober you will be.'

'Then I shall not give it.'

'Mum! You have to, for Oliver.'

'I do not care. I will not be ordered around in my own home.'

Forcing down his temper, Russ said, 'You'll get a drink when it's done, not before.'

She regarded him suspiciously. 'You are trying to trick me . . .'

'What I'm trying to do,' he shouted, 'is save your son from the mess *you* got him into. You got drunk, you rang Oliver and threatened to kill yourself . . .'

'I cannot say that. I will not.'

'You damned well will . . .'

'Mum, you can't deny you said it, or at least implied it. We know you did, or Oliver would never have got into his car.'

She was losing focus again, searching the room with her bleary eyes. 'I will do as you ask, after I have been to the bathroom,' she stated.

'Have you completely lost all sense of responsibility towards your own children?' Russ demanded scathingly. 'Has it really reached the point where even they don't matter as much as the next drink?'

'You are bullying me,' she moaned, tears starting from her eyes. 'You are being cruel and . . .'

'For Christ's sake,' Russ yelled, banging a fist on the table. 'Don't you get that an innocent young girl has practically lost her life because of you? And Oliver is going to pay if you don't tell the truth about the call you made . . .'

'But I cannot remember what I said. It is a long time ago . . .'

'Just over two weeks. You've poured so much vodka down your throat since then that it's a bloody miracle you're still alive, but as long as you are, you are going to do right by your son, or so help me God you'll be sorry.'

Trying to steady her as her agitation increased, Charlie said, 'All you have to do is give a statement and then it'll be over. You won't have to go to court, it'll be read out for you . . .'

'No, no. Then everyone will know my business. I don't want that . . .'

'You can't seriously believe they don't know it already,' Russ cut in incredulously. 'The whole world knows you're a drunk, so to try and start pretending you're not . . .'

'Dad, don't,' Charlie interrupted. 'If she doesn't want people to know . . .'

Realising Charlie was preparing another approach, Russ clasped a hand to his head and turned away.

'We'll keep it a secret,' Charlie told his mother. 'The only people who'll need to know are Jolyon and the judge, and when the judge realises that you have a problem, which is why you can't come to court . . .'

'I need a drink,' Sylvie gasped. 'I cannot think unless you let me have one.'

'I told you,' Russ said, spinning round, 'no drink until you've given the statement. After that, you can do what the hell you like.'

Sylvie looked at Charlie.

'You have to be sober for this, Mum, or it won't mean anything.'

'But I don't understand why this is my fault,' she cried plaintively. 'It is your father who was unfaithful.'

Not trusting himself to stay in the room for a moment longer, Russ stormed through to the bathroom. He began tearing open cupboards, drawers, the top of the cistern, and finally the panel under the bath, where the vodka had been hidden. Grabbing the bottle, he returned to the table, slammed it down hard and went to get a glass. 'One drink,' he told her furiously, 'and one coffee.'

Her eyes were gleaming as she looked from him to the bottle and back again. The pathetic relief of the addict was trembling in her hands, even her face, as she tried to unscrew the cap. It was too hard, so Charlie did it for her, but when he went to pour she seized the bottle from him to fill the glass herself.

'That's enough,' Russ barked as the level reached half an inch.

She tipped the bottle quickly, then snatched up the glass before he grabbed it first. In moments she'd downed more than half a tumbler of vodka.

Russ looked at Charlie, and seeing how shaken he was,

he removed the bottle from the table and went to pour her a coffee. 'That'll be Jolyon,' he said as the doorbell rang. 'You're going to do this, Sylvie, aren't you?'

She nodded compliantly.

Believing her, now she'd had her fix, he went to release the downstairs door, knowing they had to act quickly because the insatiable demon inside her would soon be crying out for more.

He wasn't wrong, because Jolyon was barely in the room before she began looking jittery again, her eyes shifting over to where Russ had put the bottle. Hating himself for doing it, he quickly added a slug to her coffee and set it down in front of her, knowing Charlie had seen and wanting to weep for what this must be doing to him.

Chapter Twenty-One

Emma didn't want to believe what she was reading. She needed nothing more than to be able to put the book down and somehow carry on through the day, the week, the rest of her life, as though she'd never picked it up. In truth, she'd had no right to open it in the first place, no one had. It was a diary, private, nobody else's business, but now everyone knew – at least she did, and so, God help her, did the police.

Knowing that Clive Andrews had read these entries was so excruciating that she wasn't sure she could ever face him again. Could she face anyone, even herself?

She felt dizzied, sick to her soul and desperate to believe that the last few minutes had unfolded in a dream, a nightmare, even an aberration, but it was no more possible for her to do that than it was for her to unread what Lauren had written – in her own hand – or to change its meaning, or its course.

The course was over now, had reached an abrupt and violent end. No one could have seen it coming, least of all Lauren herself.

Feeling as though a discordant flute was shrieking inside her head, mockingly, terrifyingly, she tried to make herself look down at the handwritten pages again, but flinched and looked away.

No mother would ever want to read this.

Lauren was not this person. She could not have written these words, felt these feelings or lived these experiences. It wasn't that she was too young, too old, too naive or even too intelligent to have been sucked into something like this. It was simply, please God, that this couldn't be the reason why she'd ended up in the middle of nowhere the very same night, same time even, that Oliver Lomax, drunk and distressed, had been on a mission to try and save his mother.

Yet it was the reason; it had to be.

The hand of fate was too cruel; it reached so maliciously for the undeserving that Emma could only wish it had found its own throat.

What had happened to Oliver Lomax's mother? Had she succeeded in the attempt to end it all? Emma presumed not, or Clive Andrews would have told her. Was she still suicidal, depressed, riven with remorse for what had happened to her son, and to the girl he'd all but killed with his car? Emma didn't want to care about that family; they meant nothing to her. Yet whether she knew them or not, their lives, their futures were intertwined now in a way that was as irrefutable, irrevocable, as the unthinkable events that had projected Lauren into their world.

Lauren had obviously taken great care to conceal the man's identity; in the diary he was only referred to as S, and there was nothing on her mobile phone to give it away, apart from the mysterious number.

Emma still didn't know for certain whose number it was, but after this it was easy to guess. She'd call Clive Andrews in the morning to ask if she was right – he must know by now who the phone belonged to. So why hadn't the police acted?

Andrews's words, when he'd told her about the diary, came back to her. 'Lauren's age means that no crime has been committed, but we will need to contact the school.'

Emma gave a sob of despair. She didn't know what to do. Should she show the diary to Will? No, she couldn't. No father should ever have to read this about his daughter, especially not written by her own hand. The mere thought of how he'd respond caused Emma to shrink inside. He'd blame her, of course, but she could cope with that – what frightened her was the kind of action he'd want to take. His anger, his need for revenge would be justified; God knew she felt it too, but how was it going to help Lauren now?

Hearing her mother coming out of the bathroom, she

put the diary under her arm to take with her, into her own room. This room was where her mother was sleeping; she didn't want her happening upon these chilling lines written by a granddaughter she'd always considered so sensible and pure.

Having to force down the wall of hatred that was rising up from her anger, Emma tried to breathe normally as her mother came into the room.

'Are you all right?' Phyllis asked. 'You're very . . . Something's wrong, isn't it? I didn't hear the phone ring.'

'It didn't, and I'm fine. I . . . I'm just thinking about the operation and how sad it was she didn't come round when the anaesthetic wore off. I was hoping she might.'

Phyllis's frown relaxed. 'I thought you were. I was too, but it's good you were there. I'm sure she senses it.'

Emma's head went down. Her mother's new sensitivity was welcome, but also jarring. 'I should . . . let you get some sleep,' she said, moving away.

'Emma, what is it?' her mother said softly. 'I can tell there's something.'

Surprised, even unsettled by how easily her mother seemed to read her, when they were hardly close, had never even confided in one another before, Emma turned back. 'It's nothing,' she said. 'I just . . .' Tears started in her eyes and she put a hand to her head. 'I'm sorry, I can't discuss it. I . . .'

'Yes you can,' Phyllis told her, firmly. 'Whatever it is, I might not be able to make it better, but we won't know unless you let me try.'

Emma's eyes went to hers, unsure of this woman who'd always shut her out before. She was inviting her in now, but Emma was afraid to take a step forward. She'd done it in the past, only for her mother to turn suddenly cold or dismissive. She wouldn't be able to bear it if she did that now.

'I'm just tired really,' she said. 'And a bit confused, I suppose.'

'About what?'

Emma sighed. 'I guess what I should tell Will about the missing blood sample, and Oliver Lomax's mother . . . It doesn't matter. I don't have to think about it tonight.'

305

'Shall I make you a hot drink?'

'No, thanks. I'll be fine. Are you going in tomorrow morning, or am I? I can't remember what we arranged now.'

'We thought I should go in the morning, but if you'd like to change . . .'

'No, it's fine. Let's keep it like that.'

It wasn't that she didn't want to see Lauren, she simply didn't know at this point how easy she was going to find it to look at her and see the same daughter she'd always believed she'd known almost as well as she knew herself.

In order to be at the hospital for the start of visiting at ten, Phyllis had left the house just before nine, taking the two books Emma had given her to read to Lauren, *A House is Built at Pooh Corner* and *Alice in Wonderland*. Later, Phyllis would show Emma the chapters she'd read aloud, and Emma would settle down to pick up from where Phyllis had left off. This was the routine they'd fallen into, but today, inevitably, was going to be different.

A few minutes ago she'd spoken to Clive Andrews and had her worst fears confirmed – S was indeed who she thought he was. After the call, she'd gone upstairs to fetch the dreaded book, not sure what she was going to do with it – torment herself with more of the exploits?

Waves of nausea and despair came over her as she recalled some of the more lurid entries, so beautifully crafted in Lauren's flamboyant prose; words carefully chosen, playful, charming, eloquent in their own right, but so *appalling* when their meaning formed the kind of scenes she was describing. Emma couldn't read them again; she might even tear the book up and burn it. It wouldn't erase the past, but at least it would prevent anyone finding it in the future.

She'd never dreamt, when she'd bought Lauren this expensive, leather-bound journal, that it would be used for something like this.

How had Lauren and Donna managed to keep it to themselves? What kind of mother was she that she had never even suspected? Had Ruth Corrigan? Surely not, or she'd certainly have said something to Emma by now. She recalled the guilt (and pride) she used to feel when her friends in London battled with their wayward teenage daughters, while Lauren – and Donna – had seemed almost perfect by comparison. If anyone had known – thank God they hadn't, and if she had anything to do with it they never would.

Hearing a knock on the door, she quickly slipped the diary into a drawer and went to find out who it was. She was half expecting Mrs Dempster to come and remove more dead flowers from outside the house, but to her surprise, it was Polly. 'What are you doing here?' she cried, as she let her in. 'Shouldn't you be inundated with children at this hour?'

'We're not quite back up to capacity yet,' Polly grimaced, planting a kiss on each of her cheeks, 'so Jilly and Margaret can manage for a while. Is everything OK? Actually, straight to the point: your mum called to say she thought you might need to talk and as you won't open up to her . . .' she tilted her head to one side, 'maybe you will to me? Or has she got it wrong?'

Closing the door, Emma said, 'No, she hasn't got it wrong. In fact, she seems to be getting things amazingly right at the moment, for her. Would you like a coffee? I was about to make one.'

'Look at me and you'll see a person who's gagging. I should have thought to bring some pastries. Anyway, on a more relevant note, it was a great relief to get your text yesterday saying that the op went well.'

Emma reached for the kettle, feeling slightly dizzied by the thought of Lauren's compound fracture. It seemed so minimal when compared to everything else she was going through, and oddly comforting, since it was something that could be repaired. 'Apparently all the rods and pins are in place now,' she said. 'I haven't had the conversation yet about how her comatose state might affect its ability to heal, but obviously I'll have to at some point.'

'And what about Will? Did he put in an appearance?'

'No, but he says he's coming at the weekend, and he's emailing and texting all the time to check how she is. Did you know this, have I already told you, no it was Harry and Jane I told . . . Apparently, Will actually spoke to Yuri Nelson, the consultant intensivist, on the phone about organ donation. Just like that, not a word to me, he just rings up and has a little chat, giving his permission, as if he's talking about a bloody church collection.'

Polly's eyes dilated with shock. 'Is he even allowed to do that without your agreement?'

It was a good question, and Emma wished she could give her a different answer. 'Actually, it's not relevant because Lauren registered herself a couple of years ago, and now she's eighteen they don't need anyone's permission.'

'Oh God,' Polly groaned in sympathy. 'But I'm sure it's not going to come to that, in fact I know it won't.'

Emma smiled her gratitude and tried to remember what she was supposed to be doing. Making coffee. Had she put the kettle on yet?

Watching her, Polly said, 'I'm getting the impression your mother's not worrying unnecessarily. You don't seem yourself, at all.'

Emma tried to make a joke about being a bad actress, while dropping several spoonfuls of the fresh coffee her mother had bought at Sainsbury's yesterday – Emma was down to Aldi instant now to try and reduce her budget.

'Emma?' Polly prompted gently.

'Actually, before I answer, I need to ask if Melissa's been any more forthcoming about Lauren's big secret.'

Appearing surprised, but then regretful, Polly shook her head. 'I'm afraid not, but believe me, I haven't given up trying.'

'Well, you can now,' Emma told her, 'because I know what it is, and it's not . . . It won't be . . .' She swallowed hard. She had to tell someone; she couldn't go on carrying this alone, and she'd always trusted Polly before. Moreover, Polly wasn't family, so for her the shock wouldn't be quite so shattering. 'The police found her diary,' she said. 'The things she's written . . . If it weren't her handwriting, her book, I'd swear someone else had made the entries, but they're definitely hers and now I'm not sure . . . I can't even *think* what to do about it.'

Looking confused and worried, Polly asked, 'What sort of things is she saying?'

As she started to recall them, Emma's insides turned rigid; she couldn't speak the words aloud, she just couldn't.

'Oh my,' Polly murmured, appearing more anxious than ever.

'Don't worry, I'm positive Melissa's not a part of it,' Emma said hastily, 'but Donna is.' Taking the diary from the drawer, she opened it, then closed it again, as if the horror of the entries was escaping the page like poison. 'If you have the time,' she said, 'I can go through to pick out the less . . . the sections that aren't quite so . . . Well, you'll see what I mean.'

'OK, that's fine,' Polly assured her. 'I'll carry on with the coffee and come and join you when you're ready.'

The first entry Emma chose to show Polly, though less explicit than most, still left little to the imagination, and had, according to the date, been written with great exuberance about a week before the accident.

I've never felt this nervous – or excited – before. Or totally wicked in every sense of the word. Absolutely no one knows where I am right now, apart from Donna who was supposed to be coming too, but she's gone down with flu. Mum thinks I'm babysitting at Dad's; Dad thinks I'm at Mum's for the weekend. Not even Melissa knows, but I'm thinking about telling her next time I'm down there.

Of course S knows where I am. This is his friend's place. I so love it here.

Just thinking about his real name makes my insides flutter like a glorious capriccio. I can almost play its sound, lively, thrilling, utterly and completely orgasmic.

I adore nothing more than orgasms with him. I want them to happen over and over and over again. In the dark of night, when no one else is awake, I sometimes use my fingers to revisit the places he's touched on my body during blissful moments in the day when doors are closed and eyes are turned the other way. Playing solo is exquisite in so many ways, each note sounding perfectly, each phrase vibrating torrents of pleasure all the way through me, but nothing, simply nothing, can compare to the

moment when the fugue of our desire soars pianissimo, scher-
zando, fortissimo, fortissimo, fortissimo . . .

He always teases me about the musical terms I use, and yet
he seems to embrace them as hungrily as he embraces me. I
watch him in class, touch my tongue to my lips and know what
is happening to him. He wants to take off all my clothes and
spank me for being mischievous. Later he will.

This will be the first time we've spent a whole night together.
He sent me a text earlier saying he was looking forward to the
undoing of our inhibitions, the careless tossing of them to
the winds, and the incredible journey to abandoned fulfilment.
He wants to find me clothed only in the glow of the flames when
he arrives, so I have already removed everything I was wearing.
I feel beautiful and alive and daring almost beyond bearing.

I love you S; do as you will with me, and let me do as I will
with you.

The second entry Emma decided on had been written only
hours, perhaps even minutes, before the accident.

In spite of arriving in the dark, and never having been to this
part of Somerset before, I managed to find the cottage and the
keys with hardly any problems at all. This place is almost as cute
as I imagined it to be, small, with only a kitchen-cum-living
room downstairs and apparently only one bedroom upstairs, but
I haven't been up yet to investigate. I think it must have been a
while since anyone was last here, because it smells a bit fusty
and seems to have no heating that works. Thank goodness Mum
made me bring a coat. Even so, I've wrapped myself in a throw
from the back of this very lumpy sofa, and my feet are snuggled
inside a bedspread that I found in an old chest under the stairs.

I wonder how many people he's bringing, I think he said only
two, which is good, because there aren't many places to sit. I
think I shall stand in front of the window to play, with the
curtains pulled of course. I have to admit I'm a little nervous
about performing on my own, without Donna. I've chosen three
pieces: 'Andante in C major'; 'Syrinx' and 'Fantasie'. He said
they should all be classical for tonight's connoisseurs. I can't
wait to tell Donna about it tomorrow. She's so mad with her dad
for making her stay in London, but we had a really fab time just
the three of us earlier in the week when he came to watch us

rehearsing. I wrote about it the day it happened, so I won't go into detail again here, even though I love thinking about it and can't wait for it to happen again. Donna's mad keen for it to happen again too. It's funny, but we never undress in front of one another normally, only in front of S which is so unbelievably cool. In the summer he wants us to play our guitars in the middle of a field, naked, and we can hardly wait.

He should be here soon. He sent a text about an hour ago to say he was about to leave, which I read a thousand times before I erased it, because he also said that he'd be able to stay on for a while after the others have gone. I know it can't be for the entire night, but that's OK. I mean, it's not, because I want to be with him every minute of every hour of every day, but as that can't be possible I'm happy, delirious to know that he wants to see me so much that he's making it happen again this weekend.

I can hear the sound of audience laughter coming from a TV next door, and every fifteen minutes the tinny chime of an old carriage clock on the mantelpiece whirrs into action. I'd love to call Donna or Melissa to while away some time. Melissa's been dead cool about covering for me tonight. She was totally blown away when I told her who I was seeing. I know I can trust her, and she knows she can always trust me.

A car just pulled up outside, and a host of butterflies has taken off inside me. I'm so dying to see him. I'm going to fly into his arms and kiss him all over his face and he'll laugh and scoop me up and twirl me round and around.

Disappointment reigns. Whoever it was has gone into another of the cottages, so I'm still waiting. He really should have been here by now, so I wonder what's keeping him. Maybe one of his friends has let him down, but that shouldn't really make a difference.

It's almost one o'clock in the morning now and I've just received a text telling me that he's really, really sorry, but he can't get away after all. I feel so crushed that I want to cry, I feel foolish too, and angry and I wish I'd never come.

It was how Emma felt when she finished reading, that she wanted to cry too, and scream and rage against the pervert who'd led her daughter to write these words. The passages she'd chosen were bad enough, but Lauren's graphic descriptions of the sex act itself, the size and rampancy of his penis, and what, on several occasions, he'd persuaded her to do with her flute were paragraphs she'd never show to anyone, or ever read again.

It took Polly no more than two minutes to read the selected entries. By the time she'd finished she looked every bit as horrified as Emma had expected.

'So now we know why she took her flute,' Emma said hoarsely.

Polly swallowed dryly. 'So do you . . . Do you know who this S person is?' she asked.

Emma nodded. 'Yes, I do. He's her English teacher. His name's Philip Leesom. The S stands for sir.'

'Jesus Christ,' Polly muttered, not even wanting to imagine the more explicit details of the journal; what she'd read was lurid enough. 'So that's where she was, the night of the accident, waiting for him and . . .'

Emma's fury was barely containable. 'She drove all the way to Glastonbury to meet him, to *perform* for him and God knows who else, and in the end he didn't even bother to turn up. If he had, her path would never have crossed Oliver Lomax's, but how can I wish that he had when this is what was going on?'

Polly had no answer to that.

'If it weren't for him,' Emma raged on, 'she'd have been out with Melissa that night, which is where she damned well should have been.'

Polly put the diary down; her expression was grave and full of sympathy. 'So what are you going to do?' she asked.

Emma threw out her hands. 'I don't know. If I tell Will . . . He'll want to kill him.'

'Maybe you should let him.'

Emma didn't argue. 'Or maybe,' she said fiercely, 'I'd rather do it myself.'

Much later in the day Emma was sitting with Lauren, gazing down at her still bruised face, though the purple was fading to yellow now and the cuts were starting to heal. She was like the calm at the eye of a storm, with so much raging around her, tearing up truths, shattering trust, changing the shape of beliefs, yet nothing was able to reach her. It frightened Emma to sense an invisible barrier between them, one that left her on the outside looking in at someone she loved who seemed like a stranger.

That was absurd, she told herself. Whatever Lauren had done, no matter how deep her crush had been on that man, or brazen her actions, she was still the daughter who had made Emma's heart sing, her life worth living. She must hold on to that truth, and never let that man's corruption overshadow it. What he'd done was in the past, and could never happen again.

Since arriving she'd barely spoken to Lauren; had simply sat staring down at her, wishing there was a way to erase every word of what she'd read from her mind, scour out the appalling images that those heady, graphic descriptions conjured of her precious daughter as the sex object of a man who had the trust of every parent at the school. He had so grossly abused his position to seduce two silly, impressionable young girls, one of whom, Lauren, had been a virgin until she'd naively, joyously yielded to him.

What a heartbreaking entry that had been to read. Emma didn't care that he'd been 'tender and loving, passionate, sweet, funny and touchingly emotional' when it was over. The thought of his tears made her want to be sick. She kept wondering how much longer it would have taken him to persuade Lauren and Donna to become intimate with the friends he invited along to watch them perform. It had certainly seemed to be heading that way, from what Lauren had indicated.

It made her want to wrench out her hair and scream to recall the way he'd flirted with her. Worse was the way she, like one of his adoring ingénues, had responded. Had she been in line as one of his next conquests? Was that what the book recommendations and a coffee at the library had been about? Or did it just give him a kick to know that he could be on friendly terms with the parent of a girl he was sexually abusing? She shuddered with revulsion, and wondered how she could ever have found him attractive when, since reading the diary, she'd felt sullied by the mere thought of him, *contaminated* by his

313

duplicity, his evil. If it weren't for him and his arrogance, his manipulation and filthy lechery, Lauren would not be lying here plugged helplessly into a system of life support, while he, exhibiting no signs of a troubled conscience, remained free to continue his career of debauchery and violation.

Well, it was at an end now, that was for sure. Emma had decided what she was going to do. By this time tomorrow he would be fully aware of what the outrageous exploitation of his position was going to cost him.

Chapter Twenty-Two

Emma hadn't expected it to feel strange sitting on a train, but it did. It was like revisiting an old habit she'd picked up again after many years. It seemed startling to see the weather spreading out over the countryside too, as though it hadn't been happening where she was, and was now doing its best to show how friendly it could be. She felt disconcerted watching busy people going about their day, apparently as familiar with their surroundings as they were with the language they spoke. This was the world outside the bubble she'd been in for the past three weeks: here sounds weren't muted and the air seemed clearer, less clouded, a place where she could almost float.

She hated leaving Lauren trapped in the bubble, but her grandmother was with her and she was receiving the best care the hospital could offer, so slipping away for a few hours should be all right, and this was something she had to do.

It felt freeing, and yet unnerving, to be travelling at high speed through fields that sparkled in late winter sunshine and stretched as far as the eye could see. She was remembering other journeys she'd made on this line or on other trains, so many down the years, almost always with Lauren and usually with Will. She could see Lauren, aged three, standing on Will's lap clapping her hands in delight as they passed cows and sheep; or chatting to other passengers about where they lived, or the different places they'd been for their holidays. She could hear her girlish laughter, her music, her excitement for new adventures or friends. She was always so full of sunshine and exuberance. Her whole life had seemed charmed, from her looks, to her nature, to the God-given talent and compassion that had made her who she was – who she'd been – until twenty-three excruciating days ago.

Emma felt herself starting to freeze inside. Lauren had changed before that, without her noticing. Things had happened to her, been done to her, to turn her from a girl into a woman, an innocent into someone who'd seemed to exult in the acts she was performing for a man who was unashamedly exploiting her schoolgirl crush. It didn't matter that she was eighteen; he'd broken every possible rule of moral conduct and teacher responsibility there was to break. Lauren Scott wasn't there for him to use as his plaything and whether she had been a willing party or not, he simply could not be allowed to get away with what he'd done.

Feeling the tightness of more anger clenching her insides, she put her head against the window and forced herself to breathe slowly, deeply. She knew how she was going to handle this, had worked out exactly what she was going to say, but the emotion tearing through her heart could easily steal her resolve and send her reeling into a quagmire of useless despair. She needed to stay in control, make sure that he understood every word she was saying and was left in no doubt at the end of it that his career was over. The evidence of his corruption was tucked safely inside her bag, photocopies of the extracts she'd shown Polly yesterday. She hadn't been able to bring herself to return to the more explicit entries, nor had she wanted to run the unthinkable risk of them having some kind of prurient effect on him.

Opening up her mobile as it bleeped with a text, she was glad to see it was from Polly. *Still think you should have let me come with you, but I'm there in spirit. Please don't rule out calling Will. I understand it might turn violent if you do, but can't honestly see the harm in that. B . . . deserves it. Call as soon as you can. Will be there to meet you off train. Px*

A part of her was wishing that she had let Polly come with her, or Will, but this was something she had to do alone, even though, like Polly, she wouldn't have minded at all if Will knocked Philip Leesom to the furthest-flung reaches of kingdom come. However, she simply couldn't bear Will to know how Lauren had behaved; nor, if the time ever came and please God it would, did she want Lauren to have to face the shame of her father knowing that she was capable of even writing such explicit sex, never mind engaging in it. She knew she'd eventually have to tell Will at least some of what had gone on; he was still agitating for answers to where Lauren had been that night, and better she broke it to him than the police. By then the diary and all evidence of it would be long gone, and so too, she hoped, would Philip Leesom.

Out of nowhere she found herself thinking of Oliver Lomax and his family, and wondering what they were doing now. Had anything improved for the mother? Had the blood sample turned up? She didn't really care, but she couldn't *not* care either, when, as far as she could tell, Oliver Lomax was no more to blame for his mother's addiction than Lauren was for Philip Leesom's exploitation. They were victims, both of them, of people they trusted and loved.

It was just after three thirty when Emma walked through the arch beneath the soaring clock tower of the school's main building and began threading her way through the corridors – high, bright passageways, enlivened by vibrant teenage art and noticeboards promoting all kinds of meetings and activities. She passed no one – most students were still in class, or taking study periods in the library, or in the sports hall in another building. She knew, from Lauren's roster, that Leesom was taking Upper Sixth for a double period till four, a class Lauren would have been attending if Leesom hadn't been the guiding hand of this stage of her journey through English literature. Given the choice she'd obviously prefer that Lauren was still under his influence rather than where she was now, but she didn't have the choice. That had been taken away from her the night he'd enticed Lauren down to Glastonbury for the sole purpose of the sick entertainment of him and his friends.

Though she was shaking inside, now she was here she had no doubt she could go through with this, though God knew she longed for it to be over.

317

On reaching the windows to his classroom, big and wide, allowing a clear view in from the corridor, she stopped and spotted him almost instantly, leaning against a wall next to the board, his large, muscled arms folded, his beautiful Byronic head tilted to one side as he listened to a student reading or reciting, or perhaps commenting on a text. Emma didn't know, nor did she care; she simply fixed her eyes on his sickening face and waited.

It took almost no time for his head to come up; from the way his expression changed she knew that he knew straight away why she was there.

If he didn't come out, she was ready to go in, if necessary she'd begin the showdown in front of the class, but he didn't waste any time in excusing himself and coming to the door. As she moved forward she caught a glimpse of Donna's frightened young face, but she couldn't deal with her now. All her focus was on Leesom, and as he let himself out into the corridor, rapidly closing the door behind him, she brushed aside his ludicrous attempt at surprise and concern, and headed for his office.

'I didn't realise you were coming,' he babbled cravenly as he followed on behind her, his usual aplomb deserting him. 'I sent an email. Did you get it? I was hoping . . .' His voice trailed off as someone passed from the other direction.

Finding his office door locked, Emma stood aside and waited for him to open it, trying not to think of the diary entries recounting how he'd turned the key from the inside to make sure he and Lauren weren't disturbed. A flash of pure rage fired up inside her, making her want to smash her fists straight into his head and ram it into the door frame as he leaned forward to insert the key.

She stepped into the room ahead of him, waited for him to follow, then taking the door she slammed it shut.

'Emma, what's happened?' he cried, looking extremely nervous.

'You know what's happened,' she told him in a danger-ously low voice. 'I'm not going to demean myself by spelling it out, all you need to know is that today is your last at this school, or any other. You will *never* have access to young girls again to corrupt and abuse them the way you have with my daughter.'

'Emma, wait, wait . . .'

'This is the end of your career,' she pressed on. 'I want you to come with me now to the headmaster's study to explain why you are handing in your resignation and why it must be effective immediately.'

A guilty colour was creeping up his neck; his moodily romantic eyes were sharpening with fear. Yet somehow his voice was smooth as he said, 'Emma, I don't understand. Why are you . . . ?'

Her voice was shaking, so was she. 'I have written evidence here in my bag of the things you've done to Lauren. They are so disgusting they make me want to *kill* you. If her father knew, you can be sure he would.'

'Please, you have to listen to what I'm telling you. I don't know what you . . . This evidence . . . I . . .'

Emma's eyes bored into his. 'It's her diary. She wrote it all down.'

Shock stripped the colour from his face. 'But – but you must understand that young girls of Lauren's age are very fanciful, hormonal . . .'

'Don't you dare try that with me! There was nothing fanciful or hormonal about *your* friends' address on her mobile phone. And what the hell is fanciful or hormonal about where she is now? I'm holding you responsible for what's happened to her, I hope you realise that. If it weren't for you she'd never have been on that road, and that wretched boy would never have hit her. *You've ruined her life*. She'll probably never be the same again, and *you* are wholly to blame for that.' She sobbed, caught her breath and forced herself to go on glaring at him.

'Emma, you've got it wrong,' he told her urgently. 'I swear I've never laid a finger on her in the way you're thinking . . .'

'Then call Donna Corrigan in here. Let's see if you can deny it in front of her.'

'But there's no need for that . . .'

'I can always get her myself.'

'Please, Emma, try to think of what you're doing. Is this

really what you want for Lauren? She's a good, sweet girl with . . .'

'Don't speak about my daughter in that tone,' she seethed, clenching her fists to stop herself slapping him. 'I never want to hear you utter her name again. Now I want you to come with me to Mr Gibbs so we can get this over with.'

He shook his head in helpless dismay. 'I'm sorry, I can't do that, because you're making a terrible mistake . . . What are you doing?' he cried as she marched to his desk and snatched up the phone.

'I'm asking the head to come here.'

'No, don't,' he protested, coming to wrest the phone from her. 'We can sort this out . . .'

'And I've already told you how we're going to do it. There's no room for negotiation.'

'But there has to be. Think of the girls we've just left. They're about to sit some of the most crucial exams of their lives. Do you seriously want me to walk out on them now?'

'What I want is that you never set eyes, or hands, on any one of them ever again. They're far enough into their studies to make it without you now, and even if they weren't, A levels or no A levels, do you seriously think there's a parent alive who'd want you within a mile of their daughter if they knew what you'd done to mine?'

'But I haven't done anything to yours. Whatever you've read, whatever Lauren's written, it's all in her mind.'

Emma could feel herself losing ground, becoming undermined by his insistence. How sure was she? Where was her proof? She suddenly couldn't think.

Seizing the moment, he said, 'I'm afraid this isn't the first time I've been accused of an improper relationship with a student. There was another girl, the year before last, who told her friends we were romantically involved. It was all a fantasy; a way of making herself seem special, more important, I suppose.'

'Lauren would never do that. And she wouldn't have the first idea about any of the things she's written about if you hadn't taught her.'

He was shaking his head; his eyes were burning a plea.

'I'm afraid you're underestimating the imaginations of eighteen-year-old girls, but what's more important here, as I see it, is the degree of stress you're under at this time. I can quite understand why you're getting things out of perspective, anyone would in your position. And I'm truly sorry that you had to find this diary of Lauren's, because obviously what she's written has added greatly to the dreadful ordeal you're going through.'

She was hearing his words, even thinking that he could be right, because somehow he was making a certain sort of sense. Half out of her mind with fear and worry, might she be capable of misconstruing or not even understanding what was in front of her eyes? Her heart twisted with anguish. She was losing her thread, forgetting what she needed to say. But then she remembered her call to Clive Andrews, the address he'd told her was on Lauren's phone, the number it had come from, who it was registered to, and suddenly it was as though everything around her was erupting all over again. She couldn't take any more. She barely knew what she was saying or doing as hysteria streamed out of her uncontrollably. She looked around desperately for anything she could throw at him. She wanted to smash the place up, the way her own life had been smashed up. Her daughter was dying, might even already be dead, and *she* was keeping her alive because she was too selfish to let her go. She didn't know what to do any more. Everything was crashing in around her. She was a terrible mother; terrible things had happened to her child and now she was being punished by a god too cruel to care. And this man, this pervert, was trying to make out he was innocent and she was mad and maybe she was . . . She could see the car coming, she needed to get out of the way, but she couldn't . . .

'*Lauren!*' she screamed. 'Lauren, please don't go . . . Oh God, I want my baby, please, please don't take my baby . . .'

'Sssh, ssh, there now,' a woman's voice was soothing. 'Get her some water,' she barked over her shoulder. Warm arms enfolded her, and Emma felt deep and painful sobs cutting right through her. She had no energy, she didn't know where she was; she couldn't make sense of anything. Who was this woman? Where had she come from?

Trying hard to breathe she sat forward, her head reeling as she dropped it into her hands. She had to get a grip, pull herself back together. 'I'm – I'm sorry,' she whispered raggedly. She'd disgraced herself, broken down, exploded, but that didn't change what had happened, what he'd done to Lauren . . .

'There's nothing to apologise for,' the woman told her. 'The strain you're under is immense.'

Emma raised her head as the woman knelt in front of her and took her hands. She was still sobbing, huge, racking chokes of grief. *Her baby was dying. Maybe she was already dead. Please God, no, no, no.* She recognised the woman now. It was Felicity Barker, the deputy head.

'I was passing and heard you shouting,' Felicity explained.

'Where is he?' Emma asked. 'Do you know what he's done?'

Felicity Barker regarded her regretfully.

'Please look in my bag. You need to see . . .'

Felicity looked up as the door opened and Philip Leesom came in with a large glass of water. He looked tense and pale; his eyes darted tentatively between Emma and the deputy head.

'Are you feeling better now?' he asked Emma, nervously offering her the water.

Ignoring him, Emma said to Felicity, 'Please take me to Mr Gibbs.'

'But, Emma,' Leesom protested.

Emma turned to him, her eyes flashing again. 'He needs to know about the kind of education you've been giving my daughter . . .'

'But I've tried to explain . . .'

'There are no explanations, no excuses for the fact that you texted her, from a mobile registered in your name, the address of that place outside Glastonbury. You even got her to take her flute so she could play for you and your friends.'

His chiselled jaw slackened with shock as an ugly rush of colour stained his neck. His eyes darted to Felicity, who was looking more alarmed now than confused.

'Yes, she took the flute,' Emma told him fiercely. 'She was willing to do whatever you wanted, because she was completely besotted with you, and knowing it you didn't hold back, did you? You took advantage of her in every possible way. I know Donna's got a crush on you too, I suspect half the girls in the school have, but the only one you were meeting that night was my daughter, who's now in intensive care, fighting for her life. Tell me you feel at least some sense of remorse, or responsibility for putting her there. Let me hear you admit that you have a shred of decency left in you to care about the fact that if you hadn't told her to go there that night this would never have happened. Oh God, you're going to start lying again, I can see it in your eyes. You're going to twist things round to make me look deranged with grief. Well, I am and I admit it, but it doesn't change what you've done, or who you are, and I'm telling you now, I will not be leaving here today until I know that every girl in this school is safe from you.'

Looking at Felicity, Leesom threw out his hands in despair. 'I don't know what to do,' he said. 'I can't admit to something I haven't done. I understand why . . .'

'It's all written down,' Emma reminded him, her voice shuddering with more emotion.

'Then please let me see it. If it's about me I surely have that right.'

Knowing he'd use the fact that his name wasn't actually spelled out to defend himself, she said, 'You can see what I have here, but then I want Donna Corrigan to see it too.'

His eyes were suddenly shot through with unease. 'But why?'

'Because she won't find it as easy to lie as you clearly do. In fact, I believe that reading these diary entries will terrify her, which is very probably what's terrifying you about inviting her in.'

Felicity's expression was harsh as she stared at Leesom.

'But this is absurd,' he protested. 'Felicity, you can see what a state she's in. We can't let this go any further.'

Felicity began to reply, but then he was shouting as Emma started for the door.

In one swift move he was grabbing her and spinning her round. 'Emma, wait, you have to listen to me,' he urged. 'Doing this won't solve anything. Lauren will still be where she is at the end of it, and you will have ruined my life for . . .'

'Do you think I care about your life when you've already ruined hers?' Emma broke in scathingly. 'Even before the accident you'd taken her down a road she should never even have known existed . . .'

'For Christ's sake,' he shouted desperately, 'she wasn't a virgin, and she's *eighteen*, old enough to know her own mind.'

As Felicity gasped Emma's face turned white. An admission at last, and to her disgust, not even the slightest tremor of remorse. 'That's just where you're wrong,' she told him quietly, 'because she was a virgin, and she wasn't old enough to know her own mind. That's why she was here, at this school, being educated, shaped for her future . . .'

'And she was doing brilliantly. You know that . . .'

'She was also doing things that should be making you grovel on the floor in shame, not stand here trying to defend yourself as if you had some sort of right to abuse your authority and your position.' Her head was spinning, but she had to make herself hold on. 'I told you when I came in here that your career is over, and now I'm not prepared to waste any more time arguing with you.'

He continued to block the way, staring hard into her eyes, ashen-faced and trembling.

'Philip, move aside,' Felicity commanded, coming to join them.

'Please, you can't listen to this,' he implored.

Felicity was holding Emma's arm, and pushing Leesom out of the way she steered Emma into the corridor. Neither of them stopped walking, or spoke a word, until they reached the headmaster's study.

As soon as the head's secretary saw them her face froze in shock, giving Emma an indication of how ravaged she must look. A beat later the girl was welcoming Emma politely and doing as Felicity instructed, going to get the head out of his meeting.

'Mrs Scott,' Gibbs said warmly and worriedly, as he came through to the office. He glanced quizzically at Felicity. 'Has something happened? Has Lauren . . . ?'

'We should go into my study,' Felicity said, and keeping a gentle hand on Lauren's arm she waited for Henry Gibbs to lead the way.

Once the door had closed Gibbs turned to Emma again, looking deeply concerned. 'I do hope this isn't more bad news,' he said.

Swallowing hard, Emma glanced at Felicity, who gave her a small nod of encouragement.

'I have something to show you,' Emma told him, and knowing she had to do this quickly she took out the extracts from Lauren's diary and passed them over. 'There's more,' she said, as he glanced down at them, 'far worse than this . . . The S she refers to is for sir, who is Mr Leesom. I've just come from his office and I . . . I hope you're going to see this the same way I do, that he must never be allowed near any of the girls again.'

Henry Gibbs's expression was starting to register both alarm and confusion as he quickly scanned the pages. 'I'd like to think I'm not understanding this correctly,' he said, glancing from Emma to Felicity and back again.

'I'm afraid you are,' Emma informed him. 'Both Lauren and Donna have been his victims. I don't know if there are any others. What I do know is that Lauren's suffering enough already by being where she is, so I'd prefer it . . . I'd rather this didn't turn into a full-blown scandal. I know I haven't helped matters, breaking down the way I did . . .'

'You mustn't blame yourself,' Felicity told her.

Gibbs's eyes were on the pages, absorbing more of the horror.

'If you'd like to speak to the police to add certainty to S's identity,' Emma said, 'you'll find the number of our family liaison officer written at the top of the first sheet. Obviously, I shall have to tell Lauren's father what's happened at some point, and I'm sure he'll want to sue the school, or do something equally drastic. If I can tell him that Philip Leesom has already left and won't be coming back, that might go some way towards appeasing him.'

Gibbs was clearly lost for words.

'Obviously we need to speak to Philip Leesom before we can take any action,' Felicity said reasonably. 'As you know, we have exams coming up . . .'

'For some, not for Lauren.'

Gibbs's eyes were on hers and Emma didn't look away; he needed to know just how determined she was.

'Leave it with me,' he told her. 'You have my word that I will deal with this fairly and promptly.'

An hour later, feeling more drained than she ever had in her life, Emma was on the train starting her journey back to Bristol. When her mobile rang she expected it to be Polly, or her mother, but to her dismay she saw it was Will. She knew she shouldn't answer, that he was the last person she needed to speak to right now, but somehow she managed to click on instead of turning the phone off.

'What are you doing? Where are you?' he demanded when she said a weary hello.

'Why do you need to know?' she countered.

'I've been trying to get hold of you, so I rang your mother and she told me you're in London, at the school. So what's going on?'

'Nothing that I can talk about now.' She was watching the platform seeming to travel past as the train pulled out of the station, and feeling as though she was in some kind of dream.

'But it concerns Lauren, obviously, so I have a right to know.'

'I'm not saying you don't, I'm just saying that this is not the time to discuss it. I'm on a train, other people are around.'

'Then call me when you get home.'

'I think it's probably best if we talk at the weekend. You are still coming, I take it?'

'Of course. And please stop with the trying to make me feel guilty. I've got a job, children, a wife . . . I can't just sit around here pretending everything's normal with Lauren when . . .'

'No one's asking you to. In fact, with the way you feel about things I'd rather you were never anywhere near her.'

'Whereas you would rather keep her alive in any kind of state, just as long as you're not left on your own. Haven't you got how selfish that is yet?'

Feeling guilt and confusion spinning through her again, she said, 'I'm not having this conversation now,' and clicking off the line she let her head sink back as wave after wave of conflicting emotions sucked her into an impenetrable darkness.

She must have slept for a while, because the next thing she knew the train was stopping at Reading station and her phone was ringing again. In no doubt that she'd ignore it if it was Will, she tried to recognise the number, felt sure she should, but for some reason she couldn't place it. At least it wasn't the hospital, because their number began with 0117, and the one she was looking at was 0207. So clicking on, she said, 'Hello, Emma Scott speaking.'

'Mrs Scott. It's Henry Gibbs.'

Surprised to hear from him so soon, she straightened up in her seat as he continued to speak.

'I thought you'd like to know that I have contacted your family liaison officer who was most helpful, and as a result Philip Leesom is here in my office with me. He understands that there can be no possibility of him remaining at the school after this. He will be leaving immediately.'

Feeling thrown by such a rapid response, Emma tried to make herself think. In the end all she could manage was a whispered, 'Thank you.'

'There's one other thing, before you go,' Henry Gibbs said. 'Though I am as keen as anyone to keep the number of people who know about this to an absolute minimum, I do feel that Donna Corrigan's parents must be told. We can't have them finding out some other way and then realising that the school has kept it from them. I am willing to speak to them myself, but if you'd rather do it . . .'

'If you don't mind, I think you should,' Emma told him. Knowing how devastated Ruth Corrigan was going to be, and how shaken she still was herself by it all, she simply didn't feel able to cope with anything else.

'As you wish,' Gibbs concurred. 'And do I have your permission to show Mrs Corrigan the entries from Lauren's diary?'

Recoiling at the mere thought, since she felt that this would be far more damaging to Lauren than to Donna, Emma said, 'Only if you consider it to be necessary, and then maybe you could limit what you show her to the sections that directly relate to Donna.'

'Of course.' Then he added, 'I'd like to extend my sincere apologies for what's happened, Mrs Scott, and all the distress it's caused you. I hold myself as responsible as anyone – the girls' moral welfare is every bit as important as their education, and I'm afraid we've let you down badly. I hope, at some point, we will be able to find a way to make some sort of reparation.'

Wondering how on earth that would ever be possible, Emma said, 'Please tell Ruth Corrigan that I'm deeply sorry, and if she wants to speak to me she knows how to get hold of me.'

'I will – and be assured that I'll be in touch again soon to ask about Lauren, and of course to keep you informed of developments here, should there be anything further.'

After thanking him again, Emma rang off and closed her eyes. She'd have liked nothing more than to be able to sink back into a deep and dreamless sleep now, but someone had tried calling her while she was talking to Henry Gibbs, and it might have been her mother.

It turned out to be Clive Andrews, who presumably wanted to talk about his chat with the headmaster. Deciding that could wait, while news of Lauren couldn't, she pressed in her mother's number first. The chances were she wouldn't get hold of her now if she was sitting with Lauren, since she'd have to switch off her phone. However, to Emma's relief she answered on the second ring.

'There's good timing,' Phyllis told her. 'I'd just popped out to call you. Is everything all right?'

'I guess so,' Emma said, knowing her mother was baffled and worried by this impromptu visit to the school. 'I'll tell you about it when I get home.' She wouldn't have to go into any detail, or show Phyllis the diary. The fact that there had been any kind of impropriety at all would be enough for her mother. 'So how's my girl today?'

'Actually, that's why I was about to call you,' Phyllis replied. 'Something happened that . . .'

'Oh my God,' Emma gasped through a surge of panic. 'Please tell me it wasn't . . .'

'It's all right, it's all right,' Phyllis came in quickly. 'It's not what you're thinking.'

'Then what? Is she all right?'

'She's fine, or the same as she was yesterday. It turned out to be a false alarm, but I thought . . . I was absolutely certain at the time that she squeezed my hand.'

Emma stopped breathing.

'The doctor said it was possible,' Phyllis rattled on, 'but after he'd checked her over he said it was probably just a reflex action, because I was squeezing hers. It happens, apparently.'

'But it might have been more,' Emma cried, unable to let go of this tiny gift of hope so quickly. 'Did he agree she could have been trying to communicate?'

'Well, he didn't exactly disagree, but it hasn't happened again since, so maybe he was right, it was me getting overexcited by a muscle contraction.'

'I'll have Polly bring me straight to the hospital,' Emma told her. 'If she can't do it, I'll get a taxi.'

Chapter Twenty-Three

'I do not need you to keep telling me this,' Sylvie was protesting, as Russ topped up her glass of wine before screwing the top back on the bottle. 'I am not stupid. I understand what you are saying.'

The sad truth was, she did understand him when she had a drink inside her, coupled with the promise of more; fully drunk she was virtually insensate, and sober – if she was ever completely that – she was too twitchy, or just plain wrecked, to be able to make much sense of anything. Russ had discovered this way of getting through to her on the day she'd given her affidavit, and Jolyon had confirmed that this was often the case with alcoholics; they simply couldn't function properly unless they had a certain level of alcohol inside them.

So, luckily, Jolyon had accepted Sylvie's statement in spite of her being under the influence of at least four large vodkas by then, but the point was she'd managed to sound perfectly coherent, even, to a degree, contrite, as she'd given her version of what had happened that night. Yes, she'd agreed, I'm afraid I did call my son, Oliver, at around one in the morning on the date you mentioned (she really didn't remember either the time or the date, but fortunately hadn't argued when Russ had told her). After insisting on adding why she'd got so drunk that night (because she'd just learned of her husband's affair with her best friend), she'd gone on to admit that she really hadn't felt it was worth carrying on. So her call to Oliver had been to say that it would be better if she left, which could, in most people's books, be construed as a threat to commit suicide. This meant that Jolyon was going to find himself on firmer ground when it came to the citation of special reasons in Oliver's defence.

He was going to need it more than ever now that the wretched blood sample had turned up, and with the way Oliver seemed so determined to make himself culpable . . .

That was for later; for now, Sylvie's continued refusal to go into rehab was the big issue for Russ, since if she was available, she would probably be summoned to appear in court – a veritable disaster in the making. In her present state she didn't see a problem with it, and there was a chance she could pull it off if called to the stand at the right time of day; however, the risk was too great. If she turned up drunk and started denying everything, or worse, accusing Russ of forcing her to sign the statement; or if she was too hung-over even to stagger out of bed, the consequences for Oliver could be dire.

So somehow Russ had to get her into a clinic, and since the only way of being able to hold a halfway reasonable conversation with her about this was to give her booze, that was what he was doing.

'I have been thinking very hard,' she told him, her hands cupped around her glass as she stared down at it.

He waited, willing her to surprise him with something along the lines of: *You're right, I should do more to help Oliver out of the mess I've got him into.* What she said was, 'I have decided that we should start doing the golden angels again.'

As his teeth clenched, he found himself longing to slap her.

Her eyes came to his, sunken and shadowed, but glowing with a peculiar sort of pride. 'It was a very good thing,' she went on, 'which made people happy, and now that they know we are behind it, they will understand that Oliver is from a good family. It will help his reputation a lot, I think.'

Not bothering to remind her of the fatuous interview she'd given, he replied, 'It's completely out of the question. It'll look as though we're trying to buy sympathy for him . . .'

'But I would like to do it.'

Not wanting to get into a pointless fight, he said,

'Perhaps, when this is over. Now can we please go on with what we were discussing?'

A look of irritation crossed her blotchy face and she took another mouthful of wine. 'Charlie told me that they will probably not be able to prosecute Oliver for the drinking and driving, because they have lost his sample of blood, and if they cannot do that then he will not be going to court.'

'As a matter of fact they've located it,' he told her. 'Jolyon called me yesterday, so I'm afraid that little fantasy is over. If it proves positive, and Oliver's certain it will, they will press ahead with all charges, including dangerous driving, which actually never went away. This means we are going to be even more dependent on your statement than before, which is why, in order to help Oliver, and yourself, you *must* check into a clinic.'

Waving a dismissive hand, she drained her glass and held it out for a refill.

Ignoring it, he said, 'I've already spoken to someone at a place not far from here . . . Where are you going?'

As though he wasn't even there she walked behind the bar into the kitchen, pulled open a drawer, then turned around. 'Do you see this?' she said, brandishing a paring knife. 'I could stab you to death with it right now and no one would blame me, because they would understand that you have driven me to do it. Eek! Eek! Eek!' she squealed, imitating the *Psycho* violins as she stabbed the air.

Only too aware of how unstable she was, he got to his feet and moved to put the table between them. 'Would you please put that thing down?' he demanded.

She laughed, girlishly. 'You are really afraid I will do it, aren't you?' she teased. 'You think, my God, she is so crazy she will do anything.'

'Exactly what is the point of this?'

She pouted as she screwed up her nose. 'The point is, my dear husband, I want you to refill my glass, and then I will put this *petit couteau* back in the drawer. I think this is a very good deal, *non*?'

'For Christ's sake, Sylvie.'

'I mean it,' she warned, thrusting the knife forward. Her eyes were glittering meaningfully, but she was smiling as though amused by her own joke.

'If you want more wine, you pour it,' he told her, realising that it would be impossible to continue while she was waving a knife that she might even be prepared to use.

Sighing with satisfaction, she popped the parer back in the drawer and returned to the table.

Watching her pick up the wine he felt tempted to grab her hand, snatch the bottle away and make her buckle to his will, but why even bother when he knew very well that it would do no good? She was way past any amount of force he could exert, mentally or physically, probably wouldn't even care if he turned the tables and actually tried to kill her – just as long as she had a drink in her hand when he did it.

For one awful moment he felt his emotions struggling to get the better of him: frustration, despair, fear for Oliver, disappointment with himself, concern about where this would end. Somehow he managed to hold them back. 'I can't talk to you any more,' he told her. 'I've threatened, I've begged, I've reminded you that you're a mother, I've offered to let you come home . . . I've done everything I can think of to try and help you, but you're so past that that every word I utter, every attempt I make to get through to you, is nothing more than a waste of breath. None of us, neither me, nor Charlie, nor Oliver, even begin to matter in comparison to your need for a drink. It's the centre of your world, the only reason you get up in the morning, and what puts you to bed at night. As long as you have your fix we can go straight to hell. Well that's where you can go now, Sylvie, all on your own, because I don't know what to do to try and save you any more, and I'm not prepared to let the boys go on trying either. If you haven't already forgotten what you've done to Oliver . . .' He broke off as her landline started to ring.

She didn't answer, only watched him as she took another sip of her drink, so he picked up instead, knowing it was likely to be Charlie.

'Allo? Sylvie? C'est toi?' a familiar voice asked at the other end.

333

'Olivia,' he said to his sister-in-law. 'It's Russ.'

'Russ! *Comment tu vas? Qu'est-ce qu'il se passe?* I am at the airport, the plane has landed two hours ago, but I am still waiting.'

Confused, Russ said, 'Which airport? Are you in England?' Was he supposed to be picking her up and someone had forgotten to tell him, or an email hadn't come through? Was Olivia here? Christ, what he wouldn't give for Olivia to be here.

'No, I am in Cape Town. I thought Sylvie was coming. Charlie called to tell me what has been happening . . . Russ, I am so sorry . . . If I had known, I would have come. She has the same problem as *Maman*, I think. Where is she? Please tell me she is not lost.'

'No, she's right here, Olivia,' he said, pronouncing her name deliberately as he looked at Sylvie. He should have asked for Olivia's help before, but he'd been unable to admit he couldn't cope. He could now though, he had to, or Sylvie was going to end up taking them all down with her. 'I hadn't realised she'd arranged to come and see you.' How freeing even the thought of that was.

'Yes, well, Charlie was the one who arranged it, but when I spoke to Sylvie yesterday evening she assured me she was taking the flight this morning. I thought when I hear nothing from her that she must be on it. Is she all right? What has happened?'

'Nothing's happened, exactly,' Russ replied. 'If I'd known about it I'd have taken her to the airport myself.'

'Let me speak to her,' Sylvie demanded.

Ignoring her, Russ said, 'I'm sure there are flights every day. Can I try to get her on one tomorrow?' This really felt like trashing his responsibilities, but he needed to.

'Oh yes, please do. Charlie has told me all about Oliver and what has happened. This is a terrible thing, and I want to do my best to help.'

'If she can stay with you for a couple of weeks . . .'

'Yes, of course . . .'

'I want to speak to her,' Sylvie cut in, making a grab for the phone.

Holding her back, Russ said to Olivia, 'I'm going to

pass you over to her. Whatever she tells you, please bear in mind that she is drunk, and I'm afraid this is the condition she'll undoubtedly be in when she reaches you tomorrow, or the next day, depending when I can get her on a flight.'

'Do not speak about me as if I am not here.'

'Just email me the details as soon as you have them,' Olivia told him.

Handing the phone to Sylvie, Russ took out his mobile and went into the bedroom to call Charlie. 'Where are you?' he barked when Charlie answered in a muted voice.

'Waiting to go into this meeting,' came the reply.

'What meeting? Oh God,' Russ groaned, as he remembered Charlie's interview with the senior clerk to a Lincoln's Inn chambers. 'Sorry, I'm not thinking straight. Call me when it's over.'

'It's OK, I've just been told they're running half an hour late, so I can go outside for a minute. Is everything OK? Did Mum get off all right?'

'She didn't go, and why on earth didn't you tell me you'd been in touch with Olivia? I'd have made sure . . .'

'You were out at some screening when I left last night, but I told Oliver to let you know. Don't tell me he forgot.'

'He must have, or maybe he left a note that I haven't seen.' He knew how unlikely that was, since he'd been back and forth from the house most of the day, and Oliver had had plenty of opportunities to tell him in person during the morning when they'd both been in the office. Where Oliver had gone this afternoon was anyone's guess, but he'd been disappearing quite regularly lately. Knowing he'd have to deal with that later, Russ said, 'I'm going to try and book her on a flight tomorrow or the next day, and I need to ask, is there any chance you can go with her? I understand it's a big ask . . .'

'You're dead right it is.'

'But I can't leave Oliver at this time, and he can't leave the country . . .'

'I get that, but I've got a life too and I seriously don't need to be in Cape Town right now.'

'It's just to make sure she gets there, as sober as possible, and then you can come right back again.'

With an exasperated sigh, Charlie said, 'It depends what happens today, OK? If they're going to offer me a pupillage then I'll have to put that first.'

'Of course, I wouldn't argue with that, but if it's not starting until next week or the week after, will you go?'

'It sounds like I'll have to. She is such a pain for not going today. She said she would.'

'You know how unreliable she is, but it doesn't matter. She's talking to Olivia on the phone now, and when I ring off from you I'm going to get Connie to come over and help her pack.'

'You need to take her home with you tonight, or God knows what kind of state she'll be in by the morning – and you don't want a repeat of the other day, having to turf some lowlife out of the flat before you can start sobering her up.'

'I didn't realise . . .'

'I'm not stupid, Dad, I knew what was going on, and I don't want it happening again any more than you do. It's why I ended up calling Olivia – after that, she was the only one I could think of who might be able to do something to bring Mum to her senses.'

Starting to feel dreadful for palming his problems off on his son and his sister-in-law, Russ said, 'I'll make sure Olivia understands it's only for a week or two, just to give your mother a change of environment and a rest.'

'They have clinics in Cape Town, you should ask Olivia if she can try to get Mum into one there.'

'If I thought there was a chance Olivia might succeed where we've failed . . .'

'Whatever, it has to be worth a try.' Then, in an even brusquer tone. 'Are you OK? You sound shattered.'

Russ's eyes closed. He'd hardly slept since the night of Oliver's accident, but he wasn't going to burden Charlie with that. 'I'm fine,' he told him, 'just worried about your mother and Oliver, you too with this big meeting coming up. Do you think they are going to offer you a job?'

Sounding dismal, Charlie said, 'Not before I've had my results.'

'But they must have confidence in you, to have called you in. How did they know about you?'

Charlie laughed. 'You're kidding me, right?'

Russ frowned. 'No, why would I?'

'Because you're the one who asked Jolyon, about two years ago, if there were any doors he could open for me.'

Vaguely remembering that this was part of a conversation he and Jolyon had once had, Russ said, 'Of course. Sorry. I'm glad he was able to help, and I'm sorry we didn't get a chance to talk it through before you left. Do you feel well prepared?'

'I guess so, but talking to some mates earlier, the competition is seriously fierce.'

In spite of knowing that every father would consider his own son to be the most outstanding candidate, Russ was confident that Charlie would get the job. 'What are you planning to do after the meeting?' he asked.

'Actually, I was going to stay in town for a few days, but now this has come up . . . Is it OK if I meet you at the airport instead of coming home tonight? I'd kind of like to hang out with some of the crowd for a while.'

Understanding how desperate he must feel to escape the pressure of his family, Russ said, 'Of course it's OK. And are you all right about Oliver using your car until we get his windscreen repaired?'

'Sure, I told him I was, and I'm really glad he's driving again. He needs to get out, because he was sending himself crazy with all that Internet stuff. Have you seen any of it?'

'Some. She's a lovely girl, very talented.'

'True, but he doesn't need to keep reminding himself of that.'

'It's going to take time for him to come to terms with it all,' Russ murmured. 'It hasn't even been a month since it happened.'

'It will be tomorrow, but OK, I agree it's not that long. I just don't think it's a good thing for him to be fixating on her the way he is, like if she doesn't make it then he doesn't deserve to either.'

Feeling himself turning cold, Russ said, 'Has he spoken to you about it? Is that what he's saying?'

'No, he doesn't really talk about it at all, but I know him, and so do you, because it's what's scaring you too.'

It wasn't a question, it was a statement that reminded Russ of how close they were, and yet how far he felt from Oliver right now. 'You don't think he'll do anything stupid, do you?' he asked.

'No, not him. The trouble is, it's like he's not really thinking straight. I mean, take when we heard yesterday that the blood sample had turned up: he seemed to think it was a good thing, like he deserves to get done for drinking and driving, when none of it was his fault, really. He was at a party for Chrissakes, and planning to spend the night. He didn't ask Mum to call him the way she did, or ring the girl up and say please be in the middle of the road when I come tearing through . . .'

'All right, all right,' Russ interrupted, 'let's not get into it again now. You need to focus on what you're doing there, and I'd better get started on trying to book this flight.'

'OK, I'll call on my way back to the flat, and if you speak to Oliver before I do, tell him I'm pissed off that he didn't pass my message on.'

'I will.'

'He's too wrapped up in all this. He needs to break out, get a perspective . . .'

'Leave him to me,' Russ said, cutting him short again. 'You just make sure you blow those guys away today. I'll wait for your call.'

After ringing off he returned to the sitting room to find Sylvie slumped in an armchair with her feet on the coffee table next to a bottle, a large glass of wine in one hand and the phone in the other. After reassuring himself she was still gossiping with her sister, he went to put on her computer and while waiting for it to warm up, he quickly pressed in Oliver's number.

'Hi, it's Dad,' he said when Oliver answered. 'Where are you?'

338

'At home.'

That was a relief, anyway. 'So where did you go earlier?'

'When?'

'You know when. Straight after lunch. You were in the office one minute, the next no one knew where you were.'

'Why's that such a big deal? Do I have to tell you everywhere I'm going?'

'No, but I'm asking and I'd like you to answer me.'

'I was driving around, OK?'

Not liking the sound of that too much, Russ said, 'Where?'

'Just places. I thought you wanted me to drive again.'

'I do, but I'd rather you didn't go back to the scene of the accident. Is that where you went?'

'Is that what I said?'

Fighting back his exasperation, Russ said, 'Try a straight answer.'

'OK, it's not where I went.'

If Oliver was telling the truth then it would be a welcome relief, because he'd been there a couple of days ago and had come home in a terrible state. Russ had found him in front of the house, still sitting at the wheel of Charlie's car, sobbing so hard that it had taken a while for him to get his story out. He'd needed to go there to be near her again – what kind of sense did that make?

'Then where did you go?' Russ asked.

'Nowhere. Please Dad, don't keep on.'

Realising it would have to wait, Russ said, 'What are you doing now?'

'Just hanging out.'

'On the computer?'

'Is there a law against it?'

'No, but what do you think you're going to prove by reading about her all the time?'

'You don't know what I'm reading about, and anyway, I'm scared they're going to flick the switch on her, or pull the plug or whatever they do when they decide it's all over. We've got to stop them from doing that, Dad.'

Taking a breath in order to try and keep his voice gentle,

Russ said, 'Oliver, I understand what it's going to mean for you if they . . .'

'It's not about me, it's about her,' Oliver cried.

'OK, but you still can't get involved. It's up to her parents and the doctors to decide what's best for her . . .'

'I know that, it's just that if they do let her go it would be like murder.'

Feeling his head starting to spin as Sylvie gave a shriek of laughter and Oliver's plight dug in deeper, Russ said, 'My understanding of it is that they won't do anything unless she has another relapse or complication of some kind.'

'So they just leave her in a coma. Great.'

'Son, if they knew how to get her out of it, be sure they would have done it days ago.' He had to change the subject, or this was going to end up in more tears and irrational shouting. 'You might be interested to hear,' he said, 'that your mother didn't get on the flight to South Africa this morning. Is there any reason why you didn't pass Charlie's message on?'

'Oh Christ, I forgot. Sorry.'

Guessing exactly where Oliver's head had been, but not willing to go there again, Russ told him, 'If I can get your mother on a flight tomorrow I'll probably stay here with her tonight, ready for an early start to Heathrow. Will you be able to bring some things over for me?'

'Sure, but I don't want to see her.'

Knowing Sylvie would be too far gone by then to care, if she even did now, Russ said, 'I'll come down to get it. It's just my shaving gear, toothbrush and a change of clothes. Now, can you do me a favour please and go back to the office. One of us neglecting our duties is enough, and at least until tomorrow I'm going to have to make your mother my priority.'

'Yeah, and it like makes a big difference, me being in the office.'

'Oliver.'

Silence.

'You're really not helping yourself or me by adopting this attitude,' Russ told him severely. 'So do as I ask and call me when you're on your way here.' Cutting the call before Oliver could take him any deeper into despair, he dropped his phone on the table and sat down at the computer.

Sylvie was still jabbering on with her sister, in French of course, which he didn't speak fluently. However, he knew enough to understand that she was reasonably excited by the prospect of spending some time with Olivia, which for Russ was nothing short of a blessed relief.

'Did you hear that?' Sylvie demanded as she rang off a few minutes later. 'I have told Olivia that I will come, but only on the condition that you come with me. No, don't argue, Russ, you are looking very tired at the moment and I think you need a break so . . .'

'Sylvie, it's not going to happen,' he broke in angrily. 'Apart from anything else, I can't leave Oliver . . .'

'He's a grown-up. He can take care of himself.'

Detesting how dismissive she was able to be over a problem she had caused, he said, 'While our son has this business hanging over him I am absolutely not leaving him on his own.'

Sylvie was in the middle of a large sip of wine. 'Charlie is around,' she finally managed.

'Charlie's got his own life. No, I'm not coming with you. The flights are booked now, you're going tomorrow, and Charlie's flying with you.'

Her eyebrows lifted. 'How splendid,' she murmured as she sipped again. 'We shall have a marvellous time, the two of us, and you will be very jealous and sorry that you didn't come too.'

Don't hold your breath for that, Russ was thinking as he clicked to print out the boarding passes. Much more likely was that he'd spend the time trying to steer his company away from the rocks after receiving six rejections for programme ideas in as many days, while doing his level best to prevent his younger son from going into some kind of meltdown.

'Mrs Scott?' a voice said quietly.

Emma lifted her gaze from Lauren's face, and felt a

peculiar rushing sensation as she moved weightlessly from the world she'd just been in with Lauren, to the one they shared with everyone else. The unit sounded busy, she realised, in spite of the late hour, voices, comings and goings, the muted rhythm of machines hissing and bleeping, a strangely hypnotic chorus conducted by the always present, never visible hand of Fate.

'Yes?' Emma replied, her fingers still wrapped around Lauren's in the hope of even the slightest tremor of a response. 'Oh, it's time to go,' she said, realising it must be nine o'clock.

The nurse, whom Emma hadn't seen before, glanced at Anna who'd been on duty since Emma had arrived, and said, 'Dr Nelson wanted me to let you know that he's here now and will be along shortly.'

Remembering that the consultant had left a message saying he wanted to see her if she came in today, Emma's heart turned inside out as she returned her gaze to Lauren's ghostly face. After the scene at the school earlier she knew she wasn't up to coping with much more today, particularly if Yuri Nelson was going to revisit the subject of letting Lauren go. But there hadn't been any further crises, and Farraday had said it would only become an issue if another drastic intervention was necessary.

Too exhausted to cry, in spite of the tears on her cheeks, she moved in closer to Lauren to brush her cheek with a kiss as she whispered goodnight.

Goodnight, Mum, love you, Lauren replied.

If only, but Emma heard it anyway, because Lauren's voice was as much a part of her as the chromosomes and genes she'd passed on to make her.

Finding another family in the waiting room, faces stricken, eyes widening with terror as the door opened, Emma quickly apologised and left. There was tragedy all around her; Death the silent stalker never left this place. How many times, she wondered, had it looked at Lauren? Was it waiting for her, even now?

As she stepped out into the corridor she saw Yuri Nelson coming towards her, and tried to evince some polite pleasure as she greeted him.

Making a better job of the same performance, he shook her hand warmly and would have steered her into the waiting room if she hadn't explained why they couldn't go in.

Understanding, he walked her on down the corridor, making small talk about the weather and some demonstration that had held him up getting here, until they reached the neuro X-ray centre where he took her into an empty office.

'Shall we sit down?' he suggested, his glasses turning opaque as they caught the light.

Doing as she was told, she watched him sit too, taking a chair the same side of the desk as her, not too close, but not too far either. Did it mean anything? She was willing him not to destroy the little straw of hope she was still grasping after the tremor her mother had felt, though she could feel it turning to dust.

'We're going to be moving Lauren to the high-dependency unit either tomorrow or Sunday,' he told her, his grey eyes looking large and kind behind their thick, steel-rimmed lenses.

She started to reply and found she had to clear her throat. 'Is that – is that good or bad?' she asked croakily.

'I guess you could say it's good, in that she doesn't need quite such intensive observation any more, so she'll be sharing a nurse with another patient.'

Emma's eyes widened with alarm. 'And a room, or a cubicle?' she said. She didn't want Lauren's privacy invaded; she needed to be alone with her daughter while she was here, but how could she expect such a luxury when they weren't private, they were NHS?

'It'll depend on the occupancy rate when we make the transfer,' he replied.

Realising she was being absurd about the privacy, that no matter who else was nearby no one could come between her and Lauren if she didn't allow it, she asked, 'So why have you decided to move her? She must be doing better if you feel she doesn't need so much attention.'

He grimaced awkwardly. 'It wouldn't be right to give

you false hope at this stage, so I should say that this isn't due so much to a change in her condition; it's more an issue of space. As you know, we have urgent cases coming in all the time, and some, most, are now more pressing than Lauren's.'

Emma could feel herself tensing. 'I think what you're really saying is that you're pushing her aside in order to save money,' she challenged.

'I'm afraid budgets are always a concern,' he admitted frankly, 'but rest assured she'll receive all the necessary care in the HDU, and if she does well there, we could soon be seeing our way to transferring her to the ward.'

'But you'll only do that if she's showing some signs of improvement?'

'If that happens then certainly she'll be moved on to the ward; but even if she remains as she is we'll probably decide that the requirement for intensive treatment has reduced sufficiently for her to . . .'

'Does Mr Farraday know about this?'

'Of course. No decision would be taken without the full knowledge of her entire neurological team.'

Her voice sounded shrill and wavery as she said, 'But the bottom line is you think she doesn't stand a chance anyway, so there's no point in wasting your resources?'

'No, no, that certainly isn't the case.'

She wanted to believe him, but it was hard. 'You think I'm cruel for saying we must keep her alive, no matter what, don't you?' she cried desperately.

Taking both her hands in his, he said, 'Please believe me when I tell you that there is no reason even to consider removing the intubation yet.'

'Only another emergency would provoke that?'

'Possibly, but as we're not there and she's been stable for the last few days, let's try not to get into a hypothesis about something that might well not happen.'

'But she's brain-dead, a vegetable, she'll never be normal again.'

'Mrs Scott, all her brain scans show . . .'

'Nothing. You're finding nothing.'

'Please listen to me. None of us knows for sure what is happening in her brain, and nor will we until she comes round.'

'And if she does, by then, it'll be too late to let her go. She'll be condemned to living in a body that won't work, with a brain that can't function, and it'll be my fault for making you keep her alive.'

'At this time,' he said gently, 'you are not being asked to make a decision, so you really can't blame yourself for anything.'

Emma looked away, then dropped her head as she tried to make herself think. What would Will be asking if he were here? 'If I object to you moving her,' she said, turning back to him, 'if I say that I want her to stay where she is . . .'

'The decision needs to be a medical one.'

'Will you tell her father that? I need you to convince him, because I know he'll say I'm not being strong enough, or taking proper care of her . . .'

'Of course I'll speak to him. Will he be here at the weekend?'

'He says he will.'

He was going to have a lot to take in, she was thinking grimly to herself when she finally went outside into the chill, damp night air to find her car. What with Phillip Leesom's sudden ugly prominence in their lives, and now this, maybe it would be better if Will didn't come. She really didn't want to have to cope with his anger and accusations any more than she wanted to go on trying to cope with the way Lauren was.

But what choice did she have?

'Emma, over here.'

Startled, she turned to see her mother standing beneath a lamp post, next to her Audi, and waving. 'I thought you'd gone home,' Emma said, when she reached her.

'I went to pick up some groceries, then decided to come back and wait,' Phyllis told her. 'You looked so tired after your trip to London, and I was afraid it might not be easy to find a taxi when you finally left.'

Emma swallowed hard as she put a hand to her head. Of course, Polly had brought her here from the station, so why was she looking for her car?

'Come on, let's get you out of this drizzle,' Phyllis said, going round to open the passenger door.

As she followed her, Emma said, 'I've just been told they're going to move her to the high-dependency unit.'

Her mother considered this, then nodded in a way that seemed approving. 'I think we'll take that as a good sign,' she decided.

Emma watched her walk back round to the driver's side and shake out her umbrella before getting in. 'Thank you,' she said in a whisper as her mother started to reverse the car out of the parking space.

Phyllis glanced at her. 'What for?' she asked, slipping the automatic into drive.

Emma struggled with her embarrassment. 'For this,' she answered with a shrug. 'Coming back to wait for me, spending so much time with Lauren . . .' She wanted to add, *I'm not sure how I'd have got through the last couple of weeks without you,* but she couldn't quite manage it. She and her mother didn't normally go in for these kinds of chats.

Seeming embarrassed too, Phyllis said, 'There's no need to thank me.'

Emma closed her eyes as a swell of emotion filled her chest. She knew it was tiredness making her long for Berry so she could rest her head on her grandmother's shoulder, and feel as though she wasn't having to carry everything alone. Berry had other commitments to attend to now, though; Alfonso's scare had weakened him and made him dependent in a way he'd never been before. Besides, she wasn't alone, because her mother was here, and Emma was glad of it, she just couldn't quite get a grip on it.

She wasn't aware of building up to a question, or of any particular feelings attached to it when it came; she just seemed to be quiet one minute and the next she was asking, 'Why have we never been close?' It wasn't the first time she'd asked, it had come up many times over the years, so it wasn't a great surprise when her mother didn't answer. It hurt, though, a lot. 'Did you hear me?' Emma prompted, suddenly unwilling to let it go.

'Yes, yes, I did, but I don't think now is a good time to be having this conversation, do you? But I do think it's something we should try to discuss when you're not quite so tired.'

The fact that her mother was acknowledging there might be an issue was a first. In the past, she'd always told Emma to stop seeking attention, or making a fuss about nothing.

'Does that mean you're ready to admit that you don't like me?' Emma heard herself saying, and an absurd rush of tears swamped her eyes. How she loathed self-pity, but it seemed to be loving her right now.

'I – I'll admit nothing of the kind,' Phyllis stammered awkwardly, 'but I will agree that sometimes it might have . . . Well, it might have seemed that way.'

Emma had to correct her. 'Not sometimes, all the time.'

Phyllis cast her a glance, but the expected reprimand for exaggerating didn't come.

Emma tried to say, *You really* don't *like me, do you?* but her lips were clamped tightly shut, trying to hold back the emotions that were choking her. Her mother was right, now wasn't the time to be having this conversation. They should revert to their usual banalities about the price of things now, or the changing weather, or what kind of bulbs Emma should plant with spring on its way. Mostly they talked about Lauren, of course, sharing memories of her childhood, spreading them out like a precious tapestry between them, something that held them together, but also kept them safely apart. They usually chose moments of joy and laughter: first smiles, first teeth, first steps, right through to the many prizes she'd won for music, dance and drama. Phyllis had been there for most of it, had even taken Lauren to her ballet lessons on Tuesdays and Fridays, and made costumes for the school plays she was in. She'd been involved in Lauren's life in a way Emma couldn't remember her ever being involved in hers.

A few nights ago they'd found themselves chuckling about the tube of suncream Lauren had swallowed, aged six, because it smelled of coconut; and later they'd recalled the passion she'd developed for a donkey in the field next to Phyllis's house – the house where Emma had grown up. Emma often wondered if her mother had as many memories of her as a child as she did of Lauren, but she'd never asked, and tonight she didn't want to know the answer.

'Do you know what I wish?' she said as they left the motorway to start across the city centre. 'I really wish Dad was here. I'm not sure why, I just think he'd be able to make everything all right.'

Phyllis took a breath, but it was a moment before she said, 'Yes, he had that way with him.' A beat later she added, 'Especially for you.'

Emma's heart twisted as she turned in the darkness to look at her mother. It was almost forty years since her father had died, and this was the first time her mother had ever even indicated that she, Emma, might have been special to him.

She felt suddenly adrift, cut loose from who and where she was. She struggled for her next words, trying to pluck them from an overload of emotion, but they were drowning, drowning, drowning. She wanted so much to take this further, to find out what her mother was hiding, but she was being reminded of the time when she was five and had started diving lessons with the school. It had taken weeks for her to brave the climb on to the board, and when she'd finally managed it the teacher and the other children had all clapped and encouraged her to walk to the edge. Once there, she'd looked down at the water, and she'd really wanted to spring up and fly like a bird before plunging head first into the pool. She was certain if her father had been there to make sure she was safe she'd have done it, but he wasn't, he'd died two years before, and she'd never found the courage to go any further.

This was how she felt now, afraid to go any further. She wanted life to stop, turn around and take her back to a month ago when all she'd had to worry about was finding a job, and her dreams for Lauren were still shared by Lauren. She wouldn't give up on those dreams, though, she couldn't; there would be no point to anything if she did, and the tears running silently down her cheeks now were no more than tiredness, nothing at all to do with giving up.

Chapter Twenty-Four

The following month passed more quickly, yet more slowly, than Emma could make any sense of. Lauren remained in the high-dependency unit for no more than a week before being moved to a side room on the acute ward, when her turban of bandages was removed, as was some of the intubation. The hair that had been shaved from the right side of her head was growing back: along with her breathing, and the healing of her other wounds, it was another sign of life, and occasionally she moved a hand, or slightly turned her head. Apparently this wasn't unusual for coma patients – some actually opened their eyes, or even sat up, others had been known to speak or try to get out of bed – but Lauren's unconscious movements remained minimal. Even so, they still inspired a hope that burned fiercely for a while, until finally it flickered and died again.

Emma had read hundreds of stories online by now, and even seen videos, of patients who'd come out of traumatic brain injury (known as TBI) comas after months, sometimes years, and a few had even made partial – or indeed miracle – recoveries. She was never going to allow herself to stop believing that this was possible for Lauren too, and since there had been no more emergencies or surgeries, the terrifying dilemma of whether or not to prolong her life hadn't been raised again.

Apart from her medical team, Lauren's visitors consisted mainly of Emma and her mother, Polly and Melissa, and Harry and Jane at weekends. Will didn't come, still refusing to engage with what he claimed Emma was forcing on their daughter, and Emma couldn't help being relieved, because seeing him always made everything seem so much worse.

Donna didn't come either; she'd been grounded until her exams were over. The diary was long gone, torn to shreds and set alight in the garden by Emma and her mother. Not that Phyllis had read it – simply knowing that an improper relationship had taken place had been enough to make her join in the burning, which, like Emma, she'd seen as a ritual cleansing of that part of Lauren's past. If Lauren was ever able to ask about it, they'd work out then what to tell her. For now, they wanted no reminders of what had happened; they didn't even mention it between themselves.

Will, however, rarely failed to bring it up whenever he and Emma spoke on the phone, which had been far too often for her liking since she'd emailed him about Lauren's diary. Typically he'd exploded with rage, had threatened to sue the school, the man himself, even her for parental neglect. Of course she was partly to blame, she'd been far too wrapped up in her struggle to start afresh to notice any telltale signs of what Lauren might be doing, though in her own defence Lauren and Donna had spun a web of secrecy around the affair that had been virtually impenetrable.

Emma knew, from Clive Andrews and the headmaster, that the police had spoken to Leesom following his instant dismissal and satisfied themselves that no molestation of underage pupils had taken place, which meant he had escaped arrest. His career was in ruins, of course, he'd never work as a teacher again, and though Emma would have liked nothing more than to think of him banged up in jail, at the same time she was relieved to know that Lauren's name, reputation, was not going to end up as damaged by an ugly scandal as her brain had been by the accident that should never have happened.

It was five o'clock on a Thursday afternoon now, and Emma was standing in the doorway of Lauren's side room, thrown to see a stranger sitting next to the bed. She hadn't expected to find anyone here at this hour; even she rarely made it until gone six, since she'd taken a part-time job at the local vet's, covering for a receptionist on maternity leave. She usually stayed with Lauren then until seven thirty or eight. It wasn't that she wanted to leave earlier than the nine o'clock end to visiting, if she could she'd probably stay the entire night; it was simply that her mother and Polly had started a routine of making dinner every evening, one night at Emma's, the next at Polly's, and Emma didn't want to let them down.

The stranger's head was bowed, his dark hair tumbling over the side of his face, so Emma was unable to make out his features, though she felt sure she'd never seen him before. He seemed too young to be a doctor, and, in a black leather jacket and faded, ripped jeans, he certainly wasn't dressed like one. If he was a physio he'd surely be exercising Lauren's limbs, but he was barely moving. His eyes seemed to be fixed so hard on Lauren that Emma could almost feel him trying to reach her. She looked at Lauren, her lovely face tranquil and almost ethereal, her beautiful hair spilling over one side of the pillow, her lengthy lashes curved in two crescent-moon fringes from the pale edges of her closed eyelids.

She felt she should make her presence known, but there was an intensity about this young man, a sense of purpose that seemed to be surrounding him and Lauren in a subtle, yet powerful nimbus that Emma didn't want to break. It was almost as though they were communicating on a level that couldn't be seen or heard, except by them. She noticed then that he was holding something to Lauren's ear: an earpiece from an iPod. The other part of the headset was pressed to his own ear, so they *were* sharing a form of communication. Maybe he was a new therapist trying a different form of stimulus – though Melissa played music to Lauren every time she came, so did Emma, and neither of them had managed to provoke a response, not even with the recording of the school's performance night, when each student taking part had dedicated their chosen pieces to Lauren.

'Hello, Emma. How are you today? Lauren seems on form.'

Emma turned round as one of the staff nurses passed behind her on her way out of the ward. It was what most of them said, that Lauren was on form, or looking good, or doing well. It was nice of them to be upbeat, even though there had been no change in her condition.

352

When Emma turned back the young lad was on his feet, his handsome face suffused with shock.

'I'm sorry,' he said, looking as though he'd run if he weren't trapped. 'I didn't . . . I was just . . .'

'Who are you?' Emma asked. She was sure she hadn't seen him before, and yet there was something about him . . .

'They said it was OK to come in,' he told her. 'I don't do anything, only talk to her.' He was coming closer, trying to edge round her.

'Are you a friend of Lauren's?' Emma asked.

'Yes, no . . . I mean . . . Sorry, I should go.'

He was almost past her when it suddenly clicked who he was, and as her heart jolted with shock she spun round. 'Wait. Please, wait,' she cried, not sure what she was going to say or do. Her mind was struggling to work out what was happening, what it could mean.

His anxious eyes came back to hers. He was remarkably good-looking, she thought irrelevantly, and tall, at least six foot. And clearly very worried about being caught here. 'You're Oliver Lomax, aren't you?' she said. *This was Oliver Lomax, the boy who'd been driving the car . . .*

'I didn't mean any harm,' he assured her. 'I just wanted to see her and . . .' His eyes went down as he ran out of words.

She should have been angry, offended, calling for security to throw him out, but for some reason all she did was ask, 'Why did you want to see her?'

He glanced over at Lauren. Emma could see he was shaking, and thought she probably was too. 'I just did,' he replied. 'I thought . . .' He shrugged awkwardly. 'It's going to sound stupid, I know, but I thought . . . I was the one who did this to her, so maybe I was the one who could, you know, help bring her out of it.'

Emma could only stare at him.

He looked painfully self-conscious. 'I told you it would sound stupid,' he said.

'Actually, I'm not sure it does,' she murmured. Or no more than any of the things she thought to herself, anyway. 'Is this the first time you've come?'

His head went down as he shook it. 'No, I . . . I come

most days, or whenever I can, just between four and five, because one of the nurses said she was usually on her own then.'

'Does the nurse know who you are?'

'No. I just said I was a friend.'

Emma took a breath, and realising she didn't know what to say, she turned to look at Lauren. She seemed so peaceful, and yet present, as if she was doing no more than sleeping. 'Have you ever . . . ? Does she ever respond to you?' she asked, not certain how she'd feel if the answer was yes.

He shrugged. 'Not really. I mean her fingers move sometimes, and I thought she opened her eyes once, but it turned out to be the way the sun was coming in through the window.' His gaze came up to hers. 'I'm really sorry if you think I've overstepped the mark. I *swear* I didn't mean any harm.'

She could tell that he didn't, and as she looked more deeply into his eyes she thought she could detect something of his suffering. He had a genuine conscience that was clearly tearing him apart. 'It's OK, I believe you,' she said.

They stood awkwardly for a moment, neither of them seeming to know what to do or say next. In the end he said, 'I guess I should go.'

'No, don't.' She spoke before realising what she was going to say. Why did she want him to stay? She had no clear idea; she only knew that she didn't want him to leave yet. 'Will you have a cup of tea with me?' she offered, thankful no one else was here, like Will, or her mother, because they'd probably think she'd lost her mind.

He seemed uncertain.

'I won't eat you,' she promised.

The unease in his eyes retreated a little. 'OK,' he answered. 'Why not?'

Emma walked over to Lauren and touched a hand to her face. 'Hello darling,' she whispered. 'I didn't know you had a new . . . friend.' Was that how she should be describing him, or even thinking of him? It wasn't feeling right, and yet it wasn't jarring either.

Lauren's lips didn't move, nor did her eyes open, but in her mind Emma could hear her saying, *Do you know who he is?*

'Yes, I've just found out.'

You know it wasn't his fault, I was in the middle of the road.

'No, it wasn't,' Emma agreed, thinking of the boy's mother and the panic he must have been in as he drove along that unlit road. Something that had never occurred to her before came quietly into her mind: at least he hadn't driven on and left Lauren to die like an animal. He could have, and some would have, especially if they'd been drinking. 'Do you mind if I go and talk to him?' she whispered, smoothing the shorter side of Lauren's hair. It was growing back as silky and honeyed as it had been before.

No, it's cool. I'll stay here and get some sleep.

'It's time you woke up,' Emma chided, loud enough for Oliver to hear.

When she turned round he was watching Lauren, not her, then their eyes met, and the way he blushed touched her with its seeming innocence and simplicity.

Moments later, as they were walking out of the ward, he said, 'I think she will.'

Emma glanced at him. He looked, she realised, a lot like his father.

'I mean wake up,' he explained. 'I think she will.'

Emma found herself warming inside. She had no idea why him saying it seemed to mean so much, it just did. 'It's good to know that I'm not alone in believing it.'

He seemed surprised. 'Doesn't everyone?'

She sighed. 'In fairness my mother does, and my friend Polly, but her father's not convinced.'

'That's because he's afraid.'

Emma nodded, impressed by his insight. 'You're right,' she said, and stepping ahead of him out of the door, into the crisp spring evening air, she found herself swamped by birdsong and felt the joy of it trying to lift her.

The cafe was only a short walk through a maze of stone alleyways and there was no one else in when they arrived, apart from two volunteers serving and a couple on their way out. Emma was recalling the last time she'd been in here, with Berry, when Will had come in, carrying his son, while his wife had waited outside. She still resented him

355

for putting his other family first, even though she didn't want his negativity anywhere near Lauren.

Never would she have dreamt, she was thinking, as she paid for a tea and a 7 Up, that the next time she'd come into this cafe would be with Oliver Lomax. She'd never envisaged meeting him at all, unless it was to inflict some grotesque revenge on him, or to see him across a courtroom being sentenced to a good long spell in prison for what he'd done to her daughter. His parents would have been buckling under the horror, receiving a taste of what it was like to lose a child.

Looking at him now, as he sat down at a corner table with her, she realised that all she was feeling towards him was relief, maybe gratitude to know that he cared about what had happened to Lauren, and admiration too for the way he'd found the courage to come and see her. She also felt a stirring of pity for what Philip Leesom's plans for that Saturday night had brought upon him, as innocent a victim as Lauren herself.

'I thought you'd hate me,' he said, staring down at his can of drink. 'I guess you do. I don't blame you.'

Being truthful, Emma said, 'I thought I would too, but I'm finding that I don't.'

His eyes flicked up to hers, then went down again. 'Why not, I hate myself.'

She wanted to put a hand on his, but was afraid it would be inappropriate, or unwelcome, so she held back. 'How's your mother?' she asked.

He stiffened and she sensed a barrier going up around him.

'I know she called you that night,' she explained, 'and it's why you were in the car. The police told me.'

His eyes stayed down. She could see pools of colour burning his cheeks. 'She's . . . She's an alcoholic,' he said, his voice catching on a breath.

'I'm sorry,' she said, meaning it for him. For his mother who, in her eyes, was as culpable as Philip Leesom, she had little pity to spare. 'Is she getting help?' she asked.

He nodded. 'Yes, kind of. She's in Cape Town with her sister, my aunt. Well, not with her exactly, because Olivia's managed to get her into rehab.'

What a pity it hadn't happened sooner, Emma couldn't help thinking.

'My dad's over there at the moment,' he went on. 'She checked herself out and wouldn't go back unless he came to see her.' His breath shuddered again as he tried to continue. 'It's all been pretty tough on him, her drinking, and I don't think I've, you know . . . He keeps trying to help me and like be there for me, but then something happens with Mum . . . Anyway, what's the point bothering about me? I've got to pay for what I've done, and all that really matters is . . .' He shrugged and kept his eyes on his hands.

It was a moment before Emma realised that it was Lauren's name he'd stopped short of saying, as though afraid he might not have the right to speak it.

'Sorry,' he said hoarsely.

He was so young, Emma was thinking, so afraid and so shattered by what had happened that she couldn't help feeling for him. 'What music were you playing to her when I came in?' she asked, realising it would be easier for him, perhaps for them both, if she steered them in another direction for a while.

He pulled out his iPod to show her. 'I made up this playlist,' he explained. 'It's got all these flute numbers, ones I heard her playing on YouTube, and some jazz-rap stuff, because I get that she likes that, and then I put on some Radiohead, which is mainly what I like, just in case she might be interested to know what I . . . I don't expect she is. Actually I don't know why I did that.'

'You've been watching her on YouTube?' Emma said.

He nodded, then alarm darkened his eyes. 'That sounds really creepy, doesn't it? I never thought of it like that.'

Emma couldn't help but smile. With anyone else it might have seemed creepy; with him, well, somehow it didn't. 'I think she'd like it,' she told him.

He looked pleased, then doubtful, as though suspecting she was just being polite.

'No, really,' she said, in spite of having no idea what Lauren might be making of it, were she able to make anything at all. The point was, she didn't feel it to be

357

sinister, only thoughtful and in a way tragic for what it was doing to him. Had anyone noticed how deeply he was suffering, she wondered. From what little she knew of alcoholics they soaked up all the attention; they broke families apart with an implosion that seemed to suck out all that was good about them. The young, the vulnerable were left damaged in the wings, wondering what went wrong, if it was something they'd done to cause this destruction of their world.

Was that what was happening to Oliver Lomax?

'How long's your dad going to be away?' she asked.

'He went last week, but he's coming home tomorrow.'

'And is your mother coming with him?'

'No, she's gone back into rehab now.'

'Well, I guess that's a good thing.'

He nodded. 'It'll give Dad a chance to focus on his business a bit more when he gets home. He's felt bad about neglecting it and things haven't been going too well lately.'

'What does he do?'

'He's a freelance exec producer, which means he represents independent producers to the broadcasters. Everyone's cutting back on their programme budgets, so it's not easy getting anything off the ground. He's worried about having to let his staff go.'

'How many staff does he have?'

'Permanently, only three, but once the commissions we're doing now are complete, we haven't got anything to go on to.'

'You work with him, do you?'

'Kind of. I've been helping out one of the producers with a series about stately homes. He doesn't really need me, but he pretends to to keep Dad happy, and I reckon it's Dad who's actually paying me. It won't be coming out of the budget, because it's not big enough.'

Emma smiled. 'It's not an easy time for anyone,' she commented.

He was staring at nothing as he muttered, 'Tell me about it.' Then, collecting himself, 'Sorry, I didn't mean . . . Obviously, it's a lot worse for . . .'

'Lauren?'

He nodded. 'And you, I guess. I wish I could change things, make it all right. I would if I could.'

'You're doing what you can, which is a lot more than most would in your shoes.'

He swallowed hard and bowed his head again. 'Yeah, well, she's kind of, you know, special, isn't she?' he said haltingly.

Touched that he would think so, Emma watched him, waiting for him to look up again, but he didn't.

'When I saw all the stuff on Facebook,' he said, 'and on YouTube, it was like . . .' He shrugged, seeming stuck for the right words. 'Everyone really hates me for what I did and I don't blame them. She had so much going for her and I came along and ruined it all.'

'Not purposely,' Emma reminded him, quietly surprised to find herself defending him.

'No, definitely not purposely, but it was my fault. I'd been drinking, so I shouldn't have been driving, and I wouldn't have been if Mum hadn't . . .' He gave an odd sort of gasp. 'I should have stopped to think before I got in the car, but I didn't and now . . . Now . . .'

Reaching for his can of soda, she popped open the tab and handed it back again. 'What's happening in regard to the drink-driving charges?' she asked.

He shrugged again and continued to stare down at his can. 'I went in front of the magistrates the week before last,' he replied. 'They've referred my case on to the Crown Court. The preliminary hearing's on the seventh of next month.'

Realising how much bigger this was for him than he was making it sound, she said, 'I heard about your blood sample being lost, but I believe it turned up again?'

He nodded. 'We still haven't had the results from it, though. Charlie, that's my brother, reckons they're screwing up all over the place because of the cutbacks.'

'So do you think they've lost it again?'

'No, apparently they've just got this enormous backlog. It'll be positive, anyway, I know that.' He took a breath, then another. 'It's doing my dad's head in thinking about me going to prison.'

Imagining it was, Emma asked, 'And what about you? Is it scaring you too?'

He swallowed. 'I try not to think about it too much. Jolyon, my lawyer, keeps saying it might not come to that, but I reckon he's just trying to make me feel better.' At last his eyes came fleetingly to hers. 'They're going to try to get me off by citing special reasons, but that won't get Lauren off, will it? And I don't see why she should be left to suffer while I walk away scot-free, especially when none of it was her fault.'

Amazed by the apparent depth of his feelings, Emma said, 'No, it wasn't her fault, but actually, I can't see how you going to prison will help her either.'

He didn't seem to have an answer for that, and because she was slightly thrown by the fact that she'd even said it, she let the silence run for a while. What did she want to happen to him, she was asking herself. Would it be right for him simply to get away with it? Of course not, but what was sending him to prison going to prove, or change?

Dreading to think of what Will might say if he had any inkling of the way her mind was working, she finished her tea and said, 'I should go back and see her. What are you going to do now?'

He seemed at a loss. 'Go home, I guess.'

'Is anyone there, with your parents away?'

'Not today, but Charlie's been around for a while. He's gone back to London now though. He's just passed his bar exams and he's about to start his pupillage at some major chambers next Monday. Dad's really proud of him.'

Detecting a note of disappointment in himself, she swallowed the urge to reassure him in a way that would probably sound patronising, even fatuous, considering the circumstances, and got to her feet.

'Will you come to see Lauren again?' she asked.

He stood up too. She could see both amazement and misgiving in his eyes. 'I'd like to, if it's all right with you,' he replied tentatively.

Her mother, Polly, Will, and almost everyone else would probably think she'd gone totally mad. Nevertheless she said, 'It's fine with me. It's nice to know she's not on her own during the times the rest of us can't be here.'

'Thanks,' he murmured, trying to hold her eyes.

She held out a hand to shake. 'It was good meeting you,' she told him, realising it was true.

'It was good meeting you too,' he replied, taking her hand.

'If anything happens when you're with her, if she shows any sign at all of waking up, will you let me know? I'll give you my number.'

'Of course,' he said, taking out his mobile. 'I'll put it straight in my phone.'

After double-checking he'd got it right, she led the way outside.

'Thanks for saying it's OK to come,' he said, holding back to show he wasn't going to follow her.

She looked up at him and gave a small nod, before turning to walk back to the ward.

Thanks to a two-hour delay taking off from Cape Town, it was close to ten in the morning by the time Russ cleared customs at Heathrow and was able to collect his car from the long-term parking. The weather, he decided as he headed out to the motorway, was doing a better job of brightening the day than his mood. However, it was good to be on his way home after a seemingly endless eleven-and-a-half-hour flight, not to mention the gruelling week that had gone before it.

Still, at least Sylvie was back in the clinic now, and promising to stay put until she'd kicked her dependency, which would be making him feel a whole lot better if he believed her. However, he wasn't going to trouble himself with it now – God knew he'd had enough of it over the past seven days, finding Sylvie more difficult than ever, even with Olivia's support. Hans, Olivia's husband, had seemed to deal best with her, showing considerable sensitivity and understanding for her condition, largely because he'd been through the same nightmare a few years back with his oldest brother. The brother, tragically, had ended up choking to death on his own vomit while slumped on the doorstep of his twenty-nine-year-old daughter's Constantia home.

The story of this undignified and desperate end and the damage it had caused his family, his daughter in particular, had, predictably, had no lasting effect on Sylvie. However, Hans remained certain that Sylvie would take it very deeply to heart when she finally came out of rehab, and would be eager to thank God, Olivia, Russ, the entire universe for how narrowly she had escaped a similar fate.

Russ could only hope Hans was right, but there was still a long way to go before this could be confirmed. When, if, that time ever came, Russ would just have to hope that discovering their marriage really was over wouldn't send her straight back to the bottle.

'Are you sure it's over?' Olivia had asked while driving him to the airport the day before. 'Perhaps it is none of my business, but you still seem to care a great deal about her.'

He didn't admit to feeling that way against his will, simply saying, 'We've been together for twenty-five years, and we have two children together.'

'So you do it for them?'

'Of course.'

'And what about this woman, her friend, Fiona? Is it serious between you two?'

'No, it never was and it's over now anyway.' He hadn't felt proud of dismissing Fiona so abruptly, particularly when she'd called a few times since that fateful night, as a friend she always stressed, to find out how he was, and if there was anything she could do. He suspected if he wanted to start up their relationship again on the same terms as before she'd be more than willing, but he didn't, and was grateful to her for not suggesting it.

Connecting to Oliver's mobile via his hands-free, he left a message on the voicemail letting him know he should be home in time for lunch, if Oliver was going to be there. When he tried Charlie he ended up leaving a message for him too, telling him to call when he could. He felt ludicrously let down that neither of his sons was available for a chat, then absurd for thinking how lonely it suddenly seemed to be now he was back. He wasn't a huge socialiser, nor was he much given to discussing his problems, but spending some time with Hans and Olivia had, he realised, seemed to lessen some of the strain. Of course Sylvie had been the main concern for them all, but he'd found himself talking about Oliver too, and how withdrawn and purposeless he'd become since the accident. Though Hans and Olivia were sympathetic, naturally, there was really very little they could do, apart from agree that hanging about, waiting to find out what was to become of the girl, clearly wasn't helping Oliver to move on. Where Hans had felt he could make a difference was in offering Russ a loan to tide him over the difficult time he was having with his business. Russ's refusal had been polite, but firm enough, he hoped, for Hans not to try broaching the subject again.

He'd have to start pulling some rabbits out of the hat soon, though, or he was going to be facing the demoralising prospect of lay-offs, and might even, if things got any worse, have to start thinking about selling up. The house was too big for him on his own anyway, and running editing rooms and production offices so far from town was just plain crazy when centralised companies half his size had long since started to fold. Being located where he was hadn't mattered during the boom years, when the facilities were regularly booked out for weeks, even months, in advance. It was a very different story now, though, without any signs of a change on the horizon yet.

Oddly, the one person he'd expected to have difficulty getting hold of at this time of day didn't only turn out to be at his desk, but was available to take his call.

'I take it you're back,' Jolyon announced, dispensing with hello. 'Successful trip?'

'I guess you could put it that way,' Russ responded. 'Do you have time to bring me up to speed with any new developments?'

'As a matter of fact, I do have a few minutes before I'm due back over the road.'

Over the road in Jolyon's case was Bristol Crown Court. 'Where are you?' he asked.

'Driving down the M4.'

'OK, well it might be a good idea to stay out of the fast

lane while we go through this. First up, we've had the blood-test result at last and as expected, it's positive. However, because of its little journey into a black hole I requested it be sent off for independent analysis, and you're probably not going to believe this.'

'It was negative,' Russ suggested, knowing it couldn't be true, but actually daring to hope.

'No, it was positive all right, but it's turned out not to be Oliver's blood at all. In fact, it belongs to someone by the name of Otis Lomass, aged forty-three, an unemployed car mechanic of Afro-Caribbean descent who lives in Montpelier. So I'd say, not even close.'

Russ was stunned. 'So the real sample is still lost?'

'As far as I know, and I can't even guarantee anyone's still looking, but I guess they must be.'

Though this was obviously good news, Russ was far too cautious to start celebrating yet. 'Does Oliver know about this?'

'I left a message the other day for him to call, but so far he hasn't got back to me.'

Sighing, Russ said, 'Sorry about that. I'll talk to him when I get home.'

'Well, when you do you can tell him that the gods really are smiling on him, because the speed test shows that he was doing somewhere between forty-one and forty-four miles an hour at the point of impact, which puts him at a mere four miles an hour over the limit.'

Russ wasn't entirely sure what this meant. 'But he was over?' he queried.

'Indeed, just not sufficiently for a dangerous-driving charge to have particularly strong legs.'

Feeling the need to stop the car, Russ kept going in the slow lane as he said, 'So what's all this amounting to?'

'Well, when we throw in our special reasons and duress, we're going to have a pretty strong case for getting the whole thing thrown out. I've arranged a meeting with the region's senior prosecutor for the Thursday before the prelim, and if it goes to plan I think we could possibly find ourselves being sent home with not much more than a warning never to get in a car when under the influence again.'

'Jesus Christ,' Russ murmured. 'This isn't what I expected at all.'

'I can't say I'd have put any money on it, either,' Jolyon responded with no little irony.

'So – so what do Oliver and I do now?'

'You just carry on as normal and wait for my call.'

After ringing off, Russ continued to drive, barely noticing the traffic around him as he tried to come up with where the catch might be, because there surely had to be one. No one walked away from a drink-drive charge, much less dangerous driving when a young girl had been badly injured – but Charlie, and Jolyon, said they did, and more often than most people realised. Had he really understood everything correctly? Oliver's charges were possibly going to be thrown out, largely due to police error, or government cutbacks, or whatever the hell was going on at the labs or the station that had labelled and sent the blood in the first place. This could mean that Oliver wouldn't lose his licence, or receive a fine, or – and this was the really big one – if Jolyon pulled this off, Oliver wouldn't end up going to prison.

Though Russ knew he should be rejoicing, or at least allowing himself some modicum of relief, he was still finding it a struggle to make himself accept that it could be this easy. Or maybe it was the way Oliver was going to respond that was bothering him, because he had a fair idea of how it would go.

Russ realised, as he stepped on the accelerator, that in spite of knowing that the Scott family shouldn't be his concern, even he was starting to feel guilty about their own good fortune, when no amount of police blunders or special reasons were ever going to help Lauren Scott.

Chapter Twenty-Five

Emma almost wanted to laugh at the look on her mother's face. However, the constant dread inside her that had all joyful emotions trapped in its thrall wouldn't permit much hilarity, and besides it wasn't that funny. It was really only mildly amusing, and, now Emma came to think of it, a little annoying actually, but she was careful not to let that show. She and Phyllis had learned over the past few weeks how to steer clear of anything that could bring them into confrontation, particularly one that might threaten the fragile fences they were managing to build. They hadn't even tried to revisit Emma's exhausted attempt to force the issues between them. Instead, they skirted around the past – the great big slumbering elephant in the room – talking only about Lauren, or Harry and his family, or what they might need from Sainsbury's or Aldi, depending on who was doing the shopping.

They were gardening now in the early afternoon, and since the sun was shining and insect life was stirring, Emma was tempted to warn her mother that she might catch a fly if she didn't close her mouth soon.

'I – I don't know what to say,' Phyllis finally stammered, her fork still buried in the soil she was about to turn.

Emma kept her eyes fixed on the seed packets she was sorting – sweet peas, hollyhocks, lobelia, poppies – four packs for the price of two at the local DIY. They were attempting to create a border of wild flowers around the lawn (that had yet to be laid), envisaging a joyful abandon of colour ready for when Lauren came home. They never actually voiced those words, but Emma knew it was what they were both thinking, and though it would break her heart to watch the flowers come and go without Lauren seeing them, not planting them at all simply wasn't an option.

'Why are you only telling me this now?' Phyllis demanded.

Not entirely sure why she'd kept her encounter with Oliver Lomax to herself for the past two days, Emma sighed as she rocked back on to the small stool behind her.

'Aren't you upset?' Phyllis wanted to know. 'Angry? What did you say to him?'

'Actually we had quite a long chat,' Emma admitted, 'and he did most of the talking.'

Phyllis was still having difficulty assimilating the news. 'But you told him he mustn't go near her again?' she asked, rather than stated, clearly not wanting to sound bossy, but managing to anyway.

Realising how hard her mother was searching for the reaction that was going to cause the least discord between them, Emma said, 'I know this isn't going to be easy to understand, frankly, I hardly understand it myself, but when I found him there . . . I don't know . . .' She gazed out over the barren garden as she tried to collect her impressions of the encounter and turn them into words. 'There was something about the way he was with her,' she said. 'He was . . . Well, let's just say it didn't feel as wrong as you might think.'

Phyllis continued to look perplexed – and wary.

Pressing on, Emma said, 'Actually, I told him it was OK to visit her again and apparently he's been back since, Jo the staff nurse told me. He goes in the middle of the afternoon, before I get there, and so's not to clash with you in the morning.'

Phyllis shook her head in bewilderment, taking a breath and blowing it out slowly. 'Well, I must admit, this is very unexpected,' she declared, which was a surprising euphemism given how forcibly she normally aired her opinions. 'Have you told Will?' she asked, evidently hoping for some support from other quarters.

'No, of course not. As far as I'm concerned he doesn't have a right to know anything, and I hope you won't tell him either. He'll only start ringing the hospital ordering them to ban the boy or threatening to sue someone for invasion of privacy, or intimidation, or whatever spurious offence he can come up with.' She knew her mother might not want to hear this, and she was fairly certain she wouldn't have herself a week ago, but she hadn't met Oliver Lomax then. 'He struck me as a decent young man who's suffering greatly over what's happened. Plus, he really seems to care about Lauren.'

Phyllis blinked, and tried hard not to look sceptical.

'OK, I know that's difficult to believe,' Emma said, 'but it's the impression I got. He really wants her to recover, and not just because it'll get him off the hook, but because he . . .' She braced herself. 'He thinks . . . she's special.'

Phyllis looked away and back again, seeming more at a loss than ever.

Though Emma understood her mother's confusion, she was becoming increasingly irritated by it. 'Tell me what harm you think he can do by going to see her?' she cried. She hadn't meant to sound challenging, but there it was, she had now, and anyway, she needed to know just in case she was missing something.

'Well, off the top of my head I don't know,' Phyllis replied honestly. 'I'm just not sure it's . . . appropriate.'

Wanting to slap away the word like a fly, Emma said, 'In truth I'm not sure it is either, but nor can I find anything really wrong with it.'

Phyllis was clearly thinking hard about this. 'Unless,' she cautiously suggested, 'he's doing it to try and create a good impression. You know, to gain sympathy from a jury when the time comes.'

Having already thought of that and dismissed it, Emma didn't like having to confront it again. 'It's not coming across that way,' she said shortly. 'He truly does seem genuinely concerned, and sorry and afraid, for Lauren much more than for himself.' She went on quickly, 'He's recorded music for her to listen to, making choices that show what care he's put into it, and frankly, when I saw them together . . .' Her eyes went to her mother's and stayed there. 'He doesn't frighten me, or make me angry or vengeful, he just makes me feel . . . I don't know . . .

Sad, I suppose, for what all this has done to two young lives.'

Phyllis seemed startled. 'But I don't think you can compare what's happening to him to what's happening to Lauren,' she protested.

'Maybe not, but they're both victims of the same accident, and frankly, something feels *right* about them trying to help each other through it. And I think she does help him, or at least being with her does.'

'Which might be fine for him, but what's it doing for her?'

Emma's eyes clouded as she pictured Lauren lying on her hospital bed, the world going on around her while she remained trapped in another sphere where no one could reach her. 'We can't know that, can we,' she said, 'but you can't think I'd ever let this happen if I thought it could harm her in any way.'

'No, of course not,' Phyllis conceded.

They remained quiet for a while, continuing to dig and plant, the early spring sunshine warming them with unexpectedly bright rays, and the sounds of children playing in a nearby garden evoking memories neither of them wanted to dwell on. An easyJet flight thundered overhead, so close that if they'd looked up they might have actually seen faces at the windows. The ten thirty from Nice, Emma decided, and tried to smile over a flutter of poignancy as she realised this was the first time in over seven weeks that she'd even particularly registered a plane, never mind embarked on her and Lauren's little game.

'Shall we have a cup of tea?' Phyllis suggested when the noise died away.

A mother's answer to everything.

Emma checked her watch. She didn't work at the vet's on Wednesdays, so she had at least an hour to spare before it was time to drive over to see Lauren, though she'd been toying with the idea of turning up early in the hope of catching Oliver Lomax again. She felt surprisingly keen to see him, yet she was also finding herself reluctant to intrude on the private time he and Lauren shared. Her mother really would think she was losing it if she confessed that.

However, unless she was fooling herself, and she accepted that she very probably was, she was starting to believe that there really was something special, even healing, about them being together. Maybe this could even prove the miracle that Lauren needed.

'His mother's in a clinic, drying out,' she told Phyllis as they washed their hands at the kitchen sink. When she looked at Phyllis's hands she wondered if she was seeing her own in another twenty to thirty years. If she was, it wasn't making her feel anything other than curious to know why her mother still wore a wedding ring when she'd been a widow for so long. Had she really never met, or even felt interested in, anyone else during all that time?

'Well, that's good,' Phyllis commented. 'Just a pity she didn't do it before.'

Remembering how she'd thought the same thing, Emma reached for a towel as she said, 'He made it sound as though he's quite close to his father, which must be a blessing, given the way things are with his mother.'

Taking the towel, Phyllis said, 'You know, I really don't think you should be getting yourself involved with that family.'

Wishing her mother occasionally failed to irritate her, Emma replied, 'I'm not involved, I'm just making an observation. And anyway, what's wrong with taking an interest in what's going on with them? Whether we like it or not, we're going to be linked to them now for the rest of our lives.'

'Well that's just a daft thing to say,' Phyllis protested. 'Of course we're not *linked* to them. Once Lauren's through this and that young man is getting his comeuppance we'll never have to have anything to do with them again.'

Deciding not to argue, since she knew she wasn't being especially rational anyway, Emma slumped down in a chair, leaving her mother to carry on making the tea. The fact that she'd missed a period last month – obviously due to stress – and was clearly lining up for a particularly bad one this month wasn't her mother's fault, so she should try not to take it out on her.

'Oh my goodness,' Phyllis muttered, as she checked her mobile for texts.

Spurred into a tart response, Emma said, 'You know, you don't have to go on staying here. I understand that you've got a life of your own.'

Her mother's expression was injured as she looked up from her phone. 'I've just won ten pounds on the lottery,' she explained, 'but if this is your way of telling me you want me to go . . .'

'That's not what I said,' Emma broke in quickly. 'I'm just . . . Well, I'm just trying to let you know that I appreciate how you've put everything on hold for me, and that you must be worried about . . .' About what? What did she know about her mother's life? 'What I'm saying is, if you want to start spending less time here . . .'

'Have I given you any reason to think that? I hope not, because it would be completely the wrong impression. However, if you feel that I'm getting in the way and that you'd like to have more time to yourself . . .'

'Why are you putting words in my mouth? I'm simply trying to point out that I'm aware that you have friends and commitments that might need your attention . . .'

'There's nothing that Harry can't cope with, and as he's happy to keep an eye on the house and pick up my mail, I don't see any reason . . . Unless you . . . I mean I can always tell him to stop if you'd rather I went home.'

'Oh Mum, for heaven's sake, why are you being like this? You're taking everything the wrong way or getting it out of perspective.'

'I'm just saying that if you don't want me here . . .'

'Except that's not what I said. I was trying to be considerate, and now you're making me sound ungrateful and selfish and like I can't wait to get rid of you, when I've told you before that I don't know how I'd have managed without you.'

'But you can now, so you'd like to have the house back to yourself? It's all right, I understand that . . .'

'For crying out loud, I don't want you to go, all right? I want you to stay for as long as you like.'

'You're just saying that now . . .'

Emma growled in despair. 'What is it with you?' she said furiously. 'Let's just forget I said anything, shall we?

We'll go back to pretending that everything's absolutely perfect and that we love being under the same roof as one another, and that we get along just fine, the way most mothers and daughters do . . . We can do that, can't we?'

Phyllis's face was crimson. 'I didn't realise I was annoying you so much.'

'You don't usually,' Emma lied, 'but right now you are, probably because it's my time of the month, but also because I've never damned well understood you and whereas I can usually cope with that, today I'm finding it hard.'

Phyllis tried to speak, but Emma hadn't finished.

'For most of my life,' she ranted on, 'you've never wanted to be there for me – if anything you've done your level best to make me feel left out, unwanted, a nuisance, a liability, you were good at them all . . . In fact, if it weren't for Berry I wouldn't know what it was like to be loved, and yet now, here you are, prepared to give up everything to be here for me, and even when I give you the chance to escape with no recriminations you don't take it. So please forgive me for not understanding you and the way you operate because you're only my mother, so why should I?'

Phyllis's head was bowed as she allowed the anger to fold around her like shadows. 'Do you really have to shout?' she asked quietly.

Incensed all over again, Emma cried, 'No, yes, maybe I do, because I want you to hear me, Mum. I want you to know that I have feelings that can be hurt like anyone else's, especially by *you*, and God knows how often you've managed that over the years.'

'You always make so much of this,' Phyllis said haltingly, 'telling yourself that I don't care when I do and I always have . . .'

'Care, maybe, because that's what you're supposed to do, as a mother, but you're supposed to love your children too . . .'

'I've always loved you,' Phyllis protested, 'but I know . . . I accept I haven't always been good at showing it.'

'Are you kidding? You've never even tried to show it, at least not with me. You didn't have a problem with Harry though, did you? You were always there for him, going to his sports days, his weekend football matches, his prize-givings . . .'

'I came to yours too. I never missed one, so please don't . . .'

'The difference was with Harry you were always so proud of him and full of how brilliant he was, while with me you'd just say well done, you worked hard at that. Or don't let it go to your head now, we don't want you turning into a show-off. The only thing I've ever done that you seemed to think at all worthy of your time or attention was give birth to Lauren, and even then you behaved as if I'd played hardly any part in it. In fact, once you started bonding with her I was more in the way than ever, and no one was happier than you when I asked you to be her minder while I was working. You could have her all to yourself then and not have to worry about me, her mother, coming between you, because I didn't count anyway.'

'Emma, please . . .'

'No, I'm sorry, but you're going to hear me out whether you like it or not. It's high time you faced up to how awful you've been to me over the years, how small and insignificant you've made me feel, how sorry I always thought you were that you'd even had me. You wouldn't even allow me to talk about my own father. What kind of mother does that to her child, tries to shut her up every time she asks about her daddy? Why was it left to Berry to fill in the blanks, to paint the pictures of who he was and how much Harry and I meant to him? What was wrong with talking about him yourself? Didn't you think I had a right to know? Are you so selfish with your memories that you can't even allow me to share them?'

'It wasn't like that,' Phyllis choked. 'The way things happened . . . You were very young, in my way I was too, and I admit I got things wrong . . .'

'But you never did anything to put them right. I kept on and on as a child, always needing to know what I'd done to make you angry, why you couldn't bring yourself to love me the way my friends' mothers seemed to love them, and that hasn't changed because I *still need to know*. No, stop, I know what you're going to say, that I'm exaggerating and getting hysterical, because that's what you always say at times like this. You tell me I'm working myself into a state that won't do any good at all, because everything's in my head and I'm so full of self-pity that it's no wonder you can't feel sorry for me; there's no room left for any more.' Though her mother flinched and tried to interrupt again, Emma still wouldn't let her. 'You're so full of sensitivity and understanding,' she said scathingly, 'so blessed with warmth and generosity that I can only wonder how I've managed to concoct such a dreadful image of you. Everyone respects and admires you, talks about how dedicated and courageous you were to bring up two children all on your own, and what a wonderful job you've made of it. Just let's not talk about Berry and how everything, probably including you, would have fallen apart if it weren't for her. Let's not mention how miserable and alone I would have been if it weren't for my grandmother; how insecure I always felt, and unworthy, because you never seemed to have time for me. The only reason I've managed to reach where I am now without massive complexes or hang-ups is because Berry made sure I didn't. She's always been there for me, making me feel special, loved, clever, all the things you should have been making me feel, but you never wanted to, did you? You could do it for Harry though, Harry who made you light up whenever he came into a room, while you barely even managed a smile for me. Even he knew it was all wrong, which was why he used to stay at home such a lot to play with me when he should have been out with his friends conkering, or swimming, or doing whatever the hell else little boys of his age do. He used to feel horrible about being the favourite, it created its own kind of pressure, but you never saw that, did you? You only saw what you wanted to see and that was hardly ever me.'

Phyllis's face was in her hands. She was shaking so badly that it was a moment before she could say, 'I don't know what to tell you to try and make things better. Maybe I should go home, but I . . . I know what Berry would say, she'd say I was running away again and I don't want to do that any more.' She brought her head up; her face was tormented with misery and guilt. 'I've wanted to talk to you for such a long time, but the gulf between us is so wide . . . Every time I try to reach out I end up clutching empty air because you've already gone. I don't blame you, why would you want to listen to anything I have to say after all I've put you through? I know I should have tried harder when you were young, that I shouldn't have allowed my own grief to come before yours, but that's the trouble with grief, it changes us, makes us behave in ways we never would have before. I'm sorry, I'm really sorry,' she sobbed, too devastated to say more for the moment.

Embarrassed by her mother's tears, and guilty for having caused them, Emma said, 'Well now's your chance to tell me why there's such a gulf between us. I'm listening, and I want to know why you've always been so cold with me.'

'It's not how I wanted to be,' Phyllis assured her brokenly. 'It was just . . . I . . . We were close before your father died, the way you were with Lauren when she was that age. You were always a daddy's girl though, but that was something I loved, so did he. He'd do anything for you, the discipline was left to me, and you turned out to need more than Harry had when he was two and three. Your father used to call you the champion tantrum-thrower; he actually seemed proud of how good you were at them. He was the only one who could laugh you out of them, while I could never get you to stop. If your father wasn't around you'd go on and on screaming until you finally wore yourself out or wore me down.

'Then one day, it was the day of the storm that . . . We were all at home feeling dismal because it hadn't stopped raining for days. Your father was due to go off on tour the following week, so he was taking some time off to be with us before he left. We'd planned lots of day trips, the zoo, Longleat, the beach, but the furthest we'd managed by Thursday was our own back garden for a picnic in the Wendy house. Do you remember that Wendy house?'

Emma shook her head.

Phyllis smiled sadly. 'You were still very young, so I don't suppose that's surprising. It's a pity though, because your father and Keith from the band built it for you. It was just about big enough for us all to squeeze into, you, me, Dad and Harry, and so we sat around your little table drinking lemonade and eating the biscuits you and I had made. You'd brought your favourite doll, Maryjo, in her pushchair, and Harry had brought his bike which he'd parked outside. The rain wasn't quite as fierce as it had been, so we were quite cosy and warm inside with not too many leaks. We had a little sing-song and then Dad told a story. He was very good at making up stories. I often wish I'd written them down. I kept saying I would, but somehow never got round to it, and then it was . . . Anyway, those brief couple of hours turned out to be our only excursion of the week, because later in the day the rain became torrential again, and the thunder was so loud I was terrified a bolt would come through the roof.

'It was in the middle of Friday morning that lightning struck the Goodleys' horse chestnut next door and brought it down. It's strange, but I don't remember it making any noise as it fell, but I'm sure it must have. In fact, none of us heard it. The first we knew of it was when you looked out of the window and saw that your Wendy house had been crushed. It wasn't the house you were so worried about, it was the doll you'd left inside. You wanted to go running out to get it, but the storm was so bad we couldn't allow you to. We tried telling you she'd be fine and that you must wait till the storm was over, but you wouldn't listen. You had to have her now. You started screaming and kicking, begging me to let you go, but I wouldn't give in. There was no point, you wouldn't have been able to get to the Wendy house anyway. So you turned to your father, telling him he had to go. "Please, please, please," you kept saying."Daddy, you have to . . . You have to." You were in such a state that in the end he couldn't stop himself giving in to you. So he scooped you up, gave you a great big kiss, then set you back down on the floor and went to get his coat. "Superman to the rescue," he cried.' Phyllis's voice had become quavery and thin. It was clear how hard it was for her to be saying all this. 'You giggled, the way you always did when he played the hero, and then off he went into the storm, in spite of knowing how impossible it was going to be to get anywhere near the Wendy house through all the branches of the fallen tree. He tried, though; he really did. I expected him to pretend for a while, then come back with one of his stories about how Prince Charming had beaten him to it and dolly was now a princess in a far-off land, but would be back to see you when the storm was over. Or maybe he was going to say that she was busy saving all the other toys from the storm and would be in as soon as she knew they were safe. He'd think of something, he always did, it just never occurred to me that he'd actually try to get her.'

She had to pause for breath, and Emma felt her heart churning with pity for the young woman who'd lost her husband so suddenly and tragically. It was almost unbearable. Were it possible she'd have gone to embrace her mother, but habits of a lifetime were hard to break. They simply didn't do things like that.

'Neither of us even thought about the power cables,' Phyllis struggled on. 'We hadn't even noticed they were down . . .'

Realising how hard this had become for her now, Emma said gently, 'Mum, it's all right, you don't have to put yourself through any more.' Her own eyes were filling with tears as she envisaged what her mother must have been seeing in her memory.

'He was a wonderful man,' Phyllis sobbed, 'the best father . . . It broke my heart to lose him, and I . . . Oh God, I'm sorry, Emma, I'm truly sorry that I blamed you. You were just a child, you didn't know any better, but I told myself that if it weren't for you he wouldn't have gone out there. He could never say no to you, and after he died it was all I wanted to say, no, no, no, as if it might make up for all the times he should have said it, and somehow bring him back. I never told anyone the reason why he'd gone out into the storm. I didn't want them to know that he'd died so needlessly – so stupidly heroically. Maybe it was because I didn't tell anyone that it all got mixed up in my head – I don't know. I only know that I felt this awful need to punish you, and my way of doing it was to keep you at a distance, withhold all displays of love, make you feel guilty somehow even though you didn't know what you were feeling guilty about. How could you, you hadn't done anything wrong, and you were far too young to understand what was happening to me. By the time I realised what I was doing to you, too many years had gone by to undo the damage. We'd grown apart – Berry kept warning me we would; she'd say, "You can't go through the motions of being a mother without putting in the emotion," and I'd tell her she didn't know what she was talking about. My arrogance was insufferable. I don't how she put up with it. I never wanted to listen to her. I didn't want to do anything except find a way to bring your father back. It was all that mattered for more years than I care to remember. It sounds like madness, I know, but I've learned the hard way that grief is a kind of madness. We never know how it's going to take us, or what it's going to make us do. It's like a life force of its own and escaping it is almost impossible. Or that was how I found it, until . . .' Her head went down as she swallowed hard. 'Until I finally took Berry's advice and got some counselling.'

Emma felt quietly stunned. Her mother had sought help? *Her mother* had been to see a therapist, a counsellor? It seemed improbable, incredible, until she remembered that this was a woman she hardly knew, so how would she have any idea what Phyllis might, or might not do? And since she still wasn't sure whether she herself should be feeling guilt, pity, anger, relief, or some other emotion for sending her father out into the storm, she found that all she could do was stay silent.

'Of course, I should have gone to see someone years ago,' Phyllis went on. 'Actually I did try, around the time you left home. I thought that once there was some actual distance between us I'd be able to see things more clearly, get a better perspective on what Berry was trying to tell me, but looking back I can see now that I was so riddled with guilt over the way I'd been with you, and so unable to imagine a way forward for us that I just couldn't bring myself to go on trying. I convinced myself that we were a lost cause; that we were never going to get past what I'd done and that never having a close relationship with you was the price I had to pay for the way I'd been. Then, when Lauren was born, I thought maybe I could try making it up to you through her. I wanted to be the best grandmother, to show you that no matter what, I was going to be there for her whenever you needed me to be. You're right, I was thrilled when you asked me to be her minder; I knew you wouldn't have done that unless you trusted me, so I told myself that maybe there was something between us, because it seemed the affection, the love I'd shown Lauren from the day she was born had made an impression on you. I never realised until now that it had made you feel left out, pushed aside. I thought the way you stayed aloof meant that you really didn't want to have a relationship with me, that you'd rather just carry on going through the motions of being mother and daughter, while I forged a bond with Lauren. I can see now that I misunderstood everything, and I know it's all my fault, I just wish I knew what to do to make you realise how sorry I am, and how much you really mean to me. I promise you, it's as much as Lauren means to you . . .' Tears were strangling her voice again, and as she turned around to start busying herself with the tea Emma could see how badly her hands were shaking.

Knowing exactly what Berry and Lauren would want her to do now, and actually wanting to do it herself, she went to stand beside her mother and slipped an arm round her shoulders. 'Thank you for telling me all that,' she said softly. 'I know it can't have been easy.'

As Phyllis started to break down, Emma pulled her round and wrapped her up tightly in her arms. It felt strange holding her mother, but not so strange that it felt wrong, only new and something that wasn't so difficult after all.

'It's all right,' she said, tears running down her own cheeks. 'It's going to be all right.'

Phyllis tried to speak, but could only nod.

After a while Emma gently eased her towards a chair. 'Sit down,' she said, 'I'll make the tea.'

'No, no, don't worry about me. I know it's time you were going.'

'It won't matter if I'm a few minutes late.'

Phyllis looked at her anxiously, taking the square of kitchen roll Emma was holding out. 'I'll be fine, honestly,' she promised.

'I know you will, but I don't want to leave now. With everything you've just told me . . .'

Accepting that it had to be Emma's decision, Phyllis sat down and blew her nose. 'I got some Earl Grey the last time I was in Sainsbury's,' she said nasally.

Emma glanced over at her. She'd spotted the tea, but had assumed her mother had bought it for herself.

'I got it for you,' Phyllis assured her. 'I know you like it and I thought . . . Well, I know it can be a bit pricey . . .'

'That's lovely, thanks,' Emma said, realising with an awful pang how quick she'd been to think badly of her mother.

After making them a large mug each she carried them to the table and sank into the other chair. 'They say everything comes in threes,' she said, trying to sound light, 'even good things, and we seem to have started off well today.'

Phyllis looked baffled.

Emma shrugged. 'Well, there's us, and the fact that we've just communicated some of our feelings for the first time in years, maybe ever. That has to be good, doesn't it?'

Phyllis nodded keenly. 'Yes, of course,' she agreed.

Emma's eyes twinkled. 'And you've won the lottery,' she reminded her.

Phyllis gave a choke of laughter.

'So I'm wondering what the third thing might be.'

At that Phyllis almost seemed to melt. 'Oh, Emma, wouldn't it be wonderful?' she said, knowing exactly what Emma was thinking.

'Yes, it would,' Emma replied, looking down at her tea. Why was she suddenly afraid that fate had brought her and her mother together to make up for taking Lauren away? 'It really would,' she whispered, trying hard to banish the fear from her mind.

'You're not going to believe this,' Angie declared as Russ walked into the office in the middle of the afternoon. 'Three green lights, one straight after the other.'

Though distracted, this immediately grabbed Russ's attention. 'Tell me more,' he demanded, registering Oliver's empty desk as he went to his own.

'All three are non-broadcast,' Angie said, busily forwarding the emails so he could read them himself. 'Strachan's Security training video; Beaumont polo club matches for all of the coming season, first fixture or chukka or whatever they call it, April 2nd, so that's where Graham is now, recceing the ground with Lance Fulmer, the director; and Winston's Oil have only approved the budget for their role-play operations. Haven't done the sums yet, but if you look out the door I reckon you'll see that big, bad wolf skulking off down the drive with his tail between his legs.'

Laughing, Russ clicked on to the emails to check the details, while Toyah and Angie danced a little jig, and Toyah's spaniel, Jack, gave a joyful howl.

'Is Oliver out with Paul?' Russ asked, as he began scanning the first confirmation of a proposal he himself had put forward.

'If he was, he's not now,' Toyah answered, glancing out of the window as Charlie's black Golf pulled up outside. 'By the way, I've got a quote for him to drive his mother's car. It's steep, so brace yourself.'

'Go on,' Russ murmured as he watched Oliver getting out of the Golf and going into the house.

'Two thousand seven hundred.'

Russ winced.

'It's a Merc,' Toyah pointed out, 'and he's only got two years' worth of no claims.'

Grateful she hadn't added 'for now', or reminded him that he'd paid for the Polo's smashed windscreen in order to avoid a claim, he said, 'Well, he's adamant he won't drive his own car again, so I guess, with a premium like that, the only alternative is to part-exchange the Polo for something else.'

Toyah and Angie looked at each other.

'I know what you're thinking,' Russ told them, his eyes back on the screen, 'shouldn't we at least wait until we know if he's going to keep his licence, and of course we will. I'm hoping we'll have some news on that by the end of next week. OK, these commissions are definitely signalling an end to our little bad patch – and let's hope that's all it was, a patch. Winston's budget alone should keep us going until August, which isn't perfect, but we're in a hell of a lot better place now than we were this morning. So, this is me breathing again, and you, Toyah, breaking out the Tetley's to celebrate. We'll wait till Paul and the others are back to crack open something stronger. I think three in one go deserves a sparkling celebration.'

'Aren't you staying for tea?' Toyah protested as he started for the door.

'I won't be long,' he assured her

A few minutes later he found Oliver on his way up the stairs, a sandwich in one hand, a can of Fanta in the other. 'A bit late for lunch, isn't it?' he commented.

'I didn't get any, so this is it,' Oliver replied, clearly annoyed that he hadn't made it to his room before his father came in.

'Don't go any further,' Russ told him as he started on up the stairs. 'I want to talk to you.'

Oliver stopped and let his head fall back in frustration. 'Dad, if you're going to start on about where I've been again . . .'

'That's exactly what I'm going to do,' Russ informed him. 'This is the fourth afternoon in a row you've vanished without telling anyone where you're going or when to expect you back, and frankly I've had enough of it. So what the hell are you up to, Oliver? And please don't start spinning me some story about being with Jerome, or Alfie, because Alfie called here about an hour ago wondering what on earth's happened to you because neither he nor Jerome have been able to get hold of you for days. Nor has Charlie, he tells me, though I got the feeling when I spoke to him earlier that he knows more about what you're up to than he's prepared to let on to me.'

Oliver's body was rigid with defiance.

'I don't understand what the problem is about telling me,' Russ exclaimed, throwing out his hands. 'Or do you like me being worried out of my mind, imagining all sorts of things that probably aren't anything to do with what's really going on? Let's seriously stress Dad out, shall we, is that what you're thinking? Let's give him sleepless nights and treat him as though he's oblivious to what's going on. Is that what you're telling yourself? Because if it is, I've got news for you, my son . . .'

Turning around, and sinking down on the stairs, Oliver put down his Fanta and sandwich and propped his head in his hands. 'I'm not trying to make you worried,' he said truthfully, 'it's just that I know you won't understand.'

'Is that right? Well, why don't you let me be the judge?'

'Because I know you'll think I'm losing it,' Oliver cried, 'or say I'm in some sort of post-traumatic stress, and I'm not. I'm just . . . It's something I feel I have to do, actually that I *want* to do, and I'm going to go on doing it whether you like it or not.'

Russ gave it a moment. 'OK,' he said levelly, 'so if your mind's made up and you're sure I can't change it, why not at least do me the favour of putting an end to all the things I've got going round in my head and tell me what's in yours?'

Oliver's eyes came to his, then went down again. He was so tense now that Russ could feel himself picking up on it.

'Come on, son, it can't be that bad, surely.'

'All right,' Oliver said in the end, defiance already thickening his voice. 'I've been going to the hospital to see . . . to see Lauren.'

It took all Russ's self-control not to show a reaction. This was so unexpected that right at this moment he genuinely didn't know which way to go.

'So come on, let's have it,' Oliver challenged sarcastically. 'I know you're going to say something about me going off my head, or not thinking straight . . .'

'I'm not going to say anything of the sort,' Russ interrupted sharply, while still not knowing what he did want to say. 'But I am wondering . . . I mean, it's just crossing my mind to ask if it's wise . . . Or to wonder what you're hoping to gain by it.'

Clearly angry, Oliver said, 'I just want to see her, OK? What's so bad about that? I'm the one who put her where she is, so what am I supposed to do, run away and pretend it hasn't happened?'

Obviously that wasn't what Russ wanted. Or maybe it was. After all, what was to be gained from Oliver forging a link with a girl whom he didn't know, and if things didn't improve, never would, especially when he'd helped to bring about this situation? 'No, not at all,' he heard himself saying, 'but . . . Well, you have to think of her family and how they might feel if they knew . . .'

'Her mother does know, and she's OK about me going.'

Russ was lost for words again. Oliver didn't sound as though he was lying, but Russ simply couldn't imagine Lauren Scott's mother wanting Oliver anywhere near her daughter.

'You don't believe me, do you?' Oliver demanded.

Russ took a breath, only to realise he was lost for words again. In the end, he prevaricated. 'How does her mother know?' he asked.

'She came into the hospital when I was there last week,' Oliver told him, 'and we went to get a drink together.'

Wondering how much more stunned he was going to become by this, Russ said, 'You went to get a drink? With Mrs Scott. So presumably you talked.'

Oliver rolled his eyes.

'What did you talk about?'

'What do you think?' Oliver retorted.

'The girl. Lauren.'

'Like yes, and she asked about Mum, and how my case was coming along . . . Actually, she was really cool, not a bit like I thought she'd be, or at least not with me.'

Russ took a breath as he tried to shift gears. Somewhere along the line he'd get a better grip on this. 'So how long have you been going to see her?' he asked.

'About three weeks, I guess.'

'Every day?'

'Most days.'

'And what . . . what do you do when you're there?' *Wasn't the girl in a coma?*

'I take music for her to listen to, and I read stuff from the papers or magazines I think she might be interested in. They say you should do things like that for people in a coma.'

Russ had heard that, he'd just never expected to encounter it this way. 'So you're doing it for her?'

'That's what I just said.'

Russ needed more time to adjust, to work out what the heck he really thought, but if he took too long it wasn't going to sit well with Oliver. 'So her mother really doesn't mind,' he said, hoping this would buy him some time.

Oliver took out his mobile. 'I've got her number here. If you don't believe me, ring her.'

Russ looked at the phone, but didn't take it. 'It's OK, I don't need to do that,' he responded. 'If you say she's all right with it, then I guess . . . Well, I guess that's that.'

Oliver regarded him sceptically.

'Except how long is it going to go on?' Russ had to ask.

As though he'd seen it coming, Oliver cried, 'I don't know. For as long as it takes.'

'Are you saying, until she comes round?'

Oliver's jaw tightened as he turned his face away. Clearly he knew it didn't make much sense, but he wasn't going to try explaining it.

'You do realise . . .' Russ began.

'That it could be years. Of course I do, I'm not stupid.'

'So are you telling me you're going to carry on visiting her . . .'

Oliver sprang to his feet. 'See, I told you you wouldn't understand, and you're already having a go . . .'

'No, I'm just trying to be clear about what your intentions are,' Russ assured him. 'And I know you won't want to hear this, but you need to find a job . . .'

'No! What I need is to do this, OK? Nothing else matters. I know that's hard for someone like you to get your head around, but for me, what counts is getting her back to who she really is.'

Russ felt oddly as though he'd been punched. 'Is it OK for me to tell you what matters to me?' he said. 'I know it probably doesn't feature very large for you, but for me *all* that matters is you and what you're going to do with your life.'

Oliver seemed beside himself with frustration. 'I knew you wouldn't get it, because you see, as far as I'm concerned, if she doesn't have a future then I don't have one either.'

Stunned again, Russ could only look at him as he realised that through the cyber connection and now these visits Oliver hadn't only managed to fall for the girl, he was starting to identify himself with her in a way that . . . Well, in a way that was unnatural, to say the least. Russ wondered what Charlie was making of it, since he surely knew. The fact that he was keeping the confidence presumably meant he had a better handle on it than Russ was achieving. However, neither of his sons had yet had to deal with any real responsibility in their lives, and their generation saw things very differently.

Oliver said, 'I know you don't get this, Dad, but she's something else. She really is.'

Russ didn't argue. How could he, when he'd already put forward his concerns and they'd apparently made no impact at all? He searched for some words of advice, but he had none. He wasn't even sure what else to ask. He only knew, sensed, that there was no point trying to reason with Oliver any more over this, because the time for that had clearly already come and gone.

Chapter Twenty-Six

Emma and her mother were being shown around the Brain Injury Rehabilitation Centre at Frenchay. Though it was on the same site as the hospital, it was a privately owned unit with an atmosphere that made it feel almost luxurious in comparison to the tired old building where Lauren was now. Of course, it was way beyond anything they could afford; however, Dr Hanworth, the senior consultant, who'd already assessed Lauren at the invitation of one of his ward colleagues, had explained that most, if not all, of the patients were funded by their Primary Care Trusts. He was of the opinion that Lauren could qualify for funding too, and virtually from the moment he'd shown Emma through the door she'd known she'd do just about anything to get Lauren here. It was so welcoming and spacious, surrounded by tree-shaded patios and with wide, light corridors leading off a hexagonal-shaped reception. Each patient had his or her own private room with posters and photos on the walls, a TV on the dressing table and their own clothes in the wardrobe. The dining room, just off the reception, was like an upmarket cafe with round shiny tables, plenty of space to manoeuvre wheelchairs in and out, and a well-equipped kitchen next door where patients and visitors could make cups of tea or even prepare food.

'We hold all sorts of events and competitions,' the centre's manager, Anita, was telling them as they wandered through to an occupational therapy room. 'Anything from *Come Dine with Me*, to poetry readings or plays, to races in the pool. We have parties for birthdays, Christmas, Easter, Halloween, you name it, which makes for a very busy time in the OT department, as I'm sure you can imagine.'

'You mean the patients make their own costumes and hats and things?' Phyllis ventured, as Emma shrank inside at the thought of Lauren being here for so long.

'Absolutely everything,' Anita confirmed. 'They're usually a lot of fun, these bashes, for all of us.'

'As I explained to you at our first meeting,' Dr Hanworth continued, as he returned them to the hexagon to direct them down another corridor with rooms either side, each displaying a patient's name and sometimes photo on the door, 'if Lauren does join us she'll have a dedicated team of supporters, starting with a key worker who'll devise her routine with the OTs, physios, psychologists and speech and language therapists.'

Realising that couldn't happen until Lauren was conscious, Emma said, 'So what do we have to do to get her a place here while she's like she is?'

'Nothing,' he replied, leading the way into the gym, where a badly scarred young Asian man was being helped on to the treadmill by his physio. 'I will make the application for you. It could take the PCT a while to respond, and I'm afraid there are no guarantees that they will come through, but in Lauren's case I really do consider it worth a try.'

'Even though we've no idea how long her coma might last?'

'That isn't a problem for us, but I have to admit that the decision-makers might see it as an obstacle to funding. They don't like open-ended situations. However, they might well agree to pay for three or six months' care, and once she's here it'll be much easier for us to make the case to keep her until she's ready to go home.'

Feeling, naively perhaps, that it all seemed so much more possible from here, Emma turned to watch a young woman being wheeled in by a nurse, her head lolling on to one shoulder, her eyes staring blankly ahead. Was she conscious? How much did she know about what was going on around her?

'How many patients do you have here at any one time?' she asked.

'We have twenty rooms,' Anita answered, 'so no more than that.'

'Are they all ages?' Phyllis wondered.

'From sixteen up.'

'Would you like to see the hydrotherapy pool next?' Andy Hanworth suggested.

Half an hour later, clutching a glossy brochure each, and some very high hopes, Emma and Phyllis were walking back across the site to where Lauren was still entombed in her soulless side room with good and constant care, it had to be said, though nothing to compare with what they'd just seen.

'We have to get her in there,' Phyllis stated, voicing both their thoughts. 'They just have to come up with the funding.'

'If she was showing some signs of recovery,' Emma said, gazing in through the windows of a large, sunny cafe that they hadn't even known existed until now, 'it would probably be a lot easier.'

'Even so, the doctor's going to try, so he must think we're in with a chance.'

Taking hope from that, Emma said, 'Did you realise it was a secure unit?'

'Mm, yes, but you'd never know it, would you? Such pretty little gardens with those parasols and nice wooden tables. Well, I was very impressed with all of it. How could you not be?'

'It seems like a world away from where she is now, doesn't it?' Emma remarked. It was heartbreaking and cruel, she was thinking, how drastically her ambitions for Lauren had changed in such a relatively short time, but she was learning to adapt, as Lauren must too, when the time came.

'. . . and you'll never guess what happened this morning,' Emma was saying to Lauren as she sat beside her bed a week later, oblivious to the comings and goings outside the little side room. Today she was barely even noticing the monitors charting Lauren's progress, nor the nasal specs that looped from Lauren's nose across her cheeks, providing oxygen. Not even the gastric tube that supplied her nutrients was catching Emma's attention. She only saw Lauren's still, tranquil features, warmed and faintly flushed by the blood running beneath the skin, and the delicate shaping of her lips that made them seem about to smile. In every other way she was healing, returning to health; she just wasn't waking up. Nevertheless the physio still came twice a day to flex and massage her muscles, sit her up, turn her over and praise her for how well she was doing, when in fact she was doing nothing at all.

'I only had a phone call from Hamish Gallagher,' Emma went on, injecting some enthusiasm into her voice. 'You remember, the manager at the Avon Valley Manor Hotel? Apparently, they want to put on a local arts fair this summer, and he's asked *me* if I'll organise it.'

Her eyebrows rose in anticipation of a reaction, and she smiled, as though she'd received one. 'I know you're saying wow, or amazing, or that's so cool, or something like that,' she said softly, 'but it's a bigger challenge than I was expecting for my first project. I'm sure I can do it, though. In fact, it feels right up my street, or I like to think it is. And I'll love meeting local artists and potters, jewellery and home-craft designers . . . I thought we could invite a few self-published writers too. They'll probably welcome some added exposure for their books. It's all got to be worked out yet, obviously, I'm just thinking off the top of my head before I go for a meeting with Hamish. He told me to call him that, which is very friendly, isn't it? No, don't start getting ideas. He's happily married to a wife who's apparently keen to help me make new contacts around the area, if I need them, and I certainly do. I'm hoping she might have access to a few local celebrities, so we can invite them along. That should bring in the crowds.' She paused, giving herself a moment to imagine what Lauren herself might suggest, while trying not to dwell on how much she would have enjoyed helping to organise it.

'Of course, musicians,' she said, realising that would have been top of Lauren's list. 'We must include them, and dancers. They'll really liven things up. Actually, I wonder if a local drama club might be interested in putting on a short play, or doing some readings. There's a lot to think about, and if I'm going to do it I shall have to start work on it straight away, which is going to be difficult now I'm part-time at the vet's. It was a case of having to go for that job though, otherwise Granny would have ended up paying for everything, and she has to be as careful as the rest of us with prices going up all the time, and her royalty payments starting to dwindle. I've a feeling she's digging into her savings already, but she won't discuss it, so I just have to make sure that I'm paying the lion's share of the bills.'

Thinking of her mother she gave a long, gentle sigh of relief. 'I expect you've been thinking about the chat Granny and I had that I told you about. I knew you'd be pleased to hear that we'd finally started making an effort to get past all the bad feelings we had between us. I guess I was so wrapped up in myself and how awful she was to me as a child that I didn't allow myself to see the overtures she says she made over the years. Yes, I'm sure you saw them, but the thing with you, Lauren, is you always see the good in people, even when it's so hidden from the rest of us we'd need some sort of X-ray eyes to get there. Not that I'm saying Granny has no good in her, because obviously she has, it just never seemed to be directed at me, or not in my mind it didn't. And you, well you've never been able to help yourself the way you give everyone the benefit of the doubt, or insist their motives are far worthier than they appear to the rest of us. It's true that you really don't see the bad in people, do you? Or, if you do, you manage to look straight past it to where the shyness, or hurt, or fear, or whatever it is, is hiding. Berry's always said it's another way you're like my father, because he had time for everyone, apparently, no matter who they were or where they'd come from.'

She paused, and her head bowed with unhappiness as she tried to reconcile her beautiful, tender-hearted daughter with the girl who'd seemed to gain such pleasure from an illicit relationship with a man more than twice her age. It was still hard for Emma to accept that it had really happened in spite of having read the diary, and in spite of knowing how complex a human personality could be. Everyone, without exception, was capable of hiding traits

391

or thoughts or failings they didn't want anyone else to know about, and it was second nature to keep secrets from those who might be hurt by them. Lauren would have known that her liaison with Philip Leesom would hurt her mother, but that really wasn't the point. What bothered Emma most was that she had been so brazen with her newfound sexuality, so proud of it and ready to embrace anything Leesom might suggest. Never once had she seemed to consider her reputation if their relationship became known, or, more importantly, what danger she might be putting herself in.

Every mother thought they knew their child inside out, until they found out the hard way that they really didn't.

Feeling tremors of unease coasting through her she wondered, not for the first time, what the accident and surgery might have done to Lauren's personality, ambitions, understanding of others. Would she still be a musician when, if, she came round, or at least someone who enjoyed music? Maybe that part of her had been crushed by the impact, or removed by the scalpel. What if her character had changed completely and she woke up not as a virtual vegetable as Will obviously feared, but as another kind of person altogether? Maybe aspects of who she'd been before would remain, but would they be the tender, sunny qualities that made her so special? Or would she, Emma, have to get to know the side of her that had thrilled to Leesom's attentions? Maybe there were other traits that even Lauren herself hadn't yet discovered. Emma would still love her, whoever she was – she just couldn't help fearing that fate's crueller side might not have finished with them yet.

There was so much to worry about, so many awful scenarios ready to crowd out the pleasure of seeing Lauren return to consciousness, that sometimes she could feel herself becoming swamped by it all. What if Lauren came round and it was discovered she'd never be able to do anything but think for herself again? How terrible it would be for her, trapped inside a body that couldn't function at all, never to be able to put her thoughts into words, or actions, or anything else that would help her to be understood, or move, or even eat unassisted. Locked-in syndrome, they called it. If that happened Will would have been proved right: she, Emma, would have condemned herself to a lifetime of caring for a daughter who might actually hate her for forcing such a miserable existence upon her. Lauren would probably consider herself better off dead.

As the days, weeks had worn on she'd found herself wondering more and more how delusional, selfish, even arrogant, she was in believing that her love for Lauren could make everything all right. Perhaps Will's way was the kindest. *If you really love someone you'll let them go.* Did that mean he loved Lauren more because he was prepared to let her go? Emma couldn't accept that, but she was starting to realise that maybe she should have tried harder to understand that all he really wanted was what he thought was the best for Lauren.

However, the decision about whether or not to let her go still hadn't been forced on them, thank God. Whatever had caused the surges of pressure in Lauren's brain hadn't troubled her for over a couple of months now, and Emma had been repeatedly assured that she was in no pain. However, she might be in a place so removed from where her body was lying that the music they were playing to her was flowing into deaf ears; maybe the force of will they were all trying to connect with was a life energy that had long since fled, never to return.

Holding Lauren's hand between both of her own, she rested her head against them as she felt herself sinking deeper and deeper into a fear she'd never allowed herself to acknowledge before. If she had any courage at all, would she be facing the fact that she was clutching at a hope that was no more than thin air? Was she making Lauren the focus of her world out of desperation, even habit, or because she truly believed she was coming back? Where were the answers? How could she find them? She needed someone to guide her, to tell her the right thing to do, not for her, for Lauren, because only Lauren mattered.

Maybe she should talk to a doctor again. Neil Duncan was in charge of her case now, at least until they could get her transferred to the Brain Injury Centre, but there had been no word about that since Dr Hanworth had sent them a copy of his letter to the PCT. Emma hardly dared even think about how much she wanted Lauren to go there, because getting her hopes too high meant she'd crash that much harder if their request for funding was turned down. If it was, what would happen to Lauren then? She hadn't asked that question of anyone yet, but knew she'd have to sooner or later, at which point she might well be faced with selling the house in order to pay for Lauren's care.

She would do it, of course, she suspected her mother would too, but what would happen after that money ran out?

Afraid that Lauren might be picking up on her negative thoughts, she forced herself to try and suppress the gloom and reach for something more light-hearted. Her first thoughts returned to the arts fair, but then she found herself remembering the travel information for India that had come through that morning. She was about to take it out to read to Lauren when she stopped. What she ought to be doing was getting in touch with the agent to cancel the trip, not sitting here pretending it was something Lauren was still looking forward to, even stood a chance of going on. A scalding rush of tears stung her eyes as she recalled Lauren's crazy idea that they should spend her first two weeks there together. What she wouldn't give to make that come true. How could she even have considered not going? No job, no other commitment would ever be as important as time spent with her daughter.

Making another effort to brighten her thoughts, she put Lauren's hand down. Lifting her head she dragged her hands over her face, as though smoothing away the tiredness. 'Has Oliver Lomax been to see you?' she asked. 'I'd like to see him . . .' She stopped as her heart caught on a beat.

Lauren's eyes were open.

'Lauren?' she whispered, mindful that this could happen and still mean nothing. But Lauren had never done this before, or not that she knew of, and there was something about her . . . This was real, she just knew it. It had to be or she would lose her mind.

Lauren's eyes moved, not to her mother, but to the lower sides of their sockets.

'Oh my God,' Emma gasped, pressing a hand to her mouth. 'Lauren, can you hear me?'

Lauren didn't respond, but she didn't close her eyes either.

Emma jumped up, started to go for a nurse, but some instinct pulled her back again. 'I'm here,' she said, grabbing Lauren's hand. 'Oh my darling, can you see me? Can you hear what I'm saying?'

Lauren was staring straight ahead. It wasn't possible to know if she was seeing or hearing anything, but *her eyes were still open*.

'Nurse!' Emma called. 'Nurse. Please someone come.'

Putting a hand to Lauren's face, she sobbed, 'Sweetheart. It's Mummy. Can you see me? Oh God, you don't know how good it is to see you.' She wanted to scoop her up, press her whole body to hers, envelop her in a tidal wave of love. She was laughing, crying, shaking so hard she could barely control herself.

Then Lauren's eyes closed.

'Oh no,' she choked, feeling an overwhelming despair well up through her joy. 'Please, please open your eyes again,' she begged, squeezing hard on Lauren's hand. 'You can do it. I know you can.'

'Emma? Is everything all right?'

Turning to Jo, the staff nurse, Emma said, 'She opened her eyes. Just a moment ago. She – she didn't look at me or anything, but they were definitely open.'

Jo's gaze went to Lauren and she started to smile. 'And they're open again,' she said softly, coming to the bed.

Emma turned quickly back to Lauren, and seeing her eyes, those beautiful, amber eyes, staring at nothing, she stood with her hands bunched at her mouth as Jo said, 'Hello, young lady. It's lovely to see you. You have very pretty eyes.'

Emma stifled a sob, then stopped breathing as Lauren's eyes came unsteadily towards her.

'Are you looking for Mum?' Jo said, taking out a small flashlight to check Lauren's pupils.

'Can you see me, darling?' Emma whispered raggedly. 'I'm right here. Oh Lauren, can you see me?'

'I think you can, can't you?' Jo replied, her voice full of affection. 'I expect it's good to see your mum, isn't it? I know she's very happy to see you.'

Emma was crying and shaking so hard she could barely speak. 'What shall I do?' she asked Jo as she picked up Lauren's hand. 'Shall I carry on talking to her?'

'Absolutely. I'll send someone for the doctor.'

It seemed an eternity, yet it was probably no more than minutes before a doctor Emma hadn't seen before was there, checking Lauren's vital signs and smiling widely as he said, 'Well, you've taken your time to wake up, Sleeping Beauty, but I do believe you're back with us now. Can you tell me who this is, standing next to me?'

Lauren's eyes went slowly to Emma.

Simply seeing her respond that way caused more joy to flood Emma's heart than she could possibly contain. Not only could she hear, she'd understood the question. 'I'm still here, darling,' she whispered, keeping a tight hold on Lauren's hand.

'Can you say Mum?' the doctor asked.

When Lauren said nothing, Emma felt herself faltering.

Going to the other side of the bed, the doctor picked up Lauren's other hand and said, 'We're going to do a little test, OK? It's very easy. All you have to do is squeeze once for yes, and twice for no. Do you understand what I'm saying?'

Lauren's eyes were on his, so it gave Emma a start when she felt a movement in the hand she was holding.

'I think she said yes,' she said huskily. 'Can you do it again, my darling?'

The movement of Lauren's head as she turned to Emma was laboured, but the pressure of her hand was more definite this time.

Emma broke into sobs of laughter. 'She said yes. She definitely said yes,' she cried.

'Excellent,' the doctor declared, his voice ringing with praise. 'Can you do the same with this hand?'

Again it seemed to take some effort for Lauren to turn her head, but she managed it and looked at the doctor.

They waited.

Emma's eyes darted between Lauren's face and left hand. Still nothing happened.

'It's OK,' the doctor said kindly, 'it would be very unusual if we had everything happening straight away. What's important is that you're moving your right hand. Is she right-handed?' he asked Emma.

Emma nodded.

Returning his attention to Lauren, he said, 'Do you know your name?'

Emma looked down at Lauren's slender young hand as it flexed once under hers.

'Is it Lauren?' he asked.

Again a single flex.

Emma could never have imagined such a slight contraction of Lauren's fingers would bring her so much relief and joy.

'And is this your mum?' the doctor prompted.

There was a longer pause as Lauren turned her head again to look at Emma. Then she squeezed her hand.

Emma gave a choke of pride.

'And am I your daddy?' the doctor asked.

Lauren continued to look at Emma as she squeezed twice.

Still gazing into her eyes, Emma leaned forward to smooth a hand over her forehead. The hand responses were vital, but it was the way Lauren was gazing back at her that was filling up her heart. Her baby was awake, alive, and though possibly damaged in ways they had yet to discover, all that mattered right now was that she was back with them, and Emma had no doubt it was to stay.

When the doctor finally left the room he was able to reassure Emma that Lauren truly was only sleeping now, tired out by her first brave attempts to communicate in a way that was already feeling like a miracle. She wasn't speaking, or making any sounds at all, but Emma didn't care how long it might be before her throat muscles strengthened (she was determined to believe that was all it would take), or before she could show them anything else she could do. All that mattered for now was the fact that when she was no longer tired she would wake up again. Not only that, she could definitely see and hear, and the tiny pinpricks the doctor had applied to numerous places around her body had all met with a response. She still didn't seem able to move her left hand, but the doctor had said that he wasn't unduly worried about that, as it too had responded to his pin test.

'We need to give the brain and body time to wake up completely,' he'd explained, 'and that might well take a little longer than you'd like.'

'But she will be all right?' Emma had insisted.

'I'm afraid it's still far too early to give you a reliable prognosis, but the fact that she's started to respond in the way she has can allow us some cautious optimism.'

Though it wasn't exactly the answer Emma had wanted, for now it was so very much more than she'd expected when she'd come here today that she was willing to embrace it as the greatest beacon of hope she'd been handed so far. Any optimism at all from a doctor was surely going to help them get her into the Brain Injury Centre – and once there, who knew how long it might be before she was able to come home?

Whispering, so as not to wake Lauren, she said, 'I'm going to make some phone calls now, OK? I won't be far away, and I've already asked if I can stay the night. They said yes, so I shall be here when you wake up again.' *When you wake up again*, and it was actually going to happen! Had Fate, God, whoever was in charge really turned a kinder side towards them at last?

She didn't want to leave Lauren's side for a minute, but at the same time she was bursting to tell everyone the good news.

Out in the corridor she connected to her mother first.

Before she could speak Phyllis was saying, 'Emma? Are you all right? I thought you'd be home by now.'

'Mum. Oh Mum,' Emma laughed and sobbed. 'You have to come. Please come. She's woken up.'

There was a moment's stunned silence before her mother started to break down. 'Oh Emma, Emma. Are you sure? Of course you are, you wouldn't say it if you weren't. Our beautiful girl. We have her back?'

'She knows me, Mum. She looked right at me and she can already answer yes and no by squeezing our hands.'

'Oh my goodness, I never thought . . . I was so afraid, but I knew she could do it. It's all down to you, Emma. You know that, don't you? You held on and wouldn't let go.'

'So did you. But I almost did let go, Mum. Today, I was thinking . . . I mean it was in my mind for the first time that I might be wrong, and that maybe I was being selfish, and then . . . then I looked up and her eyes were open. It was as though she knew she had to do it for herself now, and she did.'

'I'm so proud of her,' Phyllis laughed through a sob. 'Of you too. You know what I like to think, that maybe she went to your father to rest for a while, and now she's ready he's sent her gently back again.'

Loving the thought, Emma let it resonate for a moment before she said, 'Will you call Berry and Harry? They'll want to know right away. And Polly will too, so . . .'

'Don't worry, I'll call them all. Are we staying at the hospital tonight, you and me? Will they allow it?'

Thrilled that her mother wanted to be there too, Emma replied, 'Yes, they will, so can you bring a few things for the morning?'

'Of course. Are you going back to her now?'

'In a minute. I need to call Will first.'

After ringing off she took a few moments to prepare herself before scrolling to Will's number and pressing to connect. She didn't want to sound smug when she broke the news, but it was going to be hard not to.

Jemima answered after the fourth ring.

'Hi, it's Emma. Is Will there please?'

'Yes, he is. Is everything all right? How's Lauren?'

'If you don't mind, I'd like to speak to Will.'

'Oh my goodness, has something happened? If it has, maybe it would be better for me to break it . . .'

'Lauren is still with us, now please will you put him on.'

It seemed an inordinately long wait before Will's voice came snappishly down the line. 'Emma? What is it?'

He sounded so cold, so resentful of being disturbed, but he didn't know yet, so she wasn't going to allow him to spoil her mood. 'She's woken up, Will,' she told him, feeling another rush of joy. 'She came round. She's not in a coma any more.'

Several seconds of silence ticked by.

'Are you still there?' she asked in the end.

'Yes, I'm here, I'm just . . . Is she . . . all right?'

'I think so. I mean, she hasn't spoken yet, but she definitely seemed to know me and she can respond to questions with a squeeze of her hand.'

'Really?'

'Yes, really.'

'Well that's great, isn't it?'

The sarcasm in his tone felt like a slap. 'Actually, yes it is great,' she told him curtly. 'I've looked into her eyes and she's looked into mine, don't you want to do the same?'

'Actually, no, not if that's all she can do, because if she's a prisoner inside a body that's useless, with a brain that's functioning or not . . .'

'For heaven's sake! She only came round half an hour ago. Nobody can tell us anything for certain yet.'

'Well you call me back when they can. Until then, I'm afraid you're on your own with this, Emma, because I don't want to look into her eyes and know she's asking me why I allowed you to keep her alive. You never had my support for that, and you're definitely not getting it if she's any less than the girl she was before.'

Stunned, Emma could only stare at the phone as the line went dead. How could he have responded in such a brutal way? He didn't seem at all pleased that Lauren had woken up – if anything he'd sounded angry, even outraged by it, as if it was a foregone conclusion that she was never going to make a full recovery. Even if she didn't, surely all that mattered was that she was alive and with them and able to communicate, if only in a limited way for now.

Enraged by his reaction, and deeply hurt for Lauren, she decided she must banish him from her mind. She simply couldn't allow him to spoil this major breakthrough by trying to make her see it as a failure, or even worse, as a cruel life sentence for Lauren. Only time could tell them whether her life was going to be worth living, but at least she, Emma, was giving her a chance. If Will couldn't do that, then as far as she was concerned he didn't deserve to be a part of their lives anyway. From now on, if he wanted any news of his daughter he could damned well call up and ask for it, because no way in the world was she going to call him again.

Instead, as a way of erasing the last few minutes, she might just call Oliver Lomax to tell him the good news. He'd want to know, Emma felt sure of it, and he certainly wouldn't respond the way Will just had. He'd probably be almost as thrilled as she was, and relieved, of course, given the kind of charge he could have been facing if Lauren hadn't pulled through.

However, she couldn't call Oliver, because she didn't have his number, and besides, he might want to come straight away and that probably wouldn't be a good idea. She'd talk to Clive Andrews tomorrow and get the Lomaxes' number from him, and meanwhile she'd go and sit with Lauren and pray to a god she was starting to believe in, that her darling daughter really would wake up in the morning.

Chapter Twenty-Seven

'Oliver, will you please get a move on, or we're going to be late,' Russ shouted up the stairs while grabbing the phone before it rang off the hook. 'Russ Lomax,' he barked into the receiver.

The voice at the other end sounded slightly hesitant. 'Uh, I hope I'm not bothering you, but I wonder if I could speak to Oliver. It's Emma Scott here, Lauren's mother.'

Thrown, in fact shocked to his core, Russ rapidly tried to think what to say. Uppermost in his mind was that the girl had died. But would her mother call to tell Oliver that? She might, out of consideration – or vengeance.

'Are you still there?' she asked.

'Uh yes, of course, I'm sorry. If you hold on, I'll get him.'

Looking up as Oliver came thundering down the stairs, he watched him saunter into the kitchen, all dishevelled dark hair and freshly shaved chin with a couple of nicks. 'It's for you,' he told him, holding out the phone. 'Lauren's mother.'

Oliver's face instantly turned white. Clearly his first thoughts had followed the same route as his father's. His dark eyes were fixed on Russ as he took the receiver. 'Hello?' he said anxiously.

'Oliver? It's Emma,' she told him. 'I have some good news for you. Lauren's awake.'

It was a moment before Oliver's jaw dropped. Then he was reeling, laughing and starting to cry. 'No way, that's fantastic. Oh my God, is she OK? Dad, did you hear? Lauren's awake.'

Russ's eyes closed as he uttered a silent, fervent thank you to whoever was listening.

'What happened?' Oliver was asking Emma. 'When did she come round?'

'Last night. All those movements we've been feeling, the reflexes, muscle contractions, it seems they were all signs, it was just there was no way of telling for certain, but then last night she actually opened her eyes.'

Oliver was grinning so hard it hurt. 'That is so amazing,' he cried. 'Has she said anything yet?'

'No, not yet, but she's definitely communicating. The doctor and physio are both with her at the moment carrying out all sorts of tests, but they have to take their time over them so's not to wear her out. She's actually sitting up this morning, well almost, more than she was before.'

Oliver was scruffing his hair in a burst of excitement. Then, suddenly remembering the darker side of it all, his eyes shadowed as he said, 'Does she . . . does she remember anything that happened?'

'I'm not sure,' Emma replied. 'All we've asked her so far is if she knows where she is. She told us no with two squeezes of her hand, but the doctor's explained it to her now. I can't tell you how much she understood – I think it might take a while before we can get to that level.'

'Sure,' he murmured. Then, 'Can I see her? I mean, I know . . . I guess you'd prefer . . .'

'If you want to come I think you should. Maybe not this morning, there's quite a lot going on, and she'll probably be tired after, but later . . . Why don't you ring me around three, say? I should be able to tell you then when would be a good time.'

Oliver couldn't have looked more amazed or thrilled. 'That's fantastic,' he declared, turning to his father. 'Thank you so much. This is really . . . It's just like . . . I swear I won't get in the way, and if you change your mind . . .' He was lost for words.

'I should go now,' she told him. 'I just wanted to let you know and . . . well, thank you.'

Colour rushed to Oliver's cheeks. 'What for? I haven't done anything.'

'You care, that means a lot.'

'I really do, Mrs Scott,' he assured her.

'Oh Oliver,' she murmured, 'thank you for that, thank you so much, and I know you mean it, but we could have a very long journey ahead of us, so I won't expect you . . .'

'I don't care,' he cut in forcefully. 'However long it takes, I'm going to be there for her, OK? I mean, if you'll let me, obviously.'

With a catch in her voice she said, 'We can talk about it. For now, all you have to do is call me later and hopefully it'll be all right for you to come and see her. But remember, she won't know who you are, so please don't be upset about that, and for the time being we won't talk about the accident, OK?'

'So who shall we say I am?'

'Let me think about that.'

'Cool. You just tell me what I have to do and I'll do it. And, Mrs Scott, thanks again for calling, and for letting me . . . or saying I can come. If it doesn't work out today because she's tired or . . .'

'Don't worry, if it doesn't, we'll make it for another time.'

As he rang off Oliver's elation was brimming over.

Going to him, Russ wrapped him in a crushing embrace. 'I'm proud of you, son,' he said huskily. 'There aren't many people in your position who'd even have had the courage to go to see the girl . . . To be on terms with her mother now, and to have said the things you just did . . . I'm so damned proud of you.'

Though thrilled by his father's words, Oliver broke away from the embrace, saying, 'We're going to be late if we don't leave now.'

Russ had to smile at the new confidence that already seemed to be asserting itself. 'We already are,' he told him, 'but I think once Jolyon knows what kept us he'll understand.'

Oliver made an attempt at wryness as he replied, 'It's not Jolyon we have to worry about though, is it? It's the person who's hell-bent on putting me away.'

Senior District Crown Prosecutor Stella Finlay was a large woman in her mid-forties with such a formidable air about her that even Russ, who wasn't easily thrown by authority, had to instruct himself not to feel intimidated. As it was, he'd been around the block a few too many times to crumple at the first warning glare, and though this leading lawyer with her untidy mass of crinkled red hair, acute grey eyes and thin lips might want to see him – or more particularly Oliver – starting to cower the instant they walked in the door, she was going to get no satisfaction from Russ. From Oliver she'd probably get it in spades, not only because she was holding his future in her hands (and had made no secret of the fact that she wanted the next few years of it to be blighted by a driving ban at the very least, a stretch inside being preferable), but because Jolyon had warned him on their way in that throughout the proceedings he must show nothing but humility, remorse and a full under-standing of the gravity of his situation.

'Only speak when you're spoken to,' Jolyon had instructed. 'Keep your eyes down when she's addressing me, but don't be afraid to look at her when she's speaking to you. Be clear, honest and above all respectful. As for you, Russ, make sure she doesn't get up your back, because she has a nasty habit of it, especially when she's been cornered into something like this by someone like me.'

'But she's got to see the sense of dropping the charges,' Russ had protested. 'The case has hardly got any traction now with the lost blood, marginal speeding offence and all the special reasons.'

As someone had appeared at that point to show them through to a meeting room, Jolyon had merely slanted Russ a look that seemed to be saying, 'There are never any guarantees.'

After making the introductions, during which Ms Finlay hadn't offered the merest glimmer of a smile, Jolyon waited until everyone was seated – himself, Russ and Oliver one side of the table, Ms Finlay on the other – to begin with a thank you for agreeing to meet with them prior to next week's preliminary hearing.

'I know you'll have gone through the detail of this case by now,' he continued, 'so you'll be aware of why we're asking for all charges to be dropped.'

Her face remained stony as she raised her eyes from the

file in front of her to fix them first on Oliver, then on Jolyon. 'This really is a bit rich, Mr Crane,' she stated acidly. 'Your client was breathalysed twice that evening and on both occasions was found to be over the limit. I don't believe he's even tried to deny it.'

'That's true,' Jolyon conceded, 'but as you know very few drink-drive prosecutions have gone ahead based only on a breath test, and even fewer have succeeded. In this instance, even if the blood sample should turn up at some point in the future, Oliver's barrister will still mount a defence based on the special reasons and duress of circumstances you see outlined in front of you. You also have Mrs Lomax's signed statement giving an account of how she called her son that night and . . .'

'Yes, yes, I'm aware of what happened, but we both know there are emergency services, friends, other family members, any of whom could have gone to the rescue, and I presume your client has a phone.'

'He does indeed, but unfortunately after he received the call he panicked. His only thought was to get to his mother . . .'

'How old are you?' Finlay barked at Oliver. 'Twenty-one, I believe, with a university degree, a good upbringing and a presumably sound mind, so you know very well that whatever the circumstances, it is illegal to drive a car when under the influence of alcohol.'

Oliver swallowed loudly. 'Yes, miss, ma'am,' he answered croakily.

'As you pointed out a moment ago,' Jolyon came in, 'Oliver has never denied that he was over the limit. However, his only thought at the time was for his mother, who I'm afraid is an alcoholic and therefore, shall we say, unpredictable, to put it mildly.'

Stella Finlay sat back in her chair, regarding Oliver with an uncompromising stare. Unlike many females she was clearly not going to be swayed by his looks, or by his father's erstwhile fame. Under any other circumstances Russ might have respected her for that – under these, he'd be happy to use whatever influence he and Oliver could muster to bring down her hostility.

Speaking in an accusatory voice, she began, 'You, young man, drove your *car* into Lauren Scott . . .'

'But not on purpose,' Jolyon jumped in quickly. 'It was an accident. No one's trying to say otherwise.'

'But if he had *not* committed the crime of driving under the influence then Lauren Scott would not be lying in a hospital bed now, barely holding on to her life.'

'Actually, she came round last night,' Jolyon told her hurriedly. 'Perhaps you didn't get my latest email. I sent it while we were on our way here. Mrs Scott, Lauren's mother, rang Oliver herself this morning to break the good news.'

Finlay looked astounded. 'Mrs Scott rang your client?' she repeated incredulously.

Jolyon couldn't help looking pleased. 'Oliver has been visiting Lauren over the last few weeks,' he explained. 'He's developed a kind of friendship, or perhaps you'd call it understanding, with Lauren's mother.'

Finlay was glaring at Oliver again, clearly not thrilled at having this extraordinary development land on her without warning. 'Are you saying you have the family's permission to visit the girl you struck with your car?'

Wincing at the brutality, Oliver said, 'Uh, yes, I do now. At first I didn't, but then I met her mother and Mrs Scott said it was OK to carry on seeing her.'

'And what exactly do you do when you go to see her?' Finlay demanded, seeming more perplexed and annoyed by the second.

'I play her the music I've downloaded for her,' he replied. 'She's like really keen on music. She plays the flute and the guitar, piano too actually, and she's into all kinds of stuff . . . Jazz, rap, classical, some country . . .'

'You seem to be remarkably well informed about someone you practically killed,' Finlay stated cruelly.

As Oliver's cheeks reddened it was all Russ could do to stop himself slapping the woman down with an attack of his own. However, Jolyon's advice not to get rattled was holding firm, at least for the moment.

'I went online to find out about her,' Oliver explained. 'I mean, I know that might sound weird, but like we spent all this time . . . Well, it wasn't that long really, except it felt like hours, waiting on the side of the road for an ambulance to come, and there was like just the two of us, and I was so scared she was already dead, and then when I found out she wasn't, I felt as though . . .' He broke off and shrugged self-consciously.

'Go on,' Finlay commanded.

'Well, I felt really relieved when I found out she was still alive, not for myself – well, yes, I suppose for me – but mainly for her, and I can't really remember much about it now, I just know that that time on the side of the road seemed kind of . . . well, like it meant something, and I wanted to carry on letting her know that it meant something. Even if she couldn't hear me, but they say people in comas can hear, or some of them can, so that's why I downloaded music that we could listen to together. And I read things to her, mostly from the poets I studied for A level, because I knew she was doing English too, so I thought she might know some of the poems and if she didn't she might like the ones I did anyway.'

Finlay's eyes slid suspiciously to Russ and back again.

Russ remained silent, though he could tell that the prosecutor was sure someone had put Oliver up to this; to her it was one of the most unlikely stories she'd ever heard.

'And now you say her mother called to let you know that she's come round?' Finlay said, scraping the edge off her scepticism by making her statement a question.

Oliver nodded. 'This morning,' he replied.

Tearing her eyes from his, she told Jolyon, 'This doesn't actually change anything, I hope you realise that.'

'Maybe not in a legal sense,' he conceded, 'but I thought it was important for you to hear from Oliver himself about how he feels . . .'

'We're not dealing with *feelings*, Mr Crane, what we have here are two criminal offences that have to be tried in a court of law, whether your client has a conscience or not.'

'It's not just about his conscience though, is it?' Jolyon challenged. 'It's about common sense, human understanding, compassion and whether or not there is anything to be gained from continuing with this prosecution.'

'Well, as your client's lawyer I'd expect you to come up with something fatuous like that, but I'm afraid the charges against him are far from trivial. In fact, they're extremely serious . . .'

'Indeed they are, so let's forget the lost blood sample for the moment, which has nothing to do with Oliver, and talk about the charge of dangerous driving. The report shows that Oliver was, at most, only five miles over the speed limit at the time of the accident, which happened during the early hours of the morning, on a deserted country road where no one in their right mind would have expected to come round a bend and find someone standing in front of them. Added to that was the boy's urgent need to get to his mother. He was highly emotional, in a state of great fear, but he still wasn't sufficiently over the speed limit to be classified as driving dangerously. You know that, and I know that, so I'll leave it there for now, and go on to point out that in spite of his fear for his mother, and knowing he was over the legal limit for alcohol, he did not abandon the girl and drive on.'

Finlay wasn't buying that for an instant. 'His windscreen was smashed, how could he drive on?' she almost scoffed.

'He could have punched it out, or simply run away from the scene, but he did neither. What he did was call the emergency services, and then he stayed with her right up until help arrived. All of this, plus how concerned he's been about the girl since, shows him, in my opinion, to be a young man of great courage and character. This will all be presented to the judge and jury, naturally, and by default to the press, all of whom, I'm afraid, will be sure to wonder why public money is being wasted on a prosecution that was badly compromised from the start by the missing blood sample, a negligible speeding infraction and so many mitigating circumstances to be cited in his favour that I couldn't even make up any more.'

To Russ's astonishment, Finlay still wasn't budging. 'And how do you think the press, now that you've cited them, would respond to a young man being allowed to walk away from charges for two serious crimes? And what of the Scotts?' She was looking at Russ now. 'You're a father, so let's talk about feelings again. How would you *feel* if the shoe was on the other foot and it was your child who'd been hit by a drunk driver? More to the point, how would you feel if the law abandoned you and let the drunk driver go home without facing any charge whatsoever? Would you consider yourself and your family to be well served, Mr Lomax?'

'No, I don't expect I would,' Russ replied stiffly, 'if I wasn't aware of the circumstances behind . . .'

'Excuse me interrupting,' Jolyon came in hastily, 'but if we're going back to feelings, you'll be aware of why the Scotts themselves might not actually *feel* it to be in their best interests to go ahead with the prosecution.'

Thrown, Russ turned to look at him.

Jolyon's eyes were fixed firmly on Finlay.

Finlay's mouth was pursed in profound disapproval.

Undeterred, Jolyon pressed on. 'Questions will be asked about what Lauren Scott was doing in the middle of nowhere at that time of night. Of course, we know her car had broken down, but people, and I'm referring to the press now, will inevitably start digging around trying to find out where she'd been . . .'

'Yes, I get what you're trying to say, thank you, Mr Crane,' Finlay cut in, 'and where Lauren Scott was coming from or going to, that night, isn't one bit relevant to this case.'

'Maybe not in a legal sense, but we both know that the Scotts have already suffered enough over this. Now that Lauren has woken up and is, hopefully, on the road to a full recovery . . .'

'But you don't know that for certain.'

'No, not yet, but whether she is, or isn't, doesn't change the fact that her family's only concern from here on will be to get her well. They really won't want all the detail of why Lauren was where she was, at the time Oliver came driving through to save his mother, being bandied about in a court of law, much less in the tabloid press. As I said, they've already suffered enough, so to exacerbate that in a way that could easily be avoided would surely be an indefensible position to take.'

Finlay was clearly furious. 'We'll discuss this further at

a later date,' she told him tightly. Then, turning to Oliver, 'And what about you, young man? What more do you have to say for yourself?'

Straightening his shoulders, Oliver forced himself to look at her as he replied, 'Well, what I really want to say is how sorry I am for everything that's happened. I wish I'd stopped to think before I got into my car that night. If I had . . .'

'If you had, none of us would be sitting here and the Scotts would be going about their lives, free of the tragedy they're now having to live through.'

'Yes, of course,' he said quietly.

'And do *you* think it would be just and fair that you should walk away from your actions without having to face any consequences?'

'No, of course not.'

'But he is facing the consequences,' Russ told her, unable to let it rest there. 'As he said earlier, he's been going to visit Lauren, playing her music in the hope of stimulating her, reading her poetry . . .'

'Yes, I heard,' she said brusquely.

'This morning, when Mrs Scott called to tell him the good news, he promised he'd help in any way he can with Lauren's recovery. Knowing him as I do, I have no doubt that he means this, because he has never been lacking in integrity. Moreover, his own life has essentially been on hold since the accident, as though in some kind of solidarity with Lauren. There hasn't been a single moment of the day when he hasn't either been suffering in his own way over what happened, or been finding out all that he can about her. She's not just a victim for him, she's a real person, a young girl not so very different in age or background to his own. A gifted student by all accounts, who might, at some point in the future we hope, be able to resume her studies. You asked him if he thought it was *just and fair* for him to walk away from his actions, and I can assure you that he will never walk away from them. He has never even tried to. What he wants now is the chance to be able to help her in a useful and productive way, whether it's playing her music, talking to her, or being there through her rehabilitation, and if Mrs Scott is prepared to give him that chance, I think we should too.'

'But this isn't about what you all *want* . . .'

'If you decide to go ahead and prosecute,' Russ cut in, 'then please tell me what possible good will come of it. It'll change nothing for Lauren, apart from deprive her of someone who cares enough to help her through . . .'

'I'm sure she has plenty of family and friends.'

'I won't disagree with that, but have you considered the fact that there might actually be some sort of special connection between my son and Lauren Scott after what happened?'

'Oh, please, Mr Lomax. I expected better of you.'

'And frankly I expected better of you. What exactly would be the point of sending my son into the future with a criminal record that will probably ruin most of his chances for a decent career, maybe even a worthwhile relationship? Who the hell is that going to help? Not Lauren, that's for sure, or her family unless they're hell-bent on revenge, and her mother's reaction to Oliver is hardly suggesting that, is it? And now let me ask you this, do you really think Oliver deserves to pay such a high price for wanting to save his mother?'

A harsh silence reverberated around the room. Finlay's eyes remained impenetrable as she stared back at Russ. Several moments ticked by before she spoke. 'Where is his mother now? Why isn't she here today?'

'She's in a rehab clinic close to her sister in Cape Town.'

Finlay's eyebrows rose in a way that said almost nothing at all.

Turning back to Oliver, she said, 'I hope Mr Crane hasn't led you to believe that this is going to disappear as easily as he seems to think it will. The crimes you've committed are very grave, and certainly can't be dismissed just because your father and Mr Crane are prepared to vouch for your character. I'm sure that at heart you are a decent young man, and I'm very glad to learn that you're feeling some sense of responsibility for what you did, but the facts remain that you were driving a vehicle while under the influence of alcohol and you were breaking the speed limit when you ran into Lauren Scott. So whether I'd like to or not, I'm afraid it isn't in my power simply to make it all go away. The law is the law whether you agree with it or not, and you, Mr Crane, should know better than to try to manipulate the course of justice with such reprehensible tactics as you've employed here today.'

Jolyon looked stunned. 'What on earth can be deemed reprehensible about acting in the best interests of my client?' he demanded.

'A thinly veiled threat to go to the press with everything you know about Lauren Scott, is what,' she retorted sharply.

Jolyon frowned in confusion. 'I beg your pardon, but I made no such threat . . .'

Sitting forward, she said, 'I'm not a fool, Jolyon, and I certainly don't enjoy being treated like one.'

'Then with respect, Stella, don't behave like one. You know me far too well to believe that I would leak information to the press.'

'If you thought it would get your client off . . .'

'But this wouldn't. In fact, the only harm it would do would be to the Scotts, and the concern I voiced earlier is that the press would get to find out about it the same way I did, through the police. It's a complication whose only purpose would be to dish up a rather unsavoury scandal for the edification of tabloid readers. That's certainly not what I'm about, as I'm sure you know, and nor would it be a relevant, or indeed mitigating factor, in helping to secure the right outcome for this young man.'

Though Finlay's mouth had paled around the edges, she took the rebuke on the chin as she said, 'I apologise if I misunderstood, but I'm afraid it still doesn't alter what I've already said. Your client has been charged with two offences and I am simply not in a position to be able to dismiss . . .'

'Then why did you agree to see him today?' Jolyon almost shouted. 'It's not like you to waste anyone's time, and you knew before we came that we weren't going to tell you anything you didn't already know. So the reason he's here is because you wanted to assess his character for yourself, and now, having met him, and heard him, you must surely be more certain than ever that this prosecution is never going to hold.'

'What I was going to say,' she informed him when he'd finished, 'was that I am not able to take a decision without first consulting my superiors. When that process is complete I will let you know the outcome.' She rose to her feet.

'But in the meantime next week's prelim will be rescheduled?' Jolyon insisted as he stood up too.

'Indeed it will. Thank you for coming, gentlemen. Jolyon, I believe you know the way out.'

No one spoke as they trudged back to the lift, still reeling from the last few minutes and what might, or might not, have been achieved.

'Well, I'm glad no one let her get up their back,' Russ commented wryly, as they rode down to the ground floor together.

Jolyon had to laugh. 'It actually didn't go badly,' he said, looking at Oliver.

'What did she mean about consulting her superiors?' Oliver wanted to know. 'I thought she was the top person.'

'In this area she is, but ultimately she's answerable to the Director of Public Prosecutions, so if she does decide to do as we want she'll need to cover her back.'

'Against what?' Oliver asked.

'This hasn't been a low-profile case, so if the charges are dropped the press will lap it up and she won't want to be facing the DPP after the event. Much better that the man himself, or someone up close to his level, has approved the decision, then the flak is less likely to knock her off her perch when it comes at her.'

'So you're still confident things will go our way?' Russ asked, as they walked out into the drizzly rain.

Glancing at his watch, Jolyon said, 'I'd say it's seventy thirty in our favour. Now I have to run, I'm afraid. I've got an assault and battery going on even as we speak.'

'Hang on, before you go,' Russ cried, grabbing his arm. 'What was all that about where Lauren Scott had been the night of the accident?'

'Ah, yes,' Jolyon replied awkwardly. 'I only brought it up to prove a point. I'd forget it if I were you. It's not relevant to anything. Now I'm afraid I really do have to go. I'll be in touch as soon as there's some news.'

414

As he dashed off towards the arch leading into Bristol's legal district, Russ turned to Oliver. 'Do you have any idea what he was talking about?'

Oliver merely shrugged and shook his head. Taking out his phone to turn it on, he said, 'Charlie's going to be dying to hear how it went. Then, if it's OK with you, I'm going to put the rest of my day on hold in case I can go to see Lauren.'

Chapter Twenty-Eight

'I'm sorry it couldn't happen sooner,' Emma was saying to Oliver as she met him in the corridor outside the ward. 'When she came round last Thursday I'm afraid I got carried away. I wanted her to see everyone and hear how happy they were that she was back . . . It was all too much, of course. She wasn't nearly strong enough, but she's definitely starting to pick up now. Just please don't expect too much, because it's still very early days.'

'Of course,' he said awkwardly. His eyes were worried as they came to hers. 'Does she know I'm coming?' he asked. 'I mean, have you told her who I am?'

Emma regarded him kindly. 'No, I haven't, because for the time being at least, she doesn't seem to have any memory of the accident.'

'I guess that's a good thing,' he said, standing out of the way as a nurse went speeding past towards the ITU. 'Does she remember anything else? Like, does she know you?'

All weekend Emma had veered between floating on air, and fearing that each tiny breakthrough was going to be the last, and that hadn't changed. However, she was able to say, 'Yes, she seems to know all of us who've seen her, but so far that's only been my mother and her aunt and uncle who came down at the weekend. Polly and Melissa, who are friends, came on Sunday, but she slept right through their visit. It was very disappointing for them, but they can always come again.'

He nodded and looked down at the chocolates he'd brought, not wanting to come empty-handed. 'Can I give her these?' he asked. 'Dad said we're not supposed to bring flowers into hospitals, so I thought . . . I didn't know if she was able to eat yet, and I thought these would keep better than if I brought fruit. Or maybe the nurses would like them.'

'That's very considerate of you,' Emma told him warmly. It was bewildering to be feeling so much affection for this boy when if it weren't for him, and his mother, she and Lauren wouldn't even be here. Yet she only had to recall Philip Leesom's part in it all to make her feel far more sympathy than resentment towards Oliver. 'She's only taking fluids at the moment,' she said, 'but everything's happening by degrees.'

'Can she talk?'

Feeling the threat of a cold grip trying to claim her, Emma said, 'No, not yet. She can make sounds, though, and she definitely understands what we're saying to her.' Then, realising how nervous the five-day wait had made him, she put a reassuring hand on his arm. 'Are you ready to go in now?' How wonderful that he cared. How could she not admire and respect him for that?

He swallowed as he nodded. 'She's awake, is she?'

'Yes, she's awake, but be prepared for her to nod off while you're talking to her. She's had several visitors this morning, doctors, physios, occupational therapists, you name it. She's insisting she's not tired, but I'm not convinced.'

Clutching his chocolates in both hands he followed Emma into the neuro ward, past the nurses' station and to the open door of the side room, where Lauren was propped up against pillows with her right leg still in a cast. Her eyes, the exquisite amber eyes that he'd only seen in photos and on videos until now, were open and looking right at him. It made his breath catch and his insides seem to float.

She looked lovely, Emma thought, in spite of the odd lengths of her hair and the dismaying paleness of her skin, which had previously glowed with such vitality.

'I'm sure it'll come back,' the doctor had told her, 'you just have to be patient.'

Emma wasn't finding it easy to heed this caution, especially when Lauren had looked healthier while she was still in a coma. Jo, the staff nurse, had assured her that was only because of the strain she was under now, trying to get used to her new surroundings and coax herself into doing things she hadn't done for some time.

'She will speak again though, won't she?' Emma had insisted. 'And walk and be able to feed herself?'

'Certainly the signs so far are good.'

Though it hadn't been the categorical yes Emma would have preferred, she was quick to remind herself how much more she had to hold on to now than she'd had a week ago.

'Darling, this is Oliver,' she said, standing aside so Lauren could get a clear view of her visitor.

Lauren's eyes were already on his, and Emma watched with pride as she appeared both pleased to see him and yet perplexed, as though she wasn't sure if she was supposed to know him or not. She couldn't be exuding emotions through her eyes if nothing was happening inside, and while she might not know who Oliver was, her inherent politeness was definitely still intact.

'Hello, Lauren,' he said, going towards the bed. He stopped and turned to Emma, as though seeking permission to go further.

'It's OK,' Emma told him. 'If you pick up her hand she'll be able to talk to you.'

Showing Lauren the chocolates, he said, 'I don't know if you like these, but if not you can always offer them to your visitors.'

Lauren's eyes dropped to the chocolates, then went back to his.

Pulling up a chair, he sat on the edge of it and touched his fingers tentatively to hers.

Lauren glanced down at their hands; then returned her gaze curiously to his. Her lips parted and a small noise came from the back of her throat.

'She can't move her hand to yours yet,' Emma told him, 'so you have to do it.'

Without breaking their gaze, Oliver covered her fingers with his and held them gently. 'You won't remember me,' he said softly, 'but I like to think of myself as a friend.'

He looked down as her hand made a small movement beneath his.

'She's saying yes,' Emma explained. Her lips were trembling slightly as she smiled. There was something quite magical about watching them together, as though, oddly, they were finding each other after a long and lonely search that neither of them had even known they were making.

'How are you feeling?' he asked in barely more than a whisper.

Emma gave Lauren a moment before quietly reminding Oliver that he needed to ask questions that could be answered with a yes or no.

'Sorry,' he apologised.

Lauren's eyes were searching his again. To Emma's astonishment she began moving her hand and actually managed to lift it several inches from the bed before it fell back into his.

'That's the first time she's done that,' she told Oliver excitedly, wishing she knew what Lauren had been trying to do. The important thing was, though, *she had raised her hand.*

Lauren turned to look at her. 'Mmm, mmm,' she said.

'Yes, I'm still here,' Emma assured her, knowing by now that the mmms meant Mum. 'You're wondering who Oliver is, aren't you?'

Lauren squeezed Oliver's hand once.

'She said yes,' he told Emma.

'Well, like he said, he's a friend who's been getting to know you while you've been here. He plays music for you to listen to and he talks to you about things.'

Lauren took her eyes back to Oliver as he said, 'I've downloaded k.d. lang's new album. It's called *Recollection*, and I reckon you'll really like some of the tracks. They're kind of cool, country, but not, if you know what I mean.'

To Emma's further amazement a light of humour showed in Lauren's eyes as she squeezed his hand twice to say no.

He blushed and laughed. 'OK, so I didn't describe it so well,' he admitted. 'Would you like to listen to it anyway?'

Again she squeezed twice.

Seeing how crushed he looked, Emma quickly said, 'I think what she's trying to say is that she'd rather you told her something about yourself. Is that right?' she asked Lauren.

Lauren's grip tightened on his hand as she parted her lips to try to speak again.

'I guess that was a yes,' he teased her.

Lauren's eyes shone as she turned to her mother.

'Would you like me to leave the two of you alone for a while?' Emma offered.

'Ouch!' Oliver cried. He turned to Emma. 'That was a definite yes.'

There was the hint of a smile on Lauren's lips now, and her eyes were so bright that Emma wasn't sure who she wanted to hug more, her daughter or this boy who was doing more to light her up than anyone else had managed so far.

'I can hardly get my head round it,' she said to Polly on the phone a few minutes later as she sat down in the cafe. 'Within minutes of him arriving she'd actually lifted her hand, and when I left just now she was still smiling, more or less, not at me, at him. They're small things, I know, and anyone else might not notice them, but right now, to me, they're feeling huge.'

'Because they are,' Polly declared joyfully. 'Slowly, but surely, everything's starting to wake up again. Like the doctor said, we just have to be patient. It's going to happen though, I just know it.'

Emma wanted to hold on to that and never, ever let it go, but she couldn't forget the doctor's warning that she had to be realistic. It simply wasn't possible, he'd told her, for a human brain to sustain an impact of that force and survive in the same condition it had been in before. The most damaged of the cells had been removed during surgery, and though it was possible others would take over the tasks the old ones had performed, they had yet to find out to what degree the new ones were able to assume their new roles. 'She's probably not going to be exactly the same as before,' she said, staring sadly down at her tea.

'You have to give her a chance,' Polly said, 'it hasn't even been a week yet.'

'I know, but it threw me badly to realise that she didn't know what the flute was when I showed it to her on Saturday. And she can't remember the name of her school, or even who her friends are. Let's hope that seeing Melissa will help to jog her memory a bit.'

'I'm sure it will. She hasn't had a problem with anyone else once she's seen them.'

Emma smiled mistily at that. 'Did I tell you, I asked her at the weekend if there was anyone else she'd like to see and she said no? So does that mean she's forgotten about Will?'

'If she has, then I'm sorry to say, he only has himself to blame. On the other hand, I can see why you'd be worried about that when he's such a significant part of her life.'

'Or was, given that we've no idea what he's going to be in the future. If she doesn't make a full recovery, and he doesn't want to pursue a relationship with her, I can promise you this, I will not be doing anything to try and help her to remember him. In fact, I shall go out of my way never to see or speak to him.'

'In some ways it might be easier not to have him fussing around and stressing you out. You're so not going to need it, especially when she comes home.'

Feeling herself melt at the thought, even as she tensed with apprehension, Emma waved as she spotted her mother coming towards the cafe. 'What's happening later?' she asked Polly. 'Is it our turn to cook?'

'No, mine, but, wait for this, can you believe, I have a date? So I'm hoping you won't mind too much if I leave you to your own devices tonight.'

'Absolutely not,' Emma assured her with a pang of excitement, which might have been tinged with envy. How long had it been since someone had invited her out on a date? How wonderful it would be if that was all she had to think about for the rest of the day. 'I'm assuming it's Alistair Wood,' she said.

'Then you'd be wrong. It's Keith McIntyre, who happens to be one of Alistair's business managers. He takes care of the company's interest in the nursery, which is how I've got to know him – well, we've met twice, actually, and spoken a few times on the phone. His call came out of the blue yesterday, I didn't have a clue he was even interested.'

'So are you?'

'Kind of, I suppose. He's quite sweet and to put it bluntly, I'm so out of practice where dating's concerned that I thought what the hell, I might as well give it a go. It doesn't have to lead to anything, and it'll get me out for an evening, maybe even broaden my limited horizons. I'll find out if he's got a brother, or a friend, shall I?'

Emma gave a splutter of laughter as her mother dumped her bags on a chair and went off to fetch a fresh pot of tea. 'Don't make it a priority,' Emma advised her. 'Just have a great time and don't forget to call in the morning to tell me everything.'

'It's a promise,' Polly assured her.

As Emma rang off her phone bleeped with a text. Seeing it was Donna she sighed uneasily, knowing she'd have to call the girl sooner or later, but now, in the middle of this coffee shop, wasn't the time to explain why she didn't want her to visit Lauren. 'Is everything OK?' she asked when her mother came to sit down.

'Yes, Mrs Dempster managed to get her shopping done in record time, bless her. She knew I wanted to get away to come here. She bought us a packet of summer bulbs to plant ready for when Lauren comes home. She's very thoughtful, isn't she?'

'She's a sweetheart,' Emma agreed, 'and I think she's really enjoyed getting to know you.'

'She used to be a fan of your father's.' Phyllis smiled softly. 'She had all his records apparently, but they've managed to get lost along the way. Would you like a top-up?'

'Yes please. Did you stop by to see Lauren?'

Phyllis's eyebrows rose as she nodded. 'I take it that's him, the one who's in there with her?'

'It is. Did you speak to him?'

'Well, I said hello, of course, and told him who I was. Then I thought I'd best leave them to it, they seemed so engrossed in whatever they were listening to.'

'k.d. lang, I expect. How did she look to you?'

'She seemed quite . . . bright. She's obviously enjoying having someone her own age around.'

'Not to mention someone of the opposite sex who's very good-looking. It would brighten anyone's day to have that sort of attention.'

Phyllis's eyes grew troubled. 'Yes, he is good-looking, and I suppose he's doing the right thing now, but I'm afraid I'm still finding it very hard to forgive him for what he did.'

'It was an accident,' Emma reminded her, trying not to sound impatient. She didn't want to bear grudges, or be around anyone who did, because such things were going to serve no purpose now. They needed to move on, to embrace this new phase with open and thankful hearts, and an unshakable determination to put all negative and destructive feelings of bitterness or vengeance behind them. It was what Lauren would want, she felt sure of it. It was what she wanted too.

Phyllis nodded. 'Yes, of course it was,' she agreed. 'How long is he staying for?'

'I thought I'd give them another ten minutes, or until we've finished this tea. It'll be enough for today. He can always come back tomorrow, if he's free. And if he wants to.'

Regarding Emma's worried face, Phyllis said, 'You're thinking her inability to speak yet, or move on her own is going to put him off?'

'It might, which would be a pity when she's obviously taken a bit of a shine to him, but better now than later, I suppose, considering what he's facing. We've no idea how much longer he's going to be able to visit. In the meantime, Donna's asking if she can come at the weekend, and I have to work out a way of letting her down without hurting her feelings.'

Phyllis swirled the teapot around. 'You're still determined she shouldn't come?'

'Aren't you?'

'Of course, I just thought you might change your mind. They've known each other for most of their lives.'

Emma looked down at her cup. 'At the moment Lauren's saying that the name Donna doesn't mean anything to her, but seeing her could change that and set off the kind of memories we'd really prefer to stay lost.'

'I'm not going to disagree with that,' Phyllis commented, starting to pour, 'and I'm sure Donna's mother will understand if you explain it to her. It might be easier than trying to talk to the girl yourself.'

'You could be right,' Emma responded, though not much relishing the thought of speaking to Ruth Corrigan either.

Setting down the pot, Phyllis took a sip of tea and asked, 'So what did this morning's circus of medical practitioners have to say for themselves?'

Emma's smile was distant. 'Much the same as yesterday, but I definitely got the impression that they want Lauren out of the ward and into some sort of rehabilitation facility as soon as possible.'

Phyllis sighed. 'And still no news from the PCT about whether they'll fund her going to the centre here?'

Emma shook her head. 'Dr Hanson's chasing it up, apparently, so we have to keep our fingers crossed. She lifted her hand just now.'

Phyllis beamed with amazement. 'She hasn't done that before. What prompted it?'

'Oliver, I think. I'm not sure whether she was trying to touch him, or what it was about, but at least we know that some more of her muscles are starting to work . . . We've come a long way already.'

'Indeed,' Phyllis murmured. 'Before we know it, she'll be skipping down the garden path and calling for her flute or guitar like nothing had ever happened at all.'

Emma loved the image, and savoured it for a few moments, before the consultant's voice of caution drove her to say, 'Remember, we have to prepare ourselves for the fact that it probably isn't going to happen that way.'

Phyllis put down her cup and gave a small but determined sigh. 'Perhaps not, but I think we have to try to keep as positive as we were before she came round, don't you?'

Emma wasn't going to disagree with that. 'For some reason I'm not doing such a great job of it at the moment,' she confessed. 'I get these great highs, but then . . . I think it could be the way Will's behaving that's getting to me. It's almost like he doesn't want her to get well, and yet I know that can't be true.'

'The bottom line?' Phyllis invited.

Emma nodded.

'That man can't handle the thought of having a daughter who might be disabled. I don't know if that's because he feels as though it will in some way reflect on him; or if he simply doesn't have what it takes to deal with the fact that his dreams for her have been derailed.'

'None of us wants to see her disabled, mentally or physically, but do you see us trying to hide from it?'

'No, but we're made of stronger stuff. If you think about it, he's never had much of a backbone.'

Emma's eyes widened in surprise.

Phyllis waved a dismissive hand. 'He's a very likeable chap, there's no doubt about that, at least when he wants to be, but frankly I've always thought you were wasted on him. I couldn't have said so back when you first met him, obviously, it was the last thing you'd have wanted to hear then, especially from me, so I did my best to get along with him.'

'And succeeded.'

'To a point where I apparently made you feel shut out again, but I can assure you it wasn't intentional.'

Emma shook her head in dismay. 'I've misread a lot of things about you over the years, haven't I?'

'Possibly, probably, but it often happens between a parent and child, especially if the parent's as mixed up and uncommunicative as I was. I'd like to think that from here on we're going to work a bit harder at understanding one another. I know I'm certainly going to try.'

Emma's eyes softened. 'So am I,' she assured her.

Phyllis smiled. 'That's good, because the way things are going I think you're going to need me around quite a lot for the foreseeable future, which brings me very neatly to something Mrs Dempster mentioned earlier. Apparently her next-door neighbours are going to Australia for a year to try it out before making the big commitment, so their house is going to be up for rent starting from the beginning of June.'

Emma was puzzled.

'I think I should take it,' Phyllis explained. 'Your house

isn't big enough for all three of us once Lauren comes home, and I can hardly commute between my place and yours, it's much too far. So, if I put mine up for rent and take the one next to Mrs Dempster, that shouldn't only work out for me helping you with Lauren, but it should also allow you to take the job at the hotel.'

Emma could only blink; she hadn't seen this coming at all.

'I've been thinking it over,' Phyllis continued unabashed, 'and you really can't let the opportunity of this summer festival pass you by. If you make a success of it, and I'm sure you will, it'll put you in good stead with the hotel for future events, which you're going to need. You have to earn money somehow, so why not earn it doing what you enjoy and you're good at?'

Finding her voice at last, Emma said, 'This is wonderful of you, Mum, it really is, but I can't let you take responsibility for Lauren when . . .'

'Why ever not? She's my granddaughter, so if that doesn't make her my responsibility I don't know what does. And I won't be doing it alone; Berry will come to stay whenever she can, and you'll be working from home some of the time, and I'm sure physios and carers will be coming and going until she's able to move herself around . . .'

'We don't know yet what she's going to be able to do, and besides, there's still the small matter of my job at the vet's. I can't just let them down.'

'Polly's already on to that. She's sure she can find someone to step in and fill the place until the girl comes back from maternity leave, which . . . You'd better answer that,' she said as Emma's phone started to ring.

Tearing her eyes from her mother, Emma checked the number, and clicked on. 'Hello, Emma Scott speaking,' she said, still dazed by the way Phyllis was taking over, and finding she really liked it.

'Mrs Scott, I hope you don't mind me calling,' the voice at the other end said. 'I got your number from when you rang here last week. It's Russell Lomax, Oliver's father.'

Feeling a quick catch of surprise, Emma stared hard at her mother as she said, 'Hello Mr Lomax.'

Phyllis's eyes widened.

'Would now be a convenient time to talk?' he asked.

'I guess it's as good as any,' she replied. 'What can I do for you?'

'Well, first I'd like to thank you for what you're doing for Oliver. It means a great deal to him to see Lauren. I hadn't actually realised it was happening until you found him there and he told me about it afterwards. Frankly, I'm not sure what I'd have done in your shoes, but the fact that you've treated him as kindly as you have . . . It's a great deal more than we deserve in the circumstances.'

'I don't imagine it's been easy for him either,' Emma responded. 'Certainly, when I spoke to him, I got the impression he's been finding it difficult.'

'Yes, he has, and he's been getting himself quite worked up about coming to see her. I think he was terrified you were going to put him off altogether. I wouldn't have blamed you if you had, I don't think he would either, but we were both very glad that you didn't. I just hope it's going well.'

'Well, it seemed to be when I left them together. In fact, I can tell you that your son managed to put a smile on her face, which is the first one we've seen since she came round.'

There was a note of relief, and maybe pride in his voice as he said, 'I'm very glad to hear that. The last thing I want is him upsetting her, or causing you any unnecessary distress . . .'

'It's really not happening, so please don't worry. I think him being here is good for her. My only fear is that she'll become attached to him, and with the charges he's facing, if he should find himself . . . unable to come any more . . .'

'Actually, that's my other reason for calling, but it's something I'd rather not discuss on the phone, if you don't mind. I can meet you, at your convenience of course, maybe somewhere close to the hospital, or perhaps in town.'

This was so unexpected that Emma couldn't immediately think what to say.

'I understand I'm asking a lot,' he went on, 'but if you could spare the time . . .'

'I'm sure I can, but . . . I'm just trying to think . . . when would be best.'

'Please don't feel rushed into giving me an answer. You have my number, so you can give me a call when you're ready.'

'OK, I will,' she replied, feeling certain she'd want to ask more as soon as she rang off. However, for the moment, she could think of nothing, so she simply responded to his goodbye and disconnected.

Chapter Twenty-Nine

It was another ten days before Emma and Russ were finally able to meet, the delay being caused by Dr Hanson's success in getting the funding for Lauren to be transferred to the Brain Injury Rehab Centre. The hospital, in need of the bed, had wasted no time in discharging her, so she was now settling into her own room on Maple Corridor, with posters and photographs on the walls, a bird feeder outside the window, her clothes hanging in the wardrobe and her guitar and flute propped in a corner. Her first week's schedule of therapy had already been drawn up, and though she was understandably disoriented, and seemed a little scared whenever Emma left, she'd just these last two days started to show signs of relating to Lizzie, her key worker. Lucy, her speech and language therapist, was highly encouraging in her first assessment of how well she was managing to communicate at such an early stage. She was still not speaking, but she was nodding and shaking her head with what seemed to be growing ease, and over the past week or so she'd begun uttering various sounds that, though not intelligible, were at least proving that the muscles in her throat were strengthening. She was also managing to swallow puréed foods, and was able to raise her left hand as well as her right, though she was hardly waving, or even reaching her own face without a certain degree of difficulty, but it was all progress.

The other really good news was that her leg was now receiving proper attention, and though it would still be quite some time before she'd be able to stand, much less walk on it, the size of her splint had already been reduced and she was starting to learn how to flex the muscles that hadn't moved for too long.

Throughout almost all of her small triumphs Oliver had been there, either sitting with her and encouraging her to engage with her specialist team, or just keeping her company after the others had gone. When the doctors did their rounds, or other visitors came to see her, he waited across the corridor from her room, giving her a droll sort of wave if he spotted her looking for him, and returning to her side as soon as he could. Occasionally he even sat with her when she slept, holding her hand, and sometimes dozing off himself. Seeing them together never failed to warm Emma's heart; and she knew the staff at the centre were equally moved by the image these two youngsters created. Having found out who he was, doctors, nurses and therapists alike were as touched by the bond developing in front of their eyes as they were entranced by the effect this dedicated young man was having on their new charge.

While Emma hadn't broached the subject of Oliver's looming trial with Oliver himself, she'd learned from Clive Andrews just over a week ago that the preliminary hearing had been postponed. Andrews hadn't said why, or until when, only that he'd be in touch again as soon as a new date had been set. She guessed that must have happened now, since she'd received a message from him this morning asking if he could come to see her sometime today or tomorrow. She presumed he wanted to discuss the case with her before it began; prepare her for what might happen, and possibly even try to dissuade her from attending. He wouldn't have a problem with the latter, because she had no intention of going. In fact she wished it wasn't happening at all, because she was dreading having to explain to Lauren why Oliver had stopped coming to see her.

Spotting Russ Lomax waiting in a secluded banquette at Graze, a large, friendly cafe on the corner of Queen's Square in the centre of town, Emma tucked her mobile in her bag and hurried across to join him. How strange it seemed, to be meeting this man whom she'd only ever seen on TV until now. She'd never even dreamt that their paths might one day cross, and certainly not in the way that they had.

'I'm sorry I'm late,' she said, shaking his hand as he stood up to greet her. He was as tall and well built as she'd expected, and his looks were so clearly the forerunner of Oliver's that it was hard not to comment. What she noticed most about him, however, were the deeply etched lines of tiredness around his eyes. 'I got caught up on the phone before leaving the house,' she explained unnecessarily.

'It's not a problem,' he assured her. 'I'm glad you could make it.'

To her surprise she felt herself colouring slightly as she sat into the bench seat opposite his. 'I see you already have a coffee,' she said, glad he hadn't waited for her to arrive.

'Let me get you one. What would you like?'

'A cappuccino, thank you,' she told the waiter who was hovering.

Left alone they glanced at one another awkwardly, then both started to speak at once. He insisted she went first.

'I was just going to say that Oliver texted about half an hour ago to let me know he'd arrived at the hospital and that Lauren had almost knocked him out with her smile.' She laughed at the joke. 'He's very considerate,' she added.

Russ's ironic look seemed to say, that's certainly what he would like you to think.

Emma smiled too. 'They're always better with other people, aren't they?' she said.

He nodded. 'But Lauren's not just any other person to him, as I'm sure you are very much aware by now.'

'I have to say he's impressed us all with how dedicated he is, and patient and good-humoured. Half the time I don't know what he says to make Lauren laugh, but whatever it is, it never seems to fail.' Thinking of Lauren's frantic gulps of mirth tore her heart between happiness and grief, for they weren't anything like the infectious, mellifluous sounds she'd made before. Would that change? She hoped so, but even if it didn't, it would never alter how much she loved and admired her daughter for her courage and spirit. 'Even the specialists are crediting him with how well her recovery is going,' she went on.

Russ's eyebrows rose. 'I'm afraid he's immodest enough to tell me so when he comes home,' he informed her. 'And

431

then, lucky me, I get to hear it all over again when he calls his brother to make sure he's up to speed too.'

Emma's eyes danced. 'He has good reason to feel proud of himself,' she declared, liking the sound of how close Oliver was to his father and brother. Did it in any way make up for the loss of his mother? That was what they said about alcoholics, that it was as though their families were the victims of another kind of death or loss when they drowned themselves in their addiction. Her eyes went down. 'We shall miss him a great deal,' she said, 'once the trial . . . I mean when . . . if . . . he stops coming.'

Russ waited as her coffee was delivered, and when they were alone again he said, 'Actually, that's what I want to talk to you about.'

Emma forced a smile as she looked up. 'It's not only what kind of punishment he might get, is it?' she said. 'And whatever it is, it's going to affect his visits to Lauren. It's that he's devoting all his time to her, when I'm sure you're anxious for him to find a job and get on with his life. Except he can't with this trial hanging over him.'

'It's true, I am keen for him to sort himself out, but we've discussed his need to be there for Lauren and I guess I understand why he doesn't feel right about carrying on with his life when she's still struggling to rebuild hers. So I've agreed that I won't push him to do anything about his future until Lauren is able to start considering hers.'

Emma felt quietly stunned. Surely he must realise it could be months, even years before Lauren was in a position to start studying again, or even be able to take care of herself. However, Oliver's devotion and his father's support wouldn't mean anything if the judge handed out a custodial sentence. Even a driving ban would make it extremely difficult for Oliver to continue visiting as often as he had over these last few weeks, so whichever way they looked at it, things weren't going to continue the way they were.

She ached to think of how much Lauren was going to miss him.

'Returning to the subject of Oliver's trial,' Russ went on, glancing down at his coffee. 'When I rang you to make this arrangement my intention was simply to tell you what we were hoping to achieve from a meeting we'd recently had with the senior prosecutor. I thought it only fair, because of how deeply it was likely to affect you. Now that we've achieved our aim . . .' His dark eyes came earnestly to hers. 'Are you aware . . . ? Have the police spoken to you yet about the prosecution?'

Emma shook her head. A small panic was starting inside her. What was going wrong? What more should she be bracing herself for? 'I had a message earlier from our family liaison officer,' she told him. 'He wants to come and see me. I'm guessing, from what you're saying, that it's about . . . whatever you're about to tell me.'

Russ nodded, and she couldn't tell whether he was sorry or relieved to be breaking the news himself. She was surprised, and then unsettled, by how uneasy he suddenly seemed. 'Our lawyer heard last night,' he said, 'that the charges against Oliver are being dropped.'

Emma's heart gave an unsteady beat. She was trying to make sense of his words, but it was hard, because charges like that didn't, couldn't, just go away. It simply wasn't possible.

'I expect you've heard about the missing blood sample,' Russ continued.

She nodded. 'But I thought they'd found it.'

'So did they. I'm afraid it was a total screw-up from start to finish. Heaven only knows what's happened to the blood Oliver gave, but no one's able to put their hands on it now. Obviously, without it a prosecution for drink-driving is seriously compromised.'

But there was the dangerous-driving charge. The offence that had actually put Lauren where she was. She didn't speak the words, but he must have read her mind because he said, 'I'm not sure if you're aware of the speed Oliver was driving at when the accident happened, but he turned out to be only marginally over the limit, which doesn't in itself nullify a prosecution, especially given the extent of Lauren's injuries. However, put together with the lost blood sample and the special reasons our lawyer was planning to present as a defence . . . Special reasons effectively means . . .'

'Actually, I know what it means,' she interrupted. She'd

433

come across it only once, a few years ago, when someone who'd worked for her had escaped a drink-drive prosecution because he'd been rushing his sick child to hospital at the time he'd been stopped. In Oliver's case, they'd clearly been planning to use his mother's threat to commit suicide. She didn't blame them, she was sure she'd have done the same in their shoes, but there had to be some sort of justice for Lauren. The police couldn't just turn away from this as though it had never happened.

'Is that why he's been going to see Lauren?' she asked brusquely. 'To make it look good in case he did end up in court?'

Russ shook his head. 'He goes because he genuinely cares.'

Certain that was true, she looked down at her hands, sorry now for the harshness of her accusation. *No grudges, no recriminations.*

'I realise how difficult this must be for you,' Russ said gently. 'I'm sorry, that sounds patronising. What I'm trying to say is, I truly don't think there's anything to be gained, for anyone, from this prosecution going ahead. If Oliver is being as supportive to Lauren as . . .'

'He is, and I understand why you, or your lawyer, would do this. You have to as a parent, and he has to because it's his job. I just don't . . .' She shook her head. What was she trying to say? Her mind was all over the place; she couldn't make this seem right, but at the same time was it really so wrong?

'The decision was taken at the highest level,' Russ explained, 'so I don't think the police, or CPS, were in any way dismissive of Lauren's rights. In fact, I got the impression when our lawyer rang with the news that one of the reasons they decided to drop the charges was actually to protect Lauren.'

Emma frowned as she looked at him.

'I don't know the detail,' he continued, 'and I'm not asking for it. All I can tell you is that when my lawyer reminded the senior prosecutor, here in Bristol, of where Lauren had been prior to the accident, that seemed to put a different complexion on matters. It was felt, it seemed, that you wouldn't want that information to become public.'

Emma could feel the fire in her cheeks as she lowered her eyes.

'I only mention it to try and help you realise that your interests were given careful consideration before a decision was arrived at.'

'And you personally weren't told anything about where she'd been?'

He shook his head. 'All I know is that it apparently has no legal bearing on the case, but it was deemed important enough to be given some weight when they were deliberating whether or not to press on with the charges.'

Emma sat back in her chair, feeling shaken and disoriented. She was no longer sure what she'd expected before coming here – possibly to be thanked for her treatment of Oliver, or maybe to be asked to persuade Oliver to give up his mission and get on with his life. It certainly wasn't to find out that there was to be no prosecution for the offence against Lauren – and learning that her liaison with Philip Leesom had played a part in robbing her of that right was making Emma feel sick and murderous towards him all over again.

However, that wasn't how the Crown Prosecution Service was seeing it. They were dropping the case in order to protect Lauren from the scandal of her own behaviour. Of course, that wasn't the only reason. If the blood sample hadn't been mislaid and the special reasons weren't so compelling, they'd never have considered Lauren's sensibilities for a moment. So what was she supposed to make of this? Should she be feeling angry, outraged, relieved, betrayed? She felt all of those things and more, she just couldn't be sure what the more was – apart from increasingly concerned about how Will was going to take it when he found out.

Given the way he'd turned his back on Lauren over the last two months, Emma was finding it hard to accept that he even needed to be told. He had no right to play Lauren's defender now, and even if he did, what possible good could he do with his empty threats and puerile temper? She could easily imagine him screaming from the moral high ground that he was going to sue the Lomax family out of existence, or the police, or the Crown Prosecution Service, and no doubt he'd throw Philip Leesom in for good measure. He'd make a total fool of himself, as he always did in these situations, and at the end of it nothing would have changed and he probably wouldn't even have been to see Lauren.

So no, she wasn't going to tell him anything of her own volition. If he rang and asked she'd give him the answer, but until then he could leave his head stuffed in the sand and with any luck he might not bother bringing it out again.

For Lauren's sake, she wasn't sure she actually meant that, but she knew that Will's presence in the rehab centre would only be disruptive, since he'd be unable to resist telling everyone what to do, or accusing them of being inept in some way. And if he became frustrated with Lauren's inability to speak, or feed herself with any degree of accuracy, he might end up setting her recovery back by days, even longer, for all Emma knew. She couldn't allow him to upset her like that.

If Lauren were showing signs of missing him, or even wondering about him, Emma knew without a shadow of doubt she'd be trying to persuade him to come, but so far all mentions of Daddy had been met by little more than a blank stare. It had made Emma start to wonder how much Lauren knew. How much of what had been happening around her had she taken in while no one was even certain she could hear? She remembered the rest of her family with no trouble, and Melissa and Polly, and she definitely seemed to respond more to certain books and music than others, though it wasn't easy to be sure whether they were her favourites from before, or whether she was hearing them for the first time and liking them. She couldn't tell them, and she was so sensitive to other people's feelings that she'd very likely pretend to be pleased just to make them happy.

There was so much going round and round in Emma's mind that she could hardly believe the time when she glanced at the clock – or that she'd actually been sitting here spilling everything out to Russ Lomax. They'd been in this cafe for almost an hour now and he'd simply allowed her to go on talking and ranting as if listening to her, offering no judgement or advice, was something he did every day. She could see the kindness and compassion in his eyes. It was obviously where Oliver had got it from. They were good people, the Lomaxes, who'd come out of nowhere to devastate her and Lauren's lives, and now they were doing everything they could to help put them back together.

Embarrassed and still a little emotional, she said, 'Sorry, I didn't mean . . . I'm not sure why you had to suffer all that . . . You must be in a hurry to leave . . .'

'Even if I were, which I'm not, I'd have to insist on buying you another coffee first,' he said drolly.

Looking down at her own, Emma was shocked to see that she'd stirred at least five unopened packets of sugar into the cup – and she didn't even take sugar.

'Stressed or what?' she said, with an anxious tilt of a smile.

He laughed and turned to signal the waiter.

'No, please, I'd like to get the next ones,' she said, putting a hand over his cup.

'Tell you what, let's argue about it later,' he suggested. 'The same again,' he told the waiter, and as he sat back in his seat Emma realised her phone was vibrating. Relieved to see it was only Polly, not the hospital, she let the call go through to messages.

'I was wondering,' she said, 'how Oliver's mother is getting along. He told me she was in a clinic in Cape Town?'

Russ nodded and a light inside him seemed to fade. 'She was indeed, until about a week ago, which was when, I'm afraid, she absconded with a fellow inmate – I guess that's not what they're called, is it?'

Emma shook her head. 'Probably not, but I don't know the correct term, so let's go with that one. Does it mean you don't know where she is now?'

'Oh no, she's at his place in Camps Bay, and she's saying she won't go back to the clinic unless I send the boys out to see her.'

Emma couldn't help but feel his frustration and dismay. 'So what are you going to do?'

'Nothing, because allowing her to blackmail us like that will just make her carry on doing it.'

Though she could see the sense of that, she could tell how difficult he was finding it. 'She has family out there, doesn't she?'

'Yes, her sister and brother-in-law, who are being as supportive as they can. I spoke to Olivia last night after she'd been out to Camps Bay to see for herself what kind of state Sylvie's in. Thankfully, the man, whoever he is, seems to have a decent home and a family that cares about him too, but that said, they were both drunk when Olivia got there, and apparently Sylvie's thinner than ever.'

'Because she doesn't eat?'

'Hardly at all. Alcoholics often don't.' He took a breath and let it go slowly. 'To be honest, I'm past knowing what to do. I've been to AlAnon a few times over the last year or so, and though it's helpful to hear other people's stories, the bottom line remains the same: until she's ready to help herself . . .' He broke off as the waiter came to set down their fresh coffees.

'Does Oliver know that she's checked out of the clinic?' Emma asked when they were alone again.

Russ shook his head. 'Olivia doesn't think I should tell the boys, and I'm inclined to agree for now. They've got their own lives to lead – Charlie's just started a pupillage at a very good chambers, and you know as well as I do how involved Oliver is with Lauren's recovery. They can't be rushing off to Cape Town to satisfy the whim of a mother who probably won't even remember that she asked them to come by the time they get there. Actually, I'm not even sure they'd go. They're incredibly angry with her, especially Oliver, for obvious reasons. It's not easy being the child of a drunk, watching someone you've loved so much turning into someone you find yourself starting to hate. And we do hate what she's become. It's impossible not to, particularly when there are so few signs now of who she used to be.'

Sensing the depth of his impotence and sadness, Emma found herself wishing there was something she could do. Of course, there wasn't, but knowing what he and Oliver were doing for Lauren, in spite of their own problems, was filling her with a need to reciprocate in some way. But how, when he was clearly a very proud and private man and when she didn't really even know him?

By the time they finally left the cafe the lunchtime crowds were starting to pour in and they were both amused by how long they'd been there, and slightly embarrassed by how much they'd talked about themselves.

'I hope I haven't bored you to death,' he winced as they walked to where their cars were parked on the leafy square.

'Not at all,' she hastily assured him. 'It seems to me we were both in need of airing a few things, and sometimes it's easier with a stranger than with someone you know.'

He nodded agreement. 'Actually, I hardly talk about myself at all,' he admitted, 'which I guess could be considered one of my many failings. Sylvie has a full list of them, and apparently they're what drove her to drink.'

Appalled, Emma turned to look at him. 'You don't believe that, surely,' she protested.

He smiled. 'I'm not that much of a masochist, but I'm sure I haven't always been easy.'

She gave a sigh. 'Marriage is a very tricky business, isn't it? But having said that, I know very well that the breakdown of my own was entirely Will's fault, because when I'm not busy being a mother, I'm simply being perfect.'

With a shout of laughter, he came to a stop beside her as they reached her car. 'I've enjoyed meeting you,' he said, shaking her hand. 'It probably wasn't polite to sound quite as surprised as that, but I must confess to some trepidation before I came.'

She nodded understandingly. 'Yes, I am pretty scary,' she said with a chuckle. Then, more seriously, 'I appreciate you telling me about the charges. Of course I have mixed feelings about the decision to drop them, but with all things considered, what makes far more sense to me than Oliver losing his licence or being sent to prison, is that he goes on helping Lauren.'

Russ smiled. 'How do you think Lauren's father is likely to respond when he finds out about the charges?'

Emma grimaced. 'It won't be pretty, that's for sure.'

Russ nodded and let go of her hand. 'You've been very gracious over this, thank you.'

Had she been gracious, she was wondering, as he walked away and she got into her car. Or selfish? Possibly a little of both, with some plain old pragmatism thrown into the mix. After all, the decision had been made now, she couldn't change it even if she wanted to, but she really did think it was the right one. There were certainly going to be plenty of people who'd disagree with her, but fortunately those closest to Lauren, who were able to see for themselves the difference Oliver was making to her, wouldn't be amongst them. And they were the only ones who mattered to Emma. She felt pleased for Russ Lomax, too, that he no longer had to live in dread of his younger son being sent to prison, or visualise the nightmare of living with a young man whose freedom to drive had been taken away.

He was a good man, she decided, taking out her phone to check her messages, and a caring father who she couldn't even begin to imagine failing his sons the way Will was failing Lauren. He'd also, she realised, as she scanned the first few texts, been discreet enough not to ask about where Lauren had been the night of the accident. He must be curious, who wouldn't be when it had featured in such a momentous decision, but he'd apparently understood that the issue wasn't open for discussion. She'd have liked very much to believe that it would never come out, but since every message on her phone was from a journalist asking for her reaction to the decision to drop the charges, she'd be a fool if she did.

Chapter Thirty

Lauren had been undergoing her gruelling schedule of rehabilitation for just over a month now and had not only become one of the most popular patients at the centre, but one of the most determined to master all the tasks she was set. It hadn't taken her long to be able to read almost as well as she had before; or to write, though with a very clumsy hand, and she'd recently moved on from simple twenty-piece jigsaws to considerably more complicated ones. Her speech was coming along fairly well too, though it still sounded as if her tongue was too heavy for the words, and to her frustration her ability to apply her make-up hadn't yet reached a point where she could avoid stabbing herself in the eye, or drawing crooked clown lips around her own. Trying to look her best for Oliver wasn't a prescribed part of her daily routine, but caught up in the romance of the young couple as they were, a nurse or occupational therapist was always happy to help out, carefully guiding her hand as she darkened her lashes with mascara and coated her lips in a frosted-rose gloss. All the staff had become so fond of Oliver that visiting hours no longer seemed to apply to him.

A week ago Lauren had been declared strong enough to take her first shaky steps on crutches; by yesterday she'd managed a full ten metres without toppling, and with Oliver waiting at the end of the track to scoop her into a proud embrace. Emma had been there too, watching from the sidelines and loving him so much for how gentle and yet assertive he was with Lauren.

The press had gone to town with the dropping of his charges, naturally, lambasting everyone from the police, to the CPS, to the government, for such a 'travesty of justice'. One paper had wondered, on its front page, if someone at the labs had been paid to 'misplace' the blood sample, but as they could find no proof of it, the mischievous speculation was taken no further. Emma herself had repeatedly declined to comment on the decision; getting involved in any kind of statement at all, she felt, would inevitably lead her into a minefield of questions that would inevitably lead her to the very place she didn't want to go. Will, however, in typical Will fashion, had loudly and publicly warned the police and the Lomax family that they hadn't heard the end of this yet. Whether he was actually planning some sort of action Emma had no idea, because he still hadn't deigned to call her; and her resolve not to call him remained firm. However, she'd rung Russ Lomax, after catching Will holding forth on the news, to ask him to let her know if he ever did hear anything from her ex-husband or his lawyer. So far he hadn't, and Emma was staying hopeful that Will would once again prove himself full of nothing but hot air.

Exactly how much Lauren now remembered of where she'd been before the accident wasn't easy to tell, when she was still finding it hard to communicate lucidly or at any length. At Emma's request, Melissa had tentatively broached the subject with her, but when Lauren hadn't seemed to understand what was being asked of her Melissa hadn't pushed it. Of course nothing had been said in front of Oliver – that was something he really didn't need to know. However, when Emma had met Russ for a coffee again a few days ago she'd ended up telling him about Lauren's relationship with her teacher, not in any great detail, but in a way that she hoped might shift a little of the blame from his wife. It wasn't that she particularly cared about the wife's conscience, but if it lifted some of the pressure of guilt from Russ's shoulders then she felt it needed to be done. He had seemed relieved, but also outraged by Leesom's exploitation – and deeply sorry that Emma had found out about it the way she had. 'I just hope the man's conscience is even more crippling than the loss of his job,' he'd declared angrily before they'd parted.

442

Leesom had been replaced already, by a woman with an incomparable track record who'd be joining the school at the beginning of the next academic year. Emma had been told that by the headmaster when he'd rung to say that it would be an honour to have Lauren back as a student when she was ready to resume her studies. There would be no fees to be paid, of course, and if any extra tuition was necessary the school would be happy to provide that too. Though Emma had appreciated his confidence in Lauren's recovery, and the sincerity of the offer, she knew in her heart that she would never be sending Lauren back there. It was doubtful anyway that Lauren would want to go, since it would mean leaving Oliver, and with the way things were Emma couldn't imagine her ever wanting to do that.

There was always the possibility, of course, that Oliver might find himself a job in London, but since that bridge didn't have to be crossed any time soon, Emma wasn't going to allow herself to worry about it now. Particularly not when she had so much else to keep her awake at night, such as Lauren's recent decision to write her father a letter, in her own hand (though thank goodness she hadn't brought it up again since). Emma didn't even want to think about how Will might react to the large, misshapen scrawl, so she was hoping Lauren wouldn't force the issue. She was now getting to grips with organising the summer arts festival, and had become so immersed in it since its official green light that her gratitude to Oliver, and her mother, for always being there for Lauren had long since broken all bounds.

Watching Oliver now as he seated himself sideways on to Lauren's wheelchair, Emma perched on the edge of the bed, and felt anxious for him as he took Lauren's hand in his. He'd been wanting to tell Lauren for a while how they'd first come into one another's lives, but it had taken him until last night to ask Emma's permission to do so, and also to ask if she'd be there in case Lauren became upset and didn't want him near her any more.

Emma didn't think this was likely. However, she really wouldn't have wanted this to be happening without her, so she'd rearranged her day to make sure she was there.

'Yr-yr king veh ry see . . . us,' Lauren stammered, gazing quizzically at Oliver.

You're looking very serious. It often took Emma a moment to work out what she was saying, while Oliver seemed to understand straight away.

'Actually, this is a bit serious,' he told her. His back was turned to Emma so she couldn't see his face, but she could easily picture the earnestness in his eyes and slight tremble of his mouth.

Lauren looked over at Emma. 'Mmm-um,' she said.

'Yes, I'm here,' Emma assured her, 'and I promise there's nothing to be afraid of.'

After a pause, Lauren's eyes twinkled merrily. 'No-ot frayd,' she declared. Her gaze returned to Oliver, and Emma could see that in spite of her brave words she was starting to become apprehensive. What was going through her mind, Emma wondered. Did she think Oliver was about to tell her he was going to stop coming? Or that she might never be able to speak or walk properly again? Or that she'd done something to hurt someone without realising it? What were her big fears these days? Was Leesom in there somewhere, and the dread that Oliver might have found out? Emma hoped to God not.

Taking a slightly shuddery breath, Oliver said, 'You know you had an accident, that's why you're in hospital.' Emma saw his hands tighten reassuringly round Lauren's.

Lauren nodded. 'Hi-it by . . . caaa-r.'

Oliver's voice was faint as he said, 'That's right,' and Emma could almost feel his heart thudding.

'What we haven't told you until now,' he pressed on, 'is that I . . . Well, that I was driving the car.'

Lauren frowned and her head dropped jerkily to one side as she tried to peer into his eyes. It took a few seconds for her to muster the words, 'Donnn't unn . . . stand?'

Swallowing, he said, 'I was driving the car that hit you.' He braced himself and went further. 'It's because of me that you're here.'

Lauren still looked puzzled, and turned to Emma as though asking her to explain.

'Oliver was driving the car that hit you,' Emma repeated

444

gently. 'It was an accident, of course. You were . . . It was a dark night and he didn't see you in time.'

Lauren's eyes went back to Oliver. She rocked a little as she worked herself up to speak again. 'Yooo-ou ran mmmee ov-er?' she said.

Oliver nodded and Emma's heart folded around his pain. 'I'm sorry,' he whispered shakily. 'I . . . I didn't really know where I was, and then . . . I . . . I didn't have time to stop, and the next thing I knew . . .'

For a moment nothing happened, then, to Emma's dismay, Lauren pulled her hand from his.

'I'm sorry,' Oliver said again, 'but I couldn't go on lying to you . . . Well, not lying exactly, but not telling you how . . . how we . . . met, I suppose.'

Lauren was regarding him intently, but it was impossible to gauge what she was thinking. In the end, in her tragically mangled way she said, 'So you come to see me because you feel guilty?'

'Of course I feel guilty,' he cried, 'what kind of person would I be if I didn't?'

'Yooo-ou feel sreee fr mmmmeee.'

He clasped his hands to his head. 'I feel sorry this has happened. I wish to God it hadn't, but then I wouldn't know you and all I want is to know you and be with you.'

Emma waited for a moment, and when neither of them spoke again she said, 'I know this has come as a shock, darling, but try to think of what it's been like for Oliver too. It was a terrible experience for him . . . He didn't know . . . He couldn't be sure at the time whether or not he'd killed you. And you were in the middle of the road on a very dark night. Your car had broken down. We think you were trying to get a phone signal, and that was when Oliver came along.'

Lauren's eyes were still on Oliver, even though he was hanging his head.

'If you want me to go,' he said wretchedly.

Lauren started to lift a hand. It took a while, but eventually she rested it on his hair.

He glanced up at her, and seeing the tender look in her eyes he caught her hand and pressed it to his cheek. 'You know how I feel about you,' he whispered huskily. 'You mean everything to me.'

Lauren's lips moved before the words finally came. 'Annnd yooo-ou to mmmeee,' she told him. 'I'mmm gl . . . dint die. Woodunt know yoooo-ou if I did.'

I'm glad I didn't die. I wouldn't know you if I did.

Feeling a lump forming in her throat, Emma decided to wait for another day to tell Lauren that Oliver's family was behind the golden angels scheme. All she could do now was drop a kiss on both their heads before discreetly leaving them alone together.

'So how did it go?' Russ demanded as soon as he answered the phone.

Realising he'd been on tenterhooks, Emma smiled as she said, 'They're fine. She was a bit thrown by it at first, but I've come away with a feeling that this is actually going to bring them even closer together.'

Russ's sigh of relief was audible. 'That daughter of yours is a very remarkable young lady,' he declared. 'The more I hear about her, the more impressed I become.'

'Well, your son is a very remarkable young man. It took guts to do what he did today. He could have left it to me, but he insisted on doing it himself and it really was the best way.'

With a note of irony in his voice, Russ said, 'I'm glad it worked out, for them, of course, but for us too, because I don't know about you, but I'm not good at broken hearts.'

Emma had to laugh. 'Is anyone?' she said. Then, 'Oliver mentioned last night that if it did go well today he'd like to bring you to meet Lauren. Are you up for that?'

'Of course, it would be my pleasure.'

'It would have to be here, at the centre, of course, and I was thinking . . . Well, she has a birthday in a couple of weeks. The staff are going to put on a little celebration for her, and her great-grandmother is hoping to fly over from Italy to join us, so I was thinking that perhaps it might be a good time for you to come. It won't make too big a deal of it if there are others around. However, you need to be sure you can handle all us women at once.'

Sounding amused, he said, 'I'll do my best. If you just

let me know the date and time and dress code if there is one, I'll be there.'

Laughing, Emma replied, 'Well, if you want to dress up I was considering hiring a clown for the day.'

Silence.

Trying not to laugh again, Emma went on, 'But I'm sure she'll tell me at nineteen she's too old for such things.'

'God, there's a relief,' he choked.

Emma was still smiling as she drove out of the hospital car park a few minutes later, in a hurry now to get to Weston-super-Mare for a meeting with North Somerset Health and Safety Executive, who were going to end up shutting the arts festival down if they carried on the way they were. After that she needed to be back at the hotel to meet with Hamish Gallagher's wife and a local artist who was something of a national celebrity. Her schedule of meetings was growing by the day, making the demands on her time so great that she had no idea how she was going to fit everything in.

Something she'd never allowed to happen, however, was a single day to pass without seeing Lauren, even though it was sometimes no more than a snatched few minutes watching from the wings as she underwent one of her gruelling therapy sessions, or a brief goodnight at the end of the day. She knew Lauren loved her being there almost as much as she loved to hear about the festival and how the arrangements were coming along. Many of the ideas for advertising and promotions had come from Lauren and Oliver. Oliver had provided the greater part of these, since this was where his interests lay, but there was no doubting Lauren's enthusiasm for the event, or her determination to be there for the opening day.

Emma would love nothing more than for that to happen, and since the date was still two months away she was daring to hope that it actually might.

It was the day before Lauren's birthday already, and Russ had just popped into a jeweller's in Clifton to pick up the gift Oliver had ordered the week before. Following his son's strict instructions, he then sent a text to confirm that he had the precious item and that it was presented exactly as he'd requested. That done, finding himself with some time to spare before the meeting which was the main reason for coming into Bristol, he decided to call round to pick up Sylvie's mail.

Since he dropped in at least once a week and Connie kept an eye on things too, there wasn't much to sort through, mostly junk, a couple of invitations to charity events, and a bank statement that he only glanced at, until the bottom figure eventually registered with him. Looking at it again, he felt both puzzled and disturbed. He was sure that the last time he'd checked this particular account it had been in credit to the tune of fifty thousand pounds. Now a mere two hundred and forty pounds remained. The missing forty-nine thousand seven hundred and sixty had been electronically transferred to an account at the First National Bank of South Africa. If the account had been in Sylvie's name he'd have probably thought, or hoped, that she was using the money to pay the clinic. As it was in the name of one Johann Fortrum he couldn't help feeling more than a little concerned.

'Yes, yes,' Olivia confirmed, sounding slightly harassed, when he got hold of her, 'that is the name of the man she has been staying with, but I have some news, Russ.'

Something in her tone warned him that he wasn't going to like this much.

'We picked her up from the hospital an hour ago,' Olivia went on. 'We only got the call this morning, but she has been there for the past two days after having her stomach pumped.'

Tension shot through his body as he imagined another suicide attempt. 'What was it?' he asked, trying to quell the shameful hope that she might one day succeed.

'A mix of drink and antidepressants, apparently. I don't know if it was deliberate, but she is saying now that she might as well be dead because you and the boys won't come to see her.'

Russ's eyes closed as the wretched waves of guilt and resentment washed over him again.

'I am sorry to tell you this,' Olivia continued. 'Hans said

I shouldn't, but I am afraid she might try to do something again.'

Bring on the emotional blackmail, Russ thought bitterly. Not Olivia, Sylvie, because that was what it was about, he felt sure of it. 'What's happening with the clinic?' he asked. 'Is there any chance of getting her back there?'

'I am not sure. I would like to think so, but probably not immediately.'

'So will she carry on staying with you?'

'For the time being, I think, but Johann has been in touch. He wants her to go back to him.'

Groaning inwardly at the mere thought of her returning to some sort of love nest with a fellow drunk, he said, 'Will she go?'

'It is hard to say. You know how unpredictable she is. I think possibly it will depend on how much drink we will allow her to have. Hans says she must have some to be able to function, but I know a glass or two with meals will not be enough for her, and it is very alarming when she becomes abusive.'

This was starting to sound as though Sylvie was becoming too much for her own sister, and if he was right about that then he didn't know what the hell he was going to do. Leaving it for the moment, he said, 'Do you know anything about this money? Why has she transferred it to him?'

'All I can tell you is that she has been talking about opening an account here so she could have her independence. Perhaps she had some difficulty with it, she would not be able to produce all the correct documentation to prove she was not laundering the money.'

'So she dumped it into his account?'

'*Peut-être.*'

Sadly, it made sense. 'Nearly fifty grand to a drunk,' he muttered. 'Just think of the parties.'

'Maybe he will give it back.'

'Tell you what,' he responded, 'I won't be holding my breath for that. Can I talk to her?'

'If you hold on I will go to see where she is.'

'Hang on, what kind of state is she in? Is it even worth talking to her?'

'I think so. She is still very tired after her ordeal, and her throat is sore, as you'd expect, but I know she will want to talk to you.'

Feeling terrible for wishing he hadn't bothered to ring, Russ glanced at the time as he waited. He was going to be late for his meeting now, and distracted when he got there, and stressed and increasingly furious about the fifty grand which she'd virtually just thrown away. Not that he cared for himself, it was her money, she could do what she liked with it, but she had one son who might soon need some help funding the purchase of a flat, and another who was earning nothing while he tried to help the girl he'd almost killed, thanks to his bloody mother.

There were times when he felt that if she didn't finish herself off he might just do it for her.

Sylvie's voice was husky and frail as she said, 'Hello Russ. How are you?'

Even the sound of her irritated him, made him want to shake her and tell her that everyone was at the end of their tether because of her. She wouldn't hear him even if he did, because she only ever heard what she wanted to. So all he said was, 'I'm fine. I hear you're not.'

Her sigh was tremulous as she said, 'I am glad to speak with you, but please do not be telling me off for what I have done.'

'I guess you'd rather I congratulated you.'

'Oh Russ, you are always so cross with me. It is because of this that I am so unhappy.'

'You're unhappy because you're screwing up your life, and until you do something about it nothing's going to change.' How many times was he going to say that for her simply to ignore it? Why was he even bothering?

'I am trying, but you make it very hard for me. I want to see you and Charlie and Oliver, but you will not come, so I think I must fly home.'

God forbid! 'No, what you must do is check yourself back into the clinic, get with the bloody programme, and *then* maybe we can talk about you coming back.'

There was a long silence, so long that he thought she'd

hung up. Finally, she said, 'I will do this, I will return to the clinic, if you will take me there.'

Clenching his fists as he gave a silent growl of frustration, he replied, 'I'm not playing this game, Sylvie. I need to see you making an effort, staying at the clinic, and showing us all that you're serious about helping yourself. Then, and only then, I might think about coming over.'

'But I am serious.'

'Staying less than a month before running off to shack up with some bloke who's as big a lush as you are isn't saying serious to me.'

'You are jealous about Johann?'

'For God's sake, Sylvie, what the hell do I have to be jealous of?'

'He is a very good man. He takes care of me.'

'Oh yeah, so you end up in hospital having your stomach pumped. That's great care. What you actually mean is he opens the next bottle, or pours the next glass.'

'Please stop being so harsh with me. I do not deserve this.'

Reminding himself that getting worked up was going to achieve precisely nothing, he stated, 'Three months at least. That's how long you need to be in the clinic before I'll even consider coming to see you.'

'But Russ, that is too long. I miss you and I know this is a trick, because after I do this you will find another reason not to come. I need you here now, today, or I do not know what will happen to me. There will be no reason for me to go on.'

Hardly able to contain his fury, he said, 'Don't you dare start threatening me like that. You tried it on Oliver, remember, and look what happened to him, so . . .'

'Oliver, my baby. How is he? I want to see him so much. Please bring him to see me. I beg you, please. I know he is angry with me, but I am his mother. He will want to be here for me.'

Taking the only way out he could, he said, 'I'm going to ring off now. I hope the next time I talk to Olivia . . .'

'Russ, don't go, please,' she cried in a panic. 'Come tomorrow. I will wait for you at the airport.'

'Don't, I won't be there.'

'You must be, or I swear it will be the end for me. I cannot go on without you all . . .'

As he put the phone down he could still hear her voice, pleading and desperate. He imagined her sinking to her knees, sobbing over the phone in pathetic despair. Olivia would come to comfort her, so would Hans if he was there, but how long would it take for her to escape them and return to Johann? Once there she would have all the vodka or wine she could wish for. She'd swill it back by the bottle, blaming him entirely for her misery, becoming more determined by the minute to punish him for her downfall. What kind of pills did Johann have at his place? Who was the supplier, a respectable doctor or a pusher? No respectable doctor would put serious antidepressants into the hands of an alcoholic, unless he had no idea he was confronting one.

What the hell should he do? He couldn't leave Olivia and Hans to cope with this alone. For all he knew Sylvie was already fleeing their home on her way back to her boyfriend. He had to call and speak to Olivia again. He must warn her about what Sylvie had said on the phone, in case she hadn't heard it for herself. His head went down as frustration and fear overwhelmed him. Maybe what he really needed to do was tell Olivia that he was on his way.

He thought of Oliver and how much it meant to his son to be introducing his father to Lauren tomorrow. The boy had talked about nothing else for days, and was so thrilled with the gift he'd chosen that Russ just knew that if he wasn't there to see him hand it over then some of the pleasure would be gone. He thought of Lauren and how much he was looking forward to meeting her, and of how pleased Emma was that he'd agreed to join them. He thought of what he'd bought for Lauren, and how it would surprise both her and Oliver.

It was a birthday; there would be others, and these were only gifts.

In Sylvie's case it was her life; but it could always be another empty threat.

What the bloody hell was he going to do?

Chapter Thirty-One

The following day Emma was leaning against the window ledge in Lauren's room, surrounded by balloons and birthday bunting and living every minute of Lauren's joy as she opened a huge pile of cards and passed them round for everyone to see. She was seated on the edge of the bed with Berry one side of her, and Oliver the other. Phyllis, Polly and Melissa had brought in chairs for themselves from the dining room. Berry's face was aglow with pride, since Lauren had insisted on changing into the exquisite kaftan top she'd brought her from Italy. Being fiery shades of crimson and gold shot through with dramatic indigo swirls, it went with Lauren's bronze-coloured jeans perfectly. (Though her right leg was still in a splint and unable to be fully bent at the knee, there was now no longer any need to cut her trousers in order for her to get them on.) Her hair was glinting beautifully in the sunlight, cascading down over one shoulder in all its former glorious hues, with the shorter side held up by the jewelled combs and clips that Melissa had bought for her birthday, and had come early to put in for her.

So far her presents had consisted of a new laptop from Emma, a generous selection of Lancôme beauty products from Phyllis, an expensive hairbrush from Polly and a box of her favourite white Belgian truffles from Mrs Dempster, who'd been invited along this morning, but had had to back out at the last minute. There were more presents and cards from Harry, Jane and the children, Adolfo and his family, and what seemed to be every friend she'd ever been to school with, and plenty of the teachers too. Thankfully, Philip Leesom hadn't had the gall to send a card, or to add his name to anyone else's. If he had, Emma would simply have ripped it up. Part of her had wanted to do the same with the others, as though to protect Lauren from the pain of who she'd once been, but it would have been unkind to hide so much affection and thoughtfulness from her, even though she didn't appear entirely sure who everyone was. Donna's name had certainly given her pause; however, so far she hadn't asked anything about her.

Nor had she mentioned Will, who'd sent nothing at all, for which Emma could have happily stabbed him.

As yet Oliver hadn't handed over his gift, though Emma knew all about the long, slender package with its elegant gold and silver gift wrap and matching bow, because it was currently safely tucked away inside her handbag. She was guessing it was a necklace or bracelet, but it didn't appear she was going to find out until his father arrived.

'You know, Lauren,' Berry was saying with the sparkle of a tease in her eyes, 'I'm surprised your mother never told you that there are other ways to go about finding yourself a nice young man.'

Lauren's eyes lit up with laughter as she turned them to Oliver. Her cheeks flooded with colour, and the sobbing merriment in her throat was so touching that Emma felt her own tightening with emotion.

'And the same goes for you,' Berry told Oliver. 'I don't know what the two of you were thinking, I'm sure. It was never done that way in my day, oh no.'

'That's because they only had horses and carts back then,' Phyllis informed the gathering.

Emma wasn't sure whether it was the comment or the look on Berry's face that made her laugh more.

'Mm-mm nye in shi-shi mer,' Lauren declared, holding on to Oliver's hand.

Clearly realising no one had quite got it, Oliver said, 'She's telling you I'm her knight in shining armour, which makes her my damsel in distress.'

Lauren beamed joyously as she nodded.

'I was going more for Sleeping Beauty myself,' Emma commented.

Lauren's curious laughter, which had greatly improved

from the strangled gulps of a few weeks ago, widened everyone's smile with as much affection as pride. 'Do-do li my noo wheel-s?' she asked Berry, pointing to her wheelchair.

Oliver looked at Berry to see if she needed help, but this time she didn't.

'They're divine, darling,' Berry assured her. 'If I didn't think your awful granny would come up with something tart, I'd say I'd love one myself.'

Phyllis looked mightily tempted, but in the end resisted.

Squeezing Oliver's hand, Lauren said, 'Te-eeell Gr-nee Be-eh-ree mee-meeters.'

Nodding, he said, 'She wants me to tell you that she ran the hundred metres yesterday and won.'

As everyone laughed and Lauren slapped him playfully, he went on, 'Actually she walked a hundred metres on her crutches, and if any of you have ever tried walking with those things, you won't be surprised when you start seeing her biceps getting bigger than mine.'

'A hundred metres,' Berry gushed ecstatically. 'That's marvellous, my darling. You didn't say anything,' she chided Emma.

'She wanted to tell you herself,' Emma replied.

Lauren nodded awkwardly, but happily. 'Annnd flew,' she added.

'You flew!' Berry exclaimed.

Lauren gave another of her halting laughs. 'Flew-*t*,' she said.

Berry's eyes rounded. 'Are you saying flute?'

Lauren nodded.

'Have you played it?'

Lauren looked at Oliver. 'Yooo ooo.'

'Yes, she's played it,' he answered proudly, 'and she was brilliant.'

Lauren gasped. 'No-ot tr-trooo,' she protested. 'Pr-pr-pr-tiss.'

'Practice,' he explained for Berry.

Emma wondered if he was going to tell them how he'd managed to catch the flute as Lauren had hurled it at the wall in frustration, but it didn't seem so, and she wasn't going to mention how bitterly Lauren had cried after Oliver had gone, when she and Emma were alone.

'But it's marvellous that you've picked it up again,' Berry was declaring, glancing at Emma. 'She's doing so well.'

Emma wasn't going to deny it, but she did say, because she could see that Lauren was keen for some truth to out, 'She's still having a little difficulty holding it properly, but she's definitely getting there, and she's made fantastic progress with the guitar.' She didn't add that the doctor felt doubtful that she'd ever play to the standard she'd achieved before, there was no need, and anyway, doctors could always be wrong.

'Ho-ow Ad-Ad-olfo?' Lauren asked Berry.

Berry looked delighted. 'He'll be thrilled when I tell him you asked.'

'F-f-crse.'

Berry glanced uneasily at Oliver.

'Of course,' he translated.

Berry threw out her hands. 'Of course,' she repeated in a way that made the others laugh. 'Silly me. He's not doing too badly at all, thank you, my darling. He can get around fairly well now, but the beastly stroke's robbed him of his confidence, so he's not quite the dashing blade we used to know. Honestly, old age! I don't think I'll bother with it myself. Much better to be young and gorgeous like us,' she insisted with a wink at Lauren.

Phyllis's snort of laughter set everyone off again, and as the light-hearted banter continued Emma noticed Oliver glancing worriedly at the time, clearly wondering what was keeping his father. Realising he probably didn't want to break up the party to go and find out, Emma was about to pop out to call him herself when, to her relief, he appeared in the doorway. He looked a little dishevelled and his frown was very tense, but as soon as he realised he was in the right place whatever was bothering him seemed to melt away.

'Sorry I'm late,' he said, going straight to Lauren to shake her hand. 'I'm Russ, Oliver's father, and it's a very great pleasure to meet you.'

As she put her much smaller hand in his Lauren couldn't

have appeared more thrilled. 'Annnd yooo-oo,' she said. 'Golllden annngels.'

He grimaced. 'More my mother than me,' he told her.

'Yoou llook li-ike Oll – ver.'

His expression filled with irony as he said, 'Really? I thought I was better-looking than that.'

Lauren's eyes shone with laughter.

'His jokes were never any good,' Oliver informed her.

'No-oor yours,' she informed him.

Russ gave a cry of mirth. 'So I believe Happy Birthday is in order?'

Lauren nodded. 'Ni-ine – teeeen.'

'Then may I say you are the most beautiful nineteen-year-old I've ever seen.'

Oliver groaned at his corny line as Lauren beamed happily, and turned to her mother with a wave of her hand.

Understanding her instruction, Emma dutifully made the introductions, while Lauren and Oliver, with their fingers linked, watched Russ greeting everyone and managing, Emma had no doubt of it, to win her mother and Berry over as much with his past fame as with how polite and charming he was.

'OK, it's my turn with the birthday gift,' Oliver declared, turning eagerly to Emma.

Quickly opening her bag, Emma passed over the carefully wrapped box and watched with the others as Oliver handed it to Lauren. 'Happy birthday,' he said softly.

Putting her fingers to her lips, Lauren then touched them to his. This was often how she said thank you, though only to him. With everyone else, she generally touched their cheeks.

No one spoke, or took their eyes from Lauren's fingers as she fumbled with the ribbon which, Emma realised, had been tied in such a way that it would come off at a single tug. And the box wasn't taped together, so Lauren was easily able to remove the lid.

Oliver's cheeks were turning crimson as he watched her, and as Emma caught Russ's eye she felt sure he was thinking the same thing, that perhaps Oliver was regretting doing this in public. It should have been a special moment for him and Lauren to share on their own.

'Oh – oh, Mmm-um look!' Lauren gasped, holding up a delicate gold chain with the single letter 'L' dangling from it. Her eyes went back to Oliver, and as she pressed her fingers hard to her lips, then to his, Emma heard Melissa give a little sob.

'Isss beaut-ifullll,' Lauren whispered. 'I lo-ove soooo much.'

Oliver's eyes were full of emotion as, regardless of the audience, he leaned forward to brush her lips with a real kiss.

'Pu-ut on,' Lauren insisted.

Oliver took the chain.

'Actually, before you do that,' Russ interrupted, 'I have a little something for you too that you might want now,' and reaching into his pocket he drew out a tiny red box.

When Lauren opened it she gave a gasp of tearful delight. It was the letter 'O' in gold, ready to be slipped on to the chain beside the 'L'.

Oliver looked at his father in amazement.

'Oh my, oh my,' Berry murmured, taking out a hanky to dry her eyes.

'Do you have another?' Phyllis asked.

'And for me?' Polly added.

Passing Lauren's box of Kleenex, Emma watched Oliver adding the letter to the chain, then going behind Lauren to fasten it around her neck. Melissa quickly came forward with the dressing-table mirror so Lauren could take a look.

As she touched the letters Lauren looked up at Russ, saying, 'Oll-ver's nishls.'

Oliver's initials.

Russ smiled. 'Indeed, but I was thinking of them more as Lauren and Oliver.'

Lauren turned back to Oliver. 'Thisss bessst birth-day ever,' she told him as he took her hand.

Thinking of all the jubilant and reckless celebrations she'd had in her short life, particularly in recent years, Emma could only love her the more for being able to take what she had now and make it so special.

'Sho-ow yr dad oth-errr presents,' Lauren instructed Oliver.

Deciding now would be a good time to make a discreet disappearance for a few minutes, Emma took her phone outside and quickly dialled Mrs Dempster.

'Hi, it's me, Emma,' she said when the old lady answered. 'How's everything going? Any sign of them yet?'

'Oh yes, they've been and gone,' Mrs Dempster told her with great satisfaction. 'They were very quick, no trouble at all. How's the birthday coming along?'

'Fantastically well,' Emma smiled. 'I'm just sorry you couldn't be here.'

'Yes, but it was more important for me to be here today. Have you told Lauren about it yet?'

'No, but I will.'

'I thought this would have been her best present of all.'

Thinking of the necklace that Oliver – and Russ – had given her, Emma said, 'It will be, tomorrow. I'm going to wait until then, I think. Now, I'm afraid I have to go. Mum and I will pop over to see you when we come home.'

After ringing off she quickly checked her emails, replied to those who couldn't wait, then spoke to Hamish Gallagher's assistant who was gamely doubling up as hers now that the festival was only six weeks away. She truly didn't have a minute to call her own these days, but nothing in the world would have kept her from Lauren's little party today. Luckily, Hamish was very understanding about her family commitments, as he called them, and even weighed in himself to help out if needed, as he was most of the time now. Should everything go to plan over the next two weeks he might just find himself taking over altogether, she thought, while knowing she could never leave him in the lurch like that. She'd simply have to find a way of splitting herself in two.

After making a final call to a caricaturist who'd submitted a late application, she was about to head back inside when she heard someone calling her name. Fearing she already knew who it was, she turned around and felt her heart sink like a stone to see Will jogging along the road towards her.

'Emma, what a relief to see you,' he declared. 'I've been wandering about all over the place without a clue where to go.'

'Well, you wouldn't have, would you?' she retorted sourly.

His face instantly tightened. 'It's her birthday,' he snapped, 'so do we have to do this?'

Wanting to slap him off his ludicrous attempt at the moral high ground, she said, 'You've got a bloody nerve. Anyone would think . . .' She grabbed his arm as he made to move past her. 'Oh no,' she told him fiercely, 'you can't just come barging in here like you've been a model father for the last three months.'

'Let go of me.'

Keeping her hand right where it was, she said, 'You've got some big-time explaining to do . . .'

'I don't have to explain anything to you.'

'Not to me, to her, and as you so rightly point out, today is her birthday, and guess what? I am not going to allow you to spoil it. She's surrounded by people who really care for her, people who've . . .'

'Hah!' he laughed scathingly. 'How did I know you were going to throw that at me? Like I don't care for her. Well, you know damned well it's not true . . .'

'All I know is that you haven't even bothered to find out how she is since she came out of the coma. Your own daughter, Will, and it was too much of an effort simply to pick up a phone or send a text. How could you treat her that way? Just what kind of man are you?'

Though there was anger in his eyes, she could see his unease as his head went down. 'Actually, I don't know,' he answered hoarsely.

She blinked in astonishment.

'The truth is, I hate myself for what I've done,' he went on lamely, 'but I don't know . . . I didn't think . . . I've wanted to ask about her, I swear it, but I've been too afraid . . . I didn't want to hear she was paralysed or mentally . . . retarded or . . .'

Emma's contempt felt lethal. 'And it would make a difference if she was?' She didn't bother to wait for an answer. 'If you want to see her, Will, then you'd better start facing the fact now that a lot of things have changed around here. She's not who she used to be, at least not yet, and the chances are she never will be. Her brain was badly injured . . .'

'I know that . . .'

'Then accept it, because it's not going away, *ever*. It's made her who she is now and let me tell you, in my book, she's even more special than before because of how hard she's trying and how much courage she has. So much more than you, you spineless bastard. She puts you to shame . . .'

'Listen, I'm prepared to admit I haven't handled things well, but I'm here now. I want to make up for it, to show her that . . . that I really do love her.'

'And how do you propose to do that?'

Though he took a breath to fire back a reply, he ended up shaking his head helplessly. 'If you can tell me . . . Maybe she can tell me? Is she able to talk? Will she know who I am?'

'Oh for God's sake, of course she'll know who you are, and the answer to your other question is no, she can't speak the way she used to. She can't play a musical instrument either, or walk without crutches. All that might change, because she's improving all the time, but you need to start understanding right now that she will never be the great musician you wanted her to be, or the fastest runner on the track, or the best orator in the room. But she's still Lauren. Nothing has damaged her heart, it can still be every bit as hurt as yours or mine, and I'm telling you this now, if you do anything to hurt her, one word, one look, one gesture, I swear I'll kill you.'

His smile was rueful and didn't reach his eyes. 'A mother protecting her young,' he muttered.

'You'd better believe it. Now there's something else you need to know. She's having a little party at the moment before the much bigger one that the staff and other patients are throwing for her later. Berry's in her room with her, and Mum, Polly and Melissa – and Oliver Lomax and his father.'

He frowned, then, connecting with the name, he gaped at her incredulously. 'I didn't hear that right, did I?' he demanded.

She only looked at him, challengingly.

His upper lip curled. 'That little scumbag is in there with my daughter?' he raged. 'Have you completely lost your mind?'

Grabbing him as he made to storm off again, she spun him round and said in a voice sharp enough to cut out his insides, 'Before you go any further, let me ask you this: where the hell have you been during her recovery?'

His face stayed rigid with anger.

'Nowhere, that's where you've been,' she seethed. 'Absolutely bloody nowhere. Now let me tell you where Oliver Lomax has been, and that's right here, at her side every single day of the week, throughout every single new exercise she's given, every new challenge she has to rise to, every little setback she has to overcome. He's never let her down, not once, and nor will he. He gives her strength, he makes her believe in herself, he does things for her that neither you nor I will ever be able to do. Are you hearing what I'm saying? They have something very special between them, Will, and if you can't handle that then you'd better turn around right now and walk away.'

He shook his head, as though he in some way pitied her. 'What the hell am I supposed to say to that?' he cried. 'We're talking about the kid who ran her over, right?'

'Indeed.'

'The kid who was drunk while he was driving and has now somehow managed to walk away from it all.'

'But he hasn't walked away from her.'

'This isn't making any sense, Emma.'

'Maybe not to you, but it makes plenty to me, and it does to her too. She knows he was the driver, she also knows how much he cares for her. That's what matters to her now, not what happened before. He's put the light back in her eyes, Will, he gives her the kind of determination that she might not be able to muster on her own. So if you can't put your own ego and prejudices aside, then the only kind thing you can do for her now is leave her alone.'

He took a deep breath and held on to it for an excruciatingly long time, looking as bewildered as she'd ever seen him, but she had no pity to spare. The only reason she was even standing here talking to him was because she knew that if Lauren had any idea he was out here she would want to see him – but not if he couldn't accept Oliver.

At last he said, 'I know I've screwed up badly . . .'

She didn't argue, because he had.

'I don't know what to do,' he said angrily. 'It's too hard to accept that boy being in her life when he's the one who's ruined it.'

'But her life isn't ruined, it's just different.'

His eyes were barely comprehending. 'And this is what you want for her, to be a shadow of her former self, with a boy . . .'

'She's not a shadow, she's my daughter, the same daughter as I've always had. She's just not doing things in quite the same way as she used to.'

He swallowed and pushed a hand through his hair. In the end, his expression showed only impotence as he admitted, 'I'm afraid, Emma. I want to see her, I swear I came here intending to, but now I'm afraid of . . . I don't know, what she's going to be like, I guess, and I don't think I can handle seeing her with those *people*.'

Emma's voice was steely as she said, 'Then can I make a suggestion?'

He regarded her cautiously.

'That you go home and come back when you're ready to behave like a father and put her first.'

Temper flashed through his eyes. 'Emma, for God's sake, I'm trying . . .'

'No, you're not. You're only thinking about yourself and frankly, Will, you don't matter in the slightest. You never did. It's only Lauren who matters, and when you finally understand that is when you'll be ready to see her.'

His head went down as the truth of her words crushed him. 'Are you going to tell her I came?' he asked.

Feeling her heart starting to break as she realised that he really was going to leave, Emma said, 'Do you want me to?'

He shook his head. 'I guess it's probably best you don't, for now.' Then, apparently unhappy with that, he suggested, 'Or maybe you should decide what to do?'

As Emma looked at him she could only wonder how she'd ever loved him. 'I'll tell her if she mentions the fact that you didn't come today,' she said coldly. 'If she doesn't, it'll be like this, you, never happened.'

A while later, with the bigger party now under way, Emma was walking out of the centre with Russ, smiling at the sounds of the raucous celebrations. They both had meetings to attend this afternoon, though Emma would be back again this evening, if only to say goodnight to Lauren who'd no doubt be totally worn out by then.

Having already told Russ about her encounter with Will while they were in the kitchen making tea for everyone, Emma sighed wearily now as she said, 'Her father isn't exactly a bad man, and I know he does love her, but he's having a terrible time trying to come to terms with her injuries. And finding out about Oliver has obviously made it worse.'

'Mm, well, I can't say I'm surprised about that,' Russ commented. 'There aren't many people who'd find it easy to deal with.'

Emma raised an eyebrow. 'We seem to be managing,' she pointed out wryly.

'Ah, but we're special,' he quipped.

Laughing, Emma said, 'Do you know what I really think? I think that a part of him was glad to have you and Oliver as an excuse not to go in, because now he's made a gesture without having to face the fact that she might be less than perfect.'

'Mm, you could well be right,' he replied, 'but what is that going to do to his relationship with her when he does pluck up the courage to face her?'

Shaking her head, Emma said, 'I guess we'll just have to cross that bridge when we come to it. Did I tell you she wanted to write to him?'

'No.'

'It was a few weeks ago. She hasn't brought it up since, so I haven't either. I spoke briefly to her psychologist about it, though, and he said everything needs time to be processed, and a) she's not as fast at doing that now as she used to be, and b) she's probably not ready to deal with her father yet anyway.'

'If that's the case, then it's a very good thing he didn't join the party.'

Emma nodded. 'He'd have spoiled it somehow, that's for sure, and when I think of the various ways he might have upset her . . . He'd only have to hear her speak for the horror to show in his face, and when you consider what that might do to her morale, her confidence . . .' Such a violent sense of protection closed in around her that she lost the rest of her words. 'Thank God I ran into him outside, is all I can say.'

'Maybe you can explain to him, at some point,' Russ suggested, 'that however he sees her now isn't necessarily how she's always going to be.'

'Maybe I could, but we don't really know that, do we? They say the faster the recovery in the early stages, the more likely there are to be problems in the longer term. That means anything from seizures, to mood disturbances, to some awful side effect from the operation she still has to have.'

Frowning, he said, 'I wasn't aware of that.'

'They have to replace the part of the skull they removed for the surgery,' she explained. 'I don't think they have the original bone any more, so it'll be a titanium plate, but it won't be done until . . . Well, no one knows when, because it's not urgent, so she could be waiting for up to a year or more.'

Sounding concerned, he asked, 'But it won't delay her being able to go home?'

At last Emma felt some of her tension starting to ebb. 'No, it won't do that,' she replied. Turning to look at him as they reached her car, she said, 'I haven't told her the good news yet, because I didn't want to upstage the lovely present you and Oliver gave her today, but we've had a visit from a golden angel.'

He feigned amazement. 'Really?'

Not at all fooled, she said, 'He came to the house to measure up for a stairlift today – one of my neighbours let him in – and apparently once it's been fitted, which he said should take about a week from now, the way could be clear for her to leave the centre.' Her voice started to catch. 'Thank you so much. Thank you, thank you,' she gulped, and promptly burst into tears.

Sounding rather amused, he said, 'If I thought it was going to have this sort of effect . . .'

'We'd never have got one so quickly through the NHS,' she told him with a laugh. 'So thank you for bringing the dream of having her back at home another very big step closer.'

As he drove away in his car a few minutes later, the residue of Russ's pleasure was fading fast as he began to fear for what his decision to join the party today had done to Sylvie. He knew she'd gone to the airport to meet him, because she'd sent a text to tell him she was on her way, and another letting him know how much she was looking forward to seeing him.

Maybe we can spend a few days together, somewhere discreet and romantic. I will ask Olivia to recommend somewhere.

After that there were no more messages, and since neither Olivia nor Hans had called him he couldn't decide whether no news was good news or bad – except where Sylvie was concerned it was always bad.

Accepting that there was only one way to find out, he waited until he was in the centre of Bristol and parked before taking out his mobile and connecting to Olivia. At first the answering machine picked up, but then his brother-in-law's voice came down the line saying hello.

'Hans, it's Russ. Just checking in to make sure everything's OK with you.'

'With me, everything is fine,' Hans told him, 'with Olivia and Sylvie I am not currently able to say.'

Starting to turn cold, Russ said, 'Why? What's happened?'

'This is what I'm trying to ascertain, but Olivia is not answering her phone. She left about two hours ago to go and collect Sylvie from the airport . . . Did you tell Sylvie you were coming today?'

'No, but I can imagine she convinced herself that I did.'

'Hang on, someone is calling on the other line. Let me find out if it's Olivia.'

As he waited Russ tried not to berate himself for standing firm against Sylvie's blackmail, but if she'd done something stupid and he could have prevented it, how was he ever going to face his sons?

Coming back on the line, Hans said, 'Yes, it was Olivia, but it seems she has been unable to find Sylvie at the airport, or at Johann's house. So I am afraid that at this moment we have no idea where she might be.'

Chapter Thirty-Two

It was just after eight thirty that evening when Emma finally returned to the centre, to hear some sort of kerfuffle going on along Maple Corridor. As a chill sixth sense slid down her spine she broke into a run, knowing already it was coming from Lauren's room. To her horror, when she got there, she found Will being manhandled away from the bed by a couple of the physios, while Lauren, tears streaming down her face, shouted, 'Go way! Go way. Don . . . wan yooo heeere.'

A flood of such ferocious anger raced through Emma that she might have attacked Will were she not so keen to push her way through to Lauren.

'It's all right, it's all right,' she soothed, taking Lauren in her arms. 'I'm here now, no one's going to hurt you.'

'Make himmm goo,' Lauren sobbed. 'Dun . . . unnnerstan.'

'Could you kindly take your hands off me,' Will was saying to the physios. 'I'm not going to hurt her, for Christ's sake, she's my daughter.'

Turning to him, eyes blazing with fury, Emma hissed, 'What the hell are you doing here? I thought you'd gone.'

'I don't have to answer to you,' Will retorted bitingly.

'It's time to go, sir,' Julian, the head physio, told him.

Will looked as though he might punch him. 'This has nothing to do with you . . .'

'You were causing a scene, upsetting a patient,' Julian reminded him stiffly.

'What the hell made you come back?' Emma demanded, still holding tightly to Lauren while wanting to ram her fists into his foul, crimson face. 'I told you not to . . .'

'I'm not just standing by and taking all this nonsense about the Lomax family,' he informed her. 'If you can't see what they're up to, I can, and she has to stop seeing him . . .'

'Get out of here!' Emma seethed. 'Get out *now!*'

'Don wan him heeere,' Lauren gulped into Emma's shoulder. 'He dusn't unn . . . stand.'

'I understand perfectly,' Will growled, though his voice was softer now he was speaking to Lauren. 'The Lomax family are terrified that we're going to claim compensation for what they've done to you, and so they should be, because we will, sweetheart. That boy put you here . . .'

To Julian, her voice trembling with rage, Emma said, 'Please escort him out of here.'

'I'm her father, for God's sake,' Will cried, snatching his arm away. 'I have a right to be here.'

"No!' Emma choked. 'You have no rights at all.'

'I'm sorry, sir,' Julian said, 'but you're obviously upsetting Lauren, so we'll have to ask you to leave.'

As both physios started to crowd him towards the door he shot at Emma, 'You're a fool if you can't see what's going on. Why the hell else would that boy be interested in her, the state she's in?'

He barely even saw Emma coming until she grabbed his hair and forced him to his knees. 'I told you I'd kill you if you hurt her,' she whispered viciously into his face.

'Get off me,' he snarled. 'For Christ's sake, I'm just trying to point out the obvious.'

Grasping his collar, Julian hiked him back to his feet. 'You really do need to go, sir,' he said quietly, though meaningfully.

It was clear from the gleam in Will's eyes that he'd have fought, had he not been outnumbered.

'If you try to come near her again,' Emma told him savagely as she returned to Lauren, 'it's you who'll have a lawsuit slapped on you.'

'For what?' he cried incredulously.

'It'll be a restraining order, and don't think I can't get one, because after the way you've just behaved . . .'

'The way *I've* behaved? I'm the one trying to protect my daughter and look out for her best interests.'

'You don't even know what the words mean.'

'Lauren, sweetheart,' Will implored, from the door.

'Go way!' she shouted. 'Hate you. Go way.'

'I'm going to do my best for you,' he told her. 'I'll get you every penny you deserve . . .'

'Sssh, sssh, don't listen, don't worry,' Emma soothed, taking her back in her arms.

'Heee don unn . . . erstand,' Lauren sobbed.

'No, he doesn't, not at all.'

'Gl-ad heee din come toooday,' Lauren said. 'Heeed have sp-oil ev thing.'

Unable to deny that, and afraid that he had anyway, Emma said, 'Try to put him out of your mind and think about all the lovely things that happened today. Granny told me she and Berry danced at the disco.'

More tears welled in Lauren's eyes. 'I cannn-t dannn-ce,' she said. 'Wan too dannn-ce.'

As Emma's heart folded around her pain, she hugged her even closer. 'I know, sweetheart, and you will, I promise, just as soon as we get you better, and you're doing so well now.'

'Not!' Lauren shouted. 'Not!' She began punching her fists into the bed. 'Am stooo-pid, cannn-t speeek and cannn't do annny thng.'

Though Emma had seen flashes of Lauren's temper and frustration before, unsurprisingly today it was going much deeper. 'Hey, come on,' she encouraged gently, 'you know very well how pleased everyone is with your progress, and you are too. You're speaking much more clearly than you were even a week ago, and you're walking . . .'

'With crrrr ches.'

'But that won't be for very much longer. You're gaining strength all the time.' She had no intention of telling her that she might always have a limp, because it was only a might, and once again the doctors could be wrong.

'No gooood at annny thng,' Lauren growled angrily. 'Wisssh I died now.'

'Oh, Lauren, that's not a good thing to say when we all love you so much.'

'I'm a nuuuu . . . sance. Getting on evvver . . . one's nerrrves.'

'That is absolutely not true. You're tired now, darling. It's been a long day and a very happy one with all your cards and presents, and the party. And look at your beautiful necklace. Wasn't it lovely of Oliver to think of that, and then of his father to add the O?'

Lauren's heavy, tormented eyes turned away as she said, 'Not as expensss . . . ive as comp . . . sation.'

Wishing she'd killed Will the instant she'd set eyes on him today, Emma said, 'Darling, you mustn't credit them with the same unworthy thoughts as Daddy's having. You know how much Oliver cares about you. He's here with you every day, joining in your exercises, swimming with you in the pool, cooking in the kitchen, watching TV, doing everything with you, and making you laugh . . .'

'But Dad-deee said how cannn heee like meee when I'm innn thisss state? Am I in a state, Mummmy? Am I ugly?'

''Oh God no,' Emma cried, gathering her up in her arms and having to fight back her own tears. 'You're every bit as beautiful as you always were, and no one thinks that more than Oliver.'

'But if heee's . . .'

'Listen, you know what Daddy's like, he gets these ideas in his head and they're almost always wrong. He doesn't know Oliver, he hasn't even met him, or seen the two of you together, so how can he possibly say how Oliver feels?'

'So do yooo-ou thnk Ol-ver reeelly li-kes me?'

Emma almost laughed. 'He more than likes you, my darling.'

Lauren's eyes were still swimming in tears and uncertainty as she said, 'I reeely more thannn li-ke himm too.'

Emma pressed a kiss to her forehead. 'I know you do, sweetheart,' she whispered.

'Wan toooo come home with yooo-ou,' Lauren murmured.

Drawing back to cup her face in her hands, Emma said, 'You're going to, my angel, very soon now, because the stairlift's being fitted and all the other little jobs that have to be done are already under way.'

Though Lauren's eyes were shadowed with tiredness, a flicker of surprise showed in the darkness. 'Will Olll-ver still commme?' she asked huskily.

'Of course,' Emma assured her, and she had no doubts at all that he would, but now that Will had raised the subject of compensation she knew that she couldn't carry on ignoring it.

The question was, what kind of bitterness was it going to create between the two families once she broached it?

Sylvie had been missing for almost a week now, and the only reason Russ hadn't flown over there was because he'd fully expected her to turn up at her flat in Clifton, or even here at home without any warning. However, no one had heard a word from her, nor had there been any sign of her from the time she'd left the airport – and she had left, they knew that now, because Olivia had contacted the police yesterday and this morning they'd confirmed that there was CCTV footage showing Sylvie getting into a car and driving off.

Johann was as bewildered and worried as everyone else. He'd even told Olivia that if the police didn't come up with some answers soon he'd hire a private detective. *And probably pay for it with Sylvie's money*, Russ couldn't help thinking, though he didn't actually care who paid for it just as long as they found her.

'The trouble is,' Olivia had said a few minutes ago on the phone, 'I don't think the police are very interested. I mean, they're going through the right motions, but as one of them said to Hans, alcoholics are notorious for disappearing on binges and turning up when they're ready. In other words, they consider it a waste of police time to go looking for them unless there's some real evidence that harm has come to them.'

Though frustrated by the response, Russ knew he had to accept that the police over there really did have far bigger issues to deal with, so he'd simply said, 'I think Johann's route might be the best one to take. Does he actually know a private detective, or do we need to find one?'

'I'll call and ask him and let you know the answer. I'm very worried, Russ. I feel this is all my fault. I should never have allowed her to take a car, or even go to the airport without me.'

Feeling as though the responsibility was much more his than hers, he said, 'Let's try not to get into the self-blame game, it won't achieve anything, and we have to remember, she's an adult. We can't make her do anything she doesn't want to do.'

How true those last words were, and how often he had spoken them in one form or another, but they'd never yet eased the terrible weight on his mind, and he doubted they ever would. His biggest fear now was that she'd been dragged off to one of the townships, or perhaps she'd even taken herself there as a way of punishing him. It would be the kind of crazy thing she'd do when drunk; and he could be in no doubt that she'd found the nearest bar after he'd failed to turn up at the airport.

He wondered if the police had put out an alert for her car, and made a mental note to ask Olivia when they spoke in the morning. If she hadn't turned up by the weekend he'd have to fly out there, though God knew what he could do that Hans and Olivia weren't doing already.

In the meantime, what should he tell the boys?

Glancing up at the sound of Oliver's car coming into the drive, he reached for his mobile as it rang. 'Russ Lomax,' he said quietly.

'Russ? It's Emma, is this a bad time?'

Shaking himself mentally, he said, 'No, not at all. How's Lauren?'

'She's doing fine. Still a bit low after the encounter with her father, but she's starting to rally. Knowing she's coming home next week is helping, which is part of the reason I'm calling.'

'A problem with the stairlift?'

'No, no, not at all, it's being fitted even as we speak. No, it's about the farewell tea they're throwing for her next Thursday at the centre. Apparently they do it for everyone when they're leaving, and Lauren and I would love it if you could join us.'

Thinking of how much he'd like to be there, he said, 'If I can make it you can be sure I will, but something's come up that means, well, it's difficult to explain now.' He paused as Oliver came in through the front door. 'Can I call you later?'

'Yes, of course. Or, actually, I was wondering if we could meet for a coffee tomorrow? There's something I need to discuss with you and I'd rather not do it on the phone.'

'Of course. Just text me a time and a place and I'll be there.'

'Hey Dad,' Oliver said, dropping his phone and keys on the table as Russ rang off. 'Everything OK? I'm starving, what have we got to eat?'

Not having given it a thought until now, Russ said, 'Do you feel like popping out for an Indian?'

'Sounds cool, but can we make it a takeaway? I promised Lauren I'd start work on her farewell to the centre speech tonight. Did Emma call you about it?'

'Just.'

'I hope you're going to be there. Actually, I'm thinking about inviting Charlie, too.'

Raising a dubious eyebrow as he rummaged in a drawer for the take-out menu, Russ said, 'You'll be lucky to get him to come, he's so busy these days. Have you heard from him lately?'

'No, not much, apart from I had a text yesterday saying what good news it was about Mum.'

Russ frowned and turned to look at him. 'What good news?' he asked, feeling certain that whatever it was, it must be old, and the boys had only just caught up with each other.

'You know, that she's gone back into rehab.'

With a jolt Russ raised his head as his mind started to spin, and realising that no one had thought to check the clinic, or at least not as far as he knew, he said, 'When did he hear from Mum?'

'She texted us yesterday, or maybe it was the day before, I can't remember now. Didn't you get it too?'

Russ shook his head. 'Can I see it?' he asked.

Reaching for his phone Oliver scrolled through his messages, found the latest from his mother and handed it over. 'I wondered why you hadn't said anything,' he commented as Russ started to read.

Salut mes chéris, I waited at the airport today and none of you came which made me very sad, so I have decided to come back to the clinic to show you that I really can get myself well. I cannot make any promises, but I am going to try my best to do this, because I think you are finding it very hard to love me the way I am. I am not sure how long it will take, but please come to see me when you can, or write to me with all your news. Maman xxx

Oliver had texted Charlie to say, *Heard it all before, so will believe it when we see it.*

Charlie's reply to that: *She has to hit rock bottom first and don't know if she's done that yet. How are things with Lauren? Will call tomorrow.*

Reading how dismissive they were of their mother's words was almost as tragic as sensing the desperation in hers, yet they'd obviously discussed her further when Charlie had rung, for Oliver to have made the comment about it being 'good news about Mum'.

'Have you texted her back?' Russ asked, finding no sign of a message.

'No, we thought you'd probably done it.'

'She didn't text me,' Russ told him, picking up the phone to call Olivia, 'so please reply to her text and wish her well. And tell Charlie to do the same.'

''She'll probably have forgotten she even sent it by now,' Oliver protested.

'Oliver, just do it,' Russ barked. 'I know things have been difficult between you, and there's still a lot to be resolved, but she's your mother and right now, if she is back in the clinic intending to do her best, she needs to know she has your support.'

Ten minutes later Olivia rang back, sounding overwhelmingly relieved as she confirmed that Sylvie was indeed back in rehab. 'I can't believe that none of us even thought to try there,' she laughed uneasily. 'Oh Russ, I really hope she means it this time.'

'So do I,' he murmured, but he knew he wasn't holding out any more hope than she was.

'Thanks for meeting me at such short notice,' Emma said, as Russ joined her on the riverside terrace at the Severnshed cafe the next morning. Spread out in front of them the harbour was glistening merrily, while the flowers in their hanging baskets seemed almost ready to bust into bloom. Summer really was on its way. 'It's not actually that urgent,' she confessed, 'but I wanted to talk to you before next week's farewell tea.'

'Of course,' he said, raising a hand to summon a waiter as he sat down, 'and by the way, it looks as though I can make it, so thanks for the invite.'

Emma grimaced as she smiled. 'I hope you're still going to feel the same once I've told you why we're here.'

He looked surprised and curious, and noticing how the lines round his eyes had deepened even since the last time they'd met, she came close to backing away from burdening him with any more problems. 'How's your wife?' she asked, wanting to get as clear a picture as she could of what he might be going through.

Though his expression turned ironic, she wasn't fooled. He was as concerned about her as ever. 'I'm happy to tell you,' he replied, 'that she's back in the clinic after going missing for almost a week. As it turned out she was actually at the clinic the whole time, but had neglected to inform any of us of the sudden epiphany that had transported her there. Since then, she's texted the boys to tell them she's determined to get well this time, which can only be good news, but, to quote Oliver, we've heard it all before, so we wait to see.' He sighed as he rubbed his temples between thumb and forefinger. 'Frankly, even if she does manage to get it under control, there'll still be the shambles of our marriage to sort out, and I'm afraid trying to get her to accept that it's over for me will just set her back on the slippery slope.'

Feeling for his helplessness and getting a sense of how in limbo he felt, Emma tried, while they ordered their coffees, to come up with another, happier, reason for why she'd asked to see him. Nothing was springing to mind, however, and the real issue had to be addressed.

'Speaking of troublesome spouses,' he said as the waiter left, 'has Lauren's father been in touch again?'

Emma shook her head. 'Not with her, thank goodness,' she replied, 'but unfortunately I've had several emails from him myself, which more or less brings us to what I want to talk to you about. He thinks Lauren should have compensation for her injuries, and while the last thing I want is to cause a rift between our two families, particularly between Lauren and Oliver, I'm afraid in this instance I can't disagree with him.'

Russ's eyes were intently on hers, as he said, 'And no more should you. Lauren deserves every penny she can get, especially when you have no idea what the long-term effects of her injuries might be.'

Not wanting to think about seizures, or personality disorders, or a limp that might permanently alter her daughter's lightness of step, Emma said, 'He's talking about suing you personally, but of course that would be insane unless . . .' She regarded him uneasily. 'Please tell me Oliver was insured.'

With a comforting smile he said, 'Yes, he was, and is, so you must seek a full and proper settlement. It's why we have insurance, and why we pay such high premiums, especially at Oliver's age.'

More relieved than she could put into words, Emma said, 'I'm so glad you're seeing it this way, but I'm worried about it causing a problem between Oliver and Lauren. He might not be able to get insurance again after . . .'

'Emma, listen,' he interrupted softly, 'he's lucky to have a licence, and indeed his freedom, never mind insurance, and anyway, there'll always be someone out there who'll give him cover, so please don't worry about him. Just do what you have to do, safe in the knowledge that anyone in your shoes, including me, would do the same.'

Wanting to squeeze his hand in gratitude, but afraid it might convey more than either of them was comfortable with, she said, 'Thank you for being so understanding. I assure you I'll do everything I can to keep it out of court, because we really don't need your insurance company's lawyers throwing Lauren's past up as a way of minimising the payout. Whatever they offer, provided it's reasonable, will be acceptable, because in the end it's only money, and their relationship is far more important.'

'Our friendship too, I hope,' he replied, gazing into her eyes again.

Feeling herself starting to blush, she said, 'Yes, of course, our friendship too.'

Chapter Thirty-Three

The day had finally dawned for Lauren to come home. Emma had hardly slept all night, fraught with worry and carried away by excitement. By the look of her, as she emerged from the bedroom just after six, Phyllis hadn't fared much better.

By seven they'd given up on breakfast, remade Lauren's bed, and packed all of Phyllis's belongings ready to transport them along to Mrs Dempster's, where she was going to be staying until her rented house was ready next week.

'I think I'll just have another quick clean round,' Phyllis declared, getting out the dusters, 'we want to make sure everything's spick and span ready for when our girl comes in.'

Leaving her to it, Emma opened her laptop to plough through her outstanding emails, all linked to the festival. Though she was more or less on top of it all, there was still plenty of time for things to go wrong, and, albeit in a small way, something did virtually every day. It was to be expected, though, and since there was nothing in her inbox to raise her blood pressure, she abandoned the computer after an hour and went to find her mother.

'Ah, there you are,' Phyllis said, looking up from the seat of the stairlift she was polishing. 'Have you had a go on this yet?'

Emma gave a laugh of surprise. 'No. Why, have you?'

'Of course. I was here when they installed it, remember, they had to show me how it works. It's very impressive.'

'You only have to press a button, don't you?'

'More or less. It's going to be very handy for getting heavy stuff upstairs.'

'You mean like you?'

Phyllis laughed. 'Yes, I guess like me,' she admitted. 'Or Berry when she's had one too many. Do you think Lauren will use it?'

Emma's head went to one side as her insides did a flip. 'Let's put it this way,' she said, 'it's providing her with a big incentive to manage the stairs on her own, because she says she doesn't want Oliver seeing her in it. He, typically, can't wait to have a go.'

Chuckling fondly, Phyllis went to put away her dusters, and after making two much-needed cups of tea she carried them through to the sitting room, where Emma was starting to pump up the dozens of welcome-home balloons she'd bought the day before.

Gratefully picking up her tea, she glanced at her mother as she said, 'Are you feeling nervous about today?'

Phyllis's eyebrows rose as she nodded.

'Me too,' Emma confessed. 'I'm not entirely sure why . . . Well, I suppose it's because I want everything to go perfectly, and her to be happy, and I'm sure she will be. But I have to remember that Sam, her psychologist, warned me that it could take her a while to adapt to being at home again.'

'She's looking forward to it, though,' Phyllis reminded her. 'She's already got everything packed and told us what she wants for tea tonight.'

Emma smiled. 'It's a pity in a way that Oliver's not joining us, but I understand her not wanting him to see her struggling with things at first.'

'As if he hasn't seen her struggling already.'

'Yes, but that was there, and this will be here, where she wants everything to be the way it was before.'

'It will be soon enough.'

Knowing how unlikely that was, and becoming increasingly worried about how this new stage of Lauren's recovery was going to go, Emma finished her tea and left her mother pumping balloons while she took herself back upstairs to shower in the newly adapted bathroom. Here handles had been attached to the walls in strategic places, a special non-slip floor had been laid and the step into the cubicle had been lowered. It created a kind of wet-room effect, which Emma suspected Lauren would like once they were able to remove all aids to her disabilities, and she must keep reminding herself that that time wasn't too far away. Physically Lauren was doing very well indeed: she was moving around on crutches far more often than in a wheelchair, and her overall muscle tone was almost as good as new. Recently she had complained of headaches, which was worrying, but the doctors were putting it down to anxiety about going home, and Emma was doing her best to accept that. Even so, she couldn't help wondering what the anxiety might trigger.

It was going to be like this for a long time, her mother had gently reminded her last night; there was even a chance that the day would never dawn when they didn't fear that any little ache or pain, tantrum or excessive tiredness was the first sign of a new, delayed reaction to her injuries. They couldn't even be sure that her normal life expectancy hadn't been reduced because of them, though not one doctor had warned that it might be. On the contrary, their optimism for her future was growing all the time: the speech and language therapist was confident that she'd be speaking more or less normally by the end of the summer, and her physio anticipated a couple of crutches flying over Bristol in more or less the same time. What the consultant neurologist had advised both Emma and Lauren to prepare themselves for, however, was the possibility that some of Lauren's learning skills had become impaired. This was already manifesting itself in the way she was able to read and, albeit haltingly for now, play the music she knew, while finding herself unable to take in, or perform anything new.

So far the frustration of this hadn't seemed to hit Lauren as hard as Emma might have expected, though it had certainly raised her temper at times, such as the instance when she'd thrown her flute across the room, and another occasion when she'd strummed her guitar so violently that Oliver had been forced to wrest it away before she injured her fingers. Most of the time, however, she seemed utterly and unshakably determined to prove the doctors wrong by focusing her whole attention on a few bars of an unfamiliar piece, in an effort to understand them and play them from memory. Her success to date had been minimal, but what seemed to be helping were the lessons she'd started to give Oliver on keyboard and guitar.

It simply wasn't possible to know what they might be facing in the coming months or years, but, Emma knew, that didn't make them any different from anyone else. Nobody, rich or poor, healthy or sick, young or old, had been handed a list of guarantees about their futures, and though not everyone had a brain injury to contend with, there were plenty who had far worse handicaps or challenges to overcome. The only way forward was to take each day as it came, confident that whatever problems cropped up she'd find a way to deal with them.

'Are you OK?' Phyllis asked, as Emma finally emerged from the bathroom.

Seeing her mother gliding up the stairs on the Stannah lift with a pile of fresh towels, Emma couldn't help smiling. 'Yes, I'm fine,' she assured her. 'I was just thinking I ought to pop over to the hotel before we go to collect her. Hamish knows what's happening today, so I shouldn't be gone for long. What time did Polly say she was getting here?'

'She's not coming here. She and Melissa are meeting us at the centre at two.'

Remembering that was the arrangement, Emma said, 'And we're sure the wheelchair folds up small enough to get it into my car?'

Phyllis frowned. 'Well, it has the last dozen times we tried it, so unless it's found a way to grow . . .'

Emma playfully rolled her eyes. She was receiving her mother's message loud and clear: she had to lighten up, or she'd be in danger of passing her nerves on to Lauren and that could easily turn into a disaster. The best thing she could do now was try to tap into her excitement and forget about everything that could go wrong. It was a waste of energy trying to deal with imaginary catastrophes.

She wanted to thank her mother again for being here, but she'd said it so many times now that the words seemed to be wearing themselves out. Her gratitude, however, was still immense, because she knew she really wouldn't have got through any of this without her. The odd thing was, she seemed more at ease with her mother now than she did with Lauren; however, there were still moments when memories of how they'd got things wrong about one another created a certain awkwardness. She'd wondered, several times, if she should be feeling guilty about her father's tragic accident, but though a part of her was desperately sad and even angry with the three-year-old who'd made him go out into the storm, she knew it was nonsense to blame a child so young. Her mother had found that out the hard way, and it had taken what had happened to Lauren to start straightening things out again.

'You see, something good has come out of my accident,' Lauren had said in her pitifully slurred way a few days ago. 'You and Granny are friends again now, and I met Oliver.'

It was always wonderful to hear her being positive like that, but Emma couldn't help wondering if, given the choice, Lauren would trade the way things were now for the way they had been. She certainly wouldn't want to give up Oliver, but was he worth the loss of her mental agility? It was a pointless question and she'd never ask it, because even if he wasn't, there was absolutely nothing anyone could do about it.

'I'd like to be there for the farewell tea,' her mother was saying as Emma started to pack up her laptop, 'but if you think I should stay here so someone's at home when you get back . . .'

'No, no, you absolutely must come,' Emma told her. 'She'd be so upset if you didn't.'

Phyllis's eyes showed her pleasure. 'She's been working on her thank yous for the last three weeks,' she declared. 'I really wouldn't want to miss them.'

It was no surprise to Emma to find Oliver already at the centre when she arrived at a quarter to two, since he'd probably been there all morning. However, he wasn't with Lauren, he was in the kitchen helping the staff and other patients to prep for the big send-off. The dining room next door had its doors thrown wide to the lovely leafy patio outside and was already lavishly decorated with bunting and balloons, plus a witty collection of amateurish portraits (all of patients or staff), handwritten messages of good luck that were deeply moving, and a mesmerising montage of photos detailing Lauren's time at the centre. Several of the shots had been taken with her therapists and fellow residents, a few were with Emma and Phyllis, or Melissa, or Harry and Jane, but mostly they were of her and Oliver cooking, swimming, struggling with crutches, laughing uproariously, pedalling an exercise bike, intent on something they were making, pulling faces at the photographer, and in one adorable shot they were lying on Lauren's bed together, fast asleep.

'Has she seen this yet?' Emma asked Oliver, as he came to stand with her to look at the montage.

'No, we've been putting it together as a surprise,' he told her. 'Do you think she'll like it?'

'Are you kidding? She'll absolutely love it. You've done a fantastic job.'

'Hasn't he?' one of the therapists called out, as she carried a tray of cakes in from the kitchen. 'We all want a copy before he goes.'

'Did you see the one of me?' Mark, one of the patients, asked, rolling his wheelchair over to join them. Mark had been the victim of a violent assault outside a pub in Swindon, when a gang of youths had set on him with bottles, boots and deadly fists.

'An' me?' Dinah, a young mother from the next room to Lauren's, demanded. 'Breezghe sez look like frrringale.' Whatever she'd said, she seemed delighted by it, and as Emma smiled at her warmly she wondered if poor Dinah, who'd been at the centre for over a year after a fall down the steps of a multi-storey car park, would ever fully recover. How hard it must be for her husband and children, who had to travel all the way from Devon every weekend to see her. When, they must be asking themselves, would she ever be able to come home.

'I've put that one in a frame for you,' Oliver told her, pointing to a shot of Dinah with her enchanting eighteen-month-old twins. The poor little mites had hardly known their mother when the accident happened.

This place was so full of tragedy, and yet it emanated more hope and courage than Emma had ever come across before. Staff and patients alike were so special that it was almost impossible to put into words how much she admired them. She was going to miss her visits here far more than she'd realised until now.

'Ah, here's Dad,' Oliver declared, spotting his father coming into reception.

Turning to greet Russ as he approached the double doors to the dining room, Emma felt her heart lift with pleasure. She liked this man so much, and felt she might possibly have made a friend for life. 'Hi,' she said, reaching out a hand to shake.

'Hi,' he responded, taking it and pulling her to him. 'Congratulations,' he said, hugging her gently. 'This is a big day and you've done as much, if not more, than anyone to help bring it about.'

Emma grimaced as she blushed and turned to Oliver. 'I think your son deserves a lot more of the credit than I do,' she said fondly. She wanted to ask if there was any news on Russ's wife, but it could wait till later. 'So, where is the star of today's show?' she demanded, looking around at all the activity taking place in Lauren's honour.

Oliver's eyes twinkled. 'In her room getting ready. I'm not allowed in.'

Laughing, Emma said, 'I take it my mother's with her.'

'No, she popped along to the supermarket to get some more sugar. We were running low.'

Deciding to leave Russ admiring the photomontage with Dinah and Mark, while Oliver went back to the kitchen, Emma took off along Maple Corridor fully expecting to find one of the occupational therapists in Lauren's room helping her to put on her make-up. (Though she wasn't too bad at applying it herself now, she'd want it to be perfect for today, and Emma already knew how stunning she looked in the cream chiffon minidress they'd ordered from Next, with its wide pleated shoulder straps and transparent frill around the hem.)

However, when she got to the room and put her head round the door, to her amazement and alarm she found

Lauren all alone amidst her boxes and bags, still wearing her dressing gown and in floods of tears.

'Oh my goodness, what's happened?' Emma cried, quickly closing the door and going to kneel in front of her.

'Don want . . . don want . . . to go,' Lauren sobbed.

Her heart thudding with angst, Emma cupped her face in her hands and lifted her head. 'Are you saying you don't want to have a party?' she asked. 'Or you don't want to go home?'

'Wan to stay heeere.'

'Oh, my darling,' Emma murmured, wrapping her in her arms. 'I know it's going to be hard leaving . . .'

'Don want toooo.'

Though she'd been warned about this, Emma was still finding it hard to deal with when she so wanted this to be a happy day for Lauren. Pulling back to look at her again, she said, 'Don't you want to be in your own bedroom with all your things around you and the freedom to come and go . . .'

'No,' Lauren cried, shaking her head. 'Can't dooo anything. I'm no good.'

'Oh sweetheart, you know that isn't true. Look at all you've accomplished while you've been here . . .'

'I wan to stay, Mum. Please let meee stay.'

Maybe it was because she understood her fears, and sympathised with them, that Emma was finding it so hard to be able to soothe them. 'Think of how brave you've been up to now,' she said gently. 'You have to try to find that courage again . . .'

'I donn't have it any more. It's all gone.'

'No it isn't, it's just hiding behind all those negative things you're thinking, but it's a lot bigger than they are, so we'll just sit here and wait for it to put its foot down and say enough is enough, shall we?'

Lauren looked at her helplessly.

Emma smiled. 'I expect it's been feeling quite tired lately,' she went on cheerily, 'because it's had so much work to do. It'll wake up in a minute though, feeling as good as new.'

Lauren turned her head away. 'Don want a partee,' she

said tightly. 'Don wan to say goodbye to allll my friennnds. I want tooo stay here with them.'

Taking hold of her hands, Emma said, 'I know you do, my darling, but this room has to go to someone else now who needs to be taken care of the way you've been taken care of while you were here. And you can always come back to visit. You know that lots of people do, you've met them . . .'

'I'm diffff-rent to everyone now, Mumm. In heeere I'm the same.'

'Well, you aren't really the same, are you, because you're not as unwell as the rest of them any more. You can do almost everything for yourself now, and as time goes on you'll be able to start studying again and going places with Oliver . . .'

Lauren's eyes welled with more tears as she said, 'Oll-ver won't want me when I leeeave heeere. He'll find someone elllse, someone normalll.'

Realising they might now be getting to the heart of the matter, Emma said, 'Oh Lauren, that is such a daft thing to think. First of all, you're perfectly normal, and second, I can't imagine what else he could do to prove to you that he doesn't want anyone else.'

'But we're not in a reeeal worllld in heeere. Out there it'll be diff-diff-rent. I know it will.'

Going to sit next to her on the bed, Emma wrapped an arm around her and pulled her head on to her shoulder. 'Everyone's getting ready for your party. Oliver's dad is here, so's Granny; Polly and Melissa will be arriving any minute. And Oliver's got a lovely surprise for you.'

Lauren remained leaning limply against her.

'What about your thank-you speeches?' Emma prompted. 'I know everyone's looking forward to hearing them . . .'

'I wrote themm down in lllletters,' Lauren told her. 'I don wan to say it, so I've put themmm in envelopes for everrryone to read.'

Emma's eyebrows rose in surprise. 'So you don't want to have a farewell tea in your lovely dress and with all your friends around you?'

Lauren shook her head.

'I'm sure you do.'

'No. I don't.'

Emma was trying hard to think what to do. 'I know, what about if Oliver reads them for you?' she suggested. 'He'll probably be very good at it, knowing him.'

Lauren started to cry again. 'I've got a llletter for himmm too,' she wept. 'I've said thank yoooou for everrrything, but hee doesn't have to feeeel guilllty any more, or come and seeee me. Heee can get on with his life now.'

'Oh Lauren,' Emma sighed, her heart catching as Lauren began to sob. 'Let me go and get him so he can talk some sense into you, please?'

'No, don't wan tooo seee himm.'

'I don't believe that . . .'

'It's true. It'll be tooo hard.'

'But all you have to do is listen to what he has to say.'

'Please tell . . . tell himmm I'm sorrry, but I . . . can't seee himmm any more.'

'No, Lauren, I'm not going to do that, because it isn't what you want, not really.'

Lauren sat up to look at her. Through her tears her eyes were burning with apprehension and pain. 'It'lll be eeeasier now, than if I wait tillll I'm home. This way I won have to seee himmm being embarrrr-assed about me when we're with normalll people.'

'Oh dear, will you please stop talking about normal people as if you weren't one,' Emma chided. 'Now, I'm not going to listen to any more of this nonsense. I understand why you're upset and afraid, but I know you don't want to hurt Oliver and that's what you'll be doing if you tell him you don't want to see him any more.'

'Heee'll get over it, and meeeet someone else who heee can do things with . . .'

'Lauren . . .'

'No, Mum, please. I don wan to talk about it annny more. I know I have tooo come hommme but I don wan a party, and I don't want to seee Oliver.'

Hearing a knock on the door, Emma passed Lauren a tissue box and went to find out who it was. 'Maria,' she cried in great relief when she saw the nurse manager, and stepping into the corridor she closed the door behind her.

'I thought I heard tears,' Maria said quietly.

Emma sighed helplessly. 'She's got herself into a bit of a state. She doesn't want to leave here, or come home, or go to the party. She doesn't even want to see Oliver.'

Maria's expression was full of sympathy as she said, 'Oh dear, I hadn't expected this from Lauren, but you never know. Leaving here is a huge step for someone to take when they've been so safe and secure and haven't had to deal with the big bad world out there. Would you like me to have a word with her?'

'If you don't mind, and while you're at it, can you please try to persuade her to see herself as normal, because she seems to have got it into her head that she isn't.'

Maria gave a wry smile. 'Oh, she knows she's normal all right, in so far as any of us is, she's just using it as an excuse to shy away from what comes next. You leave her to me, I'll have her at that party in no time at all.'

Ten minutes later Emma was standing in reception with her mother, Russ and Polly, quietly explaining what was going on, when a grave-looking Maria came to join them.

'I'm sorry,' the nurse manager said, 'her mind seems to be made up and I think to try to push her any other way right now is only going to distress her further. So my recommendation is that you take her home without any fuss . . . I'll make sure no one's in the dining room and reception as you take her through, and I'll hand out her letters after she's gone.'

'Oh no,' Emma murmured, 'after all the trouble you've gone to . . .'

'Don't worry about that, the cakes will all get eaten and the decorations have come from the store room, so they can simply be tucked away again.'

Spotting Oliver and Melissa coming towards them, Emma felt her heart turn over. They looked so comfortable together, so compatible even, that she could only feel thankful that Lauren, in her current state, wasn't there to see them. It would probably have set her worst fears off like fireworks.

'What's up?' Oliver demanded. 'She must be ready to come out by now.'

Emma glanced at Russ and was about to explain when Russ said, 'It's OK, I'll take it from here,' and slipping an arm round Oliver's shoulders he walked him towards the main door.

'What's going on?' a scared-looking Melissa asked her mother. 'She's all right, isn't she? Nothing's happened to her?'

'She's fine, but she's not feeling up to the party,' Polly explained. 'Emma's going to take her home and maybe we can see her tomorrow.'

Melissa's eyes went to Emma. 'I guess this is really tough for her,' she said with feeling. 'If there's anything I can do . . . I mean, I know she's got Oliver now and is really close to him, but I still think of her as my best friend, so I want to be there for her.'

Giving her a hug, Emma said, 'I know you do, and thank you. I think she's probably going to need you over the coming weeks, so it's lovely to know you want to help.'

Just then Oliver shouted, 'That is such bollocks and I'm not going to listen . . .'

Russ cut him off with words Emma couldn't hear. Oliver snatched his arm away and started back inside.

'Emma, we can't let her do this,' he cried, his face stripped of colour, his eyes glittering with anger.

'She'll come round, I'm sure of it,' Emma told him soothingly, 'but for now we need to let her do things her way.'

'Let me talk to her,' he implored. 'I'll be able to make her see sense.'

'That's what I . . .'

Stepping in, Maria said, 'If anyone can, I'm sure you can, Oliver, but she's feeling exceptionally vulnerable at the moment, so I don't think we should try talking her into anything she doesn't feel up to. Apart from going home, of course, but she understands she has to do that.'

Oliver turned to his father as Russ joined them, his whole body seeming ready to burst with frustration.

'It'll be all right,' Russ told him. 'We just need to be patient.'

'But Dad, I can't . . .' He turned sharply away as his voice caught with emotion.

Russ put a hand on his shoulder. 'Let's go and get the montage, unless you'd like to take it?' he said to Emma.

'No, I think you should hang on to it for now,' she told Oliver. 'It's your surprise, so you're the one who should give it to her.'

Reaching for Oliver's hand, Melissa said, 'I know she really cares for you . . .'

'Sure,' Oliver said shortly. 'Come on, Dad, let's go.'

Understanding his abruptness was to hide his hurt, Emma watched him walk into the dining room and lift the montage roughly from the wall.

'I'll call you tomorrow,' Russ said quietly. 'Or you know where we are if you need to call us.'

Worried and feeling unable to cope with all this, Emma smiled her thanks, and as he went to help Oliver, she turned to Polly and her mother.

'Shall I go to her?' Phyllis offered.

'No, it's OK, I will. The best thing you can do now is get home before us to take down all the balloons.'

'We'll come and help you,' Polly said to Phyllis. Then to Emma, 'What shall we do about the neighbours? They're planning a welcome home of their own.'

'Really?' Emma said, surprised. 'I didn't know that.'

'Nothing big,' Phyllis told her. 'Just a bit of a cheer as we come into the street.'

Touched by the kindness and torn as to whether or not she should let it happen, Emma turned to Maria. 'She might feel differently by the time we get home,' she said.

'She might,' Maria agreed, 'but if I were you I'd just keep it nice and low-key for today. She's going to be tired, anyway, after all this emotion, and I'm afraid to say, there's probably going to be plenty more to come.'

There was no sign of anyone when Emma drove Lauren into the street an hour and a half later, which seemed odd, given how sunny it was. Normally children would be playing cricket on the green, or hopscotch on the pavements, but there was only a glimpse of someone's pony in the far field, and the tinny sound of a radio in someone's back garden. Emma wondered how Lauren was feeling, seeing the street that was her home for the first time in almost six months. If it wasn't panicking her, and it didn't seem to be, then it probably felt a bit like a dream. Emma didn't ask because Lauren had told her when they'd got into the car that she didn't want to talk. Emma suspected she was already feeling guilty and disappointed with herself for not having said proper thank yous and good-byes, but she'd left her letters with Maria, and she knew she would always be welcome back for a visit.

Would she ever want to go, or was it soon to become a place, an experience she'd be eager to put behind her?

Heaven only knew how she was feeling about Oliver, but Emma could easily imagine the clenching tightness of loss gripping her heart, while the breathless fear that she might never see him again would be making it hard even to move. Neither of them had mentioned him since Emma had gone back into the room to help her dress, and Emma wondered how he must be feeling now. Angry and upset, of course, perhaps used, certainly rejected, and most likely afraid that Lauren might not change her mind. After all he'd done to prove how he felt, a part of Emma would have liked to shake Lauren for the way she was behaving, yet how could she not understand her daughter's fears as this next crucial stage of her recovery began?

Phyllis must have been looking out for them, because by the time Emma pulled up her mother was at the kerb ready to help them out of the car. She'd brought most of Lauren's belongings home in her car earlier, so there was only the wheelchair to get out of the boot, and the crutches from the back seat.

'Doo yoo-ou think everryone's watching?' Lauren whispered hoarsely.

Feeling certain that at least a dozen pairs of friendly but curious eyes were peering from behind blinds and net curtains, Emma lied. 'I shouldn't think so,' she said lightly. 'They're probably all at work, or in their gardens enjoying the sun. Can you manage?' she asked, as Lauren swung her feet to the pavement.

Grabbing hold of her mother's and grandmother's arms, Lauren hauled herself up and took only one crutch from the pair Phyllis was holding to slot under her left arm. Her face was pale and her eyes seemed larger and darker than usual as they absorbed the strange familiarity of her surroundings.

'The kettle's on,' Phyllis told her as she led the way in through the gate. 'We'll have a nice cup of tea, shall we?'

'What's that?' Lauren demanded, stopping dead and glaring at the ramp that had been fitted over the step leading up to the door.

'It's for the wheelchair,' Emma explained. 'Remember, I told you they were putting it in.'

Her face tighter than ever, Lauren waved away the arm Phyllis was offering, and in a few short, hobbled steps she was inside the house.

After exchanging uneasy glances with her mother, Emma went to get the wheelchair from the boot. Bringing it into the hall, she was dismayed to see Lauren in floods of tears, with Phyllis trying to comfort her.

'I'mm not getting on that,' Lauren cried. 'I'mm not an in . . . invalid or an ollld person.'

Since she clearly meant the stairlift, Emma said, 'OK, let's just go and sit down for a while, shall we? We don't have to deal with it now.'

'I want to go to my room,' Lauren told her.

Emma looked at her mother again.

Moving forward, Phyllis plonked herself down on the stairlift, fastened the belt and pressed green for go. As she started to rise Lauren turned and buried her face in Emma's shoulder.

'You have to watch her,' Emma whispered. 'She looks hilarious.'

Reluctantly, Lauren turned back again, and parting her hair she watched her grandmother's painfully slow ascent to the landing. As a sob of laughter escaped her Emma thought her mother's little performance had worked, but then she dropped her head and started to cry again. 'Don wan tooo do it,' she choked.

'Well I'm afraid I can't carry you,' Emma told her.

'Going up on my bummm.'

'Hang on then,' Phyllis said, 'I'll come back down and give you a race.'

To Emma's relief Lauren seemed up for that, and as they prepared to go, Emma instructed, 'No stopping and starting, Mum. It's got to be a proper race and whoever wins . . . What shall we have as a prize?'

'A new brain?' Lauren suggested.

Emma slanted her a look. 'Not funny,' she commented. 'I know! Whoever wins gets tea at the hotel tomorrow.'

'You're suppose to beee taking usss anyway.'

'Well, then you might get double scones and Earl Grey,' Emma suggested. 'Are you ready? Get set. Go!'

To her amazement Lauren was at the top in not much more time than it would have taken her to walk up, while Phyllis was still motoring along like a snail on her special silvery tracks.

'Well, looks like you've got two modes of transport,' Emma informed Lauren, going to join her. 'The pensioner's buggy here, or your bum.'

'Thanks,' Lauren said as Emma handed her the crutch. 'If you don't mind, I'm going to lie down now,' and taking two clumsy paces to her room she closed the door behind her.

Sighing, Emma turned to her mother who was still only halfway up the stairs. 'Bring it to the top,' she said, 'just in case she decides she wants to come down on it, and then please let's get that cup of tea.'

Ten minutes later they were in the sitting room discussing everything that was due to happen over the coming days – visits from the community physio, speech therapist and psychologist; an appointment with the local GP, with whom Emma had only registered a fortnight ago; a potential full house at the weekend with Berry, Harry and Jane due to arrive – when an almighty thump from upstairs silenced them. It was followed by another, and another, and afraid of what was happening, Emma raced upstairs, reaching the landing as Lauren yelled, 'Muuuum! Muuum!'

'I'm here,' Emma told her, throwing open the door. She stopped dead in shock. 'Dear God, Lauren, what have you done?' she gasped. The room was in chaos, with drawers upended, the contents of the wardrobe strewn about all over the place, and the sheets torn from the bed.

'Where is it?' Lauren demanded savagely. 'What have . . . have you donnne with it?'

'With what?' Emma cried.

'You know what. Mmy journal.'

Emma froze. She really hadn't expected Lauren to be looking for it as soon as she came in the door; in truth, she'd been hoping Lauren would have no memory of it at all.

'Where is it?' Lauren repeated furiously. 'I wannnt it.'

Trying desperately to come up with the best way to handle this, Emma said crisply, 'It isn't here.'

'What do . . . do you mean? Why isnn't it here? It's mine. It's pri . . . private.'

'Indeed it is, but I'm afraid it's gone.'

'I don unnnderstand. Who took it? Was it yooo-ou? You don have annny right . . .'

Going to her, Emma took her firmly by the shoulders and forced her to sit down on the bed. Unprepared as she was to have this showdown now, she said, since there was clearly no escaping it, 'After the accident, the police found it in your car. Do you remember that you had it with you?'

As Lauren's face turned white, her eyes reflected the horror she was feeling. If she had forgotten, it seemed to be coming back to her now.

Emma said, 'Lauren, I want you to tell me how much you remember about that night. And I don't mean the accident, I mean where you were before and . . . Actually, I think you know what I mean.'

Lauren turned her head away, but not before Emma saw the awful rush of colour to her cheeks. 'It's my journal,' she retorted through her teeth. 'No one hasss any right to reeead it.'

'Well, they did.'

Lauren sat stiffly where she was, staring at nothing.

'That includes me,' Emma added.

Lauren drew breath to speak, but then her head dropped forward and she started to cry.

Unwilling to show any compassion yet, Emma said, 'You

remember what's in that journal, don't you? You recall everything you did leading up to the accident, and now . . . What
now? What are you trying to do? Why is it so important
that you find it?'

'It's not . . . not important,' Lauren wept. 'I don want to
doo anything.'

*Dear God, please don't let her still have a crush on that man.
If he turns out to be the reason she doesn't want to see Oliver
again I'll never forgive her.* 'I don't want any more lies,' Emma
said sharply. 'Nothing you say or do is ever going to make
me stop loving you, but I need to trust you and so I need
to know if you still have feelings for that man.'

Lauren was crying so hard she could barely speak.

'Tell me, is that why you wouldn't see Oliver today . . .'

'Shut up! Shut up!' Lauren cried, banging her fists on
her knees. 'I would nevvver do that. I hate you for saying
it. I love Oliver more thannn anything . . .'

'Then why are you so keen to find the journal?'

'Because I don want it any more. I don want Oll-ver ever
to find it, or annnyone else, like you. But now you're saying
yooo-ou read it, and the police . . . Whooo else knooows?'

'Not Oliver,' Emma assured her. Now was definitely not
the time to admit she'd confided in Russ, in fact there
probably never would be a time for that. As for her mother,
Emma felt sure Phyllis had already erased what she knew
from her memory banks, and should any residue be left,
she'd find the appropriate scouring pad to finish off the
job. Polly would never let on that she'd seen some of the
journal, nor would Mr Gibbs, and thank God she'd never
shown anything to Will, though of course he knew of its
existence.

'What about Daddy?'

'He hasn't read any of it, but he knows what happened.
I think I should tell you now that the man in question,'
she didn't want to poison the air with his name, 'has already
left the school.'

Lauren drooped even lower as she registered the news.
'So everybody knowws,' she wailed, covering her head
with her hands.

'That's not true. Mr Gibbs and Mrs Barker do, because

they had to be told. And Donna . . . You remember Donna, don't you?'

Lauren nodded wretchedly.

'Donna's been grounded since it came to light, and hopefully she's had no more to do with him. I can't imagine she has, but I haven't been in touch with her mother for a while so I'm not sure what's going on with her.'

'She's been mmy friend forevver,' Lauren sobbed.

'I know, and there's no reason why she can't be again, but you understand, don't you, that you won't be living in London any more? You'll be based here from now on, with me and Granny, and when it comes time to resume your studies we'll send you to a local college.'

'Tooo stupid for A levels,' Lauren growled in frustration.

'That's ridiculous and you know it.'

'Cann't learn anything new.'

'Maybe not at the moment, but I'm sure that'll change.'

'Don't wan to dooo music.'

Stifling a sigh, Emma said, 'We can discuss that when the time comes. Our focus now is to get you well enough to study anything at all.'

Lauren's head remained down as she registered everything that had been said, and placing a comforting hand on her back Emma started to rub. The best part of the last few minutes was what she'd said about Oliver, but Emma wasn't going to push that any further for now – heaven knew she'd already dealt with enough for one day.

'Are – are you angry?' Lauren hiccuped after a while.

Though Emma's first instinct was to deny it, what she said was, 'Actually, I passed that some time ago. After that came the shame, and the disappointment, and then the sheer bloody fury of knowing that if you hadn't been involved with him you'd never have been on that road that night and Oliver would never have hit you.'

Lauren's face was ravaged by tears as she finally looked at her mother. 'You understand, donnn't you, that it wass my fault too, not just Oliver's?'

'Yes, I understand that,' Emma replied, and pulling her into a tender embrace she decided to leave it to Oliver to tell her about his mother. 'What were you going to do with the journal if you found it?' she asked.

'Des-estroy it,' Lauren stammered over a sob.

Emma's expression turned wry. 'Then you don't have to,' she told her, 'because I've already done it for you.'

Lauren drew back to look into her eyes. Emma held the gaze and lifted a hand to stroke her hair. 'I'mm, I'm sorry, Mumm,' Lauren whispered.

Emma shook her head in fond despair. 'Yes, I'm sure you are,' she said, 'we all are, but the only thing we can do now is try to put it behind us and concentrate on the future.'

Chapter Thirty-Four

Over the next few days Lauren seemed to sink deeper and deeper inside herself, not wanting to talk to anyone, or go out, or even engage with the new therapists who came to see her. All the sheet music piled in her room, along with her guitar, flute and keyboard, remained untouched, and as far as Emma and Phyllis knew she wasn't using her computer either. Occasionally she switched on the TV, but Emma feared that it was more to drown out the sound of her crying than to keep up to date with *Hollyoaks* or *EastEnders*.

Being so involved in the festival now, Emma had no choice but to leave her with Phyllis for most of the day, though Phyllis was willingly shouldering the responsibility. She was naturally as concerned as Emma, but she was also being pragmatic, as the community psychologist had advised – Lauren was undoubtedly going through an adjustment period, he'd said after his first visit following her return home, and this wasn't at all unusual. However, if she was still so low in a couple of weeks, he'd get in touch with his colleague back at the centre to discuss how best to tackle the problem.

Though Emma was certain that this silly rift with Oliver was at the heart of Lauren's unhappiness, every time she tried to broach the subject Lauren would simply turn her face to the wall and tell her mother to leave it, or to go away and leave her alone.

'Won't you at least speak to him on the phone?' Emma persisted.

'No,' Lauren snapped.

'But why?'

'He doesnn't call mme, does he, so he obviously doesn't wannt to speeak to me.'

'But you're the one who told him you didn't want to see him any more. He's hurt, Lauren, and angry and confused.'

'Not mmy fault I'mm no good and cann't do annything.'

'But you can do practically everything . . .'

'Not new mmusic, or dance, or speaking properly . . .'

'It'll come, and I'm afraid lying here feeling sorry for yourself isn't going to help matters at all.'

This was about as far as she ever got in trying to persuade Lauren out of her gloom, and the situation was only made more difficult by the way Lauren's left hand, or arm, had started to show signs of a weakness that they'd thought had disappeared during the early stages of her physio-therapy. Emma first noticed it at a mealtime, about a week after Lauren came home, when they'd managed to coax her downstairs to join them for dinner, and the fork slipped from her hand and clattered to the floor. A few minutes later the same thing happened, and when Emma regarded her curiously Lauren shouted, 'Don't blamme mme. I can't help it if mmy stupid hannd doesnn't work, can I?'

'This is precisely why you have to start seeing the physio again,' Emma informed her more sharply than she'd intended, but she was angry and alarmed by the new development, and afraid that Lauren seemed to be losing interest in her own recovery. 'I've had enough of all this, Lauren,' she cried, slapping her napkin down on the table as her eyes filled with tears. 'Everybody's going out of their way to help you, me, your grandmother . . .'

'Stop having a go at mme.'

'You'll start co-operating again, young lady, and even if you won't do it for yourself, you'll do it for those of us who love you.'

'It's mmy life nnot yours.'

'Don't you dare throw that at me. I gave you life once, and I've done everything in my power to bring you back to it a second time, so you'll do this, Lauren, or I'm telling you now, I'll wash my hands of you and let you become the very thing you fear, someone who's useless, has no friends, no life, no reason to get up in the morning,' and before Lauren could muster any more arguments she stormed out of the room, took herself upstairs to bed and didn't even bother going in to say goodnight to Lauren after Phyllis had left to go to Mrs Dempster's.

The following day the physio turned up just as Emma, looking tired, unhappy and extremely stressed, was about to go out. 'Good luck,' she said tightly as she left him with her mother. 'If she doesn't co-operate I wouldn't bother wasting your time any more.'

'Emma,' her mother protested.

'No, I mean it,' Emma told her, still angry enough to hope Lauren could hear, and not prepared to discuss it any further she went to get in her car, tucked her Bluetooth behind one ear and called Russ, who was having his own struggle with Oliver's temper and pride. 'How's your little ray of sunshine today?' she asked when Russ answered.

'I still haven't had the pleasure,' Russ responded, 'because he hasn't ventured out of his room yet, but I'm guessing he'll be much the same as yesterday, and the day before that and the day before that, ready to storm your house and force her to see him one minute, then damned if he'll ever have anything to do with her again the next. One good thing seems to be coming out of it though, apparently they started up some kind of Internet project together while she was at the centre, and he's working off most of his frustrations by focusing on that.'

Interested to know more, Emma said, 'What kind of project?'

'Apparently I'm not allowed to know the details yet, but he claims to have come up with an innovative way of marketing on the Net. I can't imagine it's something no one else has thought of yet, but you never know, and please don't ever repeat that, because he'd never forgive me if he thought I doubted him.'

With a crooked sort of smile Emma said, 'So what are we going to do about the two of them? We can't just leave things the way they are – or can we?'

'Maybe we can, because actually, I'm not inclined to interfere. They're grown-ups, or they certainly like to consider themselves to be, so when they're ready to act that way I'm sure they'll figure out this nonsense for themselves.'

Emma sighed, 'Under any other circumstances I'd completely agree, but Lauren's depression is really starting to worry me.'

Sounding more sympathetic now, he said, 'Of course, and I'm sorry, because that really does need to be addressed. Let's give it some more thought and see what we can come up with by the next time we speak.'

To Emma's astonishment, when she walked in the door just after seven that evening the first thing she heard was the sound of a flute coming from Lauren's room. It was a piece they knew well, 'Dance of the Blessed Spirits', and it was being played so fluidly that Emma wondered if it was a recording, until a note rang false, followed by another, and then the music stopped.

'This is a good sign?' she whispered to her mother as Phyllis came into the hall. 'It's the first time she's even attempted to play since she came home.'

'Actually, she's had quite a good day,' Phyllis responded with a smile. 'She worked with the physio and ate lunch, and this afternoon we walked around the back garden naming all the flowers.'

Emma could hardly believe it.

'I think your little outburst last night might have done the trick,' Phyllis told her.

Though she'd have liked to think so too, Emma couldn't imagine it would be that easy, so she certainly wasn't going to start congratulating herself yet. 'What did the physio say?' she asked.

'That he was pleased with their first session, but he didn't work her very hard apparently. He's going to step up the game tomorrow, he said, and arrange for an OT to come in the next day or two to give her some extra help with her left hand. It's why she's finding it hard to play, the hand keeps giving out on her.'

Feeling the dreaded chill of fear creeping up her spine again, Emma said, 'Does the physio think they can strengthen it up?'

'They're going to try, but if it persists he says she might have to go back for another scan.'

Her chest tightening with the horror of any more radiography on Lauren's brain, Emma said, 'OK. I'll go up and see her. Are we going to Polly's for dinner?'

'I think it's still on. Polly's definitely expecting us, and Lauren hasn't said she doesn't want to go.'

'Of course I wannto go,' Lauren retorted, when Emma asked her. 'Havenn't seen Melissa for ages.'

Deciding not to remind her that this was her choice, not Melissa's, Emma said, 'Well, I'm glad to know you're feeling up to it. I hear things went well with the physio today.'

'Mm, he's really nice. I liked him.'

Starting to relax a little, Emma withdrew at that point, not wanting to overload Lauren with more questions or concern in case they sent her spiralling off into a black despair again.

'Do you think this could be the start of the mood disturbances we were warned about?' she asked her mother when she went back downstairs.

'It's hard to tell, but for now I'm taking the view that it's still all a part of adjusting to being home. And the fact that she's had a go at playing some music today and didn't fly into a temper when things went wrong is, in my book, definitely encouraging.'

It was in Emma's too, and when Lauren and Melissa disappeared off to Melissa's room later that evening, she allowed herself to take even greater heart that Lauren was emerging from her depression. A girl needed her best friend, especially when things weren't going well with a boyfriend.

'So what's happening about Oliver?' Polly asked, keeping her voice down in case Melissa's bedroom door was open.

Rolling her eyes, Emma said, 'Apparently he's as full of pride as she is, so he's trying not to think about her by throwing himself into some new project he's got going.'

Polly glanced at Phyllis. 'But they're going to get back together at some point, obviously?' she said.

'I'd like to think so,' Emma replied. 'And right at this moment I'm daring to feel hopeful that a nice long chat with her best mate will help bring her to her senses and get her to call him.'

'No, you definitely have to wait for him to call you,' Melissa was advising sagely. 'Men never respect you if you run after them.'

'That's wwhat I thought,' Lauren agreed miserably. 'But there again, I wwas a bit mmean, the way I said I didn't wwant to see him any mmore.'

'You were upset and scared about leaving the centre. He should understand that, and if he doesn't then he's just not right for you.'

Lauren looked unhappier than ever. 'He was there every day though, and we got really close, so I think he must care a bit.'

'Oh, I'm not saying he doesn't care, because he definitely does, but you said yourself he hasn't tried to ring you, or come over and see you.'

Lauren's head went down as she wondered again if Oliver was secretly happy to have been given a way out. 'I think Mum might have told him I've been tired and need to rest,' she said, seizing an excuse even though she had no idea if it was true.

'If she did you'll have to get her to tell him it's all right to come now, then see what he does.'

Lauren's eyes showed how lost she was feeling as she gazed at Melissa. 'You definitely don't think I should call him?' she said.

Melissa shook her head. 'No. Definitely not.'

It was the week leading up to the festival and Emma's feet were barely touching the ground as she flew about balancing everything from budgets, to schedules, to flaring artistic egos. She was almost constantly on the phone, either at her desk inside the hotel, or in the gardens where the stalls and tents were being erected, or heading into some last-minute meeting with the local council, or a major contributor, or someone from the press. There was no doubt that without the backup she'd received from Hamish and his wife, and most of the hotel staff, she'd never have been able to pull this off. She simply hadn't had the right level of experience before, or anywhere near enough contacts, which meant her stress levels had soared off the scale more times than she cared to remember, never helped by how worried she constantly was about Lauren.

At this moment she was outside inspecting the easels for an art stall. Her mobile rang and seeing Russ's name come up she quickly clicked on. 'Hi, how are you?' she asked busily.

There was the unmistakable ring of irony in his voice as he said, 'OK. My son's finally lost his head, he's about to storm the Bastille and I don't think there's much I can do to stop him.'

Laughing with relief as she switched the phone to her other ear, Emma said, 'Let him go, *please*! I'll call my mother to give her some warning. When should they expect him?'

'Well, he's at Sylvie's apartment right now, so I'd say twenty minutes, half an hour tops.'

'OK, the trusty Phyllis will be there to open the door. What happens after that will be down to them.'

With more irony in his tone, Russ said, 'I'm not sure whether I wish I was going to be there to see it or not. Anyway, if it does go to plan, perhaps I could invite you all for a barbecue at Craig Court this weekend. That includes your mother, of course, and Berry, if she's still coming over from Italy.'

'Sadly, she's had to cancel, Adolfo's back in hospital. Not serious, but he doesn't want her to leave him. And I sincerely hope you haven't forgotten that it's the grand opening of my summer arts festival on Saturday. I was hoping you'd be here.'

'Indeed I shall. Wouldn't miss it for the world. I'm talking about Sunday evening, if it's not raining. If it is, we can always eat inside.'

Waving frantically to a carpenter as he appeared from behind a handmade puppet stall, Emma replied, 'Either way sounds perfect, and speaking for myself and Phyllis, we'd love to come. Is there anything we can do, or bring?'

'Just yourselves. I'll take care of everything else.'

Signalling to the carpenter that she'd be just a minute,

Emma turned aside as she asked Russ, 'Before you go, what news on Sylvie?'

His voice was pained as he said, 'Some good, some bad. She's back at the clinic now, following a weekend break with her friend Johann for one of their jolly little binges, though I suspect it was anything but jolly. I'm not naive enough to think this is going to be over any time soon, but I can't help wishing for it anyway.'

'I'm sorry,' Emma murmured.

'Thank you, but it's the boys I'm concerned about. It's not good the way they seem to feel so cold towards their mother. Sure, it's a form of self-protection, but it's sad, and whatever they say, it'll be having an effect on them internally that will no doubt have to be dealt with somewhere down the road. Still, I can't go on fighting their battles for them, or spending so much time sorting out their flipping love lives, and I'm not only talking about Oliver. Apparently Charlie's just been dumped, and is feeling very sorry for himself.'

'Oh no, poor Charlie,' Emma sympathised. 'Lucky that he has you to turn to.'

'God spare me,' Russ retorted with a shudder. 'All these bleeding hearts, it's just not manly.'

With a splutter of laughter, Emma said, 'They must get their tenderness from somewhere, and from the little I know my guess is . . .'

'Definitely not me,' he interrupted. 'Heart of stone, that's me. Mr Can't-Be-Doing-With-It-All.'

Still grinning, Emma said, 'Yeah, right.' Then, 'Actually, I'm afraid I have to go, but I'll call you back as soon as there's any news from the Bastille.'

After ringing off she spoke briefly to the carpenter about one of the puppet-maker's last-minute requirements, then waving to Hamish who'd just turned up with a local news crew to let him know she'd be right there, she made a rapid call to her mother.

'Where's Lauren?' she asked, before Phyllis even had a chance to say hello.

'Upstairs having a lie-down. She did well with her physio this morning.'

'Great. Next bit of good news, Romeo's on his way.'

Phyllis gave a gasp of delight. 'And not before time. Shall I go and tell her?'

'No, wait till he's there so she doesn't have a chance to start fussing or saying she doesn't want to see him, and then do your best to eavesdrop so you can tell us all about it later. Call immediately if anything goes wrong,' and ringing off she headed towards Hamish and the crew, while making a mental note to bring Russ up to date with the compensation claim the next time she spoke to him. Another of the strange ironies between their two families was that Jolyon Crane, at Russ's suggestion, was now acting for Lauren to get as much as he could out of the insurance company. Emma reminded herself that she needed to email Jolyon back to say that if he thought he could double the fifty thousand already on the table, then she was happy to follow his advice. Quickly making another mental note to reposition the event map closer to the entrance, and another to put a pile of hotel brochures inside the champagne tent, and another to call Portaloo to direct them in through the back gates, she joined Hamish and a bossy little producer to start going through the timetable of music and theatre acts for Saturday afternoon.

Phyllis was at the window as Oliver drove into the street. By the time he pulled up outside she'd already opened the front door and had a finger over her lips, warning him to be quiet.

'No, I'm sorry,' he declared urgently, clearly in no fit state to fully comprehend anything other than his mission. 'I've had enough of this. I want to speak to her, and I'm going to do it right now. Where is she?'

Thrilled, Phyllis whispered, 'Top of the stairs, middle door, but maybe I ought to check first to make sure she's decent.'

Since he hadn't considered that, he hesitated. 'I don't care if she's not,' he decided rashly. His handsome young face was flushed with defiance, his eyes feverish with an almost Byronesque passion.

'No, but I expect she will, and you want it to start off well, I'm sure.'

Conceding the point, he allowed Phyllis to mount the stairs ahead of him, following close behind, casting an interested glance at the Stannah lift as he passed. At the top he paused as Phyllis knocked on Lauren's door.

'OK to come in, sweetheart?' she called out.

'Yeah, I'm awake,' Lauren called back.

As Phyllis opened the door to find Lauren lying forlornly on the bed, Oliver crowded against her shoulder and the look of disbelief, followed by pure joy, that came into Lauren's eyes turned Phyllis's heart inside out.

'What . . . I didn't knnow . . .' Lauren stammered as he burst past Phyllis.

'For God's sake,' Oliver growled as he tripped over a bag in his haste, almost landing on top of her.

Giggling and sobbing, Lauren wrapped her arms around him, seeming to yield her entire self to his awkwardly positioned, but nonetheless passionate kiss.

At the door Phyllis gave a sigh of blissful satisfaction.

'I'm not going to let you do this any more,' Oliver suddenly exploded. 'I love you, Lauren Scott, and nothing's ever going to change that, not even you and the stupid things you tell yourself. We made plans, remember, and I want to stick to them, even if you don't, but I know that you do and so don't try saying you don't, because I'm not going to let you . . .' He broke off as Lauren put her fingers over his lips.

'I'm not arguing,' she whispered.

Seeming only just to realise it, he gave a wry grin.

Her eyes were gazing deeply, adoringly, into his, as she said, 'I've mmissed you so mmuch.'

'Then why didn't you ring me?' he cried.

'Why didn't you ring me?'

'Because you said you didn't want to see me any more.'

'But you should have knnown I didn't mmean it. I was just in a strange mmood that day, and then, whenn I didn't hear from you, I was afraid you were angry with mme.'

'Angry? I was furious, and still am. How could you possibly think I wouldn't want you once you got home? I've never heard such bollocks in my life.'

She gave a girlish laugh as she coloured, and as she touched her fingers to the two letters she was wearing round her neck, he covered them with his. 'Do yooou really love me?' she asked shyly.

Phyllis sorely wished she could see his face as he lifted his head to look into Lauren's eyes, then she gave a choke of laughter as he said, in a very romantic voice, 'No, I'm just pretending. I storm every girl's bedroom like this, and . . .'

'Granny!' Lauren exclaimed indignantly.

Phyllis straightened up, all innocence.

'Yooou can go nnow,' Lauren told her.

Phyllis feigned dejection. 'Must I?'

'Yes, you must,' Lauren insisted.

Oliver turned to look at Phyllis, his eyes simmering with laughter. 'Got yourself a ringside seat there,' he remarked.

'Oh, and it's a marvellous performance,' she told him earnestly.

'Excuse mme,' Lauren said, turning him back to face her. 'Granny, why donn't you go and play with yourr stairlift?'

'Oh, I so want to have a go on that,' Oliver cried.

'I so knnew you wwould,' Lauren responded with a roll of her eyes.

'Yeah, but not right now,' he assured her.

Smiling delightedly as she closed the bedroom door, Phyllis went to take her seat on the Stannah lift and motored gently down to the hall where she picked up the phone to call Emma, letting her know that the sun was shining and the forecast for the foreseeable future looked very good indeed.

The following Saturday, due in part to the glorious weather, but also to her exceptional organisational skills, Emma remarked immodestly to Polly and Keith McIntyre when they arrived, the turnout for the festival's opening day was already exceeding all expectations. By noon the gardens were teeming with visitors, and the champagne tent had taken over a thousand pounds. As for the contributors, it would have been hard to make most of them any happier, even if they weren't all generating an equal amount of interest. Unfortunately, not everyone had good taste, or the cultural intelligence to appreciate 'irony in flight', as one woefully neglected ceramicist was heard to comment. If his work had resembled anything remotely discernible, it might have helped, but as it didn't all Emma could do was sympathise and try her best to steer people in his direction. Alas, his odd little pieces might have been reverse magnets for the way those who approached suddenly veered off at the last minute.

Griselda the tarot reader was doing excellent business in her self-imported tent next to the crystal stall, while Poppy, a local landscape artist, was starting to run out of prints already and taking orders for more. She'd even sold three originals, one to the hotel, another to an established fan from Farrington Gurney, and the third to Russ, who'd snapped it up after learning, from Lauren, that it was Emma's birthday in a couple of weeks, and that her mother absolutely loved the aerial perspective of the Clifton suspension bridge and Avon Gorge.

At Oliver's insistence, Lauren was being pushed through the crowds in her wheelchair as he didn't want anyone knocking her off her crutches, especially not when he'd entered them both for a five-mile walk at the end of September. It was to help raise funds for Headway, the brain-injury charity that was now playing its own crucial role in her recovery. This, happily, seemed to be back on track now that Oliver was in charge again, though the problem with her left hand still hadn't been completely resolved.

However, Emma wasn't going to allow herself to worry about more CT scans today, or the duraplasty Lauren still had to endure to repair her skull, or any of the countless neurological problems that could crop up in the future. Like it or not, this was how life was going to be for a long time to come, always wondering if any little slip, or memory loss, temper or misunderstanding was a result of her injury, or something that could happen to anyone at any time.

'It would be lovely to have it all resolved by the end of the month, or even the end of the year,' she'd said to her brother the night before, 'but unfortunately it's just not like that. We have to take each day as it comes, and never forget to feel thankful that she's not only still with us, but functioning as beautifully as she is.'

Harry had smiled fondly as he'd stood with Emma at the kitchen window, watching Lauren in the garden with his children, allowing little Phoebe, helped by Oliver, whizz her up and down the path in her wheelchair, while her brother Todd made a clown of himself with the crutches. 'What news of Will?' Harry asked quietly.

Grimacing, Emma said, 'He emails occasionally to ask for updates on her progress, which I send him, but he hasn't tried to see her again since the day he came to the centre.'

'Does she ever talk about him?'

'Not much, and her psychologist feels that it's still too early to try and push it, in spite of the long letter of apology Will sent. She knows what he really thinks, because she heard him say it, so I don't think the apology actually means anything. I'm sure she'd like to see the children though, but she's in no hurry, and for now she seems happy enough with the little get-well cards they send from time to time, and the phone calls they make on Sundays.'

Harry and his family weren't the only ones who'd driven down from London for the big event. Charlie was around somewhere, as was Alfie, who'd left Bristol a couple of months ago to join a firm of architects in Knightsbridge. Jerome, Oliver's other close mate, was now in Durban working for a civil engineering firm, but that hadn't stopped Oliver inviting him, and Emma had been deeply touched when Jerome, whom she'd never met, had sent her a message of good luck. A handful of Emma's and Lauren's old neighbours had hired a bus to bring them from Chiswick for the day, and about a dozen of Lauren's schoolfriends, now anxiously awaiting their A level results, had done the same. Donna hadn't come with them, and in spite of the relief that gave her, Emma couldn't help feeling sad about it, and was sure that Lauren did too. However, she guessed that neither of them wanted the reminder of their lapse of judgement, as Phyllis liked to put it (or shame, as Emma was more inclined to label it, but only to herself). So it seemed their friendship was yet another casualty of the affair that should never have happened.

Spotting Lauren and Oliver over by a jazz band made up of local accountants, Emma was about to go and join them when she was waylaid by a magician who'd apparently lost his wand (exactly what she was supposed to do about that she had no idea, until he suddenly made it appear from behind her ear). Then a jewellery designer, whose zany collection was attracting a lot of custom, called her over, needing to report several thefts from her stall. Emma immediately radioed security to get them to post a guard next to the designer's glittering exhibits, then went to help a dear old doddery self-published author to pick up the spiritual guidance booklets she was so proud of and had managed to spill from their display stand.

As she continued to multitask her way around the fair, feeling exhilarated by the sheer success and bedlam of the day, she found herself being stopped every few steps by someone wanting to offer either congratulations, or complaints, or to ask where a certain stall could be found, or even to try and make a reservation at the hotel.

After directing an elderly gentleman and his wife to the Portaloos, she looked around for Lauren again, but with so many people crowding the gardens now it was impossible to find her. There didn't seem to be any sign of Phyllis either, or Russ, or Polly and Keith who'd now become Polly's regular Saturday night date. She spotted Melissa hurrying towards the performance stage with Alfie, while Harry and Jane were over at the pony ride with Phoebe and Todd. Hamish Gallagher and his wife appeared to be engaged in a happy little chat with the Lord Mayor, and a highly acclaimed actress who lived near Bath was attracting plenty of bidders to her silent auction, which included all sorts of film and stage memorabilia, and a copy of her newly published autobiography. All proceeds were going to Headway – the actress's own choice, since she had a brother who'd been helped a great deal by the charity after a shooting accident that had left him blind and partially paralysed. Emma had already put in a bid of forty pounds for the book, though when she was ever going to find time to read anything other than backgrounds on the *three* potential new clients who'd been in touch during the last couple of weeks asking her to organise an event for them, she had no idea.

'I thought you might be in need of one of these,' a voice behind her declared.

Turning round, she broke into a smile of delight as Russ handed her a full glass of fizzing champagne. 'Congratulations,' he said, clinking his own glass to hers. 'I'm very impressed. To have accomplished all this at any time would be a magnificent feat, to have done it over these past couple of months is nothing short of super-human.'

'Aha, that would be me,' she told him teasingly as she took her first sip and felt it rush straight to her head. 'I couldn't have done it without my mother, of course. Or Oliver, or *you*.'

'Me?' he laughed in astonishment.

'You've allowed Oliver to take this time,' she reminded him. 'Without your support he couldn't have afforded to for one thing, and I daresay he's needed a lot of emotional backup too, even before these last couple of weeks drove us to distraction.'

Russ shook his head in denial. 'I told you, heart of stone, me. I've got no sympathy for him at all.'

She eyed him sceptically as she took another sip. 'It's good to see them together again, isn't it?'

He nodded. 'I have to admit, it is.'

In a quietly conspiratorial tone, Emma said, 'Think yourself lucky that you weren't around to hear the thunderous row that erupted when he told her she had to come in her wheelchair today.'

Russ gave a shudder. 'Have you had time to look at the first draft of their new business plan yet?' he asked.

'No. It's still in my inbox. Is it any good?'

'Actually on the face of it . . . I've got no idea. I'm going to need some more explanation, but if it does turn out to have legs, I shall get his mother to fund it. Considering everything, I think it's the least she can do.'

Liking the idea, Emma clinked her glass to his this time, and looked around. 'Do you know where they are?' she asked, puzzled by Oliver and Lauren's prolonged disappearance.

'Actually, the last I saw of them they were heading off in the direction of the hotel with Charlie, whose broken heart, I'm delighted to say, seems to be staging a rapid recovery. Have you clocked all the attention he's receiving from Lauren's schoolfriends? Having said that, he appears to have grown tired of the adulation because he's heading this way. Have you two actually been introduced yet?'

'Very briefly, just after you arrived. Charlie,' she said warmly, as he reached them. 'It's so lovely that you're here. Oliver was afraid you wouldn't make it.'

'Are you kidding? There wasn't a chance of me missing it,' Charlie assured her. 'Not that I'm especially into all this arty stuff, you understand, well I am, kind of, but something's about to happen now that I swear I'd have flown halfway round the world to see, that is if I'd been halfway round the world, but I was actually just in London.'

Emma frowned in surprise. 'Not the Beatnik Boys, surely,' she said, guessing it must be about time for the ageing rockers to start wowing the crowds with their medley of sixties hits.

'No, not the Beatnik Boys,' he replied, giving a thumbs up to someone and tucking her arm through his. 'If you'll just come this way with me.'

Glancing over her shoulder as he led her away, she treated Russ to a baffled look and received nothing more than a merry salute with his champagne.

'OK, she's here,' Charlie informed Phyllis as he brought Emma to a stop in front of the stage. 'Where's Oliver?'

'I'm here,' his brother replied, hurrying to join them.

'Stand there with Emma,' Phyllis instructed him bossily, 'and don't let her move.'

'Not an inch,' Oliver assured her, slipping an arm round Emma's shoulders.

Emma looked at him, but he only grinned and gave her a hug.

'Where are Polly and Keith?' Phyllis wanted to know. 'Ah, there you are. Is everyone ready?'

'Just about,' Polly replied, checking her mobile.

'What on earth's going on?' Emma demanded.

'You're about to find out,' Polly informed her, as Oliver eased her to the centre of a clearing that the hotel staff were helping to create.

Spotting Russ coming to the front of the crowd Emma threw him another curious look, but he simply smiled and winked.

Up on the stage Hamish was tapping the microphone, sending little static booms around the gardens. When certain he could be heard, he said, 'Ladies and gentlemen, thank you for your attention.'

It took a few moments for a hush to fall like a softly billowing blanket, and once everyone was facing his way he said, 'I'm delighted, indeed honoured, to announce that we have an unscheduled performance now by two very talented young ladies.' He grinned at the murmur of expectation. 'My friends, will you please give your warmest welcome to the very lovely Lauren and Melissa.'

Emma gave a gasp of surprise, and her hands flew to her mouth as Hamish went to help Lauren on to the stage. Once she was steady, he gave her his arm and walked her carefully to the front while Melissa, carrying her guitar, followed discreetly behind.

'Thannk you,' Lauren said softly into the mic, as the applause died down. 'I've rrearranged the lyrics of this sonng a little bit, but it's onne you all know.' Then, looking straight at Emma, she said, 'Mmum, this is for you.'

Emma was already losing it as Melissa strummed the first chords, then her heart simply overflowed as Lauren started to sing to the tune of 'Thank You For The Days' in as sweet and clear a voice as Emma had ever heard.

> *'You gave me all your love,*
> *An endless love, a precious love you gave me*
> *You never let me go,*
> *I won't forget, I can't forget, believe me.'*

Emma was finding it hard not to sob.

'Love that gave me back my life,
Love that showed me how to fight
You are my world,
The one I know is always for me
Now I can survive believe me.

Thank you for your love,
The endless love, precious love you gave me
You never let me go.
I won't forget, I can't forget, believe me.

There was a moment's pause and she whispered, 'I love you, Mum. Thank you.'

As the crowd broke into an emotional and delighted round of applause Lauren continued to look at her mother, tears sliding down to her own smile as Oliver moved swiftly to lift her from the stage. Emma never let their gaze drop as she came to wrap her beloved daughter tightly in her arms. She might never get the old Lauren back, but if it was possible she loved this one even more.

'Thank you,' Emma whispered, 'thank you so much.'

Lauren was sobbing into her mother's shoulder as Phyllis, Polly, everyone swept in to gather around them.

'Wasn't she beautiful?' Phyllis wailed.

'It was very special,' Russ said, when his eyes met Emma's.

'She's good,' Charlie declared proudly.

'I told you,' Oliver responded.

'I hardly know what to say,' Emma told Lauren, cupping her exquisitely flushed face in her hands.

'You donn't have to say annything,' Lauren told her. 'I just wannted to doo this for you to say thannk you for staying with me, and believing in me.'

'I'd never have done anything else,' Emma whispered tenderly. 'You're my baby, you mean everything in the world to me.'

Lauren continued to smile tearily. Then, reaching for Oliver's hand, she sat into the wheelchair that Alfie had manoeuvred in behind her. 'Guess-guess what?' she said, looking up at Emma. 'That's not all, because I've had the mmost brilliant idea.'

Emma looked intrigued.

'Oll-ver and I, as one of our nnew projects, are going to start up the golllden angels again.'

Emma's eyes shot to Russ. She couldn't have felt more thrilled.

'Wait,' Lauren said, 'there's mmore.'

Unable to imagine what it could be, Emma smiled down at her. 'Go on,' she said curiously.

Bringing Oliver's hand to her cheek, Lauren said, 'I have decided that even though wwee can't go to Ind-ia this year, we will definitely go next year.'

Emma's eyebrows rose. 'Oh, we will, will we?' she responded, knowing she'd move heaven and earth to make it possible.

'Yep. I've made up mmy mind. We're going to India, and Oll-ver's coming too.'

Emma nodded slowly as she got the scenario. 'Well, there's lovely for me,' she commented drily.

Beside her Russ choked back a laugh.

Lauren looked up at him, and the way her eyes moved from him to her mother and back again was eloquent enough to make the rest of her plan crystal clear to everyone.

Willing the ground to open up and swallow her, Emma pretended not to understand. Checking his glass, Russ cleared his throat and said, 'Looks like we're in need of more champagne.'

Acknowledgements

Because so many very patient and generous people helped me with this book I have decided the best way to express my gratitude is in story order.

So my biggest and warmest thank yous go to: Carl Gadd and Pete Craig of the Avon and Somerset Police. Ian Kelcey of Kelcey & Hall; Matrons Trevor Brooks, Sarah McAuslan-Crine and Bernadette Greenan of the Bristol Royal Infirmary; Mr David Porter Consultant Neurosurgeon; Diana Cornish and Pearl Griffiths of the Neuro Rehabilitation Unit at Frenchay Hospital; Alison Woods, Dr Angus Graham, Dr Simon Gerhand and Michelle Jeffries of The Frenchay Brain Injury Rehabilitation Centre.

Additional thanks go to: Dr Helen Lewis, my wonderful GP; Carole Neilson, secretary to David Porter and Tina Long PA to Alison Woods.

The main subject tackled in this book is so complex that I must stress quite strongly that any mistakes you may have found will be totally mine.

I would also like to express my thanks to my editor, Susan Sandon, my agent Toby Eady, the world's best publicist, Louise Page, to Georgina Hawtrey-Woore, Rob Waddington, Jenifer Doyle – in fact, everyone who has been involved in getting this book from me, to you, the reader.